THE YOUNG MAN

. . . .

THE

YOUNG

MAN

BOTHO STRAUSS

Translated by Roslyn Theobald

Northwestern University Press

Evanston, Illinois

Hydra Books

Northwestern University Press

Evanston, Illinois 60208-4210

This translation has been funded in part by Inter Nationes, Bonn.

First published in German as

Der Junge Mann by Carl Hanser Verlag, Munich-Vienna.

Copyright © 1984 by Carl Hanser Verlag.

English translation published by arrangement with Carl Hanser Verlag.

Copyright © 1995 by Northwestern University Press.

Printed in the United States of America

Library of Congress Cataloging-in-Publiction Data

Strauss, Botho, 1944–

[Junge Mann. English]

The young man / Botho Strauss ; translated by Roslyn Theobald.

p.   cm.

ISBN 0-8101-1338-4

I. Theobald, Roslyn. II. Title.

PT2681.T6898J8613   1995

833'.914—dc20

95-31184

CIP

The paper used in this publication meets the
minimum requirements of the American National Standard
for Information Sciences—Permanence of Paper for
Printed Library Materials, ANSI Z39.48-1984.

CONTENTS

INTRODUCTION

· ·

Time time time. The children on the street keep asking me what time it is! But I'm just like them and do not live my life according to a watch, I don't even wear one. They ride their bicycles up to the curb and stop, they ask with well-mannered remoteness, their eyes turned away, as if they were from an alien society and only passing through. They ask out of an uncertainty that does not relate solely to how they have laid out their day. The practice we city dwellers have developed of hardly looking anyone straight in the eye anymore, appearing not even to notice others where possible, seems to disturb these children. They certainly notice how friendly curiosity, the very element without which they cannot thrive, does not really mean much here. They react against this and ask everyone they meet; they sense a need to come into contact with strangers, briefly, and even if only to hear them say how late it is. "Excuse me, do you have the time?"

· · ·

We humans still have not really come to terms with time. Space, on the other hand, is something we feel we understand, at least that space that envelops the planet and that we have made our own. But time remains a part of cosmic exuberance. We earthlings cannot simply play around with it at will, we can neither conquer it nor destroy it, and we cannot count it among our own. So we have set up all kinds of makeshift clocks, the superstitious and the historical, the biographical and the ideological, and out of unfathomable time the mightiest of mankind's humors and delusions have emerged. Time is ending, time is new. Once prehistoric time was gray, and once it was golden. Once we lived in a blessed era, and then again full of the anticipation of catastrophe we saw ourselves at the end of all our days. Historical shockwaves. Transformations of our desires. Nothing real about them. And often it was only the danger in a failed *representation* of the world; when stunned we stared into what we believed to be the imminent danger of world *conflagration*.

Time is a child, Heracles said, a child playing a boardgame, a child on the throne.

The world is young, physicists say, unimaginably distant from the terrible equilibrium that will devour time. It goes on along its way full of fruitful disorder and unalloyed joy in play, like the children on the street who find pleasure in feigning a disability, in limping or running around as if they had a bad leg. Everything alive is unformed.

. . .

"Come on! Tell us a story!" the street people call to me when I go to the kiosk in the morning to pick up my newspaper. There they stand from ten o'clock in the morning until long after closing time, outside in the summer and sometimes inside in the warmth when the weather is bad. They hold their little molded bottles in their fists, young men some of them, upon whose faces drinking and unemployment have pressed a mask of unrecognizable age. Slight, infirm, mid-thirties, their dark oily hair in a smart slicked-down 50s look, even in their choice of catchwords and jokes they recall, in an odd way, a distant Borgward era. History turns round in the heads of these drinkers slipped out of time, these lonely, shaken little men who know nothing and are always claiming their best friends all fell at Stalingrad; they simply speak along in a German babble, and, much older than they are, it continues its uninterrupted flow beneath time. Among themselves they are not friends and all any of them has is a dog. So many dog owners, and they are always complaining about how the taxes are too high. They only keep German shepherds, often a mangy old animal with a snow-white snout and a paw gone lame.

Tell them a story? They'd never even be able to listen for a single minute! They are constantly interrupting each other, trying to trump one unfounded pronouncement with another. Their talk keeps going astray, erratic and at cross purposes, full of the jump cuts we see in the evening on TV. "And that's just what you're like! You, you who have the whole day free, and you keep interrupting each other and never let anyone finish what he has to say. Not one of you can even tell a simple joke any more!"

. . .

The great medium and his world-crushing rule long ago succeeded in making us feel that the slippery flight of ideas and a slight madness were entirely normal aspects of perception. Here our discourse is constantly being interrupted by what is going on around us. Just now, we see two men engaged in a serious confrontation, a young agronomy professor and a official from the department of agriculture, talking about beta-blockers in pork, and estrogen pigs living and breathing in a pavilion at the Hamburg fair. We have hardly been able to focus in on them and only begin to follow their arguments before a brass band marches across our path cutting us off; and in less time than it might take for one of us to blink an eye, we're in Soest sitting at a table in a pub where the regulars hang out, being initiated into the secrets of Westphalian sausage production. Beta-blockers already forgotten, talk of poisonous feed fluttering away. Can this be information? Isn't it much more like a giant Pac-Man game, a constant lighting up and shooting down of human beings, opinions, mentalities? This is precisely the game that governs our expanded awareness: the time of madness will soon become the time of normalcy.

. . .

And the conversation we have wanted to have with a few people over the years is not being kept up. Sitting down with someone for a quiet heart-to-heart talk makes us feel estranged. Intimacy itself belongs out in the open, and confidentialities are the stuff of talk shows and interviews. It is only under the bright glare of public light that we can be brought close to another human being. Whenever we want to say something to someone in the privacy of our homes, we suddenly feel trapped in a cramped cave, a place of paralysis and darkness. We fear each other in this nonpublic gloom. We don't listen, we don't allow each other to speak.

This is why his talent makes a storyteller feel ill at ease. Not because he lacks sufficient experience – after all, he can make much of very little – but because the elementary *conditions* under which he can communicate something to someone no longer exist, or, at any rate, he can no longer believe in them. He is already too profoundly used to being cut off in mid-sentence.

But what if he still would wish to be an empathetic chronicler, despite the fact that he can neither escape nor obey the regime of total public awareness in which he lives out his days? Maybe the first thing he should do is make himself useful in form and observation, according to the way the era has trained him, for example, in the exercise of detecting things in the dimensions of their accelerating volatility and then perceiving them all the more lucidly. Instead of producing a straight-line narrative, or striving for an all-encompassing development, he will grant diversity its zones, instead of history he will record the multi-storied moment, the synchronous event. He will lay out, or allow to take form, scenes and honeycombs of time rather than epic and novella. So, instead of nurturing a quiet opposition, he will attempt to adapt ever more attentively to the situation at hand. He will improve his means within it, knowing that only successful adaptation will provide him the necessary sovereignty and freedom to recognize the true wealth of forms, the diversity, the playful capacity of his reality. As terrible as the pressure may sometimes be, he is extremely moved by society's abundance, the wealth of knowledge and sensation, of encounters and lifestyles, of consensus and differences, and by the way in which he now can observe and experience them in this politically free community during what is, in the final analysis, a favored period of German history. From time to time he becomes aware of this through a profound feeling of satisfaction and belonging. Where some only see glittering decay, he sees transitions and transformations, he sees the extravagant market of difference that arises out of the essential insecurity and openness of this society. Diversity and difference provide everything alive with the best possible protection from death and devastation.

As far as the element of time is concerned, we also require an expanded perception, a many-faceted awareness, to protect us from the unrelievedly oppressive regimes of progress, utopia, and every other so-called future. We need different clocks for this, it is true, feedback mechanisms that free us from the stubborn, old forward-hand-mentality. We need circuits closed between Once Was and Now, and ultimately we need a living unity of day and dream, of eagle-eyed competence and pliant sleepwalking.

. . .

In an epoch that has revealed a wealth of discovery never before seen, and where thousands of possibilities are open to any one of us, we are still being single-mindedly trained to focus our attentions on the social affairs of man, on our *society*. But it is impossible to lead a fruitful life in this society if it is all you ever think about! You will go crazy or simply get dumb – in any case it will consume your best energies! This kind of thinking, pervasive as it is, does not make us more courageous, and may even be robbing us of our ultimate capacity ever to form a society. One day it will be like Carroll's Cheshire cat and simply fade away into a transparent smile – meant for those who have been staring at it too unconsciously for too long. "Well! I've often seen a cat without a grin," thought Alice; "but a grin without a cat! It's the most curious thing I ever saw in all my life!"

. . .

No, the concept of decay is only an intellectual illusion, the hobgoblin of an exhausted belief in progress. We transform ourselves and one thing evolves from another, either sympathetically or antagonistically.

Still, I lament the economic collapse of my newspaper lady, just as her physical decline weighs on my heart. Up until a year ago, she, the angel of the street people paying her kind and solicitous court across the shameless display of certain publications, had been a very cheerful and attractive woman, a small, plump, platinum blond with mother-of-pearl eyeshadow, always kind and good-hearted. Now, I can hardly recognize her. Both her face and her hips are considerably swollen, her sprayed bouffant hair is hanging off to one side of her head, and with two fists she supports herself on the shop counter, laboriously struggling against the weight of her leaden drunkenness. Hardly able to find its way out from behind a puffy face that looks as if it were made up with ashes, her smile can no longer vanquish the bulges, spots, and grooves and is becoming an idiotic grimace. It was shortly after the death of her husband that she fell into this pitiful state, probably less out of grief than out of simple weariness after having provided exhaustive care for so long.

The husband, alcoholic and unemployed, came to our street every day at about eleven o'clock in the morning to pick up a daily ration at his wife's kiosk. He often stopped under my window, his face very red, breathing hard. In late afternoon, he came again to exchange his empty bottles for an evening ration, which he carried home in his plastic bag. Quiet, forlorn and unwavering, he divided his day according to these two errands. But one day he stopped coming and the kiosk shutters remained closed. "On account of a sad event my stand will be closed today" was what had been written on a cardboard sign hung out over the kiosk window. Since that day my newspaper lady, who had cared for her husband until the end of his days while never or never discernibly drinking herself, opened the door wide to slovenliness and neglect. A terrible "Don't give a goddamn!" chewed its way through the neat and orderly conduct of her life and her nice little stand turned into a dirty, stinking hole. A penetrating stench of urine, dog, and never-changed clothing now hits me in the face every morning when I come to pick up my fresh news. Many of her loyal customers, above all the older women, stopped buying their magazines here a long time ago. There are always new gaps on the shelves and on the counter, empty spaces where papers are no longer being ordered or no longer delivered, presumably because of rather hefty back payments. All that is left is her smelly little erotic court, the circle of mischievous wretches who kept closing in more and more tightly around her until she herself passed over into their fumes.

. . .

I've just come back from getting the paper but I feel as if I've been gone for a very long time. I looked into many faces along my short route. I know the people in my street by sight. Every face the filler cap of an expansive family saga. But I don't know anything about them. figures of pure recognition, that's what they are. Their everyday surfacing and vanishing is an act contrary to moving. It is a place to stay.

. . .

The entire world is playing for time, but I am losing it. I just think that in the great electronic total, the gain and loss of hours is striving toward equalization. I believe that in some wondrously roundabout way the new world-uni-clock keeps bringing us closer to the eon where there was only Same Time. Every look took its own word, and every thing found its own poet. Events do not come, the physicist Eddington wrote, they are already there and we will meet them along our way. Their taking place is merely a outward formality. An accident, winning the lottery, infidelity, they are all there. They are only waiting for us to happen to them.

In the meantime, the ambitious concept of evolution has also managed to stir up the quiet soul of physics, and the all-penetrating time-arrow has hit its target. More recent physics has removed the last bit of static and symmetry from our dream of the world. Now we can only think in terms of Becoming. From Alpha to Omega, through the living and the nonliving, the world is bound to the irreversibility of all phenomena, to non-equilibrium, to the dynamic of chaos and excessive structure. There is apparently no place for Being. It is only the Human Spirit conscious of itself, struggling to bring its inborn despair under control, that has needed the "Life Lie" these thousands of years, and – from Plato's ideas to quantum mechanics – repeatedly new and comforting proofs that there is something universally and timelessly valid.

Our intellect keeps playing with immutable ideas, even if only to be able to take a break from the perception of all-encompassing Becoming. And the storyteller is not about to give up this plaything, he will continue to be in charge of lost and recurring time, and will not even consider throwing out the precious crystal of standstill. He will continue to defy the time-arrow to the very last, raising the shield of poetry against it even if it proves to be a lost cause.

.   .   .

Spring in the heavens and rusty-red foliage still on the trees! A May, a fine churning of clouds, a bright blue with a thin white dance of the veils . . . what a twofold time of the year! But it's back to work. Back into winter. Back to my snowfields of empty pages.

But now this constant procession of people leaving their houses! They are walking along in congenial groups, or by themselves toward a common destination. They'll meet again while shopping, taking part in demonstrations, or in the sunshine on a bridge over the river. The weightless leavers, the ones on the streets, they're the ones who are defying the rule of the bureaucrats. The street, the square, the wind provides them cover and arms.

Tell them a story? Oh, they are in good spirits, they know where they're going, they are busy, after all.

So in complete silence, like footsteps in snow, I will leave my tracks and employ such a solitary tone from the very beginning that no one will ever hear me. Maybe I will succeed in finding my way back to those still and inert events that must wait such a long time for someone to come across *them* and bring them to life. Allegories. Tales of initiation. Romantic Novel of Reflection. A little brought along, a little carried away.

"They are roots chopped off and will grow back again, old things that return, unappreciated truths whose validity will be reestablished, it is a new light that is rising again after a long night on the horizons of our perception, and slowly approaching its zenith at midday." – Giordano Bruno, *On the Infinite Universe and the Worlds*, fifth Dialogue.

THE STREET
(THE YOUNG MAN)

• •

"After a project like that, you're going to find yourself spending some time in a big, deep hole." I had been warned. And that is just what happened. I didn't know what to do with myself. During the day I wandered around town and into cafés and video arcades, looking for ways to kill time, at the movies, in parks and department stores. Then, in the evening, entirely by chance but somehow inevitably, I ended up back in the vicinity of the theater. I asked about ticket sales, I watched the audience file in, I visited the actors in their dressing rooms, I sat in the cafeteria with the stage crew and played cards, often into the early hours of the morning.

But somehow I didn't belong there anymore. My play had found its way into the everyday routine of the theater. What happened on stage now appeared to be completely the work of the actors, and no one in the audience much cared who the director was. The new risks the actors took evening after evening leading to a good or less good performance, having to appeal to an alert or a dull audience, had long since displaced the intimate enterprise that had brought us so brutally close together over the six weeks of rehearsal. Of course, the actors were happy to see me and treated me like a friend – after all, against expectations, our production had achieved some modest success – but I could sense how our feelings soon abated and became vague. They were already in rehearsal for a new play and had entrusted themselves to another spiritual mentor.

I had gone to see two or three more performances, but this only tormented me. I was in no shape to provide a useful post-performance critique. It was very difficult for me to be shut out of the close, vibrant company I had been so involved with, and to be left behind all alone. I felt as lonesome as a lost dog. Plagued as much by bitter disappointment as by obsessive devotion, I was haunted by my first more or less serious theater project, and its conflicting aftermath. There were times when I would be walking around and I would catch sight of the absurd present around me, and then in broad, ragged swatches the darkest and most difficult days of rehearsal came back to me, and once more all of the most terrifying portents, the thousands of calamities, infamies, and vicissitudes I had suffered rained down on me, and each time this happened, I felt as if I were starting all over again back at the beginning. I hardly ever thought about the later, end phase, when the promise of success was beginning to become apparent. No, it wasn't even memory, my nerves were chewing again, it was pure present. Or, to use a favorite term of theater people: the *intensity* of my current circumstances has made me relive the fear and the crisis of those days with unmitigated immediacy. Of course, this was also one of the aftereffects of repetition, an aspect of time that the theater knows well, but that I found strange and alienating after having subjected myself to it for a number of weeks. These imploring repetitions that are constantly revealing something, piece by piece, developing, or maybe only regaining something that "was there" at the very beginning, at the first rehearsal, so close you could touch it, *perfect*, but only in this happy premonition. Often enough, the whole of a protracted rehearsal schedule only serves to rediscover, fulfill, and grasp the surprising heights of the *beginning*, the beginning itself. This truly sounds much easier than it is. I can testify to that. For me, at any rate, it was very difficult to develop the necessary patience, to work my way into the appropriate sense of time, or shall we say: into spiraling time that recognizes no linear progress, and not even the most fervent exuberance, the most enlightening idea, the most iron of iron wills can affect it in the slightest, not even in the theater.

. . .

But where was I to go from here? I had finished my work. I had become a director. Hadn't I achieved my goal? I tended to think: now, it's all behind me. Redeemed, accomplished. Time to get out of here. I was also thinking about my father and his desperate attempts to keep me from taking this trip, escaping, to Cologne on this hellish journey into the theater. Up until the very last moment, he had not wanted to let me go; then he had not only taken me to the station in our hometown of Kandern, but had also boarded the train with me and ridden along as far as Freiburg in a ceaseless endeavor to get me to turn around, to give up my absurd intentions.

"Don't do it, Leon. I beg you. Don't get mixed up in all of this craziness." He considered theater arts to be superfluous, much more so than even high diving or dressage. "It's enough if you read the classics at home. You just ruin your imagination if you go to the theater. Nothing but tomfoolery, that's show business." He had always felt this way about the theater, and true to these feelings, as long as I can remember, he had never gone to see a play performed, and certainly never on one of the big-city stages. As a result, I, as the second of his two sons, had come relatively late to the theater. In my case, as opposed to that of my older brother, he had not wanted to leave my upbringing and education solely in my mother's hands, and, taking me jealously under his wing, had separated me from her much too soon. Of course, this purely paternal regimen inevitably led me onto the one track with which he was at all well acquainted, and where he was fearlessly making progress of his own, namely in his own field of study, the history of religion. By the time we came to a somewhat anxious difference of opinion, though never to real discord, regarding my career, he had been emeritus for some time but still traveled twice a week to Freiburg to lecture on Coptic Christianity. He devoted his later years exclusively to the study of Montanus, his own area of specialization, and once I had completed several semesters of study he began to seek me out as partner in discussion, and then formally trained me to be his assistant. I had hardly turned twenty-two and my horizon was already crowded with early Christian Heretics and Anchorites, Stylites and Eremites, and while my cohorts were calling for revolt, preparing to overthrow fathers and liberate the people everywhere, I applied myself to the study of Aramaic and Coptic, and at my father's side diligently deciphered the newly unearthed scrolls of the Gnostic Gospels. The great passion with which the old man went about his research, the narrative flair and fantasy with which he blew the dry academic dust from these documents, had its desired affect on me. In fact, I was so inspired that of my own free will I happily immersed myself in these secret Christian writings, which constantly made reference to feminine wisdom, to "God the Mother," to an almighty erotic grace, as it seemed to me then.

Still, I had to find some balance. I was fully prepared to fulfill the demanding requirements of my job, but I was not about to let it take me over. I had already come to the conclusion that I really wasn't fit for academic life, and that I would not continue my father's work after his death, as was his secret hope.

It was at this time in Freiburg that I met a young director, a man of much different character from my own, possessed of a totally critical attitude toward the world around him, and who could hardly develop any enthusiasm for anything, least of all for the theater where he worked. But I kept seeking him out. I was not only interested in hearing his opinions and earnest protests, but I also wanted to find out exactly what he did at the Municipal Theater. Then one day he asked me to deliver a paper to a troupe of actors rehearsing Shaw's *Saint Joan*, elaborating on voices and visions, oracles and the divinely possessed. I didn't need much convincing. A few days later, I stood carefully prepared in front of the ensemble and gave my little lecture. They apparently found it interesting, or there would not have been so many of them, including the director, who strongly urged me to come to their future rehearsals and continue to advise them, if I were interested. I was only too willing to accept this invitation, and I felt warmly welcomed and profoundly attracted to this other, communal world of the theater. From then on, I spent less and less time on my studies, and dutifully divided my energies between my father's research library and the rehearsal stage of the municipal theater. And it wasn't long before I had acquired a great deal of practical knowledge. My ardor and ambition were all-devouring. So, it was hardly surprising when I was offered the post of assistant director for one of the upcoming productions. With this new challenge, my basic theater competence enjoyed a significant upswing, and my attentive participation earned me the friendship and the trust of the entire ensemble. Within half a year I was to take over my first production, unexpectedly, when the man selected for the job, a prodigy who wavered somewhere between the free theater and the radical theater of rejection, had been suddenly moved to disappear into – as it was then known – the political underground. So, here were three live actors standing in front of me, expecting me to do something exciting for our mutual production. I was to be staging Strindberg's *Miss Julie*, and we had three weeks.

.   .   .

Up until this point, my theatrical digressions had taken place at my father's critical indulgence, even if his grumbling complaints that our mutual work was suffering, and increasingly, were not to be overheard. He was of the opinion that one could hardly deny a young person every diversion and amusement. It was in this sense that he intended to allow me to pursue my interests in the theater, as a hobby, a change of pace from demanding academic labors. My mother, on the other hand, had begun to sense some time ago that my inclinations were more profound than that, and she even secretly supported them. It seemed to her that in the long run there was a significant danger in the one-sided and over-powering occupation to which my father had subjected me. She was concerned about my independent development no matter what field I might choose to work in. Her trust in me was both blind and warm. And I would have been wonderfully strength-ened and encouraged if only the heavy, dark wing of my father had not been hanging over me so snugly from such a tender age on.

. . .

My relationship with my father was now worsening day by day. There were times when my work in the theater took up so much of my time that I had no choice but to limit my involvement with the grand Montanus project. The old man now saw the approach of an open and final break between the two of us, reproached me bitterly, and was basically insufferable and morose.

But my *Miss Julie* was a success! The production got very good reviews in the local press, and even aroused some consider-able interest beyond the city limits of Freiburg. Above all, there were quite a few theater people, some of them from rather distant cities, who had come to see the promising first work, as it was being called.

Among them, one evening, were the two leading actresses of the Cologne theater, Margarethe Wirth and Petra Kurzrok, whom I knew by name, even though I had never seen them on stage. I got a message through the stage manager that the two of them wanted to meet me in the lobby of their hotel after the perfor-mance. By the time I finally got there, I was extremely nervous. I ran around rather clumsily, but was unable to locate the two celebrities anywhere. I had no idea how to hide my unease, but I was not really interested in making a show of my boredom by burying my face in a newspaper. Then suddenly, I noticed two pair of eyes sparkling out from behind a dense espalier of rubber trees: they had apparently been observing me for some time, not missing a single move I made. Naturally, it was the two actresses lurking there behind the greenery like big jungle cats, surveilling every one of my uncertain steps. I walked up to them and they extended me a friendly though formal welcome. I could see that they were a very unequal pair. Margarethe was the taller, more ladylike of the two. Her long reddish blond hair hung down loosely over her shoulders, she was wearing a pleated, three-quarter-length skirt, and a gray silk blouse under a dark sleeveless vest. She had obviously dressed for the theater. Kurzrok, on the other hand, had not changed out of her work clothes, and in a well-worn jeans suit looked almost as if she were intentionally trying to diminish herself in comparison with the clean, simple style of her colleague. But, be that as it may, the two of them obviously belonged together, and this was not only common knowledge, it was something anyone could see at first glance. They were a team as cuddly as they were jealous. I was surprised at how short Pat was, delicate and sinewy; she had an almost boyish figure and that is probably why the nickname "Patrick" had stuck, displacing her feminine name. Long dark blond bangs covered her strong, arched forehead. She had pulled her short hair back in a little ponytail and fastened it with an elastic band.

It was not long before I got a taste of their finely-honed pairs routine. They immediately began talking about their evening at the theater and acted as if I weren't even there. They were really very thorough about the whole thing. In a very delicate and snakelike way, this kind of peer critique often comes slithering up on the person who is meant to be its actual victim. To begin with, we spend a little time on the sets, notice quite a few problems, not particularly effective, actually quite awful. At this point, we risk one or another petulant question about the play itself, feel that its contemporary relevance is waning, but then we leave it at that, after all, it is possible that the subject has already met more difficult challenges than we, based on our own critical tastes, might be able to discern. Possibly, just possibly, it might be the translation that keeps this old work from having the kind of penetrating impact we had expected. And now we are approaching a very touchy area, where we begin to note certain weaknesses in the actors themselves. But we're not talking about personalities here, it is more a question of casting, or in the worst case, perhaps even miscasting. And now we have finally made our way into the realm of directorial responsibility, and everything here depends on who wants whom to do what. Because, up until this point, everything that has been mentioned could just as well be formulated to excuse the director as to blame him. So, the two famous actresses discussed their way through our *Miss Julie*, point by point, before finally getting around to the actual Dilemma of the evening, and taking the young, very young, all too young Strindberg director to task. Due to his extreme lack of interpersonal, worldly, and erotic experience, they found precious little emotional development taking place on stage, and everything else that did take place was really nothing more than a charming series of formal exercises.

Now, as before, they carried on this conversation in artful give and take, in practiced dialogue in which a fervent concurring led all too often to a sharpening of their verdict. Now and then, the delinquent was scrutinized by a hasty look out of the corner of an eye, and to him it seemed as if he'd been cuffed by a paw. No, the dear ladies truly did not have one good thing to say about my staging. I found their abusive remarks unjustified and exaggerated, and wanted nothing more than to run screaming from the hotel. In one fell swoop, with this single devastating critique, all of my previous recognition, praise in the press, and testimony to my talent lost their validity and were simply flung into the dirt. Then suddenly, the two of them interrupted their alliance and opened themselves to me. All at once, they were indulging in an unabashed display of kindness. Out of the blue, they were telling me how much they wanted to work with me in Cologne on their production of Genet's *The Maids*.

. . .

Since my father was unable to keep himself from making a big scene in front of everyone at the train station, half of Kandern was able to take part in my departure and this great turning point in my life.

"The director!" he yelled, again and again. "The director! What does that mean, anyway? A handyman and a monkey trainer, maybe that, but certainly not a creative human being. Not even a real artist!" I asked him to please speak more quietly. "Father, you don't know how important the director is these days. He is the one who gives things a real shape, and makes the theater into an unforgettable event. He can even be a visionary!" Then our neighbor lady chimed in: "Professor, just give Leon a chance to go out on his own. We shouldn't be holding anyone captive. I have never in all my living days been in a theater, believe me, but with my six boys, I always knew when it was time to let them take things into their own hands. Today, young people have got it a lot better. Why shouldn't he go to Cologne where they've got a better theater. Maybe he'll become famous someday, Mr. Leon Pracht!"

At this, my father responded angrily: "Famous! What are you talking about? Do you know Dölger? Heiler? Reitzenstein? Well! They are famous men. He can become famous in my field, too!"

Things really got going, and almost everyone in the waiting room shared an opinion about the director's profession, whatever he may have understood it to be. An employee of the gas company, the new owner of the local movie theater, Mrs. Veldstein the surgical nurse, they all gave me their resolute support and took offense at my father's obstinacy. I felt very sorry for him, being either attacked or disparaged from all sides. Unmoved, he ignored their glib involvement, leaned over to me and continued his protest at a somewhat lower volume, but all the more urgently: "So, my boy, you're just going to drop our joint work, once and for all?" I answered sadly that I believed I wasn't really made for academics and that I had to find my own way. "Well, you weren't really made for the theater, either! At least not by me!" My mother overheard this and tried to mediate between the two of us. "Just leave it be. Leon is going to do what he wants to do." I had wanted to try changing my father's mind in a somewhat gentler way, telling him that I was also entering the theater as his first student, and would put my knowledge of religious celebrations and rites to good use. He didn't pay any attention to what I was saying, he was much too upset, much too distressed about our imminent parting. "You've already had one chance to direct a play. Isn't that enough? Why do you think you have to go to another city? This is not a life for you, Leon, believe me."

Later, when he got out of the train in Freiburg and walked up to the window of my compartment, it hit me hard, too. He was standing there in front of me so discouraged and forlorn that I could hardly look at him. He had finally given up. He had to accept the fact that he no longer had control over me. When he looked up at me again, with that narrow, gray and fiery professorial head, there was a quiet and profound fear on his face. "Don't look at me that way," I pleaded, but my voice just sank into my throat. Then, quietly and for no reason I could discern, he said: "Take care that you always speak your mind, my boy." I didn't understand what this incomplete, vague advice was supposed to mean. But I nodded and gave him my hand. An understanding had emerged from the tender confusion of his words. Silently and smoothly, the train began its journey. For a long time my father stood there waving a small, trembling good-bye in the air. A big, strong wave of the whole arm, meant to erase the departure, so to speak, did not seem appropriate. That was reserved for children and lovers. But the old man accepted my departure, and his hand was not raised in opposition to the rapidly increasing distance.

· · ·

In Cologne, people had been mulling over the following thoughts: Alfred Weigert, the lead director of the house, as well as the personal director, body and soul, of Pat and Margarethe, should finally be given the opportunity to stage his *Wallenstein* in all three parts. At the same time, the orphaned protagonists would be able to fulfill a long-cherished wish, and appear together on the stage in roles of equal stature and show what they could do without the guidance of the great master. Of course, this would be a limited production, on a small stage, not without literary merit, but first and foremost would have to meet the demand for cameo roles, solo parts. Genet's *The Maids* seemed an obvious choice; and since the two stars were also free to choose their own director, and wanted by all means to have "new experiences," as they had put it then, they set off on their search for a young, ambitious talent. What they expected from me was not clear. Maybe they were simply hoping to be able to exercise greater freedom than the master allowed, and thought I wouldn't get in the way of their bad habits, and would do nothing but support them. But I did not see myself as hired help. I had my own ideas, I came with big plans.

The third person we needed, to play the role of Madame, was more or less warmly forced on me by Pat and Margarethe. She was an older actress whom both of them praised highly, although she was much more a good-natured nanny and certainly would never generate the brutal toughness, would never be the kind of idol and lady who could make the murderous desires of the two maids seem plausible. It was clear that this fellow player was only meant to be a docile adjunct. Pat and Margarethe wanted to deliver the battle on their own, and I was to be the ring judge, responsible for the fair conduct of the fight.

But: how different were my thoughts regarding my placement with these two wonderful artists! I saw myself as the new Montanus, and just as this visionary journeyed through Phrygian towns and cities with his two prophetesses, Priscilla and Maximilla, proclaiming the advent of the new Jerusalem, so I was determined to lead a movement of renewal along with my two actresses, at least in the theater and in the actor's art. During the many lonely weeks I spent preparing for my assignment, planning and working through even the minutest detail of staging, I felt more and more strongly that this advance with Pat and Margarethe was meant to be my mission, a legitimate travesty of the Montanian triad. Through my work with my father I had become so familiar with Montanus, and it was such a strong and profoundly internalized image, that I came to be convinced that the two actresses had emerged full-blown, as it were, from my studies. I truly believed that their appearance in my life was not abrupt and by chance, but that it had come about through elemental transformation. All too easily, I overlooked the fact that the real Montanus of this sparkling pair was named Alfred Weigert, their animator and wonderworker, the squire of their souls; he already existed.

. . .

I knew exactly how it had to look, my theater, my maids, my ecstatic play. And I didn't refer to it with any lesser nomenclature. The Anti-World, the migration of myths, the passage, the stage as entrance into the great remembering, dance of the reflections with the spirits, the ceremony of the gestures, under the magnifying glass, called to the hunt, luring the audience into the "back room," inducing states . . . . Oh, the terms piled up and swayed. In my conception, the piece takes place in the not too distant future. Actually, following the breakdown of all human communication. Humans have withdrawn back into their ceremonies, hidden, encapsulated. Games are their emotional survival niches. The place: a cave in time . . .

My God. And what came out of all this in the end? A staging on the whole rather oddly bourgeois, despite some superior acting.

The real surprise of the evening was much less the young director than the discovery that a poète maudit has grown old, a Genet has become dusty gray. And for this, I had wrestled with the infernal and the heavenly powers, I strode through helplessness and cold, fire and swamp. But that's how things are in the theater: a winding instrument into which we blow our entire souls, so that in the end we will at least get some kind of small, decent tone. Nothing more, but even for that we need lung capacity.

TWO

Early Monday morning. One hour before the beginning of rehearsals, I arrive at the theater. The design assistant and two stage hands have already put up a rehearsal set that basically corresponds to what Volker, the set designer, and I had agreed upon. It looks awful. I'm not interested in having a whole lot of silly junk on stage. None of this oppressive boudoir pomp, and I don't much like flowers either, even if I am disobeying the dramatist's stage directions. Work everything through again with V! What I've got here is not quite the lived-in future I had imagined.

This auditorium is one damned skinny passageway! How am I supposed to fit my snug little self-contained niche into this long, narrow pipeline? Theater, birthplace of plays, should always be at least halfway surrounded by the audience . . . . In less than an hour my irrevocable descent into the world of emotions will begin. I am getting more nervous; anxiety, naked fear – or, to take these words literally, like a dream: the fear of standing here naked. Although I am armed to the teeth with notes, plans, sketches, in which I have worked out every position, every piece of stage business, I suddenly feel myself unprepared. Will I be able to act quickly and appropriately if something unexpected happens, if changes are suddenly called for, in the stage set, for example? After all, I know what reality can do when it kicks in full force and does not conform to what I had expected, how it can throw me into a profound emotional paralysis.

I leave the little table onstage where we will soon begin the first reading of the play. I gaze into the abyss of the empty auditorium and it makes me dizzy. You will be more composed if you are looking from profound depths up into the heights, from somewhere in the middle of the third row, your arms spread out over seats to the left and to the right. It smells of dust, molleton, heated varnish. Although I know I have descended into a pit and will be working beneath the day in order to mine the valuable mineral of this play, I feel that my place is being much to brightly lit, is much too exposed under the diffuse rehearsal lights. From all sides, I am being stared at by the sober, pragmatic demands of an uncertain reality. Workers who are not real workers. Technology that has no practical application. Schedules that must be adhered to in order to orchestrate pseudo-action, and even the newspapers and milk cartons on the stage manager's desk are no longer everyday objects. I sense that this whole pit is full of unwritten rules I neither know nor understand, and that I could not even blindly follow because I don't have the instinct. But they are there, I can tell by the enormous decline in my emotional freedom of movement, my fantasy, since I have been sitting here in the theater waiting for the actresses to arrive.

.   .   .

Matthias, my friendly assistant – he is about my age, even if somewhat more of a worldly dreamer, and always hidden under his Bob Dylan cap – reminds me that Ms. Adams, who is playing the role of Madame, has been scheduled to come an hour later. Apparently, this is something I did by mistake. Of course, for the first reading everyone should be here right from the beginning.

.   .   .

Pat comes in through a door at the back of the auditorium. She rushes in, she stumbles, she is completely disconcerted and can hardly manage a hello. She gives us her report on a brutal gang attack that she was forced to observe on her way to rehearsals. Six or seven teenagers, a gang of rockers, had stormed a hygiene shop, smashed everything to pieces, looted what they could, dragged the owner out onto the street by his hair, beat him with chains and kicked him . . . . What is a hygiene shop? A sex shop? "Yes, something like that! But out in broad daylight, just imagine. Everything's kaput, just like good old New York around here. You can't even go out alone on the streets in the morning . . ."

Margarethe comes in across the stage. She allows herself a protracted entrance. She leaves no doubt as to how she intends to triumph as Solange. Her hair has been dyed a fox red and combed out into a full, bushy mane. Her long legs are displayed under a skirt that doesn't quite reach to the knees. All her olfactory senses alert, she nervously sniffs her way through the stage pen. Pat manages to unburden herself a second time of the story of the rocker attack.

"What's so wrong," Margarethe responds, "with the boys just defending themselves against these pigs?"

"You think that's OK? Well, good going."

"Of course. But before we turn into a society of vigilantes – "

"It's the same society that's sitting out there in your audience every night!"

"I don't care. I act for everyone who wants to see me."

"Huh? It just might make a difference whether these people are looking up to you on the stage, or pulling you down into their lewd fantasies."

And so it went, back and forth in rapid succession. Neither of them seemed to have a firm opinion about anything, and they were constantly changing positions, all depending upon which point of view the other was defending at the moment. The only thing that seemed to matter was repartee. I simply wasn't there. They were already acting and had been the whole time, they were acting right over my head and I never got a chance to say one single word. Since it no longer exhibited any recognizable content, and appeared to be going further and further astray, it seemed to me that this might well be nothing but a sly and well-rehearsed opening scene, being performed with the sole intent of confusing me and testing my limits. I should have cut them off long ago and gotten down to work. Instead, I kept trying to figure out what they were talking about; but before I could make any contribution to the discussion, they had already changed the subject again. They weren't interested in what I thought, in any case, but only in how I would react to their impudent delay. Their skirmish was growing more and more insipid, they had begun to repeat themselves and almost broke out laughing. But they waited in vain for me to interrupt them. I didn't do it. finally, they stopped on their own, and, in one synchronous turn, they opened up to me just as they had at the end of our first meeting in a Freiburg hotel lobby. But this time I was met with a much cooler gaze, almost dismayed, as if to say: Well, young man, you want to take over here and you can't even get us to shut up?!

first reading. The five of us are sitting at a small table on stage. Pat begins reading the role of Claire. She avoids any emphatic accentuation. She is extraordinarily careful about putting a new text into her mouth, there may be madness hidden in it somewhere and she's not about to wake it now. But after a few minutes, she stops herself and goes back to the beginning of a sentence that reads: "You probably hope to seduce the milkman with them [rubber gloves]?"

Pat groans and squirms: "The milkman! Here he is! I knew it, a stumbling block. And what in the hell are we going to do with this virgin's nightmare?"

"It's a very tired cliché," Margarethe says, quietly pushing the text away as if she has just made a very disappointing discovery.

At the very same moment, Pat turns to talk to me, the rehearsal leader.

"Can you please tell me how, today, in the year 1969, I can sell the audience on the milkman as a lover? Convincingly, I mean. So that they don't start tearing their hair out."

This frontal address made me flinch. Stunned, I almost answered: "I don't know how, either." Actually, I had never expected I'd be trying to answer such a trite question. I knew the text right down into its most intimate shadings, but it never occurred to me that this ridiculous milkman would ever be a problem. Matthias thought maybe we could make him a postman or a newspaper carrier.

"No, no!" I jumped in, vigorously, since it was much easier for me to dismiss my little assistant, grabbing onto his fortunate blunder, than to answer the maids directly. "For me, he's the milkman, and no one else," I spoke right up. "You see: when does the action of this play take place? We all know that it was in the 1940s, probably around the same time it was written. But of course, it's taking place now, too, no, a little later – when this is all finished. It is taking place on a social meadow that was well grazed over a long time ago. There are all kinds of lost little groups hanging around, and deformed loners are crouching on barren ground. There is nothing drawing them out, pulling them forward. All development, all drive and progress have come to an end. The meadow has been grazed bare. We humans fear nothing so much as we fear time flowing apart. And it really does seem to be melting like the polar ice caps under the increased temperatures of global warming. The meltoff is driving society's outsiders into the protective circle of cults and custom. They are consumed by their desire for beautiful form, just as the maids are consumed by a desire for Madame's beautiful clothes and expensive junk. Leave the garbage behind, the sewage, the rubble, the waste dumps. We, the formless, are attempting an appearance, this is the theater, and we are protecting ourselves with its fixed rules of engagement. While others laboriously play Mama and Papa, almost to the point of expiration, doctor and patient, manager and staff, teacher and pupil, we step into the transparent room of ordered meaning, stretching ourselves out in a display window through which we can look back into an unknown world full of life. And the two sisters, Solange and Claire, are also lying in this window, waking up on a wonderfully beautiful morning, and blinking through the tall pane of glass into a sun-filled front yard where grasshoppers like dragonflies moisten yew tops and roll-up lawns. This is where they kneel and stand, the people from across the way the ladies are talking about, their distant neighbors who are to see nothing of them, but whose gazes they are unable to avoid. Peculiar beings in white overalls, like gas station attendants or runway personnel waving their planes in, men and women, and they are gawking at you, expecting a play from you, and expecting that this will be the beginning of your last play, with all of the trimmings, sublime and ridiculous, alien and familiar, mean and tender, the last play of the power of the senses, because you're going to have to see your story through to the end, take your ceremony to the limits, where it breaks apart and the irreproducible begins.

"So you will be thankful to speak about what no longer exists, wear dresses that are expensive and old; you will call to the milkman as you would to a giant from the mountains, and he will come over with his rickety cart, along the naked concrete strip, the endless runway, and his residents, the entire useless ground crew, will withdraw in fright at the approach of this powerful bear of a man. With fervent passion Solange will polish her Lady's shoes, spitting on them in cheerful humility. Like an entablature, your symbolic actions will wrap themselves around the brow of the temple in which the preparations for a murder are being made. You will experience sexual analogies as the last great symbolic language of the Old World, and it will provide you stability as well as the infallible means to your own self destruction, almost like the borrowed Greek heavens that so many ages ago lifted up and then rejected German poets and philosophers. On the outside, all existing has been damaged. A sense of everything being equally valid has devoured all form, every act of sacrifice. Every symbol. But like temple prostitutes you are serving the sanctuary of dependence and enslavement. Of bondage. Mind your transparent hideout and put yourself on display! It is only as captives that you become the most captivating entities for those on the outside, the ones standing on the runway . . ."

. . .

Oh, they listened to me! They really listened to me! Ms. Adams was even taking copious notes.

Possible that I'd overdone it a bit my first time out. Maybe I had revealed too much all at once. In one fell swoop, I'd almost given away the entire *idea* of my production. What people were supposed to – and hopefully would – think of my maids. The evaluation of an act that had not yet been seen, made before anything had even begun.

Margarethe Wirth was thinking that perhaps the play should begin as a kind of burlesque. At first, the audience should be made to believe that Claire is the lady, and not the maid, who is really only imitating her.

To my great disappointment, I could not ignore the fact that, apparently, she had not understood any of what I had laid out. But I kept my feelings to myself and answered politely that the sort of impression she had described might well arise, but only as a minor aspect of what, from the beginning, would be an ambiguous machination of roles and reflections. But I was even more concerned that Solange and Claire develop very intimate and diverse gestures that would indicate they were much more dependent on one another than they were on their Lady. That is why it would not really be all that important to come up with a faithful copy of Madame's affected behavior. To that extent, it could not really be a play within a play.

Ms. Adams asked how strong we thought the Lady should actually be. In her opinion, Madame represented the only stable position in the whole play. She did after all survive the battle of the domestics in her boudoir unscathed. She would have to (in Ms. Adams's opinion) project a very real, undeniable power. This was the only way to make the life and death struggle of the maids convincing, and to show that they were really serious about liberating themselves from psychological oppression.

I actually did have a rather clear idea of Madame's role, but at this juncture Ms. Adams's fussy questions were extremely inconvenient. I was still on too big a roll, and so full of the whole thing that for the time being all I wanted to do was win over the two stars. And I wasn't particularly pleased at having the gray supporting actress, who was of course urgently seeking contact, immediately leaping into the parade and digging the channel for the backflow I was expecting from the other two. So I stuttered around somewhat unwillingly, and suggested she think of an exalted Mama and two sisters who are intending to commit matricide. I realized that this off-the-cuff advice was hardly going to do the trick. And Margarethe protested immediately. If we were going to get involved with motives like that, we would inevitably sink into a deep psychological mud bath, and in the end the overheated characters would be nothing but interchangeable parts of a total psychodrama. I hastened to point out that I was interested neither in a psychological nor in a social development of the characters, that it was their *cultural* definition I was seeking. In our eyes, in the eyes of our contemporaries, the play and struggle of the maids already represented something of a heroic life. Therefore, their outward behavior should more closely resemble a tournament than therapeutic role play. The ceremonial, the institution of forms, should arouse longings in us before it profoundly horrifies us. Nevertheless, beneath the high ridge of rites and airs, the seething earth, the hissing of desire, must always be audible. The amorphous. Predatory lust for the role – for power . . .

Suddenly, at this point, I ran out of breath. I didn't know what to do next.

Why had Pat remained so quiet all this time? She hadn't asked a single question. She didn't seem to be at all interested in what was being discussed. She kept looking me straight in the eye and ignoring everything I said. Apparently she was trying to discover *who* was speaking, and what he had to bring to the table. She casually sized up what she could see under the rug, the backside of the design, the knotting.

Once we had finished the rehearsal, she brushed by me and

said: "Be careful, young man. Don't try stuffing all that much into this little piece!"

. . .

I left the theater chastened. My lodging, out in Nippes, was the one-and-a-half room apartment of a young actor who was working in Hamburg for a few months. And here in this cramped space you could find an example of almost everything that belonged to the bad taste of those happy years. Ridiculous posters – Frank Zappa sitting on the toilet, and Lenin in Red Square – unfinished pine furniture, metal bookshelves with a wide selection of revolutionary literature, incense, a fluffy Afghan rug spotted with candle wax. This apartment, used by a person I had never met but who was still an acquaintance, the faithful time-companion, was constantly present – how intense was my revulsion when I returned exhausted, alienated through and through from the first rehearsal. I was miserably homesick. It was my innermost wish to be sitting beside my father under the fruit trees on a pleasant summer day, finally finishing the index to his Montanus. He is calling out the names page by page and I am writing them down in the lists.

Hadn't Pat been listening at all? Maybe I was being too abstract, digging too deep. I still don't know what I can demand of them, how I can get them interested in my ideas.

From our garden we can keep watch. It is situated on a hill away from the town, and there is a road leading up to it that is hardly used except by residents from the neighborhood. Vacationers often hike up through here on their way to the woods. In a war, as there once was in our gray prehistory, I would have liked being a guard on the wall, who only looked and never shot.

Keeping watch, sitting in front of the house, is something I find elementally pleasing. Even in our modern bodies, it is possible to ferret out any number of postures that reach deeper than others, touch symbolic ground. Sitting on a bicycle takes us back to our youths, at best; sitting in front of the house on the other hand can excite us to the very core of our cerebrums, can hijack us out of history and transport us beyond any calculation of time. Yes, that's the whole point: the actresses have to develop an historical feel for their demeanor and their physicality. For example: what does it mean when a lady smokes a cigarette in the same way a bricklayer used to do in front of his boss, concealing the cigarette in the hollow of his hand? Women must always check their demeanor against a pleasure/no-pleasure schema! Even the text plays off the heightened sensitivity with which each of them observes the physical comportment of the other. Claire must know exactly how she likes to see Solange, and what she can't tolerate (legs crossed: disgusting!). "I can't stand our similarities any more," she shouts at one point.

THREE

The first week was OK. In the second week, stage rehearsals began, as did my time of trial and tribulation. Pat and Maggie did not miss a single opportunity to call my gross inexperience and lack of professional background to my attention. There was not a single rehearsal session during which I was not at some point or other thoroughly disgraced. I was just beginning to learn what kind of highly complicated battleships I was dealing with, and I was totally incapable either of steering or moving them in any meaningful way. Every bit of inventiveness I offered simply bounced off them, was dismissed as useless, pedantic, "invention," just that, invention imposed upon the work. They were doggedly determined to wrest every last scrap of plan and concept out of my hands. Of course, they had no trouble intimidating me and I responded by actually making one mistake after the other. There was hardly a single directorial shout that didn't fall flat on its face or inspire protest. Nothing, absolutely nothing went right. Solange had just begun to put on the disgusting rubber gloves, and I felt a need to step in, and shouted: "More predatory! And maybe a little more ardor!" Maggie stepped out of her role and walked over to me and said in a horribly assuaging tone: "Now, my friend, let's allow time for something to unfold, shall we! Before these sweet little things are mine, you really don't have to bother to interrupt me."

This kind of reproof always sent cold chills down my spine. This was not personal hostility, but again I had disregarded and violated a primary tenet of the theater, a fundamental rule of the craft. As a result, I became overly cautious and was more restrained than I should have been. I watched as the two of them played off one another, playing their way into the piece, charging through almost the entire first ceremonial, lines already learned, requiring no pauses at all, Pat doing My Dear Lady in excruciating exaltation, Maggie holding forth as the maid, with no less ornamentation. Everything went off at a furious pace and was totally exaggerated, and I didn't like it at all. Everything they were doing up there was, on the surface, so accomplished, appeared to be so unapproachable and unstoppable, that nothing about it was at all different from a failed premiere. But I did not dare stop them. It wasn't until Solange got stuck in a particularly suggestive way, at a line where it reads: "We're so unhappy. I could cry!" that they stopped the scene themselves and stepped out of their roles. As they had become accustomed to doing, they demanded that I immediately deliver myself of a detailed critique. But everything had gone by much too fast for me and I was so baffled that I had not been able to register any details. They demanded, in vain, to know what I had seen on the stage and how and where it might be improved. All I could do was raise a couple of objections, which they then disregarded. And once they realized that I was not going to be able to deliver the requisite "concrete" observations, they generously volunteered to repeat a few of the shorter passages so that I could better train my eye. But what they were really doing was luring me into another trap. They played one and the same sequence over and over again, each time varying the tempo and approach, and I was supposed to decide which version I preferred.

"You can have it one way, or you can have it the other way. Basically, you can have anything you want from me," Pat declared, bitterly provocative. "You just have to make up your mind."

But I couldn't and didn't want to commit myself. As far as I was concerned, there was nothing of significant difference among the options they had presented. No matter what they had to offer, it wasn't going to correspond to my expectations, to my *conceptualization*.

So the two queens tested and humiliated me hour after hour and for a number of days. They seemed never to tire of coming up with new evidence of my inadequacy. However: they did not give up on me. They did not cast me out into the desert. Apparently, they intended both through fair and unfair means to prepare me to be their match.

How should our piece, how should this reticent, deadly play begin? The way I see it, the beginning should look like the release of a covey of carrier pigeons. From behind a fantastic, plantlike wall of clothes, on which dresses grow back in after picking, the two maids come fluttering out, flit randomly around the room, and then return to their columbarium, to their nesting place. Margarethe doesn't like it. She cannot imagine how she can find her way out of all this flapping around and back into the clear, unequivocal starting position, into the Lady-maid posture. She emphasizes one more time that the audience must not be robbed of the illusion that Claire is actually the Lady, and Solange the maid. And if this opening scene does not ring absolutely true, if it is not firmly anchored, then the whole piece will simply bob up and down on the waves of one impetus or another, of any ecstasy whatever, hopelessly out of control.

I ask the two of them to at least try out my suggestion, once. And they do, but only to demonstrate before my very own eyes how utterly preposterous it is. It's hopeless. They're not the least bit interested in my ideas. They don't want anything to do with my opening. I don't know what to do next. A painful silence unfolds. They sit on the edge of the stage waiting shamelessly for my next suggestion.

> Scratchycats
> with bound paws,
> there they sit
> and stare poison.

. . .

Somehow, there must be a way to move forward. And if this really was their way of taking me into an apprenticeship, then it was inevitable that they would allow me to solve a little problem here and there. And that, after all, is why they were willing to accommodate me somewhat. But because I was not lacking in obstinacy myself, I immediately reverted back to my threatened conception, again brought out my favorite notions of gesture and physicality, and tried, when my two actresses were in the mood, to smuggle as much of them as possible into the rehearsal. From time to time, I even succeeded in getting them to accept small, isolated, practice pieces. For instance, at one particular point, Pat was to spread her fingers and run both hands through her hair.

"You have to do it in such a way that everyone in the audience feels your fingernails on his own scalp. Just imagine: a heavy, exhausted, despondent head. With fingers spread wide, yes, that's it! You literally want to weed out your head, cleanse it of all senselessness. You are seeking clarity for your thoughts and for your face. Look, you're doing it wrong. You're only pretending. You're only doing it because we agreed to do it that way. But right here, your scalp is going to have to burn, it itches so bad, or this won't work."

The modest successes I was able to achieve with such minutiae didn't lead to an abundance of high spirits on my part. But at least they gradually gave me a feeling for which of my ideas I could put through, and which I had better drop.

Unfortunately, one morning this delicate scaffolding caved in on itself with an awful rumble and roar. One single, ill-chosen word of mine and the hesitant understanding between us came abruptly to an end. Without the slightest evil intent, I had been talking about how we would present *The Maids* as realistically as necessary, as far out as possible, and noted – with all the accuracy of a technologically advanced rocket booster – in passing, that for these purposes Pat and Maggie might liberate themselves from a certain *mime mentality* . . .

Ms. Wirth leapt up, picked her script up off the floor, and hurled it down into the auditorium in my direction.

"Have you lost your mind?!" she screamed at me. "What can you possibly be thinking of? You are a disaster! For us actors, you are nothing but one immense obstacle! What in hell have you lost, anyway? And what can you possibly be looking for in the theater?"

In the meantime, Pat was running excitedly back and forth; almost in desperation, she shot out: "How can any human being be so brutal?! How could you!"

I had absolutely no idea what they were talking about. I had no sense of having said anything offensive.

"Why are you calling us mimes?" Pat yelled again. "Why are you talking about our profession with that kind of contempt?"

How, really? This offhand little word had triggered such a storm of consternation, indignation, and even smug grievance. I couldn't believe it. It seemed to me that they were grossly exaggerating their injury, and this only because they couldn't immediately come up with an appropriate rejoinder. Still, I could see that

Pat's whole body was trembling and that she had thrown herself over a chest of drawers and was crying disconsolately. Margarethe ran to her and took her in her arms.

"You woodpecker!" she shrieked. "You, down there, you sir are just like some conceited old woodpecker! But a woodpecker will never fell an oak! You, Mr. Woodpecker, will only bang around on our nerves with your pointed little green beak!" I will have to admit that at this moment I felt like someone who had accidentally started a forest fire, an avalanche, or some kind of environmental disaster. The damage seemed to have progressed into the range of the incalculable and was continuing to grow. The two women turned tenderly to one another, surrounding themselves with kisses and whispers, and expressing mutual assurance of a firm alliance. And here in the theater, away from the play, I again discovered a puzzling hybrid: something humanly moving took place and yet it possessed only a passing resemblance to the genuine shedding of emotional blood. The feeling that had broken out here was undoubtedly noble, but it owed its existence to a circumstance made of cardboard, a petty, artificial provocation. I couldn't comprehend it for the life of me.

· · ·

The next few days were pure torture. Of course Pat and Maggie continued to rehearse with great fervor, but they did so as if I weren't even there. I had to send my assistant up on stage if I wanted to communicate with them at all. When I tried going up myself and telling them something, they immediately came to a stop, looked down at the floor, and waited unmoved until I finished what I had to say. Then they picked up the scene at the point where I had interrupted, and continued rehearsing without paying the slightest attention to the suggestion I had just made. Another time when I wanted to exercise some influence, Pat simply dropped her arms to her side and moaned quietly skyward: "Alfred, Alfred! Where are you? Why couldn't you have spared us this?"

· · ·

One evening, when there was nowhere else for me to turn, I looked up Alfred Weigert, their lord and master, to seek his advice.

Alfred was a tall, gaunt man. He was probably in his late thirties, and his sometimes degenerate, sometimes highly moral demeanor clearly betrayed that he had been intensely involved in his career for quite some time, had expended large amounts of emotional substance without having adequately replenished it with nutrients from the outside. A meager head, more pointy than long, with two dark, penetrating eyes, sat atop a remarkably skinny neck, and now and then he moved it so jaggedly that anyone who saw him could not help being reminded of an ostrich. For a while, Alfred listened to what I had to say about the rehearsals, but he didn't really seem to take my problems seriously. He gave me the more or less glib advice that for a while I should concentrate my attentions on only one of them, in order to arouse the inevitable jealousy of the other. In this way they would begin to expend some of their energies on each other, rather than teaming up to concentrate on me. Of course I would have to know how to put this slippery advantage to good use, skillfully keeping the trust of the one while not ignoring the wooing of the other, who naturally would be intent on bettering her position. But what respect I would have to enjoy in order to be *that kind* of director! I, I who had not the least influence or effect on these actresses, I who was still standing longingly at the stage door, outside a place of mysteries closed to me, I of all people was to play the urbane illusionist? He could see that his counsel had hardly achieved a calming effect. And it had been offered in a rather cool manner. Apparently, he could not easily get past the fact that this rank beginner who just ran in off the street was playing around with his precious companions, obviously possessing no mastery of these noble instruments, and quite possibly doing some serious damage.

"I feel," I continued my complaint, "as if I were in a subterranean prison maze, running incessantly back and forth not being able to find my way out. The two of them up there on stage made it to freedom a long time ago. But I haven't. I don't know the ins and outs – and I certainly don't know the rules! Sure, they're good. They are very good. But I don't agree with a damn thing they're doing with this play. I have an unbending conviction that theater has to be something entirely different. Entirely different. And so I stare mutely up at them from my cell and sometimes they seem to me to have the self assurance of ghosts who are cheekily intent upon giving us an illusion of life."

"I can easily imagine how you feel," Alfred responded, "but what else can actors do when they aren't being confidently directed, except fall back into their own bad habits? You should always keep in mind: in the final analysis, actors were created for one purpose only, and that is to portray one aspect or another of humankind. Every effort made to train them to perform didactic feats is bound to lead to a grievous restraint of their talents. You can always tell when actors are doing a formally prescribed exercise on stage, representing ideas, or making any other kind of stylized appearance – the first thing you notice is they're constrained, that they're suppressing a significant part of their energies, their power to embody a character, and when this Greater Unfolding of the senses is bound and gagged it can only lead to a depressing performance, always profoundly cramped, forced and false."

"But I'm not after any kind of artificial theater!" I interjected. "On the contrary, what I want to see is the signs from an old and distant memory manifest in a *human being.*"

"But I think Pat and Margarethe are doing you a favor in trying to drive you out of the refuge of your visions and higher ideals. They have a right to demand that you engage them without crutches and supports – without a semiological agenda – as actors, as these indeterminate special beings in whom you can conjure up and make real almost anything from a ghost to a god, as long as you go about it in the right way. Beings in the twilight between Once Was and Now, bodies raised to the threshold, the actual *mediums,* the mouthpiece of Shakespeare or Molière. Only the theater is capable of the chronological synthesis that allows us – while in the meeting place of the actors – to distance ourselves as far away from home, as far from our present as we are close to arriving at a distant past. And this the boundary runs through the physical presence of the actors as well. Why is it that as soon as I see Pat and Margarethe moving around on stage, I desire them in a way that I never would in everyday life, even these two? Because, for me, their existence on stage is an absolute mystery. Because the acting human beings are so close I could touch them, while at the same time having been transported into the uncompromising realm of imagination. This is something fundamentally different from the simple sensory illusion that takes place in a disembodied, non-present cinema. The theater enthralls us with its dual bond of prostitution and virtue, of a palpable presence that is exposed but cannot be touched. Maybe you have to have a very peculiar bent, a slight sexual aberration, to relate to the theater the way I do. And then the disappointment is all the more crass when this lustful house of cards collapses. I can see this happening now in my *Wallenstein* production. But that's just the way it is: for me, actors are always the ultimate witnesses of vigorous human *being*. Aren't they the only ones among us who still come into contact with noble characters, fate, tragedy, heroism, if only in an emotional sense? Often these days, when I hold rehearsals, I find myself entertaining the suspicion that it is almost impossible to develop a credible performance of a play that demands a hero of either inner or outer stature. What kind of deformed little men am I surrounded by! Nervous weaklings, so many repressed rebels, but not a single insurgent among them! And when I think of my beloved ladies . . . I allow myself to imagine that they, Pat and Margarethe, will stand up even to historical comparison and will not have to take a back seat to anyone, including the legendary greats like Bernhardt or Duse. Their skill is certainly no less, it's just that they will never be sanctified. In general, although, or maybe because, they have only recently become involved with tradition, I believe that the interpretive arts will be much less affected by historical decline than the rest, the original arts. Actors, even directors, singers, once they have reached the pinnacle of their art, basically form a corps of peers across epochal boundaries, no matter how greatly their levels of mastery may differ. Now, I don't see any men here who fit into this category. It looks as if even Friedland's stars are being concealed by the night. These days the least talented actors are always the most eager monkeys in the troop when it comes to any kind of 'movement,' any kind of so-called awareness. They have nothing grounded in themselves, they just go panting around trying to sniff out legitimacy, an external cover for their consciences. But the people out there don't even know them. They are anything but attentive contemporaries, and thoughtful observation of their environment has been the least of the sources upon which they have drawn in the development of their talents. But that may not even be all that important for an actor, after all he doesn't impersonate another human being from the outside in. It's just that most of them have forgotten why they chose this profession in the first place: in order to be an enriched person! That's why they're so empty and distracted now. But God help us, if they go to the latest Marlon Brando film, or see some other great who is a star and nothing but a star, and then they learn just how painfully narrow they've become and complain about how little they've made of themselves. And why didn't they make something more? Because their secondhand political attitudes got in their way. Because they were already completely preoccupied with questions of political taste and other superficial intelligence of our time. They simply prefer to discuss things. These days, our actors discuss things with the public following a performance. Well, OK. Why not? But then they shouldn't be surprised when almost no one finds them attractive, that their powers as an actor are severely diminished. Whoever is within reach and often heard talking stupid nonsense will have a hard time becoming grand and unapproachable again, on stage. And even a profound Hamlet will no longer provide adequate cover: everyone will just see through the role into the face of a thoroughly average cogitating man, just like you and me."

Alfred tilted his head to the side and waited to see how I would take his words. Of course, they had tended to confuse and distress rather than encourage.

"You realize," he added, "these days I'm not very happy with our acting art and the way it's being handled here, and in other theaters. But I'm not going to worry about it anymore once my poor *Wallenstein* has made his appearance. A novel by Tolstoy, a poem by Mörike, a few pages of Lichtenberg, haven't I gotten more from them lately than from all of this theater craziness? To tell you the truth: no. Only actors give me true pleasure. When their performances are appropriately filtered through us! If they weren't always trying to get in their own way all the time! . . . For a few months now, I have been working on material for a film. I have to risk it. I'm going to take the two women with me and we'll make our own way out in the world. Enough of the herds and body-heat alliances. I'm going to write this film and I'm going to shoot it. And I'm going play the lead. That's what's going to happen. Only fear sharpens the senses."

"When I listen to you," I said, "then I can see that I'm just starting out. You already know everything and can turn away from this. But I have to do something new, and for that reason your experiences have only a limited validity for me. When you're just starting out, you have to want something new. But maybe I won't make it. Maybe I'll be a failure."

Once I had said these words, Alfred really looked at me for the first time, he had taken notice. Something inside him opened up, heart or mind, I could easily have entered.

"There is no failure," he said quietly, "there is only progress. Not even death will stop us. We are always on our way to getting at what really is behind things."

FOUR

What was I going to do now? Run away, throw everything out, get out of this poisonous smog? Things kept getting worse day by day. All the two women did was make fun of me, they continued their crude derision. As soon as I set foot on the stage they began to moan and revel in bogus complaint.

"Don't walk like that! Please don't walk around on our stage *like that*!"

Well, how am I walking? And Pat answered in the most contemptuous tone she could muster: "You are walking around like a pallbearer stepping on a loose shoelace. And it's depressing!"

There's no point. I can't do it. I'm just unlucky. No talent. Disastrous rehearsal. What I'd really like to do right now is get on the night train to Freiburg. I just stuck my neck out too far this time. And there's so much I could be doing to help my father! Instead I've got myself involved with something so ridiculous and grotesque that no sane and honorable man would touch it. A director, as I now understand it, consists of three quarters borrowed authority, of projection, of a need for dependency, and this is what the actors stuff him full of like a Christmas goose. I will never have command of this kind of constantly yawing and rolling contest for illusory power, I will never even find it worthwhile! I haven't lost anything here in this last, innermost, backyard sanctuary of absolutism in which the centralized power of the sovereign could sustain itself, entirely absorbed into its every nerve ending and camouflaged by the false tones of a modern consciousness. And what this director lacks in his own person will be lent him by the elevated position he occupies, the means make the man. I can see what's happening – the theater has served many a man as a true "fountainhead of character"; he entered an improbable toad and came back out having had that certain something bestowed upon him. As long as he didn't let himself get taken down, as long as he wasn't too skeptical and too honorable. . . . But the worst thing is: I can't get along with people. I have no talent for winning them over to my way of thinking. Even the set designer refused to do what I wanted. He claimed that my idea of turning the stage into a rundown futurescape simply wasn't doable. Of course it's doable! You just have to want to do it. But I kept my mouth shut. I was too despondent. Tomorrow I'm going to be merciless. No matter how bad it gets: I am going to be self-assured. I will convince every one of them with the wink of an eye. Otherwise there'll be hell to pay. I'm going to grab Pat and Margarethe by the scruff of the neck. My victory over them will be a moral victory. I'm going to deliver a message. They're going to learn that it's their place to serve, and serve and serve again. Not me, but the play and our common mission. I will convince them to approach our work with total resolve and devotion. I will not allow them to go prancing across the script like a couple of vain flamingoes . . . .

But what do I really want?

I don't have any science, any theory, any vision of a new acting art. What I lack is a clear direction for my struggle. Where do I want renewal? Isn't what I have in mind the perfect play – related to the concept of the perfect murder? Of course, that is something that might have been achieved at any time. Nothing fundamentally new. But is it just this aspect of perfection that I find so repulsive, its inhuman capability, that inhibits me? It makes me sick when I see them unstringing their hollow gestures pearl by pearl, when I see them lacing up and gliding off in their showy, smooth stage walk. . . .

Oh, torn apart by a thousand contradictions instead of being the child of *one* soul! I cannot get hold of them, after all. They don't understand me. I'm going to let them walk the way they walk. No, truly: they have no soul in their bones . . . . They no longer pay any attention to people, no one from the outside can affect them anymore. All of their movement is standard issue.

• • •

I could only hear them in the distance, a quiet hissing of jungle cats. Sometimes a foolish whispering.

"I think he may be suffering a seizure. He's just sitting there in a trance. I have a nephew who gets these little attacks, this . . . petit mal."

"The little evil . . . the lesser evil."

"I mean, I still don't even know what we're really supposed to be playing."

"I think this play has a lot to say about us."

"About us? I don't think so."

At this point I laboriously raised my eyes and addressed them. Heavy, almost drunkenly.

"There has to be something behind this, behind you, a room . . . can you feel it? The back room, there."

Pat put her fingertips to her temples and stretched the skin of her forehead taut.

"What could he possibly mean? Or have I become a total zombie?"

"And there has to be something behind you, too, Margarethe. Behind your back, a giant. Do you feel it? Do you understand me?"

Margarethe answered: "Hardly. I hardly understand you at all, anymore."

At this point I stood up and yelled with every ounce of strength in my body: "And I do not understand what you are performing up there!"

"Listen, Leon," she answered calmly, "there is absolutely nothing behind me. I am standing up here all alone. A simple actress. You will just have to be satisfied with what you have got *in front* of you!"

"I am your teacher, I will show you the secret realm, I am your leader!" I yelled like a crazy man and reared up to full height. But then I collapsed. I was no longer sentient. I ran out of the theater, ran half-unconscious through the streets and across the Rhine, rushed up and down the promenade like a fenced-in dog, all the time continuing to keep to the banks of the river, up the promenade, down the promenade as if I were in a struggle against the river's constant departing.

"This is the winter!" I yelled down to the water. "It is the winter who is cold and harsh and lonely. But I'll put you in your place, too, my little friend . . ."

After that I must have run into the department stores. Suddenly I found myself in an immense open room with lots of counters. There I carped about all the merchandise and argued with the sales clerks. I was painfully aware of much of my absurd behavior, but I couldn't stop it. The rest took place without my having been aware of it at all. What kind of unguided passages must I have taken! I disappeared into the cavern of the endless theater, it enveloped me like a fourth dimension. The silence, the breathing, the knowing. I saw everything I needed. I knew my part. Sometimes a bolt of lightning struck out of my stunned intelligence. But I saw it as if it were in a puddle quietly reflecting the wild heavens.

I didn't go back to rehearsal. I must have run all day. Just like the Monk of Heisterbach, I had lost my time. He had been contemplating the bible passage that says that before the Lord a thousand years is like a day, when he was imperceptibly transported and did not return to his monastery for three hundred years.

I, too, had paid a visit to the other side of time, and when I made my way back to the theater two days later, it was as if I had awakened in another phase of life.

Now I knew which direction I had to fight in. Now it was no longer a matter of some staging or other that would turn out good or bad, now all that mattered was passing the test. I could clearly see that the theater was an iron gate and I would have to stride through it in order to take the next steps on my way to "getting at what is really behind things," as Alfred had put it.

Now I was no longer afraid of the two actresses standing guard in front of the gate; they had not been called for my amusement but for my agonizing ordination.

. . .

"You have taken a great leap forward," Pat said, and gave me a timid smile. During a lengthy, exhausting rehearsal, we succeeded for the first time in touching the dark convention that would hold our maids together and spare our actresses from overtaxing their individuality. Now they smiled, Pat and Margarethe, they cooperated with enthusiasm and trust, almost as if all this time they had only been playing the whiptoting attendants of the initiation – but for me that is what they *were*!

. . .

I don't know how it possibly could have happened, but from this point on everything was easy. I now found myself in a persistent equilibrium that abolished all contention and stress, not only in me but in everyone. Together with the actors I achieved a confident balance among showing and seeing, acting, affecting, and understanding. Nothing had to be extorted, nothing hauled down from the heavens. My words, as thin as they were, seemed in a way to have been electrified, and now although I was saying almost nothing in any way different from what I had before, they were immediately converted into energy and brought about useful advances. Maybe this was also due to the fact that I had held out until the determining moment, when instrumental forces emerged out of orbiting repetition entirely of their own accord. Be that as it may, the gesticulator had become a potentate.

"You have gone through a promising development these past few days," Margarethe said, and I had become conspicuously aware that she now often took me by the hand and was happy to feel me close to her beautiful, slender body.

. . .

But I already knew that I wouldn't be staying. The theater would not be able to hold on to me. It provided me a transition, and that's all. I thought to myself: once the fairy tale bore a brave boy, and now the theater a grown man, and in this way, from seed pod to seed pod, we continually come into being. What would be next? What would my next transformation be?

More and more frequently I was being drawn out into the street in the late afternoon – into the street where I had suffered the consequences of helplessness and misfortune, into this glittering stream of eyes and merchandise that had first devoured me and then brought me back to life. The street in which I had experienced crisis and purification. And the longer I walked, and the more intently I looked, the more normal life revealed itself to me, who had been working beneath the day, the more I saw the truculent present as a painting discharging radiant exaggerated colors, one tremendous motion of time and nontime, repeatedly devoured and always on the brink, about to freeze into a monstrous sculpture at any moment, into a skittish monument, to come to a whirring standstill.

So, I couldn't help going out after rehearsals and keeping watch. And then one day I strayed so far afield I lost my way, it appeared I had come to the end of the street. Here, bewildered, I stepped out onto the flat empty meadowland, the commons that enclosed an athletic field and an expansive stadium. Through the high wiremesh fence I could see there was a track and field competition going on. But as I approached more closely, my visual focus narrowed and came to rest on the foreground. I was looking at the backs of four members of the reserve team who, having put themselves into a vague holding pattern, were standing, bent forward, a few meters beyond the wire mesh. They were runners, two male and two female. Together, all facing forward in the direction of the arena, the men stood behind the women, and each of the four was standing alone among the reserves, *ready*, in anticipation of being called up. I couldn't stop looking at them, and the longer I stared at their backs, the more I understood what Zeno had meant by the inert patchwork of time. For among the waiting runners you could hear the twang of

• • •

THE ERECT ARROW OF LOVE

Their skin remains moon white under our sun. Two women, two men. In shorts of dark red satin, in white jerseys without numbers. Reserves on the edge of the athletic field, in relaxed anticipation of being called up to the starting line. The women both have short hair, one a softly rounded pageboy, the other a rather elongated hood. All four of them of slender build, and almost all the same height. From time to time, the men run flat hands over their abdomens and then slide them down inside the waistbands of their shorts. The women are standing with their tall sinewy backs to the men. Sometimes they fold their arms under their breasts and look down into the arena, sometimes they press their hands into their hips and roll their shoulders forward. Then they look down at the ground and kick small stones away with the toes of their running shoes. But they are most attentive to the exaggeratedly impartial voice of the loudspeaker that at certain intervals announces the results of various events. One of the women gently feathers her hair with both hands. The other scratches her knee. They never slip their hands under their waistbands. The gaze of the man standing on the left has come to rest on the groove of the lower spine of the woman standing in front of him. This is where her shirt is sticking to her wet skin. She is tilting the spiked sole of her right foot inward. With his thumb and index finger, the man behind her is picking at the wing of his nose. The man next to him is resting both hands over his kidneys, his elbows positioned like ears at the alert. The woman in front of him is turning herself on the heel of her right foot once around her axis, and as she does her gaze briefly crosses that of the man behind her. She stretches her arms out wide and draws her fingertips toward her ever so slightly, to the point where they protrude like wingtips. Then she alternately heaves each shoulder forward, and the man behind her observes the ascending and descending mice of the shoulder blades under her jersey. With his index and middle fingers, the man on the left pinches a small fold in the skin of his abdomen. He stares at the strong blue vein in the flat hollow of the knee of the woman in front of him. She is standing with her knees stiffly and fully extended, the muscles of her buttocks tensed, her arms again folded under her breasts. The man raises his gaze to the pinnated down growing back in on her shaved neck. The fingers of her left hand, tucked in under her right elbow, are squeezing and pulling the thin skin over a rib bone. Where her arm bends a funny bone juts out, abnormally sharp, and covered with a wrinkled brown callus. Now, the man behind her leans forward with his upper body and braces himself with his two hands against his knees. His head draws closer to her back, only a few centimeters more before part and tailbone touch, and he is looking straight down at the loamy earth, holding his breath until his face runs bright red. In the armpit of the woman on the right, there is a dark curly patch of hair, but light at the tips, almost white. There, a drop of sweat is forming; it falls, landing coolly on the hand she has folded over her hipbone. Then, with her arms crossed, she runs the palms of both hands through her underarm hair, shakes her wet fingers out and rubs them across her red shorts. The man behind her turns around, grabs a tiny clump of dirt and hurls it against the fence. Then he turns around and faces forward again. The quiet, almighty voice that announces times, names, victories – this warm source of sound flows into the stadium. A voice so clearly enunciated at the microphone and so wonderfully amplified that well-tempered justice seems to be spreading from here to the horizon. Soon, certainly soon, they, these athletes standing here, will also be called up from afar by this caring force. But what would happen if they weren't called to compete, if in the end they weren't needed and had to fall back on their own resources? Suddenly, the women would turn around once and for all and find themselves standing face to face with the men behind them. And these men would then no longer be looking over a female shoulder in the direction of the competition – they would only be looking *as far as* the woman's eye.

But then – finally! finally, the big, just voice calls out their names, too. But the athletic field has long since been cleared of teams and spectators, and the pale moon is hanging over an empty stadium. There, the ethereal second-string runners, the late reserves make their way down to the starting line and move dreamily over the cinders round after round, striving for records in an event that is calculated according to the tempo of waiting.

.   .   .

A large cloud with gaping wolf jaws drew nearer the moon, and I hid my face.

THE FOREST

. . . .

After lunch, the young banker went back to her car and drove aimlessly through the unfamiliar part of town where she had taken her midday break. At this point she did not have the slightest idea what had brought her here and what urgent business she might have to transact. She was on her way – to whom? She had intended – to do what? She attempted – to call what to mind? There was no question, she had an appointment out in Dellbrück. Or was it in Pfaffrath? Somewhere on the northern edge of Cologne there was a client to be seen and a proposed financing to be discussed. How else would she have ended up in a completely unfamiliar part of the city? But who was it? What were they going to discuss? Very likely, it was something of the utmost importance, something worthy of her most careful attention, something so obviously significant that she hadn't even found it necessary to put it down on her calendar, or to write herself a note. Now, in search of just that kind of thing, she was rummaging through her handbag. No, the businesswoman had completely lost sight of when, where, and with whom she had an appointment.

The drafty little hole in her sense of duty simply continued to expand as she drove on and forced herself deeper into thought. The emptiness itself opened up like a gate, soon resembling a majestic portal, through which streamed – with the exception of what she sought – a myriad of colorful and distant memories, thus seriously distracting the driver. Only a very few of these memories was she able to recognize as her own; most of them did not seem even to have emanated from her and her life, but much more to be flowing over her from other lives. Just as if her useless senses, having tapped into the lives of strangers from the past, were nothing more than thieves of data and thought. In this not entirely unpleasant state, she no longer felt compelled to return to the bank, but simply continued, aware of neither plan nor appointment, to drive through the streets, soon finding herself on the far side of the city limits. After she had driven past several kilometers of flat, dusty green fields, a male figure came into view, standing along the edge of the road and rhythmically waving his thumb through the air, hitching a ride. But by the time she braked and was slowly approaching the man, he had long since turned away and transformed himself into a self-contained hiker focused on nothing but his forward progression. It wasn't that he had simply changed his mind and decided to continue on foot, but his entire bearing and his obvious enthusiasm for the march made it abundantly clear that the thought of stopping a car and asking for a ride would never have entered his mind. In an unforeseen reversal of asking and giving, the driver herself suddenly sensed a need: she rolled down the window and addressed the vanished hitchhiker, this master creator of the non-happening. She asked where the town of Heisterbach was located and if he might be able to tell her how to get there by the most direct route; she knew – it had come to her in this most recent series of strange memories – this little place had to be somewhere around here, not all that far from Cologne. The man willingly leaned over to the car window, and to her amazement she found herself looking into the face of a well-known artist, but for the moment she didn't have the slightest idea what to make of the situation. She couldn't recall his name, or even his art, she just couldn't remember. It was just a well-known face looking her way, and the famous man nodded deep in thought and then gave her the responsible answer. "Just follow the arrow," he said in his unmistakable, silvery tones. Even these few, easy words exuded fame and wealth, and the businesswoman received them gratefully; from this point on they would completely fill the void left by her lost sense of orientation. She drove on with a sense of well-being, and she did indeed find the arrows she had been advised to follow, in so many places that taking the wrong turn and getting lost was simply not possible. Whether it be the raised arm of a girl looking at her watch, the beak of a crane or even the strewn white spray of a broken bag of sugar – all of these signs had come into the driver's field of view well before a fork in the road or an uncertain turn might have caused her any doubt. Guided by these most eloquent signs, she soon left the paved road and drove straight across a plowed field following a shaft of light that had broken through the clouds and clearly indicated the way. Here, the ground became too rough for her more elegant than rugged car, and for better or for worse she had to continue on foot. She got out and soon discovered a matted field road that like a hyphen without words, gracefully emerged out of the grass only to quickly disappear again. But the mortgage banker, now practiced enough, saw in this seemingly useless trail her actual signpost, and furthermore, as a nodding row of pines beyond the field expressly bid her come into the forest, no uncertainty would arise within her. She was wearing shoes with pointed toes and high heels; she now took them and her silk stockings off and ran barefoot across the stubbled furrows. Then, once she had passed the first bushes and underbrush and was standing under a dark dome of pine, it seemed to her that she had entered the forest through its most squalid back way, as if she had just entered its bowels, this site was so completely covered in waste. Scraps of paper and rags hung from branches, like coat racks in a café, Coke cans and condoms lay everywhere on the pine-needle carpet, the rocks were covered with black spots of soot, surrounded by empty plastic bottles and chicken bones, a torn beach chair, a Day-Glo green rubber boot, newspapers, cotton, wool, Polaroid film boxes, all kinds of vile, greasy filth covered the ground. The businesswoman bent down to get under the dead, low-hanging branches, expecting to come upon a clean, open road. Then, suddenly, a shrill female voice barked at her. "Get lost, lady!" the voice echoed through the bleak stand of trees. She spun around and saw the young hermit whore, who was sitting on top of a pile of tires, warming her bare legs next to a kerosene burner. Her round face was covered with an excessive coat of stale, caked make-up and there was a crown of violet clover blossoms in her uncombed hair. She was wearing nothing but a long, worn sweater, which reached down over her thighs and then dissolved into a fringe of loose strands of wool, and, on her bare feet, a pair of thick-soled cork sandals. The businesswoman, at this point in her trek still in command of reason and pride, viewed this false and depraved fellow female with some condescension and asked how it was possible to make ends meet – in other words, how she found an adequate supply of customers out here in this forsaken wood. The young forest hooker reached for a rock and threatened to hurl it at the head of the intruder. But then she dropped the scrawny arm, awkwardly raised in readiness, and explained in a restrained voice: "No one ever passes me by out here. Everyone who comes this way takes advantage of the opportunity. That's the way things are in the forest. And I live over there in that hunting cabin. At least during the week, when the boss isn't there." The mortgage banker turned in the direction indicated by the chin of the whore, and there, on a cool Monday morning, she really did see this same young woman standing under an outdoor shower which had been set up next to the cabin. Behind a folding wooden screen, she was lathering her armpits and her raised arms. A large, multi-pound fish took form in the dense spray of the shower and swirled down off her body.

"Well, it's not really all that bad," said the businesswoman, after a brief look at the beginning of the week, "you might be envied."

"But the hunter is a crude ruler," the recluse maiden of the woods now explained, "but that's not all. His is an awful story. Of course, in his everyday life he's nothing more than the harmless owner of a textile mill, but in his innermost being and desires, he is first and foremost a

• • •

HUNTER STUFFED BACK INTO HIS HOUSE

Once a line of policemen combed this woods with bloodhounds looking for a bank robber's stash. Over there in the birch grove, beyond the long, thin line of men, the hunter was lying in wait for the small game that collects in abundance just before daybreak. The hunter, cut off from his revier by the slowly advancing police line, was overcome by a mood of quiet exasperation. This dark mood intensified the longer he had to wait, and soon it was no longer a mood but a violent surge of temper, which all but brought the whole man into a bloody rage. Forcibly prohibited from leaving his cabin in search of his prey, he saw his hobby, his recreation, his desire for freedom, first transformed into a pent-up passion. Then this same passion turned inward, a serious criminal drive to be sure, and once repressed, this drive was transformed into a bestiality barely contained. The hunter, having passed through these various stages, had all but reached the outer limits of his depravity. Excessive control and repression of a harmless enthusiasm for hunting had led to a meltdown in the nucleus of free will, a powerful compression of energy which no man can survive with his self intact. In truth, he was no longer stable, he had long since passed beyond the apex of his degeneration, he *was* already nothing more than a barely disguised wolfman or vampire, and he was no longer interested in small game.

What was to become of him now that he had reached the land's end of human being? In his heart and his jaws already a monster, he had surrendered all sense of despair and lost the capability – which can only belong to a being with a sense of the tragic, a human – namely, to put an end to his own being in order to prevent worse things from happening.

In the meantime, the police line had reached his cabin and requested permission to enter, in order to thoroughly search the place. The transformed or degenerate hunter quickly pulled together what was left of a good citizen's brittle derma and allowed the officers to march into his house and over himself. This having occurred, he immediately stepped into the open doorway. Out beyond, the birch grove, the perimeter of freely accessible wild game, the perimeter of his murderous pleasure and sport. But he takes no notice, a dull, lifeless, blurred field. Now, he is leaving the cabin headed in more or less the opposite direction. The stalker's sights close in on the back of the last, young officer, standing somewhat apart . . .

. . .

After hearing the story of the hunter, the businesswoman took leave of the recluse whore who was forced to reside ex cabin on weekends. She was able to find her way out of the dark pine grove and continued her search and her journey on a broad forest road. But coming out of the very first curve, she unexpectedly found herself standing in front of a crossing gate locked down with a chain, just like the barriers used to block the passage of motorized traffic. The timber was painted a delicate pale blue and glistened, almost transparent and impalpable. The color was reminiscent of a clear, high winter sky, from a distance like unbreakable porcelain. But the businesswoman, lacking in forest experience, hesitated to simply go under or around the barrier. Something told her that beyond this gate, she would be treading on treacherous ground. That over there she could no longer be certain of the cohesion of self, and her legs, her eyes, and her heart might well head off in their separate ways, that her precious and robust powers of reason might scatter like a flock of frightened chickens.

So she stood there, pushing her hands into her pockets and

sparring with her five senses. But when she tried turning back, just to see what might happen, she suddenly found herself confronted with a reddish gold arrow the setting sun had sent down through the treetops, and now there was no doubt, she had to keep going. In the meantime, on the other side strange happenings were under way. First, she saw an intertwined band of marchers, a lazy human snake crawling her way. The procession, dozens of men and women organized into two columns, was being led by a puffy-cheeked construction-worker king and his crude young wife, on whose shoulder this drunk and power-hungry pig was leaning as he stumbled along his way. Organized into orderly ranks, and following the two figures at the front, were the little people, who, as their quavering song made clear, were only hoping to be led out of their "desolation." The human snake was divided into close groups and cells, though this did not seem to indicate any kind of ranking, as physicists had formed up behind cooks, bus drivers, male and female, followed computer programmers, carpenters followed bartenders, and then came real estate agents, garbage men, cartoonists and many, many others; finally, fashion models, pretty but useless, brought up the rear of this well-ordered society. Perched on the shoulder of the lead man, or lead woman, of each group, there was a loud speaker facing backward, and through these speakers the hoarse, whispered promises of the construction-worker king were relayed to even the most remote of his constituents. Now and again, a lone person would pop out of one group and run over to another, either ahead of or behind his own. If, for example, a runaway fashion model managed to make her way into a clan of bus drivers, it was incumbent upon her to immediately integrate herself into the new group and conform to their customs and ways. Not until she had thoroughly absorbed the essence of busdriverdom would she be allowed to move on, or to move back to her old group. Once an alien penetrated a new group, he immediately turned into a pit bull, no matter how peaceloving he may have been before. Quarreling and clamor would arise around him and he would be dealt with harshly until he conformed. Thus, there was a great deal of activity and confusion along the flanks of the procession, while the columns themselves kept moving along in an orderly fashion. But despite all the intoxication and fracas, the head of this human snake, the construction-worker king leaning on his wife's shoulder, appeared not to have lost the least bit of authority or control. Still, at a point a few meters away from the crossarm behind which the businesswoman stood while observing this strange passage, the king suddenly pointed his chin into the wind, froze for a moment deep in contemplation, and then, turning to the left as he took his next step, abruptly changed direction. Here, the snake began to coil, rolling up in a great inward motion which finally brought the head around to the tail. The very next moment marked the beginning of the most cruel and unnatural act ever to have been played out before the eyes of the banker. Bit by bit, beginning at the tail, the snake simply devoured itself. The construction-worker king, apparently driven by sinister suspicion and unquenchable mistrust, attacked his hindmost cell from the rear, and annihilated every last member. And he didn't stop there, he continued to chew his way forward, lunging at the organs and members of his own body, one after the other, the demented sovereign devoured the columns of his true and willing followers, stabbed and bored his way through the unsuspecting backs of the little people, until his murderous suspicion – until he had reached the frontmost ranks and there was nothing left but the leadership itself, while behind there was only blood and rot. At this point, the head of the snake split in two and one eye gazed into the other, venomous and wary, for now the king and the queen stood confronting each other, their bloody weapons in hand.

"Stop! Stop!" the businesswoman yelled at them. "There's a better way to resolve this than killing each other!" With the utmost sense of urgency, she leaped over the barrier into the realm of the Same Time, but she had hardly set foot on the soil of the traveling nation before she found herself in an entirely different place. There was no trace of a cleft snakehead here. Oh, if she had only yelled out this better advice from behind the crossarm, explained it right then and there, and forgone the jump! And now, with the crossarm at her back, she could no longer recall what she had wanted to say to those two destructive beings. It must have been really great advice. But she just found herself wandering through a peaceful, leafy-moist glade, while feeling that somehow this horror hung in the same mild air she was presently inhaling. The fate of the deranged sovereigns, its terrible end seemed only to have been postponed for now, the bloody exhilaration faltering only long enough to catch its breath, before moving on to a final and complete tranquility – that is, as long as she didn't immediately come up with the appropriate word, the redeeming counsel. Thus, the woman was ready to try *anything* to find her way back to the pair, before their annihilation followed that of the society and their fates would be sealed.

This capricious realm was crisscrossed not by roads and tracks but instead by invisible streams and currents, it was not easy for her to find her way, there simply was no route for the nimble escape she desired. She had already looked around, unable to decide on any one direction, when she noticed to her amazement that she was standing right next to a towerlike structure which all this time had only been waiting for her gaze. A drab turret constructed of heavy, almost black, roughly hewn stone, it soared up nearly sixty meters high and evinced neither windows nor slits. Without the slightest hesitation, she headed into the dark, imposing ruin, hoping to find a lookout platform from which she would be able to view the entire expanse of Same Time. Next to the low entrance, cut artlessly into the rough walls, and apparently the only opening in the entire edifice, the tower guard sat dozing on his chair, tipping back up against the tower. He greeted his visitor warmly, and explained that this tower was not at all a lookout tower, but something much more like a department store, closed off on all sides, even at the top, because of its valuable and sensitive inventory, and like any other treasure house was kept in hermetic darkness. The department store even had a corporate name: it was called "The Tower of the Germans." "Here you can find just about everything that has ever been given a name in our country and in our language." This was how the tower guard proudly introduced it. Although she had no intention of buying anything, and all she really needed was a lookout, this woman in such a hurry could hardly contain her curiosity, of course she had to see the tower from the inside. The guard allowed her in, while he himself remained outside and went back to his chair.

On the inside she was immediately struck by pitch dark night. At first her eye could discern nothing, and only the diffracted daylight from the outside, lying around the entrance to the tower like a distorted rhombus, provided her the slightest orientation. Then suddenly she found herself surrounded by a myriad of tiny yellow flames hovering throughout the very damp air, and filling the entire tower to its uppermost reaches. Now, with the lights providing such a precise and concrete frame of reference, the tower actually did take on the appearance of a multistoried emporium, entirely constructed of flickering points of light. In addition, she was now surrounded by a pandemonium of hundreds, even hundreds of thousands of voices, all of which arose simultaneously out of every pore in the walls of the tower, only to be reabsorbed as if they had been inhaled. Like swarms of tiny invisible birds, the human, the German voices in the tower fluttered up and then settled again. Whispering, laughing, chattering, crying, praying, concurring, hoping and cursing, she could hear everything, every characteristic and every nuance of timbre, dialect, volume, tone, and whatever else one might demand of a voice, it was all here in stock. More bewildered than amused by this ringing specter of echoes, the businesswoman looked for an immediate escape, believing that she was the victim of some cheap carnival swindle, nothing more than hollow light and sound. But now the tower guard was standing in the exit and his broad backside blocked her way. She could hear him talking to someone on the outside, refusing to allow this visitor in. But, because the guard's ample body filled the only opening so tightly that it was almost soundproof, she couldn't hear exactly what was being said. So she yelled at his back as loudly as she could: "Let me out! There isn't anything to buy here!" "Is that so?!" he answered over his right shoulder, without missing a beat in the dispute he was conducting on the outside. "Nothing to buy here? What about the voices? Didn't you hear them?" "Of course," the woman answered, "the voices, all of those fleeting voices, it's enough to drive you crazy!" To which the guard, having rejoined the strife to the front and given his commands, responded, "The voices, my dear lady, are the wares of this store. Just take your time and listen around. Make sure you check out our sales. You'll surely find something to suit your tastes. In the meantime, I've got to do something to get rid of this barbarian, he was banned from the store a long time ago, under no circumstances is he to be allowed to take a single human tone into his degenerate throat."

At this, the detained woman turned back into the shimmering store of voices, somewhat dejected, the air saturated with tiny flames making it difficult for her to breathe. On the inside wall of the tower, not far from the entrance, a broad, flat wooden stairway rose up and turned round in a spiral like the peeling of a perfectly pared apple. She climbed slowly upward and, believing that she was passing by numerous levels and departments, she also noticed that all of the voices, which had previously seemed to be flying around in wild chaos, were in fact carefully sorted according to various criteria, and carefully stored in stone niches in the wall of the tower, just like clothing, jewelry, and household items stored on the shelves of ordinary department stores. Here, the tiny yellow flames, nourished by the gusts of voices, took on the shape of lettering and prices. In one area, voices and idioms were arranged according to profession, and she could hear the automobile mechanic, the barber, the meteorologist speaking their own particular languages; in another area, they were grouped according to tone, color, and range. On the next floor up, there were stacks of jargon and idioms from various epochs and regions. Even the most exacting demands could be satisfied. German spoken by youth of the 1920s was just as conveniently available as exorcisms or national pathos. Of course, there was also a pornography section, and under lock and key: the language of poets and philosophers, somewhat like the noblest of wines, which, in a department store, are kept in display cases or on shelves behind wrought-iron bars. And there were "open" stones everywhere: these were the pawed-over bins, the tables full of specials. Which is where the businesswoman was rummaging around at this very moment – dialects and regional speech – suddenly she heard Westphalian tones, someone from Münster! She bent down closer to the stone, believing that what she was hearing was her father's voice, just as someone abruptly grabbed her by the arm. For a fraction of a second she saw the gaping hairy jaws of the wolfman, the same beast she'd heard about from the forest whore, and was scared to death. Fortunately, it was only the store detective, a gaunt, gray-haired man who claimed he had caught her in the act of shoplifting.

"And what would I be stealing here?" she screamed, both ashamed and excited. "There's nothing here that I'd want!" The man, who had a flat forehead and a small wrinkled face, pointed at her neck: "And what's this?" "My neck." "What's inside?" "Inside? Inside . . . my voice is inside." "It is not your voice at all. Just a little while ago I heard you talking with the guard downstairs, and it sure as hell sounded a lot different then. First, it was a dark voice, and second, it was perfectly free of the slightest trace of dialect."

Unfortunately, there was some truth to what he was saying. The woman had noticed it herself: during that moment of shock – when she simultaneously believed she was hearing the voice of her father, was abruptly grabbed by the arm, and was assailed by the image of the wolf man – her voice did slip back into her old regional speech and now she was still speaking in the somewhat crisp, bright tones of her childhood. She just couldn't escape it, no matter how hard she tried or how many times she cleared her throat.

"You have committed a theft!" he repeated brusquely. "Come with me, we're going to take a closer look at this case." He grabbed her by the arm again and pulled her along with him down the stairs and then, atop a descending metal platform, they floated down into his underground office. It was an unusual room, round like a diving bell, equipped with video screens and speakers that were connected to infrared cameras and hidden microphones, thus enabling the detective to see and hear everything that was going on in the tower, even at night when total darkness and silence reigned. While the detective had no nose worthy of mention, he did have moist and wiggly lips, and when he talked they gradually became covered in bubbles of spit as large as Christmas tree ornaments. And now he had his suspect down here in his unventilated room. He draped himself over the edge of his desk, facing her, and began running his dagger-shaped letter opener around and in between his fingers. He observed his prey with greedy vigilance and threw himself into the pose of an interrogator. But the woman was perfectly willing to provide all personal information requested of her, and the only thing she refused to do was to admit to having a stolen voice in her throat. As he kept insisting on a confession, and even threatened to call the police, she soon found herself laughing out loud at his fierce efforts, and it was clear that it had been some time since the detective had gotten any convictions to his credit, and he was worried about his job. He reached excitedly for the receiver and threatened her: "I'll call your mother and tell her what's become of her pretty daughter. Nothing more than a nasty little shoplifter! Is that what you want me to do?"

Knowing that her mother could not be fooled so easily, and that she would stand by her daughter, no matter what, the business-woman simply shrugged her shoulders. Her indifference pro voked the totally superfluous tower attendant, and he became more pretentious than ever. He started delving into the so-called investigation of the motive, meaning that he didn't really investigate any thing at all, he simply hurled useless psychobabble her way. She was of course an example of the widely-known affluent kleptomaniac, who, out of some sense of sexual inadequacy, was now haunting department stores, morbidly latching on to things she didn't even want, doing all of this in order to finally be caught, humiliated, and arrested, at which point she would be able to indulge herself in the intimate pleasures of an interrogation with the detective. For his part, he furiously shoveled around in her background, attempting to do what he could to destroy her, to push her over the edge into a breakdown. But he did not succeed. For, although his little scenes were painful for her to witness, they were so clichéd, degenerating into meaningless platitudes at every turn, that they never once touched her person. Once he finally realized that he was getting nowhere with his victim, the detective immediately plopped down from the lofty heights of his exhilaration into a puddle of despair. He turned away from her, still babbling on about something or other while he rearranged the papers on his desk. For him, this case was apparently over; his rude and unhappy pursuit of a confession had again ended in failure, and the case would now have to be brought before a higher power. "I'm going to take you to the proprietor of the Germans. If you would be so kind as to follow . . . "

"To the proprietor of the Germans?" the businesswoman asked, amused. "When did this come about?"

"I am referring to the owner of the tower, and I do have a legal right to use that title. Come on!"

"One more question, detective, sir," the woman said. "How does one pay for a voice, should one decide to purchase it?"

"It's obvious that you don't know," the sub-interrogator growled, "you did after all steal one. It is well known here that we pay in units of valid identity energy. One or more fingertips are held over the appropriate little flame, and the price is then calculated in I-quanta, and booked. You, on the other hand, simply leaned down over the stone and sucked up the goods."

"I didn't suck up anything. And that's that!"

The two left the office dome through a round opening under the desk, and then climbed up a long stairway, heading toward an extensive network of canals that spread out like a municipal sewer system, under a low manhole cover dripping copious amounts of water. But it wasn't runoff, it was humanity's ground water: "the streams of life" is what they call the waters flowing here, quiet and colorful, radiant and murky, glistening and dull. Among the infinite variety of substances and materials, all in liquid form, there were those humans need for nourishment and physical strength, and others that were necessary for work. The canals flowed parallel to one another, and no matter which direction you looked, it was impossible to see where they ended. The small part that was visible here gave no indication of how the whole was organized, so it seemed that there was simply some kind of random neighborliness at work among the rivers. Dissimilar materials such as bone marrow and white rubber, tears and gasoline, venison and ink, flowed side by side through the open concrete conduits, and the inorganic gave way to the organic, the refined to the raw; but every one of them was sap. Even glass and wood, even dralon, leather, and quartz had been released from their natural state to find another in this gushing foundry. It was clear that neither heat nor high pressure could have been the cause of the current state of these materials, and that it could only have been some chemical reaction or interference unknown to this world. A damp and somewhat cool air rose uniformly out of the brooks. "This is the great reserve," the detective explained to his astonished companion, as they made their way on catwalks and iron steps across the kaleidoscopic currents, "and they also belong to our proprietor, the one we call 'the German' for short. Over there, where you cannot actually see anything, we have stored in their liquid state those materials that up there, under the open skies, are more or less thought to lack matter, those things known as spiritual property, history and art, magic and technology, and many more. There are no shortages, as you can see for yourself, and if, up there – up there in society – one or the other of these materials should disappear, *he* will always be able to replace what is lacking. And then there will be nothing to equal his power. Just about anything you need to live a decent human life is available here in abundance, coursing through the system, being kept fresh." In the meantime the two of them had come to an iron shed, which at first glance reminded one of those little structures on the tops of big office buildings and warehouses, which house the electrical plant. And the inside hardly looked like the reception area for the personal offices of the all-powerful German. Instead, it looked much more like the switching station of a power plant, there were long desks covered with switches and regulators, with monitors and flickering banks of lights, everything pulsing and informing, even though no one was present to take readings or activate controls. Data rising and falling, exploding into view and vanishing, pictograms shooting past, waxing and waning symbols of precise information, all of this bubbled and flashed, took shape and then outstripped itself, seeming both to shield and to indicate an extravagant existence in process, distant and vital. The detective sat down at one of the control panels and whispered an unintelligible code word into the metal bud at the tip of an adjustable microphone. At this very same moment, the riotous motion of little glowing dots, the spewing forth of numerals, and the flashing alarm lights all subsided. The shimmer of the video monitors stilled. Everything which had heretofore been hopping and ricocheting violently now glided gently into a smooth, measured mode, as if the frantic dreams of the apparatus had given way to a deeper, sounder sleep. To the same degree the light from the video monitors dimmed, a high, glasslike surface appeared before the eyes of the mortgage banker and began to glow more and more brightly, and soon the woman could see water lapping up against the other side. A huge aquarium, taking up an entire wall, finally emerged, and it was not long before powerful swells surged across the surface of the water. A frail, distant glow emerged out of the brownish green darkness, and the entire ambience suggested the approach of something extraordinary and huge. But, because a flutelike tone came wafting through the room at the same time, it was also possible that they were to be confronted by something colossally cute. Then suddenly, without having visibly arrived, it was already there: a bodiless monster of simply unimaginable proportions hovered and swam around behind the pane of glass. His upper face was that of a mature, even aging, man. Indeed, it was human all the way down to its cheekbones; but from there on down was the fat puckered mouth of an ill-humored giant carp. The head of the proprietor . . . of the Germans. It towered a good three meters high up over the head of the diminutive woman. The eyes of this entity were clear and trustworthy, but the fish mouth was gloomy and mean. The four long whiskers undulated lazily like parade banners. His dark-blond hair curled easily over his forehead and seemed to appear and reappear continuously. However, the arrogant mouth spoke no more than these good true eyes saw. The sense organs and the organs of expression must have been somewhere else entirely, and the true core of the proprietor's being was hidden behind this malformed monstrosity, as if behind the fool's mask of an evolution celebrating carnival. So, the businesswoman was not surprised when shortly thereafter she heard the voice of the proprietor, and the fish mouth stayed shut. What she really perceived was a sound coming from somewhere just behind her ear, and it was more courtly and sweet than any contemporary voice could possibly be. Only a supernatural being, now descended, could speak to a woman at once so powerfully and so tenderly.

"I regret most deeply," came the tones, measured and effortless, "the occasion of this meeting is not a happier one, my dear lady. And I would like to suggest that we put an end to this tedious predicament as quickly as possible."

"I agree," the businesswoman answered, heartened, and added, while bravely looking into his divided visage: "And I expect you to declare me innocent, immediately, of all those nasty accusations your overzealous employee has brought against me."

"I think," the head responded, nodding slightly, "your new voice suits you very well. As if you'd been born with it. And you should pay the appropriate price."

"I don't have to pay any price for my own voice. It belongs to me. From the day I was born. And I have absolutely no intention of buying another one. And even if I needed one for a change, I would never pay for it in I-quanta."

At this, the head laughed cheerfully behind her ear. "Let's forget the payment. All I'm asking is that you give me a few moments of your precious time, and if you allow, I would like to invite you to a little supper in 'Jerry's Air Bubble.' It would truly bring joy to my heart . . ."

His heart, his heart, thought the one so desired, and where might this Head-Only-Monster be keeping his heart?

Obligingly, as if he were thoroughly accustomed to his master's sudden shifts, the detective pushed himself away from the panel and walked over to the leftmost edge of the tank. He motioned the woman to come over to him, as she was still thinking about the repulsive head that had just disappeared as suddenly as it had revealed itself a short while ago. Out of sheer curiosity, out of an inborn spirit of adventure, she was ready to accept the invitation still fluttering around in her ear. The detective instructed her in the use of an airlock located behind the glass wall: through it, the detective assured her, she would be carried up to the appointed site inside an oxygen shaft, without ever coming in contact with the surrounding water. Now, she was also directed to remove all of her clothing, as she would be sucked into the lock from the outside through a thin and delicate rubber membrane. Not having the slightest intention of putting herself in a compromising situation, the businesswoman raised her eyebrows, somewhat involuntarily. But the detective, who, now that he had lost all control over her fate, had become a most obedient serf and drudge, explained the technical necessities so convincingly that she finally took off her overcoat, as well as everything else she was wearing, and laid them over his arm. Then she fastened her long hair at the back of her neck and crawled, completely naked, into the narrow vent. She could still hear how her helper locked the device from the outside, started the suction turbine, and suddenly she whooshed up the oxygen shaft with the speed of a bullet. Having no sooner left than arrived, albeit half-deaf, at "Jerry's Air Bubble," it was hardly possible for her to have gotten any idea of how far she had come. Here she was enveloped by a transparent oxygen tent of grand proportions and an opulent meal had been laid out in her honor. Fresh oysters, warm meat, mushrooms and fruit, wine, tea, and all sorts of breads and pastries were there for the taking, and nothing more need be ordered. Still, only half of the table was accessible to her, as the second half lay outside the plane of her canopy, continuing on through a water- and airtight slit into the turbid waters outside. And there, at the far end, sat, undulated, or simply reigned the outrageous head of her host. The exposed woman sat down at the table, still without the slightest tinge of embarrassment, certain that even though the good and just eyes of the colossus rested on her, they must either be blind or faked. And the deformed maw that disgusted her now as much as ever could not approach any closer through the solid plane. It was only the peculiar tickle of his voice, so close to her ear, that made her uneasy, and it was just as he greeted her again in his old-fashioned way that she would rather his words had reached her from a more seemly distance. Apart from that, the air in this bright and friendly pavilion was pleasantly dry and warm and she noted the pleasurable sensation of pores opening on her bare skin. Just then, something equally delicate-heavy-cool touched her bare foot and slid over it with a tortured lethargy. The carp head immediately sensed her alarm and reassured her, saying, "That's just Jerry, the owner and chef of our friendly little inn. If there's anything else you would like, please feel free to let him know. He will take care of everything. Though under certain circumstances a little patience may be required."

So, the businesswoman thought to herself, this restaurant's being run by a turtle. No wonder everything had already been set out before we arrived, and there's almost every delicacy one could imagine, except turtle soup! And fish!

She was feeling so good that she was almost overcome by an impudent desire to indicate that she just might be hungry for a capital carp.

Set up in front of the detached head there was a frame strung with silver wires, something like the kind of abacus children used to use to learn arithmetic. But instead of beads, there were rows of fist-size fish balls which had apparently been shaped from various sorts of chopped worm. This is what the well-mannered monster was having for dinner, and the all-disapproving snout of the carp crudely snapped away at the proffered meal. During this entire time the mighty entity paid her compliment after compliment and praised her beauty, and the faint eddies of air behind her ear were as soft as a kiss on the back of a hand. Strangely enough, he also praised the elegance of her attire – which she was, of course, not wearing. It may well be, the woman thought, that *in the present* he doesn't see me at all, and has not noticed in the least how comfortably I am lounging around naked on my chair. While most men undress women with their eyes, this one seems to be clothing me with his polite looks, supplying proper attire to a helplessly exposed person.

Her good mood had made her somewhat imprudent, and she wanted to get behind the facade of this man's manners and talk to him about his incredibly commanding presence.

"Just how much power do you really have?" she asked quite distantly, and noisily licked off her fingertips.

The response of the hermaphrodite was immediate and deadly

serious. And she sensed an icy wave, the essence of deadly seriousness, pressing toward her, having breached even the impenetrable wall of the tent.

"As far as German spirit extends," was the restrained, imperious reply.

"Are you aware that we've now got two separate Germanys up there?"

"I am the essence of all Germans," the answer reverberated darkly out of the colossus. "Not one of them thinks German without me."

The businesswoman noticed that her host was not about to tolerate any joking around with these sensitive issues.

Without thinking, she had touched on sacred tenets which could no more be joked about here than God could be joked about in front of a believer.

Still, she thought: he, the Most Powerful, he might as well be living on another planet, the way he's living down here. There is something terribly outmoded about this landlord of our soul!

Now, however, the voice of the head had again snuggled up to her ear, but this time there were no flattering words, instead a quiet singsong lulled the somber woman into lethargy.

A head hovers deep beneath the earth

It rules the realm, it builds the church

Towers are rising, bridges struggle forth

Across an entire land one arm lies

Iron arm of unity

Fame renewed and strength renewed

Rising from the flames of unity's might

Every man knows, every man quakes

Sun, erupt! Ether, burn!

German earth, eternal bloom!

The underwater dinner guest was deeply disturbed by this cant, her simple, contemporary mind outraged.

"What kind of gloomy verse is that! What a sick way of thinking! Listen, tower owner, I'd like to know: what era do you belong to, anyway?!"

Having said these words, she heard a powerful angry roll of thunder arise from behind her ear; the gentle breath became a storm and threw her down against the edge of the table, and in her humiliation hot tears of helplessness gushed onto her plate, an ear-splitting bolt of lightning descended on her with a terrible scream: "I time!"

At this very same moment, the enormous maw of the carp opened wide – it could easily have swallowed "Jerry's Air Bubble" whole – and the world became black, the entire restaurant wobbled and seemed to be rotating wildly around its own axis, it would not have taken much more for the tent to have torn loose from its algae anchoring and to have been carried away in the currents. But luckily, there was only one clap of thunder. The cloudburst of anger quickly subsided. Like a bowed blade of grass, the naked woman slowly stood upright and looked into the endlessly good, just, and bogus eyes of the mammoth face. And the commanding voice was again resting up against her ear, but this time it oscillated in more gentle tones.

> I come and go
> Possess and retreat
> Am wave on the shore
> Wind in the trees
> Eluding the new
> Escaping the old

"Yeah, yeah," the businesswoman sighed, "I see it already, I know what kind of shameless swoon you're trying to lull me into." Here she had come, simply out of curiosity and an innate sense of adventure, and where other men might well have used the opportunity to make indecent advances, the head creature, not any the less provocatively, ensnared her in all this German bluster. "No!" the word simply burst out. "I believe in self-determination for the German people, it is a belief I could not possibly hold more strongly!" She had of course learned from legend and history that courage always will vanquish the tyrant, and that the expression of a deeply held conviction will seldom fail to produce the desired outcome. And thus, she had the same chilling effect on her host that she might have had on an ardent suitor, having excused herself after dinner because of a certain indisposition. The lifeless mask, if one may put it this way, recoiled through and through. A gust of bitter cold swept in. "I am afraid I do not fully understand what you mean," the head replied courteously, but with an icy gray detachment. "I simply intended to engage you in a free and open exchange of ideas. But it now seems to me that I may be burdening you disgracefully with my presence . . ." At this juncture the businesswoman was about to express herself a little more clearly regarding the provocative whispers in her ear, when she suddenly felt an unpleasant tug on her big toe.

"It's Jerry," the Head said. "He would like to assist you in finding your way to the door. I do appreciate how much of your valuable time you have sacrificed here with me."

At that, the naked woman stepped onto the shell of the turtle and allowed herself to be serenely carried away. "Valuable, well, you're certainly right about that," the mortgage banker mumbled to herself, while turning her thoughts to the construction-worker king and his wife and hoping that they had continued to refrain from hacking each other to pieces. "The strange thing is, I don't even know how much time I actually have left. Basically, I feel that I'm on time wherever I am. And I've even enjoyed being down here with you and I don't feel that I've wasted the least bit of time. By the way, I didn't mean to be rude . . ." But at this very moment she found herself in the oxygen elevator, rising to the surface surrounded by a myriad of other empty bubbles.

. . .

She finally re-emerged into daylight in the middle of a deep, moss-green lake in the forest. Ducks and coots fluttered wildly away as the rolled-up body broke the still surface of the lake, gurgling and bubbling furiously. She had to gasp for air, as her oxygen supply had begun to run out during the ascent in her thin-walled capsule. With powerful strokes she swam to the near shore, overgrown with rushes. These gave way to a narrow strip of sand where she could lie down and begin to recover from her rugged ordeal. When she closed her eyes and tried to recall the mysterious Head of the Germans, what came to mind was extremely vague. The brows an eel, the nose a giant, the eyes two fiery heads of lettuce: the true hermaphroditic image had been expunged from her memory and was entirely transformed into nothing more than an emblem.

A late summer gentleness and warmth hung over this part of the forest where she now found herself; she would not be cold, even though she lay on the ground still unclothed. She gazed up into inert azure, and inconstant clouds blanketed the evening sky like billowing golden hair. There is where a strong-armed sleep was attempting to carry her away, when all of a sudden she heard frenzied male voices and serious argument. Again, curiosity and a sense of adventure deterred the businesswoman from giving in to her own exhaustion. She got up and saw, not far off in the background, a half-dozen old men standing around an oak tree immersed in the observation of one single green leaf suspended from an otherwise bare branch. The woman immediately set off in the direction of this curious band and watched while the men lined up one behind the other, the first one grasping the leaf with both hands; then the entire squad, each holding onto the shoulders of the man in front, leaned back in an apparent but unsuccessful attempt to tear the green leaf out of the tree.

With the chasteness of one thirsting for knowledge, mindless of her bare state, the woman joined the old men, who immediately stopped the proceedings and surrounded her with confused and bewildered faces. She was now looking into a circle of dumb old mama-men, leathery Indian faces, wrinkly necks, long gray braids hanging down over brown-spotted shoulders, sunken chests with protruding ribs showing through old-fashioned bathrobes. Full of determination, the woman made her way to the oak leaf, took the stem in both hands, and, with knees bent, gathered all of her strength and pulled. The leaf, however, broke loose with a most minimal application of force, almost dropping off the branch, thus setting the oak leaf picker on her backside with a generous abundance of momentum. The old men gleefully clapped their hands and broke out in foolish laughter. Only one of them remained somber, and it was the very man who had thought up this nonsense in the first place and had headed up the group effort. He walked up to her and advised her to take very good care of the leaf she was about to angrily crush in her hand. Having heard what he said, she looked at the leaf full of wonderment and suddenly became aware of the fact that she was sitting stark naked on the ground. In a split second she was on her feet, broke through the circle of giggling old men, and ran as fast as she could into a grove of quivering aspen, securing adequate protection, but hardly the hideaway she needed. Driven by an embarrassed panic, she sought to flee her lack of cover, running further and further away even though no one was following her, finally reaching a broad footpath that, like the one at the beginning of this outing, was suddenly blocked by a lowered crossing gate. The only difference was that this gate was painted red and wrapped in loose strands of barbed wire. And next to it there was a small red-and-white-striped guardhouse. From this little building there emerged a young man dressed like a lifeguard or a masseur, entirely in white, in cotton pants and a light sweater. Without asking her a thing, or showing a hint of surprise, the guard took the leaf out of her hand, went back to the guardhouse, and then reemerged with every piece of clothing she had left in the underground machine room resting over the arm of the detective.

Now, right here in front of the guard's eyes, she put everything on piece by piece, starting at her feet and working upward to her neck; and when she had finally buttoned the topmost button of her overcoat, she looked into the young man's face for the very first time. She noticed the strong, warm eyes that had been watching her all this time. And then, all of a sudden, spontaneously, she began to repeat each dressing motion in reverse order, until she was again standing bent forward in that very same posture she had assumed as the silk stocking was being slipped on over the tips of her toes, only this time it was being peeled off. And in precisely this pose, the stocking peeler offered herself to the lunging stranger. The man desired out of the blue in the blink of an eye.

Once they had taken their pleasures with each other, the guard invited her to stay with him a while longer. "Just for one cigarette!" he said, and they both crawled into the hut. There he smiled and thought out loud: "There are people whose eyes can only be opened by love. Until this happens they never know where they are in this world . . ."

"My dear sir, I don't love you," the woman replied.

"No, you don't, I know," the man answered, "and that's why you're still going to be wandering around in the unknown."

"Be that as it may." The woman cut off the conversation, picked up her clothes and looked around for a more or less sheltered spot where she could get dressed without being observed. She had hardly had time to stand up and finish dressing, when she sensed, without the slightest doubt, that she had been penetrated to the innermost depths of her body. She was, of course, deeply distressed at this realization. What wouldn't she have to suffer here in this forest? Here, where the laws of time changed course as arbitrarily as the pathways, which themselves were no more than signposts, the growth and development of the fruit in her womb might also proceed in entirely unexpected ways. It was therefore her one and only wish to find her way out of this wilderness of Same Time as quickly as she possibly could, and to reach a place where she could count on more natural processes. Weighed down by her misery, she did not even notice that she had run deep into impassable undergrowth, and she was attempting to climb up a steep bluff on whose upper slopes she had observed the back ends of campers and trailers. At least there, she thought, she would be certain to find an inhabited campground, or something of the sort, and there reenter the secure, modern world. She suddenly found herself trapped in a dense stand of bushes, and since she had been gazing so longingly at the top of the slope, she was now surrounded by impenetrable vegetation; thorny branches, densely intertwined, blocked her climb at every turn. On top of all this, the ground beneath her feet was beginning to give way, growing increasingly soft and damp, and with her very next step she sank knee-deep into a muddy marl pit. Genuinely fearing for her life, she grabbed for the nearest stand of hawthorn bushes, and desperately in need of something to hold on to, to keep her from sinking any further into the soft, grimy hole, she opened deep, bloody gashes in her hands. In terrible pain, she locked onto the thorny tendrils and slowly pulled herself onto firmer ground. At this point she no longer dared to stand upright, and crawled, more precisely, shoved herself, sliding laboriously forward under the branches, holding her coat in front of her like a shield until it was finally shredded to pieces. It was as if the undergrowth had sunk its claws into her like some multiarmed beast of prey. She held her torn hands in front of her face, she sobbed, screamed, she cursed and moaned into the air, she could see the boundaries of her torment up at the top of the bluff; why hadn't anyone emerged from his leisure to reach out to her?! Ah, wait, there was someone at the edge of the slope, but he had only come to empty a plastic bucket full of dirty dishwater down the slope that the guests at the campground used as a garbage dump.

Still in the clutches of the wild undergrowth, she was forced to struggle on with arms and legs, even teeth. Thorny branches fastened themselves around her forehead, she bit off the barbs and tore the knotted strands apart with her teeth. And this is how she slowly made her way forward under unimaginably difficult conditions. When she was finally able to stand up straight again, having firm ground under her feet, she looked around and saw she was in a hollow that contained nothing but a single, round bush rotating into itself. It had broad, deep-violet leaves and was not like any of the native plants she knew. It was more like a dwarf Brazilian chestnut tree, a para-nut tree. The businesswoman was strongly attracted to this amazing bush, and, as she approached more closely, she noticed that the dark-leafed parts were continuously devouring themselves only to sprout forth again from the inner-most reaches of the plant. Without being touched by the slightest hint of a breeze, the bush swayed, delivered itself in overabundance and then flowed back. The plant was more like a whirlpool in a pure spring, and like the powerful, undulating plumes of a firestorm, too, its wave and flame seemed to merge in its motion, flowing and erupting, creating and consuming, and just like these elements, it had the power to siphon every nearby bit of matter into its vortex. And not even the pregnant woman could with-stand the force. Ripening within her, the fruit of an accelerated life had become round and heavy and she had to lie down. She stretched out under the bush and immersed her widely spread legs in the dark spring. In a stupor, she sank in up to her waist; in a moment of profound emancipation she delivered herself and grew up under the bush. Here is where the curious eyes of the child appear, along with a mind so easily corrupted, the precocious delight in forests and streams, and a little later the almost painful gift of being able to discern transformation inside still things. She must have just reached the vulnerable age of six or seven when, at the end of a long Sunday spent in the woods with her mother, she walked onto a mountain meadow to pick a full bouquet of crowsfoot and yarrow, marguerites and bluebell. She knew her mother was not far away, lying on her stomach on a blanket next to a babbling brook, a thick book without pictures in front of her nose, her legs stretched out behind her, bare feet touching one another.

Having bound the flowers and grasses neatly together, ready to give to her mother, the child is rudely interrupted in its merry approach. It stands stock still as if rooted in place. The child's mother is lying on her back, half naked, legs spread wide, and a strange figure is bent over her. At first terrified, and then deathly sad, the little girl lets the flowers slump and is about to turn away. But then she suddenly notices that her mother's head is hanging lifelessly over the edge of the bank, bleeding into the water. The child screams in terrible pain. But only the creature, the strange wild thing, seems to hear her, and it turns around to show its gaping, bloody maw. At this moment the little girl loses all understanding, she runs as fast as she can, runs for her own life, deep into the woods, blind to every path, simply runs and keeps running until she is lost among the trees and slides breathlessly down a trunk to the ground. But hardly has she gasped a few breaths before she hears steps, branches snapping, wings fluttering, leaves rustling, her pursuer is announcing his approach. The yellow eyes of the wolfman glare out from behind every bough and every dark mass. And the child is on her feet again staggering aimlessly onward, the fear growing ever greater that in her confusion she is more likely to be running toward the beast than away from him.

So the child ran and grew up. It ran fearing for its life and got older. Now dark well-known figures were beginning to appear along the edge of the path in order to greet and encourage the frightened little runner, just as if she were competing in some kind of athletic event. She could also see the idols of her childhood and youth among the spectators. A shining Christ figure stepped out from behind a run-down hunting blind and floated down a broken ladder to the ground. She pressed the tattered bouquet firmly to her chest and cried over the loss of this sweet nurturing essence, and over the fact that she would have to continue on her way alone.

She had just avoided a poisonous shimmering pool when she caught sight of a gentle singer, her true love at the age of fifteen, sitting high overhead in the crown of an ash tree and playing "Lady D'Arbanville" down across her path. But she was unable to hear the song through to the end, the days of her youth had passed by in an instant. What an abundance of beauty and love glimmering along the periphery of her terror, so much elusive sanctuary beckoning her on this hopeless flight! Even her "first love," the gangly waiter from the ice-cream parlor, approached her tenderly with arms open wide, but she just kept on growing. Her sick father hobbled along with her a few labored steps, then gasped, fell behind, and hung the white plastic bag containing all of his possessions on a scrawny branch. Friends welcomed her and called her over to them, her little nieces ran up to her wanting to be kissed, at graduation her professor waved a hand full of certificates and awards. And now, with more and more familiar faces advancing toward her, she felt she must be seeing the home stretch and beyond it the growing throng of friends, lovers, saviors, into whose arms she would fall in utter exhaustion. But at this very moment – the businesswoman had most likely reached her present age – she ran into a broad fork in the path and hesitated briefly before deciding which way she should go.

Here, she was approached by a man in a dark beret. His head held down, he asked her for a light. She was about to reply that she could be of no help, when she suddenly discovered that she was no longer pressing marguerites and bluebells to her chest, but instead was holding a cheap, disposable cigarette lighter, which she must have lifted from the lifeguard or the locker room attendant, without thinking. She lit the lighter and held the flame out to the stranger under the beret. As she did, two crude leathery claws suddenly grasped her hand, and the hairy gaping jaws spit into her face. Exhausted, body and soul, at the end of her strength, she would have surrendered to the beast without a struggle, would even have sunk into the murderous arms, if it had not been for a powerful gust of wind that came between them at the very last moment, abruptly tearing victim and monster asunder. . . . The Head of the Germans, visible only as an electrical silhouette high in the upper air currents, a garish ring of northern lights, struck down and flashed between them. The Head jolted the monster into his magnetic field and took him back, leaving nothing behind but dark, steaming viscera.

The businesswoman recognized that the voice of the proprietor, no longer nestled adoringly up against her ear, was apparently being generated by air friction, artificial and full of static, as if emanating from a loudspeaker of the spheres. And as the halo of the skull turned blue and flowed into the sandy soil, one crackly word sprang forth: "*Gründe!*" And once more: "*Gründe!*" After that, everything was silent and pitch black. With a sigh of relief, she sank exhausted into the soft sand, and for now the memory sutured in lightning found well-earned peace.

. . .

On the dashboard clock of her Citroen the red numerals displayed 14:48 as the mortgage banker turned onto the rain-soaked Highway B 51 and drove back toward Cologne at a somewhat elevated speed in order to make up for lost time.

She still hoped to arrive on time for her appointment with her new client, Mr. Wolf-Dieter *Gründe*; he would have no reason to complain about any unreliable tardiness on her part. This gentleman, whose name had completely escaped her for some few agonizing moments, the well-to-do proprietor of a fluorescent lamp factory, owned extensive properties and forestland and wished to be advised about the potential for sale or transfer. This was the task at hand; of that the businesswoman was certain, and she united herself with the happily rediscovered name of her client. She had practically beaten her brains out, turned her mind upside down and every which way, searching for this colorless yet telling name. And during this whole time she had been driven further and further along the highway and out of the city. This isn't the kind of name you forget only once, she thought to herself, there's something about it, some kind of short-circuit, it'll be blowing my electronics again. I'll have to be very careful!

As she was about to pull out to pass a bus, she looked into her rear-view mirror and couldn't believe her eyes, in an icy horror she immediately stepped on the brakes although there was no discernible danger out in front. The fright had gripped her from behind, the unfathomable was sitting there on the backseat, the construction-worker king and his wife were each looking glumly out of one side of the car at the rain-drenched countryside. Of course the driver knew who they were and what they were about; but she just couldn't understand how these darkly symbolic, time-shy creatures had ever landed in the back of her car.

"Where do you want to go?" she asked, frightened and abrupt, not wishing to continue in any way with the acquaintance she had made during those moments she was so indisposed.

"How should we know," growled the construction-worker king who had done away with every one of his followers, down to the very last man. "You're the one who hauled us out of the woods." And his wife jumped in: "You hauled us out, and now you're asking us where we want to go! 'Back into society!' Aren't *you* the one who yelled that in our direction . . ."

"And drove us out of the woods like little lost hens?" the man thundered. "'Back into society!' Well, what now? Now, we'd like to know what you've got in mind for us back in your 'society.'"

Not being able to recall in the slightest the events they had described, the businesswoman turned beet red in embarrassment and distress. Might she, at the very last moment, as she was coming out of her sleep, out of her unconsciousness, have yelled something to the battling pair? And somehow, might this slogan have been magical enough to have kept them from butchering each other?

The woman felt obliged to accept this or some similar explanation of the events they described. She also realized that she had neither the means nor the moral right to dump the grim couple out of her car. Nevertheless, she was overcome with such an intense feeling of debility and confinement that it seemed to her as if Jerry, the clumsy turtle, had just plopped himself down on her heart. Not possible, she thought, there's no way I can escape responsibility. One must smooth the promised way for these two.

When they finally pulled up to the factory owner's villa, she explained the purpose of her visit to the outsiders. The two reintegrated citizens had very little idea of what she was talking about and simply shook their heads disinterestedly. The woman reminded them to behave themselves. They were to be her associates, and she would introduce them as her departmental colleagues. Nothing but this sort of mental gymnastics back into actuality could help them now.

Gründe, a good-looking forty-something, a man as polite as he was congenial, received them without great formality and led them through austere and orderly hallways to his library, where he had already laid out maps, drawings and calculations for the meeting. Hardly had the usual personal niceties been exchanged, the protective cover of clichés set aside, before the landowner began speaking about his plans and showing his designs. It did not take long for the experienced mortgage banker to become firmly convinced of her client's earnest temperament and entrepreneurial spirit. And even the dour facial expressions of the construction-worker king and his wife brightened noticeably, though they had some difficulty getting into these matters at first. They were simply unable to escape the energizing influence that emanated from the proprietor's lofty goals; he rekindled their almost extinguished urge to engage in practical activity and consumption. In addition, there was Gründe's knack for continuously engaging the builder, the experienced construction worker, in professional dialogue. At the heart of his plan was a plain but well-fortified "Tower of Silence," to be built in a suitable section of his forests (yet to be precisely determined). The tower was to serve both as the entrance and the center of a projected forest development, of a "truly free-range enclosure for men of good will," to use his own words. Furthermore, he dreamed of a site dedicated to pure sociability and guileless human contact. But the tower, landmark and testing station alike, was to be built first. He already had an exact idea of what it should look like inside and out. On the inside, almost plain and bare, there would be nothing but a simple stairway leading heavenward up to an opening, totally unobstructed by the likes of a platform or metal ornamentation. Eventually, this tower was to be open to anyone who entered with the intention of creating something, no matter how insignificant and useless it might be; generating anything, be it nothing more than a personal memory long forgotten. In each individual case, the tower guard, a man distinguished by the quality of his own character, as well as his ability to judge his fellow man, would have to be able to conduct a rigorous and impartial test. The objective is to separate those people who cannot be duped and are committed, beyond all doubt, to doing something themselves, from those who are only interested in being fed without preparing a single dish on their own, always hoping to do nothing but stuff themselves full of the meals others have prepared. The latter are to be denied entry to the tower as well as to the free settlement, to be built later. Furthermore, anyone answering the simple query regarding how long he might wish to stay with anything even remotely referring to the concept of time is to be summarily banned. Entry into the forest beyond is to be paid with a certain minimal quantum of required energy, a sincere expression of will, the fragment of a life plan, even one single, burning desire would suffice to gain entry, such a desire being in and of itself a positive value given the despair rampant in our world today. He, the proprietor, wanted to see if it might be possible to develop and nurture a community of self-reliant human beings in his forest; in this system everyone's needs would be met, without stifling individual initiative and will, where the individual might indeed dedicate himself to their enhancement.

But the businesswoman, whose job it would be to set up financing and tax accounting for this project, was somewhat unsettled by what she was hearing of the factory owner's plans. How much of the known and the half-known was she reencountering in his fantastic scheme! It was difficult for her to understand how it could have so much in common with her own experiences in the time of her forgetfulness, but a dark, inner association attracted her all the more impulsively to this congenial man.

Absolutely! she thought, I dreamed what he is thinking! And, thank God, the things he is planning are already behind me. I could certainly do a lot more for him than simply manage his money! But she did not continue this line of thought. She quickly lit up a cigarette in order to hide her embarrassment. But she could not forget the horrible fright she had suffered in just the sort of forest he was describing here, and how very little there was about it that was at all benevolent. What was taking shape in his brilliant mind as an idyll, was the heart-stopping labyrinth of fathomless apparition and terrifying pursuit she had just lived through. At just the same spot where, in the full light of day, he intended to provide training for peace and joyful occupation, she had raced through a hellish passage, through a barbaric night, and had barely escaped disaster. But she didn't say a word about any of this. In every way she could, she wanted to support this magnanimous man in his wise and fanciful designs. If courage and entrepreneurial spirit were to continue to be of value in human history, she understood very well that she could not allow her anxiety, or even certain knowledge of a disastrous outcome, to diminish the intense energy required for this undertaking.

Still, she had been through the forest and could never entirely deny it. Every time she was reminded of her experiences and looked into herself with shame, the hopeful face of the proprietor became blurred with the carp-mawed Head of all Germans. But all she had to do was look into his bright eyes, full of hope and clear conscience, and she again saw only a handsome and resolute man, suffused with the redeeming ideal.

The businesswoman fell madly in love with him; she managed his affairs with selfless zeal and melded with his happy being.

Thus, she found herself in possession of the two highest means left to mankind to rise up against his inescapable fate: extravagant love and dauntless energy.

THE SETTLEMENT
(THE OUTSIDERS)

. . . .

Sometimes the boredom was absolutely intolerable. Then it wasn't of much use to throw myself into the deck chair on the balcony of our little boardinghouse and pretend I was camping in a Central American rain forest, having to muster the patience of an explorer from a century past, who had probably spent month after inactive month waiting for his first encounter with a tribe of wild Indians. The old-fashioned education of such men, as well as the terrible difficulties they had to overcome on their journeys, must have given them an extraordinarily sturdy and accommodating sense of time. Of course, the kind of pioneer fever and pride of discovery that came along with these kinds of primal encounters also helped to drive away the deadly boredom. For our kind, however, stalwart perseverance and leaden indolence had become an onerous test of endurance for both the heart and the mind, an extremely outdated travail, capable of robbing us of the last iota of intellectual alertness we so desperately needed for our work. I could easily visit my "people" as often as I wanted, and I could observe their bizarre activities whenever I wished. They had settled less than half a mile away from our quarters, just beyond the brush-covered tennis courts, and lived in the cabins and bungalows of an abandoned resort village that had been built in the not too distant past here in Gründe's Forest. As far as the people of the *Synkreas* were concerned, my joy in discovery had long ago given way to what could more or less be described as fascinated loathing. I had been observing them for three years now, periodically living among them for several months at a time.

For Inez, on the other hand – my shy companion, my bright and beautiful colleague, whom the commission had generously sent to assist me – this was her first assignment to a field station. As might be expected, she was still possessed of extraordinary industriousness and curiosity. I enjoyed her genuinely helpful enterprise. For me, it sweetened the stale and inane project in whose service we were both working. Her conscientious and quietly delighted involvement with some sort of pictographic find from the *Syk* region often seemed more worthy of observation than the artifact itself. The most beautiful thing I saw on any day was her graceful, intellectual quickness.

. . .

"Has something new occurred to you?" I asked Inez, when she brought me a fragment of a spirit-fable and showed me her first attempt at a transcription.

"Hmm," was all she intoned, and wrinkled her brow slightly as she worked her way through the text again, line by line. "Oh, yes! Recently, they started using just one word, one and the same word, for something cut into pieces and something flowing together."

I glanced at the collage bulletin board, which was covered with layer upon layer of pictograms and other working materials.

"That's right," I said. "What do you think? It looks to me like they're tending more and more to abandon diametrically opposed terms and replacing them with a much more ambivalent vocabulary. They have already introduced a whole series of these multipurpose, or joke, words, whose clear and original significance has been lost forever. They cannot even be distinguished by their sentence position or stylistic coloration, and we will always have to take the entire nimbus into consideration, including its connotations and its denotations."

"They even use the same sign for photography as they do for sexual intercourse," Inez added, somewhat troubled.

I laughed and said: "They are trying to get rid of every last one of the world's painful oppositions!" Inez went to get the vocabulary list we were putting together at the request of the commission, and for the benefit of our friends, the symbologists and the pictogrammarians. She carefully entered each of her new little discoveries under the various headings. That often represented an entire day's work for me. I helped Inez, I directed her attention to the most important details, that could be used to lend our report the most convincing aura of pedantry and scientific zeal possible. That done, I sank back into the endless lethargy and moronic stupor of our sultry and stuffy forest solitude. The only timeline I could grab hold of, to pull myself through the day, hand over hand, were the meals and between-meal treats our hosts supplied regularly and in abundance. We both praised our good little boardinghouse, that was much too far off the beaten track for any other guests to find by chance, and was run in a very kind and homey fashion by an older Italian couple.

There were also more stressful days on which even Inez's zeal for learning flagged, and since she avoided any personal conversation with me, the only exchange left to us were these few laudatory words regarding our lodgings and the hospitality, and, with variations in emphasis, we repeated them more often than reason might demand.

Despite the tall, shady oaks that surrounded our balcony, it was constantly hot and muggy. An old, unhealthy heat had settled in among the trees and extracted great quantities of moisture from the plants and the forest floor. Small heat curls rose from all over the surface of the overgrown tennis courts, which were entirely without shade in this blazing sun. Given the enervated, drought-stricken nature all around us, we were in comparatively good shape. It might not have been terribly far-fetched to conclude that the climactic shift predicted in any number of futuristic scenarios had indeed already occurred in the northern hemisphere. The abrupt social changes we had experienced over such a short span of time, the cultural landslide everyone was talking about, and that had also undoubtedly taken place, and how our overtaxed minds would have loved to have been able to relate these events to a higher, grander, meteorological change! But that's not what really had happened. What we were experiencing was a long, hot, unforgiving summer, so similar to the three or four that had preceded it that our heat-numbed minds often could not distinguish among the years. Maybe this Pan weather, the endless high noon, had simply made us all the more susceptible to the mystery of a lethargy that arose after the swift disintegration of the free-market societies of the West; the same lethargy that is part of the emotional makeup of a large portion of the population of Central Europe. The first aftereffects of the heat-generating breakup were manifested in widespread group clusters and citizen associations, newly formed units that governed themselves according to old social patterns. The situation did not change radically until the sudden advent of extensive migration and new patterns of colonization that spread freely across national and state borders. Here, all of a sudden, is where the modern man of the third industrial revolution congregated into a kind of tribal society and, regardless of origin, age, or nationality, formed large families or small traveling bands.

All of this had happened so suddenly and so disjointedly that it was impossible to explain it in terms of the conventional models of crisis and change. As absurd as it may seem to speculate about the cosmic or extraplanetary influences that may have brought about this coincident jolt to the consciousness of so many citizens, it was not entirely unreasonable that in an emergency an intimidated human soul would first turn to such parables rather than to some gaunt scientific analysis. But if everyone was talking, and they were, about galactic shock waves and fluctuations (likening our minor social drift to nothing less than the supernova explosion of a used-up star, a process that usually leads to the formation of a new planet!), then I would like to translate these grandest of events into somewhat more modest, earthly terms, and note that this new dispersion of lifestyles and patterns of behavior is indeed sustained by fluctuations, by shock waves that have buffeted everyone's consciousness, emanating, as I am absolutely convinced they are, from our glistening troves of omnipotent weapons of destruction, which we have kept stockpiling on this small planet as if we one day intended to play the sun.

. . .

Of course, my consciousness was buffeted, too. But I was still in a position where I could account for it in some way. At least for the time being. While giving every outward appearance of being hard at work, I myself noticed that more and more often I was tending to gently fall away into a doze with the glittering waves of midday pitching and rolling over my head, and nothing – no self- criticism and no sense of responsibility – could bring me out of this abyss of passivity and indifference. Then, it was as if I were leisurely steering toward a *different* intelligence, as if a kindlier, more generous spirit were beckoning to me. But I never went any further than half way, I hesitated and struggled against making the entire passage, I preferred sloshing around for hours in this aqua fortis, so comforting at one moment and so painful the next, while memories began to flow more swiftly and the force of the *drain-off* spiraled. As I've already mentioned, my covert prejudices did not, at least at certain intervals, keep me from carrying out the observations necessary to complete my work among the Syks. And while at times I may have appeared distracted, or even lost in a trancelike state, I was also more "attuned" to potential peril, impending conflict, and to all sorts of devious motives behind what others were saying and doing. Beneath all of my indolence, I developed a system of accomplished, passive cunning. Perhaps I had simply adapted to the Synkreas' highly developed capacity to react, and I may even already have surpassed them in this area. I recall one day when we all – 322 men, women, and children, Inez and I – had taken cover in the community cave when a hostile band of commandos from one of the nearby small towns was paying us a visit. They had set up camp at the entrance to the cave and we found ourselves under constant fire from their laser weapons. "You ducked at just the right time, again," the Synkreas leader said to me, apparently rather indignant that I had responded to the lightning-fast salvos before he or any of his people had. The damned beams were really bad for your skin, and if you took a direct hit you'd suffer bouts of choking and vomiting for days. Most of the Syks had taken at least some fire. And my pain derived from the fact that it was important for me not to better their chief in any sphere of activity that was of vital importance to them. On the contrary, we had been given explicit instructions not to provide any behavioral models, and not to assist them under any circumstances, even in matters of life and death. We were to leave them mercilessly to their own devices, and had absolutely no authority to interfere in their lives and habits in any way. We were to confine our activities exclusively to conscientious observation. We could not even take part in their work and their games or suggest any kind of enterprise, and should they ever ask for it, we were to withhold any and all advice. Thus, our assignment was clearly circumscribed. Once a year, the central office required that we prepare a comprehensive report in which we noted all significant occurrences and changes we had been able to observe in the colony. Our officials – an interstate commission whose sole charge was to investigate and track the establishment of the new social order, and had its main offices in Frankfurt – naturally viewed the "new consciousness" with great alarm as it spread and spilled across national borders, and they simply could not imagine how something like this could suddenly spring forth from a human mind of central European origin. By the way, none of these minor peoples was yet able to sustain itself economically, not even my Syks. Like all of the others, they received ample material assistance and welfare services as well, all based on the information provided in our annual report. In return, they were to be classified as a "social experiment," and allow themselves to be constantly ogled and X-rayed from every possible angle. Of course, the commission was merely pursuing its own interests in studying "appropriate survival models in a society with limited labor demands," which might be of significance for other populations. And, in addition, they sought to keep the spread of this movement under control and to monitor its development.

As far as we were able to determine, even though Syk society required an absolute minimum of labor and acquisition of its members, they were not given to laziness and apathy, but instead cultivated an especially intense degree of social bonding, and developed a creative fantasy, something like a mature drive to play, that had become the wellspring of their communal order as well as their individual character. What was striking here was the degree to which the predominance of goal-oriented, formally logical reasoning – corresponding to the cultural output of the left half of the brain – had diminished considerably, making way for a combinatoric style of thinking, so strong that it might be referred to as a kind of "aggregating-madness." Thus, they produced ("remembered") a great number of rites and customs, all of which changed with amazing speed, and just as suddenly they produced ("remembered") a remarkable supply of fantastic fables and pieced together stories, which also were very quickly forgotten, or intentionally "recast." In this way, almost everything in their society was in an accelerated, though remarkably neutral, state of flux. And where a genuinely primitive people remained in permanent alliance with their manes and spirits, the Syks had nothing to work with but the inherited specters of the free-market society. Of course, they had broken with this past and separated themselves from it, but the cultural property of the consumer society, its historical remains and fragments, had become the primary material of their play and craft. In this sense, they were *creative* – but only as inventive *synthesizers*, as collectors and recyclers. (It wasn't any one of the researchers in the field, but some bureaucrat at commission headquarters who had jokingly coined the term "Synkreas," and it had quickly risen to the status of an official designation.)

Due to their playful way of thinking, all of their utterances and their ambitions took on a very unstable and incoherent form, thus making it very difficult for us to ascertain, and reliably describe, the fundamental structures and control mechanisms of their behavior. There was random interplay of creative production and forgetfulness, intelligence and incoherence. And after spending a few months with them, you came away with almost nothing you could really hold on to. It was impossible to know if you had been observing the closing roundelay of randomly ordered forms of human interaction, of swift repetitions, of a lively stretta before the irreversible dissolution; or perhaps it was the laborious coming of the New Man making his way through enormous deposits of junk.

. . .

My companion, shy, undiscouraged, and totally committed to the cause, often kept me from all sorts of gloomy misinterpretations and mean polemic in those moments when I could no longer bear the thought of confronting all of those confused Synkreations; her patient interest, her good-natured attentiveness and zeal for learning, simply required that I exhibit a calm and earnest attitude. But this was not the only way she affected my life at the outpost. In many suddenly dark and unguarded glances I had discerned a deep-rooted fear of love, and this observation had actively engaged my investigative curiosity.

Easily, all too easily, one might be tempted to describe the Syks with terms such as degeneration, dilapidation, downfall, and worse. Language was no longer the main vehicle of cultural expression; traditional concepts of order in social life, the supremacy of logical intelligence, all of this was in a state of flux. However, one would be guilty of a most grievous error if one were to see in this only dissipation and ruin. In truth, this change in the direction of the mental winds had brought into play a whole series of positive factors, invaluable survival skills – not necessarily new, but human, capabilities, which had long been ignored and pushed aside, regained their relevance. Thus, their intelligence (and their economic practices as well) was more directed toward imaginative interaction with found objects, and not to the development of ever newer, ever "better" products and services. Among the Syks, combinatory skills were more important than innovation. Dreams, games, collecting, integrating concepts had risen above and greatly diminished the importance of the iron rule of abstract logic, planning, progress and the dictates of tradition.

The infantile aspects of our nature, lurking over us our entire lives but constantly held at bay, that enduring source of change, paradigm of fable and fairy tale, had replaced the rational mind as the only valid expression of maturity.

And they carried on with their lives in their secluded forest hideaway, a small, compatible, peaceloving community – but still they had their hands full trying to set a boundary to their limitless freedoms in order to keep from plunging into the black hole of total social chaos. They could well sense this most horrible threat: the high degree of autonomy, which distinguished every duty and every bond and shielded them from all duress, could at any moment lead to a total voiding of social substance, and implosion. Without having to put up resistance in any quarter, be it against a state or against the raw power of nature, they could suddenly find themselves trapped in their free space, as if in the most cramped of cages, and then expiring in a system of their own making, which had been based solely on yearning and desire. Even the most peaceloving being will not stay that way forever when he has no other aim than to sustain his peaceloving conduct. He must want something *beyond* that, something more than naked peace, or he will not have even that. Without robust strategy, without a higher impetus, he cannot stay put on his own little patch of earth, he will simply sink into the morass of his own excretions.

. . .

The reservation lay in the middle of the Gründe Forest, a good twenty-five kilometers northeast of Cologne. It was easy to locate from any direction because of the high templelike structure that towered over the treetops and was visible far and wide. It formed the hub of what was once a resort and recreation center, but people no longer seemed at all aware of its original purpose and use. On the inside it was completely bleak and empty, with only a spiral wooden staircase rising into the heights, before reaching its bricked-up terminus devoid of any view. There was much to suggest that the earlier inhabitants or guests had one day quit the colony in great haste, having left almost everything in their houses just as they might have been using it. The houses were equipped with technologically advanced appliances and furnishings. In among these houses, there were also old-fashioned workshops and small factories, and besides the dwelling units there were also larger administrative structures, athletic facilities, and a health clinic. When the Syks moved in, the freezers were still jam-packed with provisions. But, as far as what really happened here in this tower and forest city, what really caused the sudden exodus of the population, not one iota of information has ever come to light.

The Syks – themselves the offshoot of a great north-south migration whose nucleus was formed of a wondrous amalgam of Icelandic fishermen, an itinerant troop of French actors, Turkish tailors, and German social workers – the Syks had made use of the existing facilities, and had moved into the housing units, most of which consisted of only one large room, and made no major modifications. Only audiovisual equipment, pictures, photographs, posters, and the like had been removed and put out of sight. Of course, the Syks weren't art vandals, but they had a profound fear of all optical materials finished and reproduced. For them, *image* meant nothing different from *imagine*, and this was bound to lead to some sort of industriousness. You produced an image and then made it vanish again, something was happening. But above all, it was the basic building block of their language, their own distinct pictogrammar, as naive as it was richly imaginative. Their speech, their language act, was a dynamic combinatory system of gestures, indicated objects, individual words, and a profusion of finely differentiated tones of emotion. The field of meaning for any expression had an absolutely arbitrary depth, and could only be correctly interpreted through a precise grasp of the speech circumstance. But their written language, their transcriptions, more closely resembled abstruse objects of art. Most of their fables were recounted on these heavily burdened collage boards, and they were much more fragmentary than their lively, multifaceted speech. These boards were the primary focus of our investigations. And it cost Inez, the judicious explorer, and me, the occasionally impetuous interpreter, a not inconsiderable effort to first come up with a halfway usable lexicon with which to disentangle the tightly packed narrative complexes, and then to attempt to render them into the "old" logic of our German language – and, as we hoped, to do so without having done injury to the idiosyncrasies of their fantasy or their contemporary simplicity.

These fables, language games, synthetic myths, which held such a prominent position in their community life, were constant testimony to a highly developed utilization intelligence, but actually served only as a vehicle to exercise the fantasy of young and old, and to stimulate emulation.

Some have raised the objection that we have assigned the "dark side of thinking" in these *mind stories* an all too prominent role. This cannot really be the case insofar as night and day, waking and dreaming have long since become a whole, a balanced cognition, for the Syks. The day-and-night equivalence in their perception has made them immune to the appeals of traditional religious power blocks, of the utopia of a benevolent natural state, as well as that of a just and redeemed world order. In this sense, to use the words of a poet, they are indeed "dreamed-out dreamers," and as such they stride on beyond our horizon.

·   ·   ·

DEALER ON A HIGH LEDGE

One morning, a gem dealer was rudely awakened by a raw, wet wind, and as she was about to get out of her bed, she looked down and saw, several hundred meters below, the pale red roofs of the little city in which she carried on her trade. Houseless, completely without any protective surrounding, her bed, which she sometimes jokingly referred to as her "holiest of holies," towered up among the skyscrapers and swayed freely back and forth in the winds on its four spindly legs.

It was as if God had pulled the legs of the little girl's bed in which she had curled up and stretched out for more than twenty years. Or looked at from the opposite point of view, it was as if her berth, like some giant jack-in-the-box, had shot away from the earth, and, upon awakening, she had found herself in the dark formless belly of a cloud. In our common, everyday language there is no word for the feeling of horror that was now required of the gem dealer, but neither was there in this world a prior example of a human being exposed to this kind of free-floating and catastrophic predicament. Even if we call to mind the breathtaking feats of tightrope walkers, swaying over canyons of houses only to be struck by sudden gusts and dashed into the sensation-hungry maw of the crowds, the lonely peril of the gem dealer was still far more dangerous and terrifying. In her first waking seconds, her mind was nothing more than one single plunge, a whirling spinning fall, a dull splattering thud. She didn't dare stir. She lay with wide-open eyes and numb, clawlike fingers in a revelation of absolute terror. This must be an instance of supernatural cruelty, when a poor being finds herself in an absolutely incomprehensible situation, remaining conscious, smelling the rain-filled air, hearing the winds hiss and blow, measuring the depths below in meters instead of fainting or having her heart stop. The bed swung in a gently circular motion; the frame creaked and groaned, but the thin posts seemed far more elastic than normal linden wood could possibly be.

Suddenly, a storm cloud broke open above her, and a mighty downpour flooded her bed, soaking through sheets and mattress and running over bare eyes left unprotected by lids crippled in fear. Shortly thereafter, a bulging cloud stretched open and a yellow ray of sunlight pierced through. It blinded her, and all she saw for some time was dancing black tendrils. But the ray of light soon appeared to be softening and expanding, and she could now see a kind of canal or furrow opening up, and then all at once she was able to discern a long row of glittering planks leading obliquely higher into the heavens. What? Still higher? Was this the only way out, climbing higher and higher up into this shaft of sunlight? Up into completely unpredictable heights, and this without *any* link to the ground whatsoever, a connection that up until now had been provided by the long bed legs, and later, perhaps, to be suddenly extinguished and carried off with the dwindling light? No, there was no way she was going to expose herself to this entirely different peril, even though she could easily have reached the lowest rung and grabbed onto it. Still, compared with the ascent into the unknown, if not into total infinity, even the elevated swaying bed seemed to offer safer haven, especially since, in spite of everything, it still represented warmth and security. With the utmost of care, she rolled over onto her right side and pressed her cheek into the wet pillow. Some distance away, a buzzard flew his silent rounds and hovered, without having to fear for his fate, in the same open skies where she found herself, the catapulted creature being held in reserve for a certain fall. Suddenly the bird stopped, and looking out across a field, shook violently and shot into the depths like an arrow. Never had the gem dealer observed the flight of a bird with such longing. When will I finally fall? she thought, when will the inevitable happen, when will the bedframe break? A human being, naked, with no support at all, unequipped by nature for these heights, abandoned in her deadly cradle, she can only fall, nothing but falling and plunging to her death. At this moment she heard a powerful flapping of wings, and as she raised her head ever so slightly, she could see the buzzard again, now sitting on the foot of her bed carrying a fat toad in its talon. In fear and loathing the woman drew legs and blanket up around her. The bird dropped his catch on the bedsheet and the croaker attempted to hop away. The griffin struck with its brown hooked beak, with its deadly weapon of a head shaped of pure masculine malevolence. Then he raised himself, puffed up his breast and gazed elsewhere through eyes flaming in anger, as if he had completely lost interest in his prey. Not until the toad made a last clumsy leap did he attack again, seizing it and cutting its slippery body to pieces. He tore the intestines, destroyed head and throat, plucked and pitched, so that only a twitching, lifeless cadaver tantalized him, and this he gulped down in jagged, wrathful haste. All that was left was a dark, slimy spot on the bedcovers, and shimmering in the middle of this was a bright shiny object. The gem dealer, who had not been able to turn her eyes away from this cruel play, stared at the blood-smeared opal, the remains of the toad's innards, which the buzzard was now picking at in an evil temper. And as he did, a myriad of tiny field spiders swarmed out of his feathers, and flitted over the bed and over the hands and head of the woman. She spit them out of her lips and shook them from her fingers. The raptor spread its wings as if he were about to attack her, but then he suddenly raised himself sideways into the air, and disappeared. Something must have distracted him and driven him away. Strongly attracted to the bright, shining orb, the gem dealer tried to sit up and grab it, but before she could reach it, a small, fishy hand appeared and took it away from her. Without her having noticed, a despicable, poisonous little man had descended on a shaft of sunlight and sat down on the bed next to her. He was a shimmering green being and belonged to a species of semi-winged creatures that cannot fly, but do know how to move in extremely nimble fashion within the electrical field of light beams. Nevertheless, in the spherical middle realm in which they caroused, they were spirits of limited capacity, and although they knew almost all there was to know about everything, they were denied any effective role among creatures of the light. In our society they would be counted among the intellectuals and accorded a certain respect. But up here they were marked men. While their bodies were subject to unending decay, their sex and their minds were in a painfully high and constant state of excitement. No Ariel and no female creature of the skies would ever have accepted them, without exception the nymphs all fled their shameless presence. But just such a creature had discovered the gem dealer, and joined her in her lofty bed. It was covered from head to toe with a greenish mold. Its cheeks were ashen gray and its dentures consisted of a string of lackluster gold teeth. The woman was overwhelmed by disgust, and hastily threw herself onto her stomach and pressed her face firmly into her pillow. To no avail; it appeared that the little man's voice could wander freely over her body without his having to move at all. His brittle whispers tickled her ear, then the backs of her knees, and her underarms. In her nameless fright she experienced no shame, she simply lay there with her nightgown rolled up over her hips and did not even notice that the blanket had fallen off her half-naked backside. The little oily fanatic hovered over her thusly bared body and poured out a torrent of lecherous supplications, declaring that in all the eons of his living days, he had never been so close to the fulfillment of his dreams as he was now that he could see the chaste goose bumps on her bottom; it was only in search of this unnaturally blond downy hair that he had strayed through the centuries, and he had already taken on a heavy coat of mold; it was only in search of the flip side of abysmal lethargy that his soul had been under way to this singular arc of not-being-accepted, to this deafness of God become flesh, which only a cry from the depths of desire can break through . . .

The gem dealer noticed how his voice had become ever more frantic and his excitement, intensified by an obsessive need to gab, was rapidly approaching its apex. Suddenly she interrupted him and called for the opal. She told him that she was ready to please him in so many ways if only he would hand over the precious stone first. Without giving it a second thought, the ardent little man gave her what she had asked for, and she put the stone, covered in toad's blood and guts, into her mouth. In the next moment, she overcame her disgust and was herself gripped by intense desire. She grabbed the moldy pelt and set him on her hips. But just as she was about to hold him, to embrace him, to receive him, his entire body seemed to her to go dead like a rotten bough. In her hot hands, the little man twitched once, weakly, and thus were the eons of his living days fulfilled, he was used up and no good for anything more. But she was not ready to stop and she pulled and pressed him to her, while the semi-winged creature turned away from her with empty chatter, launched himself into a puffed-up hysteria and, hand over hand, climbed up and away into the nearest shaft of light. Full of spurned desire, the gem dealer screamed and turned in her bed. Then the shaft of light opened and became a vast and splendid solar courtyard; grand, festive music poured down, a many-turreted palace rose high into the glistening light, gleaming golden elves glided out through open windows, and flowing together in tumultuous jubilation they formed and clenched and became one, single, magnificent male body, and slowly descended. The gem dealer opened her arms, and from deep inside her mouth she let the opal slip onto the tip of her tongue. There, two soft and firm lips met hers to receive the stone. She saw no face and felt the weight of no man's body on her own, but still two strong arms held her and a generous warmth flowed over her body. A mass consisting of light and music embraced her, and the wondrous essence kissed her with fiery red lips. Rolling the stone from mouth to mouth, they both pursued rapture. Now she also understood why she had been launched so terribly high into the sky: not that she was to plummet to the ground and smash apart, but because grace cannot descend so far for love and we must all meet it halfway. But toward what she could not hold by the hair, by the shoulders, or by the thighs at the height of her ecstasy, she most yearningly stretched open her empty arms, and the force of the overpowering moment shook the bed so violently that the slender legs could no longer support the burden, they splintered and broke, the angular frame of their consecration settled into a twisted crooked maze, the skyscraper-high construct finally did plummet into the depths. But at that very moment, a knotted rope caught her raised hands, and she allowed herself to be delivered from her stratospheric peril by the helicopter at the other end. The gem dealer submitted passively to her serendipitous rescue. All she sensed was the emptiness in her mouth, and in an expression of cruel release her face had frozen into a mask. Like a being newly born and arrested in eternal shock, she glided back to earth.

. . .

Shortly thereafter, a most varied group of scientists gathered on the spot to thoroughly examine and discuss this, the most bizarre case of levitation they, or anyone else, had ever heard of. In front of the remains of the shattered bed and the towering frame, all pieces having been carefully secured, there immediately arose a chaos of voices propounding one theory or another. Where the theologians were still arguing the question of whether this was a divine elevation or an example of the devil's work, the sociologists were already certain that in our crowded society more or less volcanic zones had formed, and that suddenly, at any time, an unstable individual might be catapulted into the air like a chunk of lava. The parapsychologists, on the other hand, focused principally on the gem business of the levitated person in question. They believed that in her daily contact with mysterious materials from the distant past, the woman had been irradiated by an unknown beam that had, with an effect similar to that of a champagne cork shooting into the air, torn her out of her sphere.

Then one day, a young freelancer whom the experts had chosen to be their spokesperson stepped out in front of the querulous public and announced the interim findings of the investigation.

"It will be very difficult," he began, "to understand this incident in its *entirety*. We are fully capable of deciphering and clarifying almost all of the motives and each of the individual aspects of this occurrence. These days, complementary findings from the most varied fields of knowledge can be called up at lightning speed, combined, reconciled with precision, and, on this basis, results can be projected. Therefore, practically speaking, we are not missing any of the significant links in the chain of motives in which the occurrence can be set and sketched out. What we are missing is the capability to discern which order of existence this event ultimately belongs to. We are like an archaeologist on a dig, who has found all of the fragments and pieces of a vessel, really *all* of them. And look here, they all fit together, precisely, they can be seamlessly assembled into a beautiful, coherent whole. The only problem seems to be that the pieces all come from different epochs and ages, and the vessel, which we have been able to reconstruct in such an exemplary and harmonic fashion, cannot possibly have existed at any one *single* moment in man's history."

The young man amused and baffled his audience with the analogy. But one of them gave him quite a thoughtful response. "No," he said, "there can never *have* been such a vessel. Because, in the final analysis, it would be the *complete* vase in which we could contain all history and simply carry it off."

"Well, you can see for yourself," the speaker answered, somewhat perplexed, "we are doing our best not to let things come to that. And, for the time being, we are leaving the invaluable material of our investigations in pieces, we will be displaying it from a totally open and unbiased point of view, open to its very fundament, if you know what I mean. We will not be reconstructing the vase, whose pieces originated from all epochs of our history, even though we are unfortunately capable of doing so."

TWO

Nothing could possibly have been more alien to the Syks than anarchy and lawlessness. The life of the "right half" (the cerebrum), as we well know, the site where image, space, music and synthesis are more strongly represented than number, word and analysis, protected them not only from narrow, goal-oriented thinking and a link-up to the digital world system, it also afforded them a half childlike, half philosophical spirituality incompatible with any radical political movement. On the contrary, the Syks were not only capable of obeying the *Law*, they were profoundly and entirely given to doing so, submitting, hearkening, and in almost the same way the ancients were of the scriptures, in awe of treetops and of the fundament of a stony brook, but also of the sound of motors, the whir of bicycle spokes, or electronic interference in an amplifier. Their sense of hearing, or their intuitive compliance, was perhaps their most highly developed, most responsive organ. Through this they gained admission to the law *and* to imagination. But just as they collected used and found goods everywhere, employed and then discarded them, they found great joy in altering and completely supplanting the politics of their social system according to the random forces of the moment. Their entire social order was dreamlike and governed by the law of free and open transformation. It had no enduring or underlying constitution. If today's discovery was the great personality, a shaman bestowing peace and order, then by tomorrow there would be a collective council in his place. They found mimicking a totalitarian mini-state to be quite satisfying, and for a time they even submitted themselves to the bitter severity of a religious dictatorship, only to turn a few weeks later, and greatly relieved, to the election of a democratic parliament. As we might expect, these transitions all took place without recourse to revolt or struggle for power, everything happened according to the "random forces of the moment" and the demands of shared cultural memory. Furthermore, the Syks believed that the more political systems they tried out, or had in their repertoire as it were, the better prepared they were for any possible changes in their social milieu. And given such an occurrence, they would not defend their little patch of territory through resistance, but rather, through studied adaptation, they would enhance and strengthen it.

Throughout all of these transitions, it was obvious that a human being might be overcome by many different political impulses, and often several at once. From the inside out, the Syks diligently revealed them, put them into practice and behaved in a law-abiding manner until the next regime came into being, until the next constitution.

Conventions of dress were equally inconstant. For a time, colorful and decorative finery characterized the general appearance of the group, brightly trimmed fantasy costumes of their own design, for both men and women. Then one day the collective taste seemed to undergo a drastic change, and there was not a single swatch of color to be seen. All of the Syks started going around in plain mousy gray; they all wore the same unadorned, unisex pilgrim's robe. Then, there followed a phase in which women were intent upon differentiating themselves from men in every possible expression of style. This even led to their going completely naked and unclothed at certain events, where they appeared only in paint and their male escorts wore designer suits of the most elegant of fabric. But even here, unconstrained disposition took shape according to law and natural demands. And the touch of naked skin on costly fabric was meant to revive ebbing sexual attraction. There was no question that fashion served to provide an artificial stimulus and to restore dwindling desire. A progressive decrease in polarity and contrast had accompanied the growing crusade for conciliation. The great Synkretic harmony had no positive impact whatsoever on the allure of one sex for the other. So, in order to obey the demands of nature, all kinds of artificial and what often appeared to be absurd stimuli were applied, ritual measures taken, in order to generate the necessary "stimulative framework" for an act of consummation. In any case, a bared body was no longer an adequate seductive force. A new type of character virtually came to be a fixture among us, the somewhat sleepy-sterile type, the quiet naked creature dreamily leaning up against a nearby doorway while guests gathered, and then, at some time, joining them, sitting down, like a child in the midst of adult conversation, on someone's lap, indifferent, undemanding, interested only in being lulled to sleep in the sheltering murmur of conversation. The status and the allure women once possessed, when in the more violent male-dominated societies they still represented the ideal of all that was other, was lost to the Syks forever and could never be regained, even through the most artful of staging. Moreover, with this alarming drift came the establishment of a phenotype: forms of a feminine intelligence achieved preeminence in *both* sexes, and were making a major impact on the customs and the memory of the colonists. It no longer mattered which aspect of intelligence we were dealing with, the essential inconsistency and forgetfulness, the spontaneous creativity, intuition and practicality, we have always believed these to be feminine attributes and now they were setting the tone of our everyday lives. Thus the struggle for equal rights for women, so protracted in the old society, had been decided in this out-of-the-way corner of the earth in a completely unexpected manner: all knowledge had become feminine. At the same time, a man's image of the desirable woman (and a woman's self-image as well) had basically gone up in smoke, and along with it the idea and the sense of the most natural of opposites. A feminine presence was at work in everyone's creative will, in everyone's public mentality, everyone's dreamy perception.

Enduring bonds such as marriage, family, relatives, life companionship were not particularly encouraged among the Synkreas, or they simply played a subordinate role. More important and of great significance for social integration were the small, impermanent groupings, the communities, the "body-heat alliances," as they were called. They were each organized around members of the tribe who found themselves in an enhanced state of *affiliating*, i.e., whose intellectual energies were for a time more highly excited or more abundant than those of their neighbors, thus making it possible for them to adequately look after four or five other persons, and they were indeed required to do so. Such a unit included children as well as the elderly, women, younger and more mature men, and the empowered personage at the center could be of any age, man or woman, there were no restrictions here. Once such a practical grouping began to lose its power, it would be dissolved without reluctance or rancor and then transformed into another. Affiliating and envelopment: those were the key concepts of their faith and their trust in the world. The Syks presumed that every existence sought inclusion in the Great Melt-River that contains all human and natural knowledge, extraterrestrial and divine intelligence, too. It encircled the universe as well as each individual human life. In order to combine with it, the river of all goods and all spirits, to achieve affiliation, the best thing any individual could do was to involve himself in a creative activity, be it in play, in social modelling, in collecting and inventing rites and trends, be it in the production of idea-stories, or even only in intuitive obedience, in total immersion in nature, in being amazed, in comprehending available objects. According to the deep convictions of the Syks, there was nothing isolated in this world, everything was imbued with *one* spirit, that of unceasing creation, the source of everything existing, from the origin of the universe to the lowest cackle of a hen, and its history would have no end, even if it should at some time pass beyond humankind, wiping out the current species. They said: I am descended from the big bang. Radioactive decay millions of light years away, and the blink of my eye, now constitute an endlessly protracted unit. Still, the distance between the two is so unthinkably vast that it can only be known and experienced in magical contact and in dreams. Therefore, man is not the crown of creation, but he is certainly the first step on the endless path of the universe coming to an awareness of itself. For the world behind our physical life on earth is full of higher consciousness from which we are totally barred by the limitations of our own kind. Only after death will we enter the world of the greater spirit, passing beyond our species and on to the "continuation of mankind." Once beyond the development of human consciousness, all further evolution will be of a spiritual creative nature and not of an earthly material one.

If a Syk achieved affiliation, he hardly felt himself to be an individual any longer, but much more a component, an element of a primal intelligence, enveloped, all-sensitive. If he failed – and that was what normally happened to everyone – then he sought refuge in the proximity of one empowered, and joined him. If he were to remain alone, he would have been totally isolated and suffered enormously, drifting like a plastic capsule afloat on the organic stream, and perhaps being washed up on a deserted bank.

Preparation for affiliating was at the heart of the tender pedagogy that the tiny populace afforded its none too numerous progeny. Through play and picto-fables, even the youngest learned about envelopment in the womb of creation, and that they had nothing to fear from the unfamiliar. The older ones were also taught that beauty and complexity, science and faith are not mutually exclusive. That the history of the development of life (on earth) is not on a downward trajectory leading from abundance to scarcity and impoverishment, from paradise into the wasteland, but on the contrary is evolving from the simple into the complex, from singularity to plurality, from poverty to unimaginable riches; and it was therefore incumbent upon humankind, in mind and heart, not to become poorer and coarser (nor more cunning and more specialized), but rather to observe *and* play all the days of their lives. They must find the same joy and respect in artistic symbols as they do in useful plants, because the abundance of forms in art and in nature are merely two branches of one and the same life principle. Therefore, every creative process and every actively engaged affiliation must, by definition, work to conserve its kind, and serve to expand and further develop the entire species. There is no division and no conflict between nature and intellect, between matter and mind! Everything is contained in one and the same law of transformation, in a perpetual genesis of differentiation, of tree from song, of fire from electrode, of amoeba from the sublime. God, so the Syks say, is only the shortest name for the story that is only beginning and knows no end. And this story is taking place in the spontaneous order of a termite mound as surely as it is in the most minute elements of a semiconductor. It is not through rivalry but through a finer compatibility with its mechanisms, in *obedience* to its higher technical components, that mankind will be transported beyond its present level of understanding, and only then, having achieved a new, a truly "synkretic" state of consciousness will technology again come to serve man and protect him from its destructive consequences. Technology's constant leaps forward into realms where we have no overview, where its devices still confront us with the most awful threats imaginable, will no longer unnerve us once we have expanded the range of what we are able to observe.

From the Syks' perspective, human beings in the old free-market societies were invariably trained to recognize a mass of conflicts, resolve them and survive unscathed, to the extent that was possible. And by the end of more recent history, their intellectual and working lives had simply disintegrated into thousands of contradictions. Most of all, they preferred to study that which was unreconciled, and this was also the focus of almost everything they were able to perceive. Fear of their own insignificant death had a much greater influence on the realm of their thought than did magnificent and richly diverse life, itself. They were dying their existence more than they were living it. In their struggle for association, the Syks had managed to make significant advances in compliance, in sensory and nature-based adaptation, but they had almost completely lost their facility for disputative conflict resolution, and, in fact, harbored no penchant for conflict at all. Beginning with their educational system, there was absolutely no allowance made for it. The young did not oppose the old. Being experienced, initiated, possessing mastery of play, these were acknowledged values and questioned by no one. In spite of their obvious delight in invention, being able to make use of the past was more important to them than innovation. And so it was, that we were unable to observe one single instance of resistance, opposition, or outsider behavior among them. The elementary virtues were once and forever: observing, admiring, serving, and praising. They did not even have a picto-term for concepts such as arguing, fighting, and competing.

Of course, we cannot forget that we are dealing with a subsidized little people who no longer had to be concerned about its own welfare, and who were acting as "trailblazers" for an old used-up, success-oriented society still struggling for some vestige of serenity. At those times when I was overcome by weariness and entertained the most contemptuous of thoughts regarding the colonists, they would suddenly become just one more crazy sect among many others. Then the synkretic prescription of utilization and collage, of dream and piety in science, all part of their trademark outlook, seemed to me to differ very little from any other cleverly concocted nostrum that a gigantic feel-good industry was constantly heaping on the market. Still, when I studied their fables and genuinely involved myself in their naive, inquisitive, sometimes even rash and reckless thinking, I could not deny them my respect. They had indeed achieved something that the rest of us might envy. They thought only as expansively and as deeply as it did their souls good to do. They thought – in order to enhance their sense of well-being.

Along the road of intuition and association, the Syks had been touched by laws, but they were not able to describe them, they had no scientific training. The unity of mind and matter, which they so faithfully propounded, was something the empirical sciences had not yet learned to fully appreciate. The "right side" of the Syks had slept its way to a contemporary wisdom; they had been fed the formula and they kept it dreamily under lock and key. What had Görres, the great Romantic, said? "In the depths of sleep, we are united with the infinite substance and lost to nature."

The tale of the natural sciences had revealed itself to the Syks and was transfigured into a compelling parable. The end of a long, complex fable we received from a young craftsman says: "I was a freighter in a lonely harbor that had long ago been abandoned by its inhabitants. Only a jackdaw was left to christen the ship. It pecked a cord in two that had been attached to a loaded catapult; the champagne bottle was hurled against my bow and smashed to pieces. I, the freighter, was silently launched. Captainless, my name glided out onto the open world sea. Bearing no ill will, I took leave of the [sic] *old* society."

And then, a little later: "Our life is so short, but still, in each of the hundred billion cells of our body, we sense a cosmological time, and in our dreams and our ecstasies we reach far back before the beginnings of human history. Therefore, we should feel our life worthwhile, even if it is only this wondrous window through which we gain a fleeting glimpse into the vast distances of time. Only to know that we are enveloped, dead or alive."

· · ·

You may have gotten the impression that we were already in possession of an elaborate blueprint with whose help we had completely perceived and taken the measure of the realm of the

Synkreas, and that we might soon be able to make our findings accessible to one and all. But, in fact, that is not the case. This communal settlement, somewhere between a childishly esoteric secret society and an artificial tribal unit, still presents us with a whole series of formidable puzzles. To this day, there is so much that remains a mystery and so much that we may never understand. Many of their facilities, much of their behavior, appear to us to be thoroughly absurd, and separated from their oft- avowed "Unity of the Whole," a concept they set above all else and according to which, strictly speaking, there can be no dead-ends, nothing split off, nothing unnecessarily duplicated, unassimilated, nothing entirely unique.

And what a headache it had been trying to figure out the damned cage! A cage, an enclosure made of extremely fine wire mesh, long, rectangular, about two-and-one-half meters high, a thick rubber pad for a floor, its posts driven deep into the ground. Set somewhat off to the side of the actual residential area, not far from the empty, stone tower in the clearing, it was the secret center of all events that took place in the settlement. But we didn't know its precise significance, we simply couldn't figure it out. The structure was almost always watched by two, sometimes even three, guards armed with long wooden poles, all keeping a very close eye on the interior of the cage. From time to time they broke out in a horrible yowl and banged their poles against the wire as if they were intent on intimidating a wild animal inside. But there was – we must have checked this out at least a hundred times – there was nothing inside the cage, it was absolutely empty. Whenever we tried to engage any Syk in a conversation regarding the unusual circumstances, the only response we got was a shrug of the shoulders. As far as the Syks were concerned, the cage was jam-packed and alive, *their beasts* inhabited the space, that much we had been able to learn. And that was all. Still, I could not get the cage without content out of my mind, and I kept stealing back to it. But it wasn't until much later, after having made a major discovery in an entirely different field of study (which we will discuss later), that I dared lay out even a preliminary explanation and shed a little light on the bizarre goings-on around the cage. I had come to the conclusion that it must be spiritual animals they were holding here in captivity, and that these were actually the fluida, the forces of the currents that nourished the personal energy of each individual, as well as the mental and social coherence of the group. These forces were pictured as more or less living creatures, which, though they were invisible, filled the cage in great numbers and transformed it into a "communications power station." But when and why did the guards bang on the wire with their poles? They appeared to be striking out whenever the fluida began to get dangerously entangled and threatened to strangle one another. Was this an accurate and elegant explanation? I don't know. At least one thing was clear: the cage was considered to be a place from which all possible sorts of threat and upheaval in the community might emanate. It was always spoken of with great reverence, often with unconcealed fear and trepidation. In order to ward off the worst possible turn of events, they called these spiritual animals "their beasts." I took the liberty of translating this as "beasts of asocial being," since, obviously, it was *also* the influence of something essentially absent, which they were attempting to keep under control in their cage.

. . .

For some time, no less puzzled, we observed a process we recorded under the heading of "Lutz-work." It was a widespread and at first glance curious phenomenon among the dilatory of the forest city. Someone who undertook to do an obviously unnecessary and useless piece of work would immediately refer to it by his own name. Energy, purpose and value were totally expressed by the fact that a man by the name of Lutz (or whoever else) was carrying out the task. Someone would stand in front of his house or at a workbench and take apart an absolutely intact umbrella or a cassette deck, separate the working whole into all of its component parts and then spend hours, sometimes days, putting it back together again just as it was before he started. What could he possibly be doing? To begin with, he was "destroying" a finished and functioning manufactured product, and, in the process, absorbing its design, its form and its soul, in order to create new work through his hands and his intelligence. Could there possibly be some magical sense concealed in this economically empty and superfluous activity, or was this simply a make-work project carried out by someone who was essentially unemployed, and solely for his own personal gratification? A small chore he took upon himself and wrested out of his boundless indolence? If you were to ask a Syk engaged in this sort of activity: "Nol, what are you doing now?" he would answer with total sincerity and deeply involved in his enterprise: "I am doing my Nol-work, sir." It always sounded as if he had lost his name to his work and would only be able to get it back once he had brought his task to a successful end.

We called it Lutz-work even though the name Lutz, or any other of our common names, was never used among the Synkreas. Instead, there was a (limited) number of artificial, one-syllable, unisex names that they had distributed among themselves, and which all gave the impression of somehow having been cut off in the middle: Rin, Zuk, Ter, Pak, Om and Quan. Usually accompanied by a pictogram or an emblem. And here, it is well worth noting that one of the strongest taboos we ever observed in the settlement was the prohibition against addressing one another by name. Even salutations were generally more inhibited and abashed than they were open and frank. They hardly ever looked each other directly in the eye when they met. We never understood this either. On the one hand, they functioned within conventions we could only dream of. But then, they exhibited inhibitions and quirks that were so similar to the behavioral disorders of the Old Society that they could easily have been mistaken one for the other. There were even phases in which their shyness spread in fits and epidemics, like an infectious disease. Then the entire little polity would suddenly be overwhelmed by a wave of shame, and everyone went running around with lowered head, or face covered with both hands, hurrying to get to their masks in order to find safety behind them. These masks were in no way artful. Most of them were made of simple cardboard and had slits for air and eyes, and the fronts were painted or cut out to resemble famous historical personalities or other idols. The disguise served neither as totem nor as ornament, it was meant to ward off not to please, it lay like a soothing gauze bandage over a burning rash of shame.

. . .

Bearing witness to such a forced carnival, such tangles and webs and panicky impulses, would we be justified in questioning whether or not the Syks were really on the right path? Was this still the source of blessings, the *colony* without social convention?

In the "new orchard," that is, in the lap of a considerably run-down, overdeveloped natural setting, we examined the innards of cultural refuse feeders, and we should indeed take great care not to take the last for the first, the collectors and mixers for the doers and entrepreneurs.

At this point, as further documentation of my confusion, I shall submit a passage from a so-called manifesto that circulated for a time among young Syks. At first glance, it reads like the meditations of someone on a cocaine high, like rules of good behavior for cool teenyboppers. The world as advertising and design; silent future of a progressive narcissism of the second, third, god-knows-which generation . . .

While you are cleaning the thin wires of an egg slicer, maybe you will dream of a long, white beach. Can't believe what the perfectly clean little thing is emitting your way! What it is releasing inside you. There is still the dream of a white beach. But no one goes there anymore. Too many people, too much garbage. Stay home, wash your walls, polish your shoes and your silver, look in the mirror and be pleased with your daily change of clean under-wear. The most important thing for you is: be clean, well-dressed. Everything else will come of its own. You will feel good. But you will only feel good when you are perfectly clean and look absolutely up-to-date. Be happy when nice people drop by. But don't let anyone in with dirty hair. People should be nice and know how to dress. Be sure that you are always playing the right music, and that it isn't too loud. Loud music is nasty. If you are at a loss what to do with your guests, then take out your photo album and your awards. That's always a lot of fun. When people use improper language, train yourself to adopt a certain manner, be wary and ask them what they really mean to say. You must be the absolute master of your style and that is why you must not allow inappropriate language and indecent expressions in your milieu. When you leave your beautiful, clean apartment and meet people on the outside, you will inevitably be confronted with a profusion of impressions you may wish to avoid. If a problem should arise, be polite and flexible. Avoid all conflict. You always know: "I suit myself," and that is what's most important. Never forget that you are a handsome man, from the crown of your neat-ly combed head down to the soles of your designer shoes. You are a master because you possess an absolute sense of serenity. And this you possess because you have style. It is your shield and your standard. Style is your radar system. No matter where you are

living, your greatest concern will be for perfect clarity and the
cleanliness of your surroundings. Your noble nature must be
apparent at first glance. There are no universal prescriptions, no
instructions; you either have it in you or you don't . . . But, by all
means, avoid the following: velour carpeting, lampshades, cur-
tains. These are three things that will cause severe interference in
your reception field and can almost cripple your psychocom . . .

Nothing really exists except you. Absolutely nothing. The radi-
ator's white radiator ribs spread apart. The earth trembles – and
settles again. No, it was nothing.

. . .

So much for this excerpt from the young colonists' Primer for
Cleanliness. But what were we supposed to make of the term
"psychocom"? There was no question that we were currently sta-
tioned at a location that had disconnected itself from the dubious
blessings of telecommunications more resolutely than any other
on the face of the earth – could it be that we had stumbled upon a
no less perfidious and totalitarian network? And here, what had
first read as a silly tract on the utility of cool self-love, was now
putting us on the trail of some rather unusual observations. We
have already mentioned the Syks' well-developed receptivity for
spiritual and mental energies; we learned a lot about this while
examining the cage and states of associating. We were also beginning to get a clearer insight into their strangely abbreviated and
fragmentary speech. What remained unsaid during the course of
communication gradually became perceptible and revealed a highly developed system of information, which operated both in the
background and in the interstices of their purely vocal expressions. To put it more succinctly: their communication was a montage of segment-language and directly emitted impulses. Where
at best we are able to read another's movements, posture and
expressions (often only to feed our suspicions regarding his "true
intentions"), through their fluida, through sense-bearing emissions, the Syks received precise, undistorted information from
others, and were able to respond promptly in the same manner.

Of course, this capability was extremely susceptible to interference. It required continuous training, as well as strict preliminary and prophylactic regulation, in order to maintain it in good
working order. Among these measures were many of what had at
first seemed like such silly precautions in the manifesto, for exam-

ple, keeping your apartment absolutely spotless, and decorating with as little material as possible; or – with the help of a self-induced incense high – to transport oneself into a state of inner emptiness, which is undoubtedly the prerequisite condition for psychocom. Before he could enter into the free, horribly exposed exchange of fluids, beams and tiny particles of being, the participant would have to be a Master, someone who had already achieved a state of unconditional serenity. Only in that state would he be able to communicate purely: from one unconscious to another. And the resulting communication would be the only communication possible, all ambiguity, conditions and hidden meanings having been excluded from the outset. The Syks lived and communicated with just such a sharp and blinding inner transparency. A normal intellect, a healthy soul would hardly have been able to stand it. Until now such clarity, similar albeit much less developed, could only be observed in schizophrenics. In the Syks' case, however, perceptive facility is confined, exclusively and inevitably, to the unconscious aspects of communication and behavior. As if viewing life on an X-ray screen, they register nothing but hidden motives and impulses and are no longer capable of detecting the outer lay of skin, the protective convention.

It is quite obvious that our old-fashioned language, the circumscribed logic of the left side, with its grinding rational consistency, has certain concrete advantages when compared with their highly developed psycho-electronics. It shields us against an unbearable excess of interpersonal information, of "background turbulence."

The Syks, on the contrary, believe that it is just this conventional, abstract, word-based language that threatens their consciousness, and may one day pull them to pieces. In the entire settlement there was only one site where writing could be found, and found in wild abundance. And that was in the cave where they all retreated in cases of collective attacks of anxiety, or when confronted with some external menace. The cave walls were scribbled full of words, entire sentences, quotes, sayings and parables from various literatures and cultures. Covered and reverently decorated with canvasses consisting purely of script, and wall texts, too. But this was not in any way an attempt to hoard language treasures, it was much more a banal witchcraft aimed at protecting themselves from the vengeful return of language.

In the grotto, they sought protection from all sorts of difficulties and misfortune. As incomparably swift as their communications were, their fear of everything abrupt, assuming it came from an external source, was profound. The sudden, no matter what its source, could protect them. But its spirit, and they were absolutely convinced of this, had its seat and was most treacherously concealed in the old written language, and an onslaught from these quarters was the one thing they feared most in their world. At any moment, this repressed and outwitted force might rise up and make its retaliatory strike thus ending synkretic play forever.

But where did they seek help and protection? From which power? The spirituality of association did allow for the existence of a personal deity, but in its splendor it might only be adored and not petitioned. We spent a long time rummaging around in their diverse and sundry articles of faith before we finally observed how, little by little, as if out of the dense mists of all transformation, a pure and glowing light began to emerge. A savior figure becoming slowly visible, unspeakably so. This was not just one more spirit entity, but the devout summoning of a physically massive godhead, positively bursting with power. If here on earth they had already become dependent on a "cage full of spiritual animals," as well as a variety of other airy and bothersome stratagems, then, from beyond the horizon, they were expecting nothing less than a body of naked splendor, the advent of the Great Overseer in all his incomparable physical magnificence. And why should this surprise us? With so much social capacity being vaporized, with words swirling in currents, given so many concept-stories and exchanges of fluida, the air in the settlement had already become so thick and heavy with disembodied matter that you could have cut out the approaching body with a knife. The way the warm tongue of a cow once licked Buri, the Giant, free from a salty block of ice.

THREE

Oh, larcenous people, the Germans! From whom we have descended, and who have brought us down. I see it in my beautiful companion, who is always making the most exquisite effort, and is certainly the most alert and perceptive person one could imagine – even she has been: robbed! This society has looted our knowledge; looted the pride and the province of every individual, every searching and progressive mind. The society is holding them captive, saddling them with its lifeless dilemma.

Oh, pale, bloodsucking people! They have stolen it from those of us on the frontiers; and from those meant to soar, they have sucked the marrow from their bones and parceled it out among their mousy gray inmates. Because, without our inner substance, pulverized and broadcast far and wide, they could not even nurture their rotten thinking sos and liking tos.

. . .

Inez had every reason to be unhappy with me. Like the unhappy woman who has to drag her drunken husband out of the bars every night, she had to keep coming after me, always having to look for me somewhere among the Syks, where I may have crawled away into some quiet corner or snuggled up to one of the "body-heat clusters." For days and nights on end, I was absent from the boardinghouse and was not to be seen at the site of our mutual scholarly endeavor. Something was going on inside of me. A powerful shadow had taken me under its warm wing, was sheltering me and pulling me along; my blessed compliance. I could no longer even observe what was happening, let alone prevent it. I just loafed around, much more awkwardly and lethargically than ever before. I had little more than a blurred notion of what my duties were, of the official assignment I was to carry out on behalf of some commission or other. I used every opportunity I had to escape over there, into the colony. It had become an irresistible attraction, and each time the expectation of finding soothing tranquility and the fulfillment of wondrous desires grew stronger. A magical garden was blossoming in my sober field of research, and I strode in full of good cheer, partaking of the finest conventions and in the continual protection of a refreshing dawn. So I went to the Syks.

Not that Inez would have confronted me with harsh reproaches; she was much too tolerant, and too intelligent. But in her own quiet way she showed her concern, that seen close up the objects of our research might begin to appear all too indistinct, and that I might be losing my faculty for critical evaluation. With a shy hold on my arm, she took me, the one who had until now been her mentor, and led me like a young truant back to the terrace of our boardinghouse, where the lists of vocabulary items and rough drafts of translations lay spread out across a wide table, waiting for my inspection. For a while I was able to pull myself together, I sat down at my desk and held sheets of paper in front of my eyes. But still I could not focus on the familiar subject matter; I simply glossed over all of those things that were my responsibility, I didn't understand them anymore. Had I lost interest in working together with her, Inez asked, somewhat sadly. "No, no," I responded in subdued tones, and retreated behind a helpless smile.

At times now, I found myself having to struggle with an erratically twitching tongue. My speech became halting and began to rotate. I could no longer contain a tendency to repeat words over and over again within the briefest span of time, circular motion of sentences, and I even began to notice the effect in my limbs, which led to my sometimes playing the half clumsy, half elated dancer. I could feel it coming on and it always made me feel terribly self-conscious: the gurgling, the proto-articulation of a new, as yet uncomprehended song that was overtaking my numbed words.

. . . endless swell of looking, gentle rocking gait of finding out. Time's sail is struck. With the tips of my tranquility, I touched . . . the *new* . . . the redeeming *new*, leaving us in its wake . . .

Then, former good cheer. Good old irony. Still, as if under glass. Harmless. Inez observed deciphering. Over the span of one minute, she twice pushes the hair out of her face with the tips of her fingers. Hardworking, downright industrious. What guidance could I possibly give her now? Who does she see when she looks at me? Beautiful keeper of journals! I see you, I am observing you very fastidiously from my glassed-in back room. What is it you still seek to understand without knowing? Aren't you yourself wondrous enough? Authorized to go over and become a native? Why are you hesitating? Is this the threshold upon which I am to take you and hold you in my arms, so that you – under the guise of desire – can cross over more easily? But where would we go? You, as fair as fable, dark and tender apprentice, one and only true stranger I have met in the forest among all of the simply transformed – my desires can do you no harm; a dark being will not be more revealed just because she sleeps with someone.

Ah, capable young worker, how quickly she's picked up on her job! Exhibiting so much independence, so much good sense! Specialist in charge of secrets, responsible for the unarticulated and for reconceived writing; responsible for . . . *poets without society, allegories without hierarchy!*

But in no way does she resemble Aphrodite's foolish administrators, Kleta and Phaenna, Miss Clamor and Miss Shimmer, who promise the insatiable dreamer heaven on earth . . . Inez! Come with me! No road in this forest leads back out. We must cross through it, and it through us . . .

. . .

Yes, I wanted to take Inez over to the other side, as I understood it. But, with the entire defiant grace of her zeal for her work, she resisted my sleepy words, my unformed seduction. The chaste huntress, allegory of the authorities as well as a cruel passion for knowledge, turned me down, silently, unequivocally. Again, I found myself in the position of having, as I had always done before, to leave and make my way to the Syks alone, but this time I was steadfastly determined never to return to our boarding-house again, even on Inez's good arm. As I stole away one midday shortly after lunch, while my companion was resting in her room, I left no sign of my departure, nothing that might have suggested irrevocable flight.

I knew very well that there would be no place for me among the Syks. Being like-minded and a sympathizer was not reason enough to be granted entry into their community. Since the founding of their colony, they had not admitted one single person from the outside into their ranks. And they would not likely make any exceptions, even for their first chronicler, their generous defender and paymaster. I was not a member of their tribe, I had not migrated with them, had not melded with them, nor had I wafted in their winds. I had merely come under their influence . . . . Nevertheless, continuing in the role of condoned observer, I hoped to be able to stay for as long as I wanted, and to integrate myself unobtrusively.

. . .

But this time I did not arrive in an entirely faultless state. The shameless thoughts with which I had pursued Inez hung around in my dimly lit head like bats on the roof of a cave, densely snuggled up together and highly excitable; I was dragging a heavy lecherous infection across the border with me.

. . .

I was first drawn to the former tavern of the resort town, where at this early hour of the afternoon there was usually a crowd of settlers casually assembled and taking things easy. The simple pillared structure with its high bowed windows also served the Syks as a site for taking the cure. They strode around, aimless and aloof, now and then drinking some of the strong, iron-rich spring water that was swirling in a constant flow into a broad marble basin. Everyone stood here quietly lost in his own thoughts and appeared to be seeking some respite from community tasks. I sat down quietly on one of the dark wooden benches that were set up on the long side of the hall, and whose backs were carved with a decorative motif. Out of the languid promenade, my gaze immediately isolated the one person who until now had always avoided me with persistence and craft, and had been able to dodge all of my official inquiries. She was a young woman and her name was Zinth. Apparently, she harbored a genuine mistrust of me and my activities. Still, whenever I looked her way, it seemed that instead of mistrust it might be a deeper, agonizing knowledge of my person that made her shy away, a forsaken lover from a gray and distant past evading me. Now, of all times, in my weakened condition, in a state of highly impure pursuits, she had to come to my attention! I felt my cheeks turn red, I pulled out my notebook and buried my face in it. She was not particularly pretty, actually she was somewhat too small, her legs were short, but her entire air set her very much apart from the waning and faded sensuality of the rest of Syk women. All of a sudden, my mind was occupied with the coarsest of superficial stimuli, with her full, round head of curly hair, in a style that no one else wore here, her high cork sandals, thick reddish green eyeliner. I could hardly ward off an attack of common avarice, a jolt of decidedly unfeminine intelligence. I feared that my heat waves would betray me immediately and I tried to hide my distress behind an anxiously furrowed brow, and in my determined scribblings. What could it really be, I inquired philosophically of myself, that made us desire so fervently, that a small, halfway interesting creature dressed in a decidedly modest smock, protruding slightly at her breasts, who had been walking back and forth through the hall without taking the slightest notice of us, and yet unmistakably the longer she keeps walking, the more filled she is, one might say inundated, with the awareness that she is being covetously observed – what could possibly make us demand so crudely, that for a moment this especially small, remote-controlled person dumbly let herself down on us, occupy us like the flat seat of a chair, without even displaying the slightest hint of affection, and through an explicit, instinctive motion of the hips contribute to an almost inhuman sense of fulfillment? What is it that makes us, with an almost brutish lack of inhibition, desire from every pore of our physical being an act or an episode with a person whose expression would remain unshakably that of someone wandering aimlessly around a hall?

It is the primal desire to be visited and taken in total detachment; the essence of the unalterably alien who loves us without reflection and reflex, without batting her eyelashes . . . . Ah, it is *your* requirement, bordering on frenzied madness, to be able to work your way through to the indestructible virginity of another and find him untouched by you. "Stop!" the ensnared Zinth shouted at this very moment. "Just leave me alone." She was shouting in my language, loud, angry, profoundly intimate: "Can't you just please leave me alone?!!" She was standing off by herself some distance away, hidden from the others she had so thoroughly frightened with her screams. Those who had until this moment been detached loners immediately began collecting into small groups, the way they always did when threatened by any sort of danger, when the abrupt took place. Only Zinth stayed by herself. And this frightened me. Who was she? Didn't she belong to anyone? Why did she remain isolated from the others? Could such a gap be allowed to exist at all in this seamless community?

Shortly thereafter, two envoys from the ruling community council entered the drinking hall. They approached in calm strides and sat down on the bench next to me. The others were given a signal and they gradually left the hall and dispersed. "Zinth," I suddenly shouted, startled by an obscure memory, and the representatives of the people had to hold me back. "Zinth!" I didn't know what her name had been before. And she didn't hear me. She quietly followed the others out without even turning around. Everything that then followed was as predictable as it was mysterious. The policemen informed me in a most affable way that my sister-in-law – no, they were talking about the wife of my brother – had arrived, and that she was waiting for me "out in the chalet." The chalet, as I well knew, was situated outside of the precinct, beyond the borders of the colony on the opposite side of the forest from our boardinghouse. It is where the Syks housed their guests, members or friends from earlier days who might not be allowed immediate access to the settlement.

Still: my brother's wife? Who could that be? As far as I knew, my brother, the manager of a hotel chain, had been living abroad for many years in several different countries of the Near and Middle East. But we had not been in contact for some time, and it was quite possible that he had gotten married in the meantime without my knowing anything about it. The two men took up position on either side of me and escorted me through the settlement, where the Syks were standing in front of their houses; they turned away, shy and uneasy, as we approached, just as if I were being led away to my execution, or was being forced to make some other onerous passage. But I was not at all that distressed, and even though I sensed that I would never return to my beloved little people, a restless curiosity had suddenly seized me, and my new sense of expectation was greater than the pain of departure. We strode past the cage full of spirit animals, where the keepers were leaning up against the wire netting and dozing next to their poles, and then we passed the stone tower, the unfathomable ruins of an earlier founder period, and finally ended up in a dense evergreen forest that I knew to be the natural southeast boundary of the reservation.

Because of the unceasing heat, the underbrush was extremely dry and brittle, and clouds of a dusty humus powder puffed out from under our feet. Most of the time, all three of us held our heads down. No one spoke anymore. The forest path gave way to a large, paved parking lot, split in two by a wire barrier; this was the fortified border of the settlement. My quiet escorts handed me over to a sentry who stepped out of his guardhouse; dressed in casual whites, he looked much more like a young tennis player than a soldier.

The leavetaking was brief, I was not supposed to know it was my last and final good-bye. Now that the guard had taken custody, he directed my attention up to the heights where a small house was standing on a grassy hill, alone, as it seemed, and was to be regarded as the chalet in which my presence was eagerly awaited. But, when shortly thereafter every lock on the border gate was closed behind me, it finally hit, and I felt myself banished like a mangy street mongrel, like a diseased lecher exiled from this happy, idealistic alliance.

The sun had just set. A bank of clouds hung dark and gray over the hill. Maybe a thunderstorm would finally form and break through this oppressive dome of heat. There was no path leading to the little house with its flat roof, and I had to climb up the hill in broad curves through the desiccated grass. When I finally reached the top and turned around once more, I could see the soaring tower in the woods, and next to it the peaceful settlement of the Synkreas, now from an unfamiliar angle and a painful distance.

• • •

MY BROTHER'S WIFE

From the time I stepped inside the secluded house in which my brother's wife was waiting for me, I was a fugitive in flight, having suddenly appeared, my back pressed up against the door, and, before a single thought could cross my mind, I bolted it securely shut. From the very first moment on, there was no evading possible between me and this being. The woman wore a calf-length dress of brown raw silk, with white trim on the short sleeves. Nothing she wore suggested she was a foreigner. But her bronze skin and the narrow, finely sculpted face left no doubt as to her Levantine origins. Her eyes, rather widely spaced, drawn out toward the temples, had a dark, warm glow. "What I have seen!" these eyes said, for a long time, and I would like to have had a glimpse of what they had captured. Languages only separated us. We stood here, facing one another mutely in the closest and most confined of spaces. So much energy, so much contrived resistance in those first few minutes to lean into the storm that was pressing us together, struggling like the two ends of an unfurled scroll to hold ourselves apart! The undertow would have quickly overwhelmed us, had not a regard of like magnitude emerged, as if to preserve us from sinful offense. Almost crushed between these two forces, we were immediately plunged into a deep, primal agony, utterly cut off from all easy and contemporary morality. Wells of feeling and behavior long run dry now burst forth, and a gentle stream of established comportment and solemn formality ran through our stunned limbs. For the moment, it calmed the violent state in which we stood confronting one another. It dampened the terrible rumble and the anxious whimpers that had accompanied the birth of the world in another's eyes.

Mute, austere, and uninterrupted came the sweeps and turns

of devotion between the related stranger and me. Salutations in countless nods and bows, the relief of kneeling side by side with raised and lowered brow, with arms outstretched in supplication or in defense; the repeated kissing of feet, a discarding of ballast. This was our only way out of the closed and confining space, and we negotiated it swiftly and very timidly. Without halt, we rushed through remote plots as if through endless corridors, through time-corridors that led us to the most obscure of customs and behaviors, and even far beyond them into the dark patterns of prehistoric knowing. Once exalted by gesture, and suffused, any misshapen movement was almost unbearable in this cramped, one-room house (which otherwise included only kitchen and bath). Not one step, not one stance without measure and example, without paying homage to a higher decorum. Of course, there were moments when we touched, but it was always the kind of touching whose ritual, even *public* character, lay over our taut derma like a blanket of insulation. So I might well hold my brother's wife by the hips or the neck, as long as we rendered an appropriate figure of gratitude or expectation; however, to simply stroke her on the cheek in passing would have been impossible. We could never have parted. Even the consumption of food and drink was guarded in reciprocal service, accompanied by offerings which we periodically made to an embittered demon who would leave us nothing but the choice between sin and madness. As long as we spent the day in established forms of association, the night, during which we shared a common bed, could not bring us down. There were often moldy, damp, and cold dreams that led us down into a vault where the scene was dominated by funerals and lying in state. The room of our civilized intercourse became a catafalque overladen with flowers, our extravagant chasteness gave way to the quiet splendor of last things.

Still, we were approaching the moment when our richly varied comportment, like a prism refracting and deflecting our senses, had clearly reversed its effect and was now concentrating our desires in the extreme. One day, filled with humility up to our very eyeballs, chained to one another by an utterly frenetic deference, we were no longer willing or even able to tolerate as much as a hand's width distance between our two bodies. With eyes glazed over, and much shaking and quaking, we intensified the ceremony until its rhythms carried us beyond the boundaries of our species, uniting us with other living beings, and just as if we had stirred up that part of our inheritance we have from the bees, we trembled back and forth, up and down, in the abrupt dance and vibrations with which they communicate during flight.

Still: it had become unbearable; the journey too far, the tension too overpowering, I broke loose from my moorings. Without moving, shapeless and nothing but there, I stood in front of her. In this abrupt calm, an ample calyx cushioned my shock, like an airbag that erupts from the steering wheel before impact, as if to shield me from a brutal realization, and gently anesthetize me with its dust and fragrance – but it was already too late. I tore my clothes off and bared my skin. The woman kneeled down in front of me and enclosed my rigid projection in her two hands. She rendered her services with such skillful and innocent ardor that it seemed as if this would not have even the slightest effect on our decorous relationship. On the contrary, to her there seemed to be no rift at all. Still, while she was holding me, she turned her mute, motionless face up toward mine and looked straight into my eyes as she performed her act. But having disappeared into unimagined heights of ecstasy, I no longer recognized who was looking at me from down there, and what he was trying to comprehend.

I have never felt a more potent thrust of my vigor than at that moment, as white lashes struck an upturned face that did not even twitch and never ceased its submissive watching.

Not much later, I was so full of shame and remorse that I could not even imagine how to hide from her. I was well aware of having violated a law whose roots I presumed to sense in the deep religiosity and cultural devotion of this woman, and whose might I could after all discern in the passionate respect we had both been paying it for such a long time – I was well aware of having violated this profound and foreign dictum irreconcilably. But my generous lover came to me with water and towel, she washed me and dressed me with practiced care. And hardly had this been accomplished when the control mechanism of our opposite-one-another existence went back into high gear. The delicate nearness, the fine behavior, unfolded again and was resplendent in the richness of its forms, no different from a dew-covered garden under the first rays of the morning sun. The law, the gentle code, quickly grew in over the offense, seamless and fine, like fresh cell tissue over a wound. The secluded little house – on what sort of mystery-filled land and over what groundwaters must it have been built that so many sensations, never before felt, have arisen here in a human being? – was filled again with our sometimes devoted, sometimes courteous gestures and little rites, it again revealed an utterly immense time-space. And so things continued for a good long while without further tension, the game now moving its figures around with a lighter, sometimes even lazy hand.

One morning I was awakened by a draft of piercingly bad air. When I looked around, I found that my brother's wife was no longer lying next to me and was not even in the same room. Then, suddenly overcome by nausea, I leaped out of bed hoping to get to the bathroom in time. As I rushed through the narrow door, I was stopped in my tracks by a terrible shock. The being to whom I was bound through the most elating of dances received me in a horribly transfigured state, in unimaginable filth and degradation. It lay apathetically in a tub half filled with excrement and kept vomiting over its own chest. It looked out at me from behind a lifeless, seemingly smirking visage, and something which I didn't understand came gurgling out of its dark runny mouth – these were the first sounds, the first words, I had ever heard from my playmate. Overcome by a horrible disgust, I turned and blindly rushed out, I ran to the door, looking for any way out of this filthy chalet and the murderous stench. But the door had been locked since my arrival, the key carelessly misplaced. I ran to the windows, tore open the curtains, but instead of venetian blinds I found a heavy steel plate had been lowered and was barring us, the soiled demon and me, from air, freedom and light. My throat knotted up, I felt as if I was going to suffocate at any moment in this caustic, contaminated cell. Already half senseless, I stumbled back to the bathroom, and there I tripped over empty containers, chemical canisters, in which my brittle playmate had apparently collected and locked up all of her waste throughout these solemn days. I fell to the floor, and when I turned around I saw that the woman was standing up in the tub and beckoning me with a heavy, reeking gaze. No! Not one more glimpse of this monster! I pressed my face into the tiles and tried to suck fresh air out of their pores. I don't know how long I lay there motionless, stunned by disgust and fear; but at some point I was gently relieved of an extremely eerie feeling, and a first wave of mercy flowed through my heart. Pity swelled, as only anger had done before, and kept growing stronger until it finally developed into the pure image of salvation, a redemptive zeal, a hardly more minor obsession than that which inhabited the unnatural himself. And wasn't this just what we were seeing, a nobility struggling with hellish depravity? And, even if both of them together made up the true essence of her being, was it not my role to rush to her better side to help, and to free it from the clutches of wickedness? Weren't her gurgling noises, which I didn't understand, and at first had taken for grunts of the ugliest and most abnormal contentment, in reality choking cries for mercy and help? So, like a good Christian knight, I stood up and strode over to her slough. I will have to admit that the creature I saw cowering there was endlessly far removed from the sphere of humankind, on the brink, no, already in the midst of the pulpy flow of damnation, but it was still holding its arms out wide in order to be taken and saved. I was beholden only to my own high purposes to climb down into these beseechingly open arms, to bring joy to this creature and tear it out of an everlasting orbit of filth. I had hardly bent down over this distorted figure before she grabbed onto my body and embraced it with grimy limbs. The violent chase of our bodies that now ensued, and served only to bring down the monster of her defilement, led us through a horrible ecstasy and into a blind frenzy, where slaying and becoming are one, and screams spit fire. Then, it happened, at the same moment I mortally wounded the beast, I passed out and sank into a deep unconsciousness.

I don't know how many hours I rested. But when I came to again, I was lying alone on a snow white sheet with the windows of the chalet wide open in front of me; I was looking out onto a sunny, gently rising meadow and into the massive crown of an old oak tree. Half hidden in its shade, there was an old woman sitting on a folding chair and paging through a newspaper.

I also saw that I was dressed in clean clothes, and there was not the slightest trace of the deed I had carried out in such base filth. It must have been late in the afternoon; a soft light was settling over the warm, undulating hill. It seemed to me as if this little landscape had spread itself out before the house solely for my care and recuperation; I closed my eyes again and my renewed life spirits soared out into the open, and flitted around like butterflies rummaging through blossoms.

A little later, a rather angry wind blew into the oak and

prowled around in its dark leafy dome. It raised a rustle of a thousand voices, but not from the leaves. Endless ribbons danced in the tree, narrow bands of tape from broken cassettes and reels tangled around the branches. The entire memory-innards, streamers of knowing and governing, knotted up into thick, curly piles. Stored sound and data, unbound, the orderly archives of passing time, useless and entirely snarled, an immense collection fluttering in the wind. Also unbound, the magical alliance of abbreviated beings known as society, which has been holding our characters in check for some time. The words, the names, the knowledge, they fell away from the inmates like pearls off a broken strand.

The thunder of Perfect Reason rumbled deep within the tree, and shortly thereafter, the bird Bren, the gray, underground griffin crawled out of a crack in the trunk. But he couldn't fly away because his huge mud-encrusted wings were as heavy as stone slabs. Unhappily incapacitated, he beat his wings resoundingly against the branches. And the griffin was carrying a pointed cap of light, sunny flames on a flat head. This seemed to depress him deeply, he bowed his head beneath it and held his neck askance.

How could this be? Is the flame a burden to the candle? And light a burden to our heads? This is what I asked myself as I watched the noble and clumsy earth griffin, who, trapped among the branches, was not able to wield his power. Again he spread his wings, and with his black weight, it seemed as if he was about to break out of the dense leafy story at once. But his attempt was unsuccessful. At the height of his trembling stretch, from under his dark plumage – just as if a frightened heart had beat it out of his breast – a shining ring of light, a rolling glow, growing larger and brighter, it floated out of the tree and descended slowly down onto my bed. And the face that emerged before me, this sultry good fortune, this human face! What an enormous joy: here they come, here they are! With eyes so wide open and so gleaming, that a whole world of people was reflected in them, lips opened so promisingly that all the spheres hearkened . . . . "The new, the new!," I stammered and started to get up, "the new overtaking us all . . ." At that moment I sensed the profile of a very familiar figure close to me, and I was gently laid back down on my bed. Inez, my lovely companion, bent over me and comforted me. "You, my darling," she said, her arrival gentle and decisive. "My darling." But I lay far, far beneath her in the rubble, a whimpering little heap of insentience listening to her soft voice still floating among the currents. "The new, the new!" I stammered again, and pointed anxiously outside, where every evidence of the apparition had disappeared from the tree.

"No," Inez answered, "not the new. There is really nothing here that deserves that name. Just look around. You'll see how useless that word has become for us." I didn't understand what she said. She told me to get up, took me by the hand and slowly led me out. We left the house, this horrible pressurized cabin of desire in which I had been so severely tested. Approaching its entrance, it seemed to me as if my lovely companion were drawing open the slack, gray curtains I had been staring at for so long, while spinning and whirling with the related stranger through highs and lows, through circles and dodges, through the vast realm of love's vocabulary. "Look," Inez shouted, "here you've got every variety of rose ever known. And over there, freesia and fuchsia, hyacinths and gladioli. You see, everything that is apt to give you courage is known by a true, old name." And under the chalet window, there was actually a narrow hedge of roses in which a great variety of hybrids appeared to have come together for a kind of family reunion. Many other flower beds joined in, which I, seeing only the marvelous oak from the horizontal perspective of my bed, had not previously observed. And clematis, countless blossoms, spread out over the wall of the house, blanketing it in deep sky blue. Little by little, I began to recognize the outline of the individual rooms and spell out the rich species of this garden which the Syks had laid out up here, intending that it serve as a cheerful passage back into the old order, should anyone wish to, or have to, leave the settlement. I brushed the strange fairy-tale dust off each plant and determined its precise identity. And with every flower named, I sensed the tender approval of all matter, an infinitesimal signal from deep in immeasurable, hurtling space, seeming to slow as it progressed through dense, unbroken linking from layer to layer, from the most vast and distant down to the most proximate, while in reality, even at rest, continually quavering internal growing of plant material and minerals, never really stopping, never and nowhere ceasing, just as it will continue to generate other reason beyond ours, mankind's own. But left totally on his own, what vast realms of order this intellect of the moment perceives! Only the indifferently employed, males, no matter what their lineage, who have always believed that they have no choice but to wrest their existence from their society, they remain unaffected . . .

· · ·

For a moment I was suspicious when Inez asked if I would go with her to the commission in Frankfurt, as they had urgently request-ed to see "her report." *Her* report? Hmm. I just shrugged my shoulders and didn't say anything. She could take me along and go wherever she wanted. I couldn't go back to the Syks anymore. And being near Inez was far and away the next best.

· · ·

Once on our way we soon came upon the old woman, still sitting under the oak tree reading through her magazine. Seeing us approach, she looked up and affably nodded our way. Then she took a slip of paper out of her apron and handed it to me. I was more than a little astonished as I looked it over and discovered that I was holding a very carefully prepared bill for my stay in the chalet. No minor sum, either. And on an attached sheet, under the heading "Treatment and Care," was a detailed list of the services I had been provided. Every item, every procedure "my brother's wife" had dispensed was recorded in the usual shorthand, along with the amount due. Just as if I had been staying at a luxury-class spa. Of course, I could have immediately claimed the charges were improper and refused to pay, after all I hadn't come to the chalet and to my dubious relative of my own accord. And how could I have known that the exit from the realm of the Synkreas inevitably led through this hygienic lock, this exorbitantly expen-sive soul wash? Naturally, I did not avail myself of the opportunity to object, and settled the account without delay. These ticklish money matters might have infuriated me all too easily; I would have been moved to scorn and mixed feelings, and in no way did I wish to spoil my farewell from the Syks with such emotions. Scorn and mixed feelings are the treacherous agents of the left hemisphere.

Even when I discovered another, identical chalet at some dis-tance beyond the German oak, and then, within a broader radius, a few more, thus allowing me to assume that the Syks had set up an entire resort village for their cult-cures, I still kept my compo-sure, calmly and good-heartedly accepting everything I saw. I gave myself over to the care of my beautiful companion, knowing myself to be united with her in the best spirit of the colony.

On our way to Inez's car, packed and ready to go, we came to an athletic field enclosed by a high wire-mesh fence. There was a group of young men and women who had divided up to play a game of ball, and they were so full of such graceful zeal that I wanted to stop and watch for a while. I walked up to the mesh and took pleasure in the swift passes and the combative rush of the young women players all clothed in white. Then, suddenly, I recognized my quiet, enigmatic hostess among them. Here was my brother's wife cheerfully engaged in a spirited game of tag ball, all the while shouting encouragement to her side. Once she caught sight of me, she immediately waved and came sprinting over to the fence in a short skirt that showed her long dark legs. She pressed her lovely exotic face up against the wire. She smiled questioningly, and even a little embarrassed; uncertain how I had been affected, and to what extent I had gotten over everything. But I walked straight up to her and kissed the tips of her fingers protruding through the wire mesh.

She, who had led me through the dizzying pass and far beyond the shuddering frontiers of lust, wasn't she now all the more deserving of my undiminished admiration, especially seeing as *she* had acted with subtle habit while *I* had surrendered myself entirely to the singular and the never-been-there-before? And where I had consented to the loneliest godforsaken act of copulation, she had only carried out one of her expert games. How should I now acknowledge her great sensual superiority and mastery? Once as my brother's wife, by night, seductive, she now seemed an artist unmasked, radiant and exemplary. In the first rush of our encounter, I might almost have knelt down before her, but Inez stepped in, exasperated, and yanked me off to the side. She urged an immediate departure. One last time, I acknowledged the complete stranger and took leave of a Syk domain already tending toward outward chaos.

FOUR

Only very few lucid moments was all I was to be granted in the cool and heartless report Inez had prepared. It continued with remarks about my diminished self-control, my immoderate conduct, my uncritical disappearance into the field of observation, the distortion of my character, redefinition, disintegration of the entire psychological profile . . . . This, according to my lovely companion in her report to the commission.

As presented in her report, she had spent a very significant amount of time dedicated to the study of Syk culture. At some point, however, she had refocused her attention and made her teacher the actual object of study. He was alleged to have been in the grotto of the Syks on numerous occasions, and to have actually taken part in their necromancy. She had observed him attempting to work his way into the body-heat alliances of the settlers. Seen what humiliations he was forced to suffer after he had pursued Syk women, and was consequently expelled from the reservation. What a nasty, lonely and desolate awakening!

Inez, whom I had considered not only my friend but even my guardian angel, now stood before me an ambitious, bureaucratic stool pigeon, a waning human visage, an informer.

If nothing else, this filthy treason must at least have shown me where I now stood, again in the depths of the beauty-evil-false, in the heart of dissension, in the free-market society.

Her report shamelessly exaggerated every point; the style was bad and extremely obsequious. We met by chance in the corridor in front of the director's office, where the laborious and stupid interrogation was taking place and would require my presence for days.

"Why did you do it?" I asked her, more sad than hostile.

"I was very unhappy with you," she answered in a similarly sad tone, to which she, the traitor, was in no way entitled. Furthermore, it sounded sullen and soulful, just as if we were both confronting the heap of broken shards which had once been love. But that possibility had most certainly ceased to exist.

"Is this the way you treat a friend?"

I was shocked at the narrow, fanatic gleam that came into her eyes.

"I want to go back to the settlement," she said, "but it is impossible to go back with you. They will never let you back in."

"Everything you know about them, you learned from me."

"Yes. And I won't forget what you did for me," she responded. And suddenly, that gentle, shy smile was there again. Just as it was on those warm evenings when we sat on the terrace out in front of our boardinghouse, and she proudly showed me her first translations. Behind all of my bitter disappointment, I now felt the contentment of memory and did not regret having trusted my lovely companion so blindly and completely. Even if everything else should turn out be false, the delight and the promise I enjoyed for so long in her company were not; I could count her among the commodities, among the vital reserve substances, which continually renew our naïveté.

. . .

My inquiry, before a subcommittee of the commission, suffered from the existence of considerable difficulties in communication. The chair was occupied by a young Danish Social Democrat, a pale and zealous smart-ass who, in my opinion, did not possess even the slightest competence for his office. He had neither the antenna nor the curiosity for anything out of the ordinary. And as far as the new settlements were concerned, he was somewhere between skeptical and totally at a loss. With his – from a synkretic perspective – repulsively unfeminine intelligence, he dismissed every significant point in my testimony, and things which should have been of consuming professional interest simply escaped him, he didn't notice them at all. But what was the purpose of this commission if it wasn't to carefully attend to and support new ways of living and thinking? And because these new lifestyles appeared to be developing more robustly in the cultural reserves than in the raw climate of the remnant societies, vast quantities of money and personnel were being expended there. Unfortunately, however, the most natural of interests had slipped into the realm of everyday politics and was pulverized beyond recognition.

With me in front of his eyes, the stuffy bureaucrat would have been able to spare himself a good piece of fieldwork. If he had only taken a slightly different approach, then my statements wouldn't have seemed as "incoherent and illogical" as he claimed. He would have been able to learn from a progressively assimilated man at the frontier what makes the Synkreas tick, and how they are doing. But the only thing he was interested in doing was exposing the deserter, the observer who had neglected his duty, the researcher-crazy, the vanished interpreter.

The clever little head bobbed up and down rather uneasily in the colorful, brackish waste water my statements had left behind. Every time something did occur to him, he would raise one accusing index finger and deliver himself of a fundamental finding. "You, dear colleague, have a odd sense of time!" . . . "You are no longer thinking democratically!" . . . "You believe in social demons!"

Essentially, his technique consisted of peppering me with his breathless analyses and goading me into some kind of contradictory response. But he was unsuccessful. I simply kept right on talking, intrepidly, in my varying style in which tale and fact, idea and deed, played a completely equal role in establishing the truth. I explained nothing and regretted nothing; of course, this is how I managed to talk myself out of a job. As might be expected, this protracted farce ended with a temporary suspension; and after an appropriate interval, it would undoubtedly be followed by my dismissal. None of this worried me very much. Actually, I was rather relieved. How much more painful would a punitive transfer to another little province have been! And now I saw before me a long, uninterrupted period in which I could devote myself to the pure and complete extermination of the half observer, of what remained of the skeptic, which in spite of everything was still a part of me. So, I stayed in Frankfurt, rented a room in a cheap boardinghouse on the edge of the Nordweststadt, and spent the end of the big, steadfast summer there. Patiently, now and then content, I surrendered to what was left of the change going on inside of me, like a mineral spring slowly filling a bowl in shallow pulses.

• • •

ONLY VERY FEW LUCID MOMENTS

"Sunday afternoon at two, empty street with front yards. Even the nearest, most reliable road you can see right out the window is flickering like a distant mirage in this hellish heat. If there is another living being anywhere at all, then it is a long way away from this man with the bare, wet torso, dragging himself to the kiosk to pick up a beer. Early this morning, as I was waking up, I slowly began making plans to haul my car off to a shady spot somewhere. And just a few hours later, I was indeed standing in front of the lousy little hotel I had holed up in, having actually got to the point where I was about to act. However, I soon noticed that I had absolutely no idea where I had parked the damned heap. So, heading off in a totally arbitrary direction, I started my search. I walked along between rows of high-rises and dragged myself down side streets where cars were shimmering in the blazing sun and exhaling their greasy substances; but I still couldn't locate my own. At some point, I found my way onto a dusty path leading out of the city, and it slowly took me into unfamiliar – even, as I was to learn, *unique* – surroundings. I soon wandered under a damp, sultry green, under a luxuriant dome of creeper and shadowy arboreal giants, and when I looked down I was astonished to see that I was now standing on a crumbling old tennis court that had long been overgrown with weeds, mushrooms, and bushes. The gravelly red surface had almost completely faded, covered in places by patches of moss; it was barely possible to make out what was left of the broken white boundary lines. There seemed to be two or three more courts hidden deeper in the dense low undergrowth. Gradually, it became clear to me that I had stumbled upon the vestiges of a deserted vacation colony which had literally been swallowed up by the forest. I wondered how long it would take before this savage growth would reach the first houses on the edge of the city, and, like a raging fire, engulf everything in its path . . ."

. . .

We have only one tonality our entire life long. We would be well advised not to deviate from it, not to attempt any useless modulations, we must hold it as best we can, as long as our breath holds out. May it break off at some point, hopeless and abrupt, without having ever modified its oscillation in the least. Today, at midday, when I left my shabby little boardinghouse in the Nordweststadt in order to find a shady parking place for my car, I unexpectedly came upon the outrunners of a primeval forest. As it grew ever denser and more savage, I lost the way right out from under my feet. After a good hour, during which I had had to fight my way through dense thickets every bit as tall as I am, I suddenly found myself standing on an old overgrown tennis court, outside the forgotten remains of a one-time vacation facility. The site had literally been swallowed up and become part of the savage forest. Still, the reddish surface could easily be discerned, as could the broken, moss-covered boundary lines, and the rusty fence pulled down and lashed by the dense undergrowth. I will come back to this story later, even though I began it more than eight years ago and essentially never got beyond the discovery of the overgrown tennis courts. Indeed, it is inescapable: I confront it over and over again; the sultry forenoon beginning of a hot, suburban Sunday; the search for the car parked only God knows where, the sight of the overgrown tennis courts, the point of progressing-no-further; confronting this story, the tone of my report perpetually the same, this "entire life long," "we must not deviate," etc., etc. No, we did not deviate. We kept struggling through the underbrush and coming back to one and the same little patch, doing the best we could for as long our breath held out.

. . .

(*Pure* annihilation? Don't be so sure of yourself. Even if you were a form of plant life or nothing but pristine tone, your purest conversion would release large amounts of the same old acidic pollutants which never cease being in the world. Indestructible and more agonizing than ever, all that remains of you is: wretched irony.)

THE TERRACE
(BALTHAZAR. FABLES ON THE MORNING
AFTER THE CEREMONY)

· ·

Then the pale king pricked up his ears. His heavy body sank silently to the ground. This was the end of the king. Just as if the cheering multitude of guests had crushed him in their deepest midst, he lost his life. The crowds, already prepared to stride out onto the terrace and greet the morning as it broke over the park, looked around and saw a man who had celebrated himself to death lying stiffly on the dark floor boards. And it was the king himself, resting on broad shoulders with his eyes fixed angrily on the ceiling. Blinding horror gripped the intoxicated congregation, and everyone – his loved ones, his staff, and his advisors – silently withdrew; no one dared approach the stiffened monarch. The queen leaned quietly up against the wall, she turned away and anxiously pressed her son to her bosom.

And now that the most recently all-powerful, most recently emperor, brandishing the pillaged grail, lay fallen and still in the hall, suddenly nothing would ever be the same again for his loyal followers. The veil was pulled from everyone's eyes, the bond was broken, the reverence torn from everyone's chest. Suddenly, the king was no more, there lay a bloody miscreant, a murderer and evildoer at their feet. This they hadn't seen as long as he lived, ruled and acted. But now, absent his commanding eyes, his manly grip, his great stride, and words, all they saw was naked, enduring evil. The gray everyday wrong, which his glowing ardor, his steely will, had concealed for so long, now emerged from the pallid body, visibly, like a throng of maggots, a verminous infestation.

Not the slightest sound of sorrow, no prayer would rise; tears would not fall and devotion was lost. Instead of heated emotion, the courtiers were gripped by an icy dread of the world to come. Everyone pushed and shoved, wanting to steal away as quickly as possible. Not a single one wished to admit having been a subject of the monster, suddenly revealed through his abrupt silence, his blind stare, his motionless repose. The *king* in this man had not survived the plunge into lifelessness. Death had not only deprived him of sight and breath, with one blow it had also robbed him of stature and renown, even history. And everyone pushed their way back through the hall exit out onto the broad terrace, and quickly down the embankment into the predawn palace park.

But the queen's youngest son asked why his father was lying so still, and not accompanying his guests outside for a little fresh air. "My child," the mother stammered, "your father is probably much too tired to go outside."

"But, if he's so tired, why doesn't he close his eyes?" The queen sighed and kissed her son. "The king is so tired that he forgot to close his eyes." At this, the child turned from his mother, walked up to the stiff colossus and closed the great eyes, with the tips of his fingers, as is only fitting.

In the meantime, the throng outside the hall, in the orchards and in the gallery, gulped down fresh air, hoping to find their way back to sobriety in the early morning dew, to clear thought and a better conscience. But they would not recover so quickly. A dull stupefaction had overcome them all and it was not wearing off. The death of the one so exceedingly powerful discharged and scattered a uniform daze across the entire land.

Not only was it denied the petty overnight retinue of the king to walk back out through the final exit of their stale intoxication, but the entire rest of the population, asleep at this very hour, did not find its way out into a clear, lucid awakening, either. Instead, it was held in a perpetual state of mild, persisting drowsiness, and from now on it would carry out its day to day work, its thought and its desires semi-unconsciously. For the next day did not break like every other – it was suspended in early dawning and the sun did not actually come up. No matter how hard they might try to shake their heads free, no one was able to remove the furry muffling from his senses. And so it was, and continued to be for many, many years, pervasively and without exception; and many believe that even today this strong and beautiful land has not yet completely awakened from its Balthazar night.

We are still being held in the embrace of his death and it continues to fill with us with fear and breath. We, in our dazed state, may all very well have been created equal, and thus have granted ourselves equal rights in a free and democratic constitution; but how healthy can our freedom really be as long as we do nothing more than vegetate in the shelter of *his* ubiquitous oxygen tent, under *his* pneumatic hull?

This society is continuing to nourish itself from the death of its greatest evildoer.

. . .

"They have created a society!" Reppenfries shouted, while letting his arm wander over the deserted palace grounds, as if everyone were assembled there in full strength for morning roll call. "They have created a modern society, and learned to exist in it, these drunken heathens, these cowards. To hide what? To protect whom? It looks like coagulated blood to me, the people's sovereignty is closing over the wound like a scab. But watch out! – time opens all wounds!"

We met again and again in the gallery, on the broad terrace behind the palace, we tried to debate, to speak and even to remember. But not one of us knew how to deal with this, how to cope with the enormous, incalculable time-masses which the absent day, the standing dawn, had piled up before us.

So, we were standing together in a circle which was both intimate and relaxed. About the same age, all of us born after the war, even though we were from significantly different backgrounds. There was Reppenfries, the medic-thinker, always flanked by his two women, the sister-in-law, Paula, and the wife, Dagmar; there was Almut, too, the beautiful renouncer, and then the "modern man," Hans-Werner, press secretary for a large chain of department stores; Yossica, the postal worker; and finally me, the dilatory seeker . . .

The seven of us were bound to this lazy site, birthplace of "more recent history," we rambled happily through the park and the surrounding orchards, rowed to the islands across the misty lake, hid ourselves in bushy mazes or behind dense stands of shrubbery, and then stepped back out onto the terrace, always perplexed, always deep in conversation, while others, no less dazed, ran their offices, took action and made deals in their assembly shops and businesses, traveled across continents or lasciviously wandered from one person to another – for it was allowed no one, wherever he might be, whatever he might think or do, to make a complete escape from the German stupor, and to break the spell with which the decaying evil had been irradiating our minds and souls over the generations.

. . .

LOVELIGHT

As alien as another is by the light of day – just as boundless is nighttime trust, once he has taken his place in darkness next to you. In a small room, on a large bed, we lay in restless sleep after many embraces – the random one and I, both condemned forever to enjoying only the "Love of the First Night," both nailed to this cross, and no longer conscious of any other desire. Stretched out on our stomachs, our breathing faces turned away from each other, we lay with arms slung across each other's naked backs. Again and again, rising up out of a shallow and fitful sleep, I sensed the reposed strength of the tall, slender body next to me, a body that now, after our deep and arrogant caresses, again belonged only to itself. It appeared that the life of this unknown person lay here before me, rounded off, and in its most perfect form. The beauty of its soft and taut surface, charged but nowhere voluptuous, was soul and chronicle enough for me; time and the idle stretch of shared years would not have been able to reveal more person than was visible here. The strong line of her neck meeting broad, fluctuating shoulders, flowing into the groove of her spine and ascending to her buttocks, dividing and sloping away down two long bowed legs to her turned-in feet with their dirty, callused heels – surrounded in its transparency, I saw all of this, and held it in my arms, the tangible aspect of an ideal phenomenon. This person existed in two senses. On the one hand, she was the innocent young woman, strikingly tall and beautiful, who never hesitated to sleep wherever she felt like sleeping, and who, during her waking hours, made use of the same cool, alienating language I did. On the other hand, there was this unfathomable back my arm was now lying across, and I was convinced that a creaturely awe of the senses would prevent any man from ever being able to *possess* this entity. I even believed that her own womanly self-assurance would never come close to grasping the power and the essence of this body; no, not even she was its mistress.

"Every inch of her too much for you!" was what I heard being hissed into my ear in my witless, jumbled state of mind. A gigantic enlargement of her armpit, although no more than a hand's width away from my face, appeared to me in my semi-somnolent state, and the soft brown hair billowed gently like grasses on the sea floor. I was overcome by a masculine modesty, a primal discomfiture at the sight of this feminine growth, and the intense, untold superiority of her devotion.

At that moment, in her sleep, she grasped my shoulder firmly in her hand and drew me to her, she clutched at my neck and tore at me like a drowning woman – and then, suddenly, she released a piercing howl, the sovereign body writhed in pain, and at that very second, under the arm I was holding around her, I felt – what a hideous sensation! – a cold, wet lump beginning to protrude; a bulge, an absurdity, an amazing specimen emerged from between her ribs, broke free, slippery, flitted out, and, before I could grab hold of it, was already able to walk around on its own and escaped into the room.

My companion for the night was no more roused from her sleep by this event than she had been by her previous screams. Instead, she gulped for breath ever more deeply and hurried as if she were struggling to reach safe haven in her sleep. I carefully ran my hand over her back, but felt nothing, no unevenness, no distension, no tear – even though this vile lump, this clammy growth had just crept out from under my arm and leaped away. I sat up, and what I saw then made my blood run cold. Not the least bit of light shone into the room from the outside. But the white, even deathly white skin of this creature lurking in the narrow doorway glowed like moonshine in the night. It was hardly taller than a bedside table and had the body of a child or a dwarf, but its head was fully developed like that of an older, careworn man. Above all, the upper component of the massive skull reminded me of the broad, sweeping forehead of a very familiar poet, while the remaining features, from the cheeks down, unmistakably resembled those of one particular despot and criminal tyrant. No, there was no doubt: across this bloodless visage there glimmered one half Baudelaire and one half Hitler. From his temples to his chin, traces of afterbirth ran down the gnome's face. He stared glumly around, unsettled and distressed. At this point, I shook the big shoulders of my companion and rudely yanked her out of her sleep. "There! Just look! What in hell have you dragged into my house?!" She sat up next to me, slouched over her knees, arms resting on her thighs, and for a while she drowsily observed the shimmering creature. Then she fell back down onto her pillow and took my head in both hands. "Sleep," she said, "sleep! He'll be gone by early morning." She lay her long, slender fingers over my eyes. "But who is it?" I asked, indignantly. "It is – " she began, but then stopped short. She rolled over on her back and folded her arms behind her head. From this position, she looked over at the pale whelp almost, it seemed to me, with affection, and for its part, it lowered its bulging eyes as if in shame.

"It is lovelight," the woman said. Apparently, she was well acquainted with the specter. I asked her to stop speaking of such an unnatural phenomenon in the tenderest of tones. "But it was created by our friction," she answered, solemnly, "the way a thunderstorm grows and lightning fires when two air masses of different temperatures clash, when the skies are truly laden with electricity . . ." She kissed my stupidly drooping lip. "But can you explain," I stammered out with great effort, "why a crippleweight is hauling around this provocatively amalgamated head, why it is, as you may have noticed, such a crass, contemptuous cross between a noble French poet and the most evil of all Germans?"

"I don't really know how these two came together," the slim woman answered, "two others might just as well have fused. But in these sudden encounters you hardly ever get a more attractive image. A frightened soul senses nothing but the essence of the infinite, and grabs onto whatever mask is at hand. And that's why the lovely infinite often ends up with such an ugly face, sometimes the most obscene monster comes slipping out of the most joyous rapture."

"I guess you've managed to bring quite a few monsters into this world, haven't you?" I asked, rather sullenly. She gently ran a fingernail around my earlobe, and kissed me. "Now, let's sleep. Early tomorrow, as soon as the first rays of light filter through the cracks around the door, he'll melt." With barely concealed affection, she looked over at him again.

"I'll call him Boris. Every hurricane gets a name. And every lovelight, too."

I turned my head into my pillow and hid my face behind a raised arm.

.   .   .

It seemed that I had hardly dropped off when it began to grow light, ever lighter, and suddenly very cold. I could feel that something, which could hardly be the cuddly thigh of my companion, was pressing up against my hips. And it was nothing other than the disgusting little gnome, who, in his clammy little fieldcoat, had squirmed his way in between us and was more or less attempting to settle into what would be a child's place. I leaped up in blind rage and lashed out at the insufferable bastard, but she – I almost called her his mama – fell into my arms and pushed me back down onto the bed with unexpected strength. She reprimanded me in the sternest of tones and forbid the slightest punishment, making it absolutely clear that I was not to so much as lay a finger on the deathly pale Boris. I was so overcome with horror and loathing that I could neither go back to sleep next to this clammy freak, nor find a conciliatory bone in my body, and all I wanted to do was to leave my bed, the room, the house. But the stranger ordered me to stay; the one night given to us to spend together would have to be completed together in order to avoid potentially unpleasant consequences. Her orders and demeanor were so uncompromising that I no longer knew my own mind and I stayed, astounded at the gruff, almost crude tone I would never have expected to emanate from that body.

I lay down along the outermost edge of the bed, tossing and turning sleeplessly within a severely circumscribed space. And I even had to watch as the Baudelairean Hitler was allowed to climb up onto her back, while she offered no resistance at all. He just sat there, his head resting on one hand, gloomily brooding to himself. After a while – dawn's first glimmer may already have been shining through – I noticed that he had curled up into a little ball and very gently snuggled up in between her shoulder blades. He no longer glowed so moon white, or now at least his skin had turned matte, and he was nothing more than a little, gray, round heap of general, with a skull no larger than a fist. Almost ethereal, almost cute, the creature lay there consuming himself, and the tall woman bore it on her patient and shapely back, which – even given the beauty of its surface – I could never imagine cherishing or desiring again.

TWO

Besides an inclination to intense awareness and furious thought, Reppenfries was possessed of another, somewhat androgynous passion: Helping and Wearing a Uniform. He had himself trained by the Red Cross as a medic, and then one day he simply disappeared, distancing himself, so to say, from the rest of the troupe, in order to become more independent and thence make his way in life as a freelance helper. And he had allowed the simple gray uniform to remain in his company, it was something he could not and would not do without. He wore it every day; whenever he left his apartment, even if it was only to go to the mailbox, he was properly attired in gray. He was convinced that at any time, in any place, a situation might arise in which he would have to intervene helpfully. In truth, however, the wearing of a *good* uniform had itself become a necessity and a secret balm. It was one of his greatest satisfactions: to be unexpectedly needed, without having first to lie in unending wait for some unfortunate situation to arise in his proximity. Incessantly ready to help, and always happy to show up in his medic's uniform among the populace, he relished both the regard and the quiet trust his appearance engendered, and he felt welcome in circles that he basically – or let's say, that he, for his part, if not loathed, at least viewed skeptically from every possible angle, and disparaged with vigor. But: as caustic as his spirit was, his hands were caring; as arrogant as his heart was, his sense of duty was strong. He was absolutely convinced that his mere presence in a street milieu could prevent certain misfortunes from occurring; it would suffice if he sat vigilantly on some street corner wearing his Helper Jacket, a quiet authority of protection and care, imbuing people with a sense of enhanced security, and thus diminishing their susceptibility to distress. His territory had no fixed boundaries, he had to roam, he had to be mobile. He got his assignments from no one. Athletic events, rock concerts, theaters and the like were firmly in the hands of his organized colleagues. But he, the deserter, the runaway Knight of First Aid, had to search out neglected danger zones on his own. He waited at construction sites and unguarded crossings, he mingled with the crowds at fairs and demonstrations, took up position in underground shopping arcades, in the red-light district and in public toilets, and was especially attracted to nursing homes. He showed up whenever someone fainted, sprained an ankle, or injected himself senseless. Got beat up. Hit by a car. Suffered heat stroke or an asthma attack. And things did often happen when he was around. Happened *because* he was near, as his sister-in-law, Paula, so possessed of sarcasm, protested.

Reppenfries stepped back from the balustrade, the vantage point from which he had been surveying the leaden, predawn, haze, and returned to our midst.

"All that," he began, while pointing with outstretched thumbs back over his shoulder, "this society of ours is supposed to be the greatest work of mankind created in our time. In this century, neither science nor politics, let alone art or religion, has anything comparable to show for itself, anything as complex and highly developed, an almost superhuman achievement, as this unfathomable, all-powerful communal body is. But what kind of a body is it, really? Hasn't it laid claim to all of our creative energies? Haven't we given much, perhaps much too much, of our best and our most dear in order to keep it well-nourished? Many a personally outstanding virtue has already fallen victim; we have given much courage, love, enthusiasm and peace of mind, and received, in return, fear, emptiness, and uncertainty. What have we created? A demigod or an insatiable demon? In any case, the grandiose and singular construct of a free, mass society has long since overtaken us, it is a thousand times 'smarter' than we are, and not even the combined knowledge of all of the experts, politicians, and wise people on this earth would be enough to begin to understand this superorganism, let alone direct it with a superior intelligence.

"It is no longer necessary to read science fiction, or to wait for the advent of biological or robotic superman, in order to encounter a higher intelligence. We are already surrounded by just such an enigmatic visitor, in the form of the mutated sovereign, the free and open society. Of course, we are ourselves a part of its intelligence, but possessing only the rationality of the initiated, we perform its rites without being able to explain them. A secret society, a secret unto itself, and us right in the very middle, so profoundly submerged in its rational goals and games that the human brain is no longer capable of seeing beyond its rules, or rising above them. Not all that long ago, we were talking about the scientific mind 'disenchanting the world.' In the meantime, we have gained somewhat more insight into the complex order of things, but only enough to be enchanted again by what we have found. Our knowledge has done nothing more than ratchet our astonishment up another notch."

"You've probably already had a very similar thought," Almut offered in her quiet way. "But, isn't it possible that the whole of our communal life is one long ritual avowed, unbeknownst to us, in order to satisfy some deity we neither sense nor see, in order to somehow, subliminally, obtain its protection?"

"And all of these horrible highway accidents have always seemed like ritual sacrifices to me," added Yossica, the young girl. Reppenfries threw her a suspicious glance, thinking she might be making fun of him. But she was totally sincere, as were the rest of us. Even the "modern man" agreed this time, though he almost always challenged the medic. "Those things that strike us as random occurrence, and inexplicable phenomena, might well appear orderly and easily comprehensible to a being in the next higher realm of sense and time. Just think of old Jacob's ladder as having very many rungs – countless intermediate stages of evolution separate the creator-spirit from this human planting here on earth. We are the garden – long past being God's own, of course, now only that of a next higher, possibly very playful, cosmic intelligence. It cast a few spores of life onto this planet and cultivated us like an allotment garden. It knows the entire plan and sees, perhaps from another time, our fate blossoming for only one spring."

"You're right," Reppenfries responded happily, "we often gaze out of our confined inhabitings and workings up into the sky and quietly ask ourselves: what might the stars be thinking about all of this? Yes, yes. We are being watched, I believe it too, we are being observed. Otherwise, we wouldn't be moving . . ."

"Obscure! No, how obscure!" the robust sister-in-law, Paula, interjected, loudly clapping her hands. She probably thought she had caught her gloomy brother-in-law making a huge intellectual blunder, and wanted to expose him immediately. Unfortunately, Dagmar had just walked up to her husband and tucked the wayward corner of the ponderer's shirt collar back into his uniform jacket. This wifely intervention, considerate on the one hand, tactless on the other, sent the thinker-medic into a sudden rage.

"I have got to concentrate, and you're here fiddling around with my collar! It's an impudence, you sit here and listen to me until you see a chance to fix something or other. What that means, of course: you haven't really been listening at all, you've just been lurking out there waiting for the right, or, much more to the point, the wrong moment to aggrandize yourself by conspicuously grabbing the collar of a hardworking man, only to prove how easily your sphere can lord over his!"

"But that's not the way it happened, at all!" Yossica the mail clerk shouted indignantly, feeling her sense of justice impinged upon. "It wasn't until the others had started jumping in and interrupting you, and you weren't even all that concentrated any more, that your wife grabbed your silly collar and tucked it back in. And, besides, she really meant well!" At this, the wife Dagmar indicated that she no longer needed the young woman's sympathetic intercession. "Watch out! My husband's an active philosopher!" she said, somewhat sarcastically, in a tone not unlike her sister's, but as she was a warmhearted person by nature, it seemed put on. She couldn't even abide little Yossica's mild rebuke of her husband. And she would be much more likely to defend his coarsest attacks on her than to make common cause with others against him.

In the meantime, Reppenfries had pulled himself together and was continuing with his expository remarks.

"So, we have made," he picked up his line of thought, "of ourselves, of our nation, nothing other than a thoroughly modern society. Social concepts govern our lives to the very outermost boundary of our senses; they shadow our entire thinking, the more proximate as well as the more remote, they regulate our political and personal morals. They truly provide protection and cover – but they also shield us from all forms of wisdom and more profound consciousness. Usually, these concepts are especially welcomed by our youth (and this includes the concept of a state); they lend an aura of intelligence and provide for a rapid upswing in understanding. Still, they contribute very little to equipping us with the stability and sagacity we so urgently require in our lives. The science of the here and now is hardly even the stuff of an evening's diversion. And this can as well be applied to the evening of a life as it is to more recent times. Where in the not too distant past, our people had surrendered themselves to a fate of despotic *captivity*, contemporary social man, upon achieving awareness, surrenders to the no less devastating horror of total *dissociation*. Our so recently formed fellow-man cannot escape suffering the fate of Antaeus, who, as we all know, lost both strength and life when Hercules lifted him up off the earth. His chest is crushed by the feeling of having completely fallen victim to the commonsense, the demons of society. He may do, think, dream, even suffer and fear, whatever comes his way, but he senses that no matter what it may be, he is only halfway, feebly, nearly realizing it. He can only despair, for no matter how conscientious he may be, how tender and constant, no matter where he turns, he will still be nothing but a weight raised up off the earth, seized by a swirl of time, buffeted by a wind that makes *everything* fickle. What he is experiencing are the tremors of disconnect. No less, it seems to me, not one little bit less a heart-pulsing shock than to wake up one morning imprisoned, in this opposing, this Antaean nightmare: incapable of holding or adhering, of ever again feeling the redeeming earth under his feet; lifted, in order to be crushed by the wind . . . . Oh, counted and fixed, weighed and found wanting, broken apart and cast to the winds!

"Our dissociation from evil followed an evil uncoupling. Like someone born without roots, we keep losing our way in a false habitat. Runners and dancers, jumpers and fencers, hunters and fugitives, doddering or reeling, oh, the only thing on the move anywhere is movement! These words, faces, speeds – when and where are they supposed to be? And me, myself, when and where? No, it is profoundly uncertain, it cannot be determined. Instead of a modest bundle of experiences, we are carrying a high pannier full of cravings and sensitivities around on our hunched backs, a vast amount of opinion and data, nothing but untried existence, more exhausting to bear than a moderately weighty fate. Naturally, an abundant inner agenda of private joys and sufferings is continually taking place, but all without a life emerging, being lived out in the open. We tend to take the play of attraction and impulse for the very stuff of an active life, but we are like someone being trained as a pilot and never managing to make it out of the flight simulator. Our life of freedom? Freedom! Sacred word, enormous fire that has lifted and inspired peoples, states, classes, and artists! However, its blazing advance cannot be checked, and, devouring everything in its path, not even sparing those long since liberated, those who are actually more in need of peace of mind and a sense of conformity than they are of greater individualization. Freedom and its long progression from the creative fire to a life-obliterating conflagration – freedom from slavery and alien rule, freedom from God and predestination, freedom from state coercion and family bonds, freedom from others, freedom from everything – free as never before, crazy free!"

Reppenfries had delivered his last few sentences in one breath and wanted by all means to keep the "modern man," Hans-Werner, from immediately jumping in with an opposing opinion, which would only spoil the effect of what he, Reppenfries, had just said. "Wait," he shouted excitedly, "one moment, please. I would like to present a little demonstration."

To our amazement, he now took the young mail clerk aside and stood her, facing him, at a precisely determined distance; just like a hypnotist or magician performs with a volunteer he has chosen from the audience, and whose shyness he intends to make good use of in a particularly frivolous stunt. Accordingly, he addressed himself to the girl with a calm, entrancing voice, and from then on did not let her out of his unwavering sight and sway.

"Yossica, why aren't you happy?"

The girl, growing into a woman, answered trustingly and quickly in the clichéd phrases that came to her in her trance. She was no longer speaking herself; what they heard was the voice of the conjured archetypal spirit of her generation.

"All this repression is driving me crazy."

"What kind of repression do you mean?"

"I mean all of the repression. My life is full of it."

"Then, how would you like to live?"

"I would like to live freely and be able to run my own life."

"And what would you do with your free life?"

"Communicate freely, do things that are fun."

"And what do you think would still be fun for you, if you could do everything you wanted?"

"I don't know. I'd like to write songs, for example. Or learn how to be a cabinetmaker. And make nice things."

"And what's wrong with your job as a mail clerk?"

"It's dumb."

"Then find yourself an apprenticeship in cabinetmaking."

"There's no use, I can't get one, anyway."

"That's not true. If that's what you really want to do, and you have enough determination and real desire, then you can become a cabinetmaker, and even be happy at it."

"Whenever I go looking for a place, there are always ten other people standing in line in front of me. Or, somebody or other doesn't think I'm good enough. And then I get discouraged."

"You are now twenty-two years old. And you don't know what you want to do?"

"I do know. I want. I want to make something. I can feel it in the tips of my fingers. But I can't wait any longer. Or I'll lose the force."

Yossica, or whatever was speaking through her, was becoming more and more agitated. Words just kept bubbling up out of a soul as overwrought as it was deeply depressed. And she had nothing good to say either about her friends or about her colleagues at the post office, or even her manager, who, she claimed, was constantly harassing her. ("You are the Marilyn of our section . . .") Recently, when they were at a disco, her friends, so-called, had left her in the lurch when a female skinhead kicked her in the stomach. For no reason at all, she just did it. "Might have been wearing the wrong stockings, or something." And her friends, people she really thought she'd been close to, just stood there, dumb, not one of them helped.

"Young people, you can have 'em all. Everyone between sixteen and twenty-five is a Nazi. Most of them will become entrepreneurs. They just don't see anything else to do, so they're going out on their own. But for that you need lots of guts, and you have to be tough. Where do you get guts? 'Throw the foreigners out,' and things like that, that's what's going on here, it's just something in the air here in Germany, like acid rain. That's what you turn to when the going gets tough."

Although it was still the lovely Yossica standing there in front of us, babbling on, so pretty in her black handmade slacks, and her pink wool sweater – I suddenly began to feel very uneasy. It seemed to me, that emanating from this young creature were the rustlings of an old malevolence, a historical curse, rather than the anguish of youth or affluence. Suddenly, it was the deep breath of revenge that was driving this girl (and countless others of her generation) into open failure. "Anyway, I can't cope with anything I'm supposed to be coping with," she screamed, "wherever you look, it's lousy and awful. I can hardly believe, just last Easter, I was feeling so good when I was skiing with my parents . . ."

At this point, Reppenfries broke the spell and released his medium. Yossica, drenched in tears of shame and a most profound distress, bolted away, running down into the park with no intention of ever showing herself again.

We all surrounded the medic and reproached him in the sternest of terms. What could he have been thinking, taking such crass advantage of a young and vulnerable life just so he could find another occasion to shove his frail fist into the face of "society," an opponent, who, in the final analysis, was always totally unassailable, and never to be held accountable for anything, or everything. Under no circumstances could he be allowed to torment an individual person merely to illustrate the general principle of being tormented. Reppenfries vigorously rejected our accusations. He claimed not to have tormented Yossica at all, but only to have irradiated her. He had only touched her most impersonal strata, and allowed the purely non-individual core of her being to speak. At most, this may have confused Yossica, but certainly will have caused her no serious harm or pain. And, by the way, it would not do any of the rest of us any harm, either, to have him conjure up those universally common, and fundamentally contemporary, aspects that run through our singularity in broad tracks and dense belts of radiation.

"Terrible waste of children!" he added, in somber distress. "Dear members of this society: what have you done with your children?! They are your responsibility, after all! Your pursuit of unbounded freedom, which has already dealt a death blow to tree and stream, has not left your children unscathed. The destruction of interest, of youthful aspiration, of loyalty to oneself, that's hit close enough to home and it's enough to kill. Where the strength to *experience* life is broken, that is where you'll find the living dead wander. In the same way that dead waters continue to flow."

Drowning the rest of us out came the robust voice of his sister-in-law, who had until now been restraining herself. Once more, she expressly disapproved of the unseemly demonstration that the medic had carried out with Yossica, and then immediately moved on to an even more intense castigation of her relative. Reppenfries appeared to endure her hectoring with somewhat tortured equanimity. In any case, palms flat against his body, he had stuck both hands into the belt of his uniform jacket, and a weak and pained smirk drew across his face.

"Taking everything apart and then not getting it back together again. That's absolutely all there is to your genius! Drive everything into the ground, shred it to pieces, expose it, see through it – 'irradiate' it! And then just leave it lying there. We're the first ones in line, your closest relatives, your targets, and then it's society's turn, the planet, God and the universe! And now you can't even leave youth in peace! You just like the idea of abusing someone who's got so much more going than you have? Just think about who's really responsible for all of your crap! You're not suffering from what you see around you – all you're suffering from is your own sickening views. And even if you do know the bitter truth, just stuff it, and keep your mouth shut. We know it already, ourselves. We can all keep our mouths shut. But, no! You, with your X-ray vision, you want to play the great seer again, the solitary debunker! Why? Everything's been seen through, long since, shot right out of the water. The smasher of false custom, bad convention! Why? Everything's already lying there in pieces. The last Knight of the Unmasking! A Nietzsche-Again, a Nietzsche-Once-More, and One-More-Time-Again, a Nietzsche, truly, in the saddest of all forms!"

In a frenzy of resonance, even Dagmar let loose a few tough words from her good conscience. "You're going to choke on this society mania, if you're not careful! It's already bordering on craziness, you and your long lance always charging at something that's neither here nor there, something that's everywhere and nowhere. We all have to stop and smell the roses, sometimes!"

"Then, go join a garden club," the medic growled.

"Not necessary, not necessary at all. I just have to take a look at Yossica. Young people are so open and straightforward. So reassuring! They speak openly and honestly about what's on their minds. They're a lot more honest, a lot more spontaneous than you and I are."

Reppenfries, who had been showing remarkable deference toward his malicious sister-in-law, hardly challenging a thing she said, was all the more unforgiving with her sister and charge, who was his own wife.

"No one is a more wretched liar than a person who is continually pounding himself on the chest, and saying: look here, how open and honest, how spontaneous, how totally I, myself, I am! As if such an I, all on its own, without tradition, duty and underlying concept, with nothing but half-baked freedom in its head, could ever speak the truth! It can't help lying, spontaneously, in and of itself. It does not possess the slightest *notion* of integrity. It is in way over its head with this open and honest chest it keeps pounding on."

"A pity," his wife sighed, "it is really a pity that no one here has gotten sick to his stomach. Or sprained an ankle. Then you would have something to set, or someone to resuscitate. And we wouldn't have to listen to any more of your sick hatchet jobs." Well, you could argue with Reppenfries over just about anything, but without showing the proper sense of care and gravity, you could not, under any circumstances, remark on his medicdom, the dark and sacred contradiction in his nature. No one knew this better than Dagmar, his wife. She knew the risk she had taken, and you could see the fear of annihilating retaliation in her eyes.

"You are," the medic coldly stated, as he turned to her, "not worthy of the language that has passed your lips. In the most profound sense, you are lacking the moral right to speak in the German language. Of what use has it been for you to have been able to listen to me for all this time? I'm not the one who sat here and babbled on in empty-headed impudence. *I* acknowledge the authorities. I obey the greater spirit. I follow those whose experience is richer than my own. But you? You want to assert *yourself*, and God only knows that is little enough to assert."

After these words, I could see Dagmar's dazed look. It held everything: anger and pain, helpless thoughts of resistance, the onset of the irreconcilable, but also unadorned horror, fear for the future. Was the thread of devotion to be broken forever at this very second? Her eye was *one* fixed expression of many fleeting emotions. But it did not see, it was blind in this stormy testing of limits.

"You are insufferable!" she blurted out, cramming her entire soul into one false word.

Now, she became the second person to flee trembling from our midst, and she bolted to the balustrade, where she paced restlessly back and forth for some time. She was in such a state that Paula temporarily put off the retaliatory blow we were all awaiting and rushed promptly to her sister's side.

For a second time, those of us remaining felt ourselves compelled to try to bring Reppenfries to his senses and to remind him of the demands of basic human decency. In no uncertain terms, we warned him against repeating such attacks on any of us here, including those nearest him. Hans-Werner was the first to make an attempt at getting us out of the twisted and embarrassing situation we had gotten ourselves into following this rancor. He had been waiting for some time for an opportunity to challenge several of the medic's statements, and, now, with carefully chosen words, he took command, simply ignoring the excited souls around him.

"It is useless," the modern man began, "it is even dangerous, to chase after ideas, morals, or customs, and set them up as a standard for our emotions, when they no longer have any universal validity at all. When they are irretrievably gone. We all run the danger of simply going crazy if we try to hold onto something that no longer has any relevant role to play in our social existence.

"You, Reppenfries, you never got engaged, did you? But I think we can all agree that was once a useful custom, as long as divorce laws were strict, most women never had professions, and marriage was more or less viewed as a lifelong commitment. Today, if you get engaged, you may be a friend of ceremony, but what you are doing is something needlessly charming, something that has long since lost its formal intent. What was once custom has now become nothing more than atmospherics. In the meantime, to take the place of everything that has been lost, somewhere, in the eventful scheme of our reality, something entirely different has emerged, just as important and just as promising, something that deserves our complete attention, and that we seldom correctly appreciate in its first stages. We must understand that it is our emotional inertia that causes us to attribute so much more significance to the old than to the 'terribly new.' We never really accept anything, or become fond of it, until it is lost to us. Even now, in relatively young years, we condemn our awkward age, deplore the many rapid changes in our social and technical environment, which we, in almost every instance – in exactly the same way our fathers and grandfathers did – consider to be a decline. And one thing is certainly true: over such a short span of time, no other epoch has produced so much past as ours has. Even as recently as our fathers' time, no one really felt old until they had reached a rather mature, advanced age. Today, however, where experience counts for nothing, and curiosity and innovative skill appear to mean everything, a man who has hardly entered middle age will often escape into his memories, suddenly, like an old man, beginning to view the years of his youth through rose-colored glasses, with great nostalgia. A vigorous forty-year-old feels he's already past his peak, and obsolete, when he finds himself confronting an entirely new and demanding 'generation' of machines, of structures and marketing strategies. And with that, sentimental aging has taken a giant step forward. But this is a deceptive, an artificial and extremely inhibiting development, much more the stuff of attitude and emotion than necessity, and I am certain that it will soon vanish like an evil spook. Namely, at that point when we succeed in transforming the character of our own time-sense, instead of laboriously, grindingly, struggling to adapt to the changes around us. It is my belief that, inwardly, we are now standing at the threshold of a new time-principle and where the old, impoverished principle only recognized linear extension, it will be overtaken and replaced with a considerably expanded, and even reassuring measure. It is just this straight, single-strand time, also known as progress, that we have always had stuffed down our throats, a leftover from the era of revolutions, it and only it is responsible for the accelerating vertigo that we are now experiencing – because we only see things moving in *one* direction. If we were able to view all these developments from just a slightly more elevated time-point, things that now seem to be taking place in impossibly swift succession would appear orderly and controlled, and, furthermore, it would be much easier to distinguish between their good and bad ends.

"And, Reppenfries, whether you want to believe it or not: it is electronics and the complex output of our social intelligence that is bringing us ever closer to this new time-sense, and that is already clearly signaling the approach of its abundantly branching rhythms! In creating his works, whether art or machine, unknown or neglected, man has always exposed and drawn from the reservoirs of his natural capacities, his potential and his fate. His nature has always emerged through what he has created into his consciousness. And things are no different today, when, in the design of highly integrated control systems, we see elements of our own essential, biological function; namely, the process of circular feedback, which forms the basis of all organic life, even regulating the growth of the simplest cell. This is the counter-principle, the mega-principle, to the linear, to the cause-and-effect-sequence, which has held our thinking and feeling hostage for so long. Through the magnifying glass of microelectronics we are discovering the principle of a life based on integrated feedback. Once this concept has truly penetrated our thought and our senses, then it will radically transform our entire perceptive capacities and our mentality. Among other things, it will put us in a position to examine, with utmost assurance, all data of the external world, all of the changes and 'mutations,' to set them off against the values of our past, of our cultural memory, of our empirical world, and to balance them in such a way as to gain the greatest possible survival advantage. Then, there will no longer be competition between yesterday and today, and we will be living, thinking, and creating in the sphere of an elaborate, expanded sense of present.

"Let us no longer mourn the lost depths and the ephemeral heights. Experiencing the complex surface is no less an achievement of the human spirit than its extension to the mothers below and the father above. A sense of the web, the intricately interconnected, will more than compensate for the respect of the hierarchies. Stop looking to conserve, suffocating in attempting to hold on; instead, find the heart of the Great Transformation, and then, I believe, we will really be able to live. Our banished reserves cannot survive on their own. Just imagine: the entire supply of precious knowledge, noble art – imagine it had disintegrated into ashes and nothingness, all that was left was museums and archives, and there was no one among our *contemporaries* who themselves wrote poetry, painted, philosophized. No matter how frail their own efforts, how unsure the stroke they set down, they would still be uniting the archives with the beginnings, keeping it all alive through their lonely struggle. For me, Reppenfries, you talk too much about decline, breakdown and disappearance. Where, obviously, almost everything shows up again before you and your critique have been able to carry it off to the grave! Just be a little more patient. And look around you. There is so much going on! Yes, *going on*, in the process of formation, not in entropy, not being squandered away as you seem to think. No, I don't want to hear any more of those heroically hollow protowords about the end, about silence, forgetting, disappearing and whatever else might occur to you. Aren't we more attuned to the pathos than the thought, to the holy trembler you evoke from ages past? The last, the end – even they are only *plants*, especially enchanting to observe in this garden of boundless transformation. But just like your pessimism, Reppenfries, only one sensual pleasure among many others. The anguished cry of a soul, that it is soul! But life is stronger. It passes by this as it does every other form of rejection. I want you to know: the way you are viewing the now and what will follow you, you are not doing them justice. With your way of thinking, all you can adequately study is what has already come to pass, actually nothing more than *your own* past.

"And there is one more point where I would like to make my objections absolutely clear. When it comes to our highly developed democracy, you might be much better off appreciating it with all your waking senses rather than with your overly pointed views. The beauty in diversity, which we so readily admire in nature and think healthy – why are we to view it so skeptically and suspiciously when it appears in western societies? Why are we so disinclined to take pleasure in the wealth of its forms, rather than immediately locking our annoyed gaze on its deficiencies regarding some or another unfulfilled ideal? We, you and I, have lived long enough in this flexible order, survived youth and maturity, anger and fear in it, and have not had to forego an inner growth; and this under a form of government that remained totally free of the 'control of a grand personage,' as Mann once put it in his 'Observations of an Apolitical Man.' Long enough, too, for this flexible order to have permeated flesh and blood, to have sunk into the subconscious, or let's say: into the core of our intuitive powers and needs. Didn't it long ago create a kind of poetical Doppelgänger, releasing a phantasm of itself? In the meantime, the second German Republic has endured longer than a lifespan, has already borne its own past, created eras, and is beginning to take on the contours of that easy empire, where everything mean and ordinary is being transformed into beauty and stateliness. For where there is memory, there is cloudiness. And out of this cloudy sky will fall the particles of a golden age. We Germans will yet succeed at mythologizing our 'Bundesrepublik,' we began long ago.

"I am asserting that we long ago internalized our sense of order, much more profoundly than is commonly thought, that it created a phantasm, an inner presence in us, and I would like to refer once more to the natural sciences and the paradigm in which a pluralistic network has largely replaced that of the causal concatenation. I suspect that there is a whole series of more recent discoveries, particularly in the field of microphysics and molecular genetics, that would not have been made or formulated without a more profound *democratic intuition*, to which a mind shaped by hierarchical models would never have come. Thus my skepticism toward the mighty thinker-hero, who has not appeared in our era, basically because we have no use for them. These days such a figure could hardly set himself up as the lone authority, and like a Zarathustra, a mountain wanderer, step out in front of us and hurl down his proclamations; of necessity, he would have to be part of the system, and evolve out of it; he would have to discern and acknowledge this societal formation that has permeated our every nerve and our every vision. And his real spiritual adventure would begin with the desperate acknowledgment (which you, yourself, brought up just now): society, as such, is a more intelligent 'being' than I am. There is no way that he could hide behind this realization if he ever intended to lead the way to a 'transvaluation of all values.' And today, the matter he would have to penetrate would be many times more dense than that which Nietzsche once ran up against. Assuming, of course, that such a trailblazer had not simply thought his way past the science of our time, but even then he would be a tragicomical figure, a subsidiary trailblazer. At any rate, we are not now living in that special time when epochal layers are being shed, when it is possible to be 'late young' and rise up to become a great debaucher. No, Reppenfries, these days no one is better than anyone else. For that to happen, there is too much going on down here on the plains, too varied, too widely dispersed. And that's why I am not all that interested in the image of the icy mountain top and the lonely wanderer. I love the wide-open and synchronous terrain of the many. And the stumbling of people all over their junk. It will show us our next steps."

.   .   .

The medic had been listening carefully and unmoved the entire time. Several times, with brief sidelong glances, he had taken the measure of the speaker's ardent drive, and even accepted many a barb directed his way, all without taking any perceptible offense. And even in his responses, he sought more to address the accomplice, the accessory, rather than drawing out the acknowledged opponent.

"Now, I am sure you are not one of those frantic smart guys, one of those quick dealers in used views, whose awareness is hanging out of their mouths like the panting tongue of an over-heated dog. I am certain that you, too, have stumbled onto an absolute view of things, and have been crucified by the urge to confess, and how could things be any different, as long as we are trapped in this faltering morning, while our tendencies pile up until they're ready to break out in revolutions!

"I listen to you, and I have to ask myself to what extent the dis-oriented community has already struck and damaged the individual's ability to observe, how far the radiation sickness of decay has already progressed when the best minds can develop such abscesses of illusion. You say: bright, beautiful world! Where the only place I see bright colors is in the phosphorescent shimmer of decomposing substance. You evoke grand, synchronous, 'democratic' plains; I warn: do not disintegrate into a thousand tolerances, do not go down in the carnivalism of freedom! Basically, these are our differences. For me, diversity is no sure sign of fruitful abundance; profusion can also be found in decay. Just as, the other way round, the uni-and-omni-form does not necessarily signify deficiency and impoverishment, but can also be an indication of rigorous, concentrated power. Anyone who wants to be a founder must stand up against the diverse. Tolerance does not promote creative determination. Now, you say that life is stronger than all rejection. Then it is also stronger than man. It was there before him and it will be there after him. It is therefore a paradox for us to pray for God's protection while at the same time worshipping creation. For creation is well on the way to overwhelming us. Worse yet: ours seems to be the horrible fate of annihilating every living thing simply to serve the progress and enhancement of creation. But even if one day we sweep the planet clean, entirely and repeatedly, emptying it of man and animal, plant and stream, somewhere there would still be a germ ark, enough biomass from which the whole could begin all over again and play itself out, albeit under somewhat harsher conditions. And, of course, on a higher, more tested plane, over millions of years, creatures would develop who had no talent for the kind of catastrophe we fear today and are preparing, a stronger, 'more chosen' species, beyond luxury and death. 100 million years closer to God – and maybe more like Him. You see, Hans-Werner, your 'evolution,' taken to its logical conclusion, inevitably leads to a universal absence of mercy. Neither man's suffering nor the fate of epochs count for anything here. The Great Change, the *living* is passing us by, unmoved, with blood and desolation, flames and toxic substances, more indifferent than the most brutal criminal of history. The catastrophe of contemporary man, what else can it be but a minuscule occurrence, an event hardly worthy of mention in the course of the eight billion years to which the history of our planet is limited, in any case? Having turned up somewhere around its halftime, we achieved the necessary overview rather quickly, and know with great certainty that the red sun giant will come, no matter what happens; only a brief four billion years and all life on the planet will vaporize. The extermination of the earth creature has already been irrevocably set and will not be halted, least of all by man's powers. We have been bridled by the end, and it is in our nature that we be so. And what we have always known in our subconscious thought, and in our souls, what has already taken place in countless myths and mysteries, is now being confirmed in the precision of astronomy, in sober terminology, and it is, bit by bit, delivering the proof that precisely what we have dreamed will come to pass. The horizon will go up in flames, twelve suns will appear in the heavens and scorch the earth – what real difference is there between this Brahmin vision of the sun at the point of its supernova explosion, and the astrophysical depiction of the same event in terms of an inflated helium balloon? In these practically identical end-images, which both religion and science have drawn, we can experience, or at least foresee, the unity of human thought from the enlightened right down to the cyberneticists; and this unity is itself only a part of the univers-all-consciousness, which ranges all the way from primal matter to God, and in which our extraordinary species is permitted the first step toward perception, and in which it is granted transient participation. This manner of thought, in which there is reconciliation of mind and matter, science and transcendence might justifiably be considered redeeming. But even if it were to touch us, even if it were to 'lower itself down' to us, would we be prepared and able, would we the possess the cultural composure and strength to receive it and allow ourselves to be redefined? Our interests have long since been carried away by the short-term view, and now, prisoners of our lust for power and our greed for time, we are pursuing the business of disaster, ever more hurriedly, ever more blindly. But the redeeming thought, as paradoxical as it may sound, will survive even without man. It doesn't need him. It is eternal creation.

"Furthermore, we are in no way justified in drawing any conclusions regarding the ability of our own societies to transform and renew themselves, based on the unlimited evolution of species, and the indestructible power of living things. But if you still love comparisons, then, Hans-Werner, you will not deny that over the course of the billions of years of phylogenic history on earth, by far more animal and plant species have died out than are still in existence today. By comparison, the six-thousand-year era of human history appears decidedly modest, though it is filled with countless ascents and declines, dying races, decaying and destroyed cultures, exhausted epochs, overextended empires. And, we, contemporary humankind, of all beings, are to evade decline through diversity? Where do you actually see this diversity? It seems to me that instead of a 'wealth of species,' our life forms are becoming more and more homogeneous all around the planet. Powerful, new revolutions in industry are turning the deadly concept of equality into a reality. And the laws of nature have taught us, that we do the deadliest thing possible for our kind when we standardize its capabilities worldwide.

"Of all beings, how are we to achieve splendid transformation and renewal? No. Our little bit of what is us, our little bit of mind, ancestry, belief, and will to live, is just not going to fork it over. Cardinal Newman's famous social demons would have to come to our aid, these good little spirits who belong neither to heaven nor hell, but do their work in larger or smaller groups of human beings, who inspire entire nations and social classes, helping them to wise actions, in a way that an individual never could come up with, even if he were of the highest stature – and furthermore: an intelligent anticipation of our contemporary maxim, that the human mind is incapable of understanding how social systems function – ah, I fear these good demons have really left us twisting in the wind!

"We live in a feedback loop, you tell us. Then, how can you ridicule my sense of the past? I have it alone to thank for that fact that I still mind my house with an express contempt for death. That I can experience joy and anger, make my observations, form judgments just and unjust; that I am curious, as if I were not old, and ready, as if I were not tired. The eyes of the anachronist, which you consider me to be, are looking straight ahead; and no one keeps a more patient watch than a man well supported at the rear. While those who are all too contemporary, who have dived deep into the stream of happening, will of necessity notice only the most fleeting aspects of the world around them, the flowing itself, and they will simply keep blubbering on, garbled and indistinct.

"Naturally, I know better than anyone else that my assertions, too, are only fluttering particles of universal disintegration. I am also beaten and bound to all forgetting, to the enormous increase in the amount of shit that is backing up into our rooms out of all of our pipes and canals. Given current circumstances, every serious conviction, no matter how strong and how valid, is nothing more than one delusion among many, one more garish rag on a motley fool's coat. Within evil's realm of influence, ideas drawn up are no longer even desperate but only lost. You can hear the rustling of dead flashes of lightning . . . Still, I believe: every active effort aimed at protecting our natural environment from ruin defies the stupidity that has been imposed on us. Even if our contemporary spirit has been made numb and stupid with horror, it is still possible for us to take correct action. And these acts, which lead us to an awareness of our life sources, are pastorally good, instinctively right. Here, we can feel a good wind blowing, and for the time being it is more important than any grand theory.

"Though I am a resolute disciple of Blake, and not like you, Hans-Werner – a modern believer in science, an evolutionist! – I do not intend to go so far as the great mystic and other religious zealots who view nature as fundamentally bad and desecrated, as God's fallen garden. Given our somewhat touchy situation, that would be too much for our good reactionaries to take, and could, in the end, be used as a justification for thoughtless habitation of the planet. In any case, the point I would like to make here in this little aside is that man is not only a social, but also a metaphysical being, and this fact, it seems to me, is something we have simply been repressing for a very long time. There is nothing more urgent now than the protection of our planet and its ecosystems. And here, let's not forget the protection of our consciousness as well, something we need no less urgently, no, it's not merely protection we need, but rather a great healing, a thorough washing clean, in order to reconnect with the sources and the tributaries of great cultures and draw strength from them. Belonging. The destruction of interest and mind – something no one intended, but that inevitably followed the outrageous narcissism and idolization of society's rulers – its effect is just as life-threatening as the pollution of air, water, soil and foodstuffs. We should always remember: among all of the elements the only one unharmed by our presence is the most powerful: fire; and it will close the earth chapter of the world.

"Man will never come to understand himself sufficiently while on society's path; he will only discover what will next be to his advantage. Without an understanding of nature, his dependence and his participation will only cause greater and greater injury to this extraordinary organism, it will annihilate and thereby be annihilated itself. For, according to the gnostic gospels, to be unknowing is worse than sinning. Unknowing, we will become 'creatures of oblivion,' and suffer certain self-destruction. 'If you do not understand the origin of fire, you will burn in it, because you do not know your roots. If you do not first understand water, you know nothing. If you do not understand the origin of the wind that blows, you will perish in the wind. If you do not understand the origin of the body you carry, you will die with it. If you do not understand how you came, you will not understand how you will go . . .'

"And I say, too, from this day forth: if you cannot translate 'butterfly' with 'soul,' you will not be able to find your way back to the unity of nature. You will remain standing before the gate. You will be like a blade of grass, bent in the middle of life, with your head swaying loosely over your roots. Without myth and metaphor, our central organ, the heart-head, the dream of consciousness, or call it what you will, is not connected to the system of living things. These form the true symbiotic pharynx through which we are linked with ether and earth, animal and shrub. And these things are so wholly interconnected, it seems to me, that I would almost like to say: once memory returns, the waters will again run clear.

"At this point, I would like to close with a simple fable, which you will, I hope, find more pleasing that the pale and brittle figure of my thoughts, which have stretched themselves out in the sparse morning like a priggish nature lover."

• • •

BERND AND TREE WOMAN

The bank customer dropped his passbook, the returning traveler dropped his bags, the patient her bottle of pills, the tennis player his racket, the runner his torch, the demonstrator his banner, the painter his paint gun, the fisherman his rod, the nanny her child; crowded into a corner, each one cut off from his destiny in the flash of a discouragement, *divine* power failure, power cut in the Great Department Store; *Society*, an emergency aggregate, long overburdened; and the good old generators of *love* are wearing down . . .

Out on the edge of the churchyard there is a woman growing out of a tree, and from her navel on down her beautiful contours, her sensual body, transform into a tree.

"There is nothing to be done," she whispers softly, and gently bends down over the young man who has just leaped up onto her trunk and is gnawing on her bark like a stag.

Until just a short while ago, our Bernd had belonged to that clan of palefaces among the conservationists who had never ventured out beyond mass rallies in the streets, and only felt themselves truly sheltered and at ease in a forest of political placards. But then, one day, he came upon a living tree and was immediately consumed by his passion for the stately elm woman, or perhaps we might better say: he immediately pressed his reckless urban desires upon her. "No," is how the beauty in the tree responded, "really, there is nothing to be done. I bloom every year and burst forth in fresh green. I give shade and produce valuable atmospheric gases, I provide protection from bad weather and storms, I whisper and I sigh, I sway and I stretch, but I cannot embrace you. Observe my beauty, and consider the advantages I offer you: permanence and stability, unswerving fidelity and a healthy way of life. Nor need you fear my aging or my baldness, you will experience them every year only to find me with all of my charms, young again, the following spring, and your own passionate feelings as fresh as on this first day. So, as the year ends you will not be shocked at the funny, gnarled, groaning old woman, will you? As long as your life lasts, and even when you yourself are a very old man, I will continue to blossom in fresh youth at your side. So much for the superficial, natural characteristics of my person. As for the more quiet and tender advantages our love holds for you, they are surely inestimable and not to be found with any other creature. I will listen to you patiently and always respond, summer or winter, with lively concern. I will not remain silent when you speak to me, I will not withdraw when you need my support, and I will sing for you when you need comfort."

"Stop!" Bernd yelled. "You are seducing me, you are promising me the sweetest gifts of love, and turning my head! And still you will not surrender. I need a woman, I need a woman! Not a knotty old tree stump!" And embracing the trunk even more ardently, he tried to shake it, to bend it, to move it. But all he succeeded in doing was chafing his cheeks and his pants.

"Then go find another!" the tree woman answered back, brusque and cool.

"But I want you! Yes, I know: they have all had you. The lifeguard, the bank director, the switchman! Everyone here in the neighborhood has had you at one time or another. Even the cantor's five sons have been bragging about how they made their conquests, one after the other.... I am the only one you refuse!"

Then came a torrent of rage from above, and the tree woman snarled at him: "You are lying! How dare you question my natural virtue and defame me as a whore!"

"But that's what you are!" the amorous city-dweller shouted up at her, beside himself in outrage and misery.

Suddenly, at that moment, a single powerful bolt of lightning struck out of the black bank of clouds hanging over the field, and it shot through the body of the elm like a cutting torch, tearing open a gap in the tree shaft as tall as a man, and starting a fire inside that hollowed it out. Because the shattering blast had sent him reeling so high up into the air that he landed some meters away, lying unconscious in the field, Bernd saw none of this happen.

When he came to again, the sun was lying low in the late evening sky and there was no sign of the sudden, dark storm, except for the charred-out hollow in the tree. Anxious and confused, he looked up at his sweet love and saw that her eyes were fiery, and that half of her body silently pined for him. Irresistibly drawn to his tree woman, he crept up to her trunk. There, the breach was just large enough that he could curl himself up and squeeze in, and, in stunned delight, he climbed into the gaping, sooty wood. Above him the tree woman groaned, she felt her heartbeat out into tips of her crown, and her body convulsed in a shudder from the very deepest of its roots . . . .

It may have been by only a few centimeters that the wood had contracted and the fissure had narrowed. But it was enough that Bernd, who had just barely been able to crawl in and curl up into a sitting position, could no longer move. Every effort to get out of the trunk ended in failure; there was nothing more he could do.

Several months passed before the foresters came by with large iron bolts to close the wound in the tree. As they began their work, they discovered a pile of bones in the hollowed-out trunk, neatly stacked but in a puzzling arrangement – just as if the dead being had broken up in accordance with a higher design, as if his remains had arranged themselves into a meaningful sign, somehow marking the way forward.

. . .

At this point, Reppenfries ended his narration and looked into our faces with his greedy little eyes to see what effect it may have had. But for the next while the three of us were silent; we were each sufficiently occupied with the vast array of things he had said so that we did not feel immediately compelled to offer our impressions or make replies. While we wandered through the park looking at the manmade landscape, each keeping to himself, each searching his own soul, the medic took it for a good sign and seemed satisfied. I don't know what the others were feeling, but something inside of me, my feminine knowing, or what should I call it?, secretly revolted against his declarations. At times, what he said had simply been too lofty, too surly, even too false. Then I looked into his face and all I studied was this raw, fingernail-biting desire for a commanding view of things, of the transparent workings of their motions, the wantonness of intellect. I felt as if I had been captured in the magnetic field of these emissions, and slipping right by his words and his arguments, I did not register them at all, I no longer understood a thing. Nearby, the melancholy Almut was struggling with a different kind of cognitive difficulty, as she later confessed. In her mind, almost all of the medic's lofty terms were immediately transformed into lovely, flat little poker chips, which could be used in a kind of Monopoly to purchase "intellectual properties," only to lose them again. Unlike me, Almut possessed the ability to adapt to almost anything, even things that didn't really appeal to her, or were indeed offensive. There was nothing so alien to her that she couldn't become involved with it in some totally indifferent way. She, who seemed determined to remain encumbered until the end of her days, to live her life as one long penitential pilgrimage, she diffracted every mania and sensual stimulus in her proximity through her nature, and what got through was only the very palest of reflections. Physically, she was a rather thin, delicate creature with narrow shoulders, shortish lower legs, and small turned-up breasts which she exposed under a see-through silk blouse in order to make a point of how totally unattractive and unworthy of demure concealment she considered them to be. Almut's beauty resided wholly in her face, in her large, dark eyes, her soft pale red mouth, in her coal black, loosely put-up hair. But her entire appearance was veiled by an impenetrable sadness which thwarted every lustful gaze. She was probably the only beautiful woman whom I have ever met, and to whom I was deeply attracted, without ever really being able to desire her.

In spite of her constant melancholy, she was in no way apathetic or insensitive. She sensed every oscillation, every stimulus – and tempered it. An intensified, extreme behavior would immediately be adjusted downward, and set to match her own internal temperature. Her restrained nature, its balance entirely achieved in misfortune, was capable of neither shock nor enthusiasm. Such people have something of a saintly-ill aura about them, and we consider them, perhaps wrongly, better and more profound beings whom a more fundamental intelligence has touched and entranced. Still, the most striking thing about her was her beauty, and I simply didn't know how to respond to it. I was not used to sensing a temptation or an attraction without heeding it. But how, when this woman aroused nothing but a dull virtue – a vice which I had until now avoided – in every limb of my body? At the same time, however, I believed I was hearing a faint plea, a secret entreaty to come closer. But how do you find your way to a body whose every turn proclaims that you will never be able to move it even one millimeter closer to ecstasy?!

· · ·

After we had remained silent for some time, Paula and Dagmar were still holding out at the balustrade watching us suspiciously, Yossica had not yet reappeared from behind the bushes, and Reppenfries could finally no longer expect either a judgment or a response to his speech, I was startled when I heard my name being called and saw the medic abruptly turning to me to request that I stop playing the role of a mute observer and contribute to the series of statements that he and Hans-Werner had introduced.

. . .

"Now, Leon, it's about time we heard what you've got to say!"

I winced just like an ill-prepared schoolboy whom the teacher has called to the blackboard. But it didn't help me at all, there was no way I could get out of this; I had to, even I, as Reppenfries demanded, had to tell my story; openly describe for everyone the cross to which I have been nailed. But I did not even know where to begin. Was not the one principle guiding me in much greater need of care, much less comprehensible than anything the other two had related in their reports, which seemed by comparison much more like manifestos or ideologies you could have read in newspapers or heard in public debates? Wouldn't the circumstances of my situation seem heartrending to everyone the moment they were put into words? Not because they might be too bizarre and obscure, but, on the contrary, all too intimate and familiar for anyone to really be interested in hearing about them. Therefore, I warned everyone around me, and requested that they interrupt me immediately if my remarks began to disturb or offend. Of course I was addressing myself primarily to Almut, whose dark yearning face, petrified in yearning, was providing the actual impetus for me to tell my story. I would dearly have loved to know how much narrated depravity she could tolerate. Or if I might not finally be able to unsettle her prim and proper gloom, maybe even tearing it wide open. One final attempt to make myself appear desirable to her, this was probably the more profound motive for everything I was to say, and now that I was delivering my narration before her eyes I allowed myself confessions that had never before passed my lips.

THE WOMAN ON THE FERRY

I had come to Istanbul for the day to attend the funeral of a Turkish friend, a wonderful actor and a gifted poet, who was for some time a part of my innermost circle. Still young, he had died a few days earlier of injuries received in an automobile accident. The burial took place in the Grand Cemetery of Üsküdar on the Asiatic side of the city, where for the past few years E. had been living in a small house with his wife and children. It was a misty Sunday morning in early September; a heavy stormladen sky had been hanging over the lead gray Bosporus for the past few days. A stranger to the mourners, to E.'s family and closest friends as well, I kept to myself in the background and did not actually take part in the ceremonies. I waited for the funeral party to disperse before I approached the graveside and the casket, strewn with flowers and veils, and stood alone thinking of the happy times spent together in Germany that had made us inseparable friends. It was then, for the first time, that I was overcome with grief and the pain of separation, as well as the bitter sense of not having attended to our friendship over these past few years.

An hour later, numb and unseeing, I left the cemetery and walked back to the ferry, which quietly crosses the strait not far from the High Bridge and connects the Asian side of the city with the European. Grieving, mourning, I took no notice of my unfamiliar and celebrated surroundings and sensed only vaguely that a few hours' flight had transported me from my home into the Orient. My first impressions of the famed Golden Metropolis consisted of nothing more than the shabby grayness of new housing developments. So it was possible, without my becoming immediately aware, for someone to have been standing at my side on the deck of the ferry, so close that it might appear we belonged together. Not until the ferry had landed below a mosque and the passengers gathered around the gangplank did I see the flat, flesh-colored shoes, polished matte, intimately in step with mine, their tongues finely perforated, and then the opaque beige stockings, the dark brown, three-quarter-length skirt with a whimsical pleat running down the side – and nothing more; because the mood I was in would not allow me to lift my head any higher, even if I had wanted, and certainly not to take note of a stranger. But once I had left the ferry, I was forced to realize that the flesh-colored shoes had completely adapted themselves to my stride. I walked onto the square in front of the dock and they were still next to me, even though the cluster of passengers that had been holding us together had long since dispersed. I stopped, and the slender, unknown legs did the same, dressed as they were in a way so uncommon to this land. Stopping in unison, starting in unison, in such easy consonance it seemed as if these two people had already taken many thousands of steps together! But at this moment there was no possibility of my amazement overcoming my despair. Not even this engaging company could, or could be allowed to, tear me out of my frame of mind and away from my thoughts. Still, it was mysterious how these steps had adapted to my own and lulled me into a sense of trust and intimacy. Just as if our rhythms – having bypassed habit and life – had established themselves so profoundly that for the present we exuded the essence and the demeanor of many years of association. I was not being led, or led astray, by the unknown, any more than I was luring it my way; rather it was our sentient steps heading toward an agreed-upon destination. (And this could not possibly be my hotel, located on the heights at Taksim Square in the center of the city, because we were continuing along the shores of the Bosporus, apparently in the direction of an outlying district.)

After some time, I noticed how some of my most bitter sorrow was beginning to ease, and the knot of remorse had relaxed ever so slightly. I even took some slight comfort in finding that here in a strange country, on this difficult and desolate day, I was not walking alone, and, in some admittedly dark way, no longer had to worry about anything. At least as long as this profoundly shared, undemanding perambulation continued. Still, now as before, I was in no mood to lift my head. Like someone with a stiff back, constantly bent over, I simply could not bring myself to raise my eyes any higher than the level of her knees and to finally look straight into the face of this stranger who had insinuated herself into my existence.

·   ·   ·

It turned out, however, that at least she knew our destination, and its selection had not been made by the self-regulating mechanism of our mutual progression. After all, she was the one who stopped and crossed the road, and I merely followed, already lacking any will of my own. We soon arrived at a house set back from the street, the height and size of which I could not accurately discern without looking up, but it must have been one of those two- or three-story buildings, perhaps a somewhat more modest version of one of those cheap and ugly concrete monstrosities that had contributed so much to the disappointing impression the city of sultans, odalisques, and magnificent tales had first made on me.

. . .

The room, which we entered through an unlocked glass door, resembled the bar of what may have once been a coffeehouse; in any case, we walked in to the right, past a counter, above which milky white neon tubes glowed even though daylight provided adequate illumination. I could see shabby plastic barstools stacked up in a row, there was cracked linoleum under my feet, newspapers and electric cables lay around on the filthy floor, and there were many other remains indicating that it had been some time since this café had received members of the public. My guide – as I now had to think of her – stepped onto a spiral shaped metal staircase that led to an upper floor; she was now walking out in front of me without the slightest hesitation; there was nothing left of our mutual stride. As far as I could tell, the room she now opened would provide us with much more pleasant surroundings than the neglected bar on the ground floor. At least everything here gave the impression of being cared for and freshly maintained. It was furnished in an unmistakably central European style, and almost uniformly in apricot hues. Wallpaper, carpet, drapes all played in similar, finely varied patterns. The window, which I assumed was looking out onto a courtyard or a garden, was covered by half-closed blinds. Arrows of sunlight shot out of dark skies born along by a lazy storm, and one sensed they were somehow poisonous.

. . .

Now, suddenly, after our mysterious wanderings, we stood separated from one another at an abrupt standstill in this room, and the dread moment when we would be standing *across from* each other could no longer be postponed. I suddenly felt very alone and ashamed. I don't know if she noticed my embarrassment – my head was still bowed, even if now it was more in shyness and discomfort than it was in grief. In any case, I suddenly felt the tips of her fingers under my chin. She was trying to raise it. After an initial, strained resistance, I found I had no other recourse and gently gave in. But as my forehead slowly rose, my eyelids fell closed and I felt a warm breath, followed by open lips, and my entire face was enveloped by another. Our heads circled around our locked mouths, but all I could see was the stride of flesh-colored shoes, and all I could hear was the distinct beat of half-hollow heels. Then arms, hands, and knees relaxed and I did everything the impetuous exchange of caresses required of me. Embraced as I was embraced, grasped as I was grasped, pressed as I was pressed. Anyone unfamiliar with the human act of love would probably have considered our mingling to be some absurd exertion aimed at bringing one or the other unruly object under control, the way a clown sometimes struggles with an unwieldy prop.

. . .

But suddenly she interrupted our tumult and moved away from me. At that point I should have been able to see her, but I was in no condition to do so, the light in my eyes flickered and my pupils rolled back and forth so rapidly that it was as if I were in the middle of a sleep phase full of dreams. An unsteady outline was all I could discern against the backdrop of the window, and that she had put her finger to her lips as if signaling me to keep silent; and still, up until this point, we had not exchanged a single word. So what she really meant was that I should remain in my enraptured state. As she did, I also took off all my clothing. She cleared pillows, toys, and blankets off her bed and we returned to each other.

I was more than a little astonished when she began speaking to me in my own language and whispered to me in stern and tender tones what I was to do for the pleasure of her beautiful body. I was hardly able to take account of my own amazement before being overcome by the tender surprises of a passion that no longer allowed for sober inquiry or an estranging word. Our actions became more and more intense, ever more masculine, ever more unyielding, and emanating from some profound source, a victory neared for us both. A trembling from her innermost energies overcame this vital woman, an almost brusque shudder, as if she had suddenly lost all sense of me, and I, kissing her and dropping away like a ripe fruit, I sank over the edge into unconscious depths and saw her above, far, very far above, bending over the rim of the fountain, and finally, in falling, saw her face.

The Woman on the Ferry · *157*

When I awoke, I immediately wanted to embrace my lover again. But she was no longer next to me. I found myself alone in a cool, half-darkened room. The afterthirst of my ecstasy had become so burning that I immediately sprang to my feet and began the search for my glorious and impetuous companion. I pulled on a few clothes and ran downstairs to the bar. I was hoping to find a door at the back that would give me access to the hidden garden or courtyard. I also believed that I had heard the voice of a woman singing there and I could already see my beloved waiting longingly for me on the edge of an Osmanli pond, if not at least an elegant emerald green swimming pool.

In fact, I did find a small door, flush with the wall, and I immediately yanked it open but did not pass through to the outside. Instead, I found myself in a dusky, windowless chamber assaulted by musty fumes from within. It took a few minutes for my eyes to adjust and then I saw that I was not alone in this secluded place. To my absolute amazement, I came upon a group of indistinct figures sitting together around a table and bathed in the dim light of a ceiling lamp hung low over their heads. There were five men of various ages and attributes who did nothing more than open their hands, which were resting on the table, look into them, and then, after some time, close them again. In the dim light I could only differentiate their most obvious features and took account of the pale one, the gray one, the thin one, the young one, and the bearded one. None of them seemed to be from this region. They remained silent and did not move from their places, as if they had not noticed my sudden entrance at all. A malevolent gust of consumed past, as if it had blown in from a musty pool of time, enveloped me and I lost all sense of haste and desire.

But what had taken place here? What group of what men? What was keeping them together? A card game begun many years ago? A once prosperous business relationship, or a conference? A secret, unrealized agreement? I leaned up against the damp, plaster wall. It had suddenly become difficult for me to move as I was used to moving. The crippling time-dimension that applied to this mysterious space was beginning to have an effect on me. Listlessly I turned around, I slowly turned my thoughts back to the bar, and with great difficulty pondered how I might make my way back to the entrance and steal away from this house . . . .

Then I noticed a number of larger and smaller photos hanging on the wall near me, either tacked up or stuck up, and in them I was easily able to recognize the portrait of my sovereign mistress. The photos appeared to have been taken at various stages in the life of one person; at one time she was just a young child, then a mature woman (which, it seemed to me, she had not yet become), at one time in a very serious pose, then extremely frivolous, with short hair or with a full, loose mane. Next to these pictures, each time in a different hand, in chalk, lipstick, or charcoal, the single word "Mero" was broadly scrawled or smeared across the entire wall. There was no doubt that this was the name of my seductress, which up to this point had remained hidden from me. But what did this have to do with the group of five mute men at this table, all of whom, if my interpretation of the handwriting was correct, had conjured that name up onto these walls, in anger and in yearning, profaning and extolling? Here in this desolate back room, which may once have been used to conceal forbidden games or encounters, these men sat together in almost complete silence, almost motionless, and in the pale light only their intent, straight faces spoke. Still, now and then, one of them would laugh quietly out of the sleep of memory. This would infect the next man, and then, sluggishly, haltingly, work its way through the entire group. First, the bearded one would laugh, snorting, then the young one whimpering, the thin one quietly, the gray one tsss-ing, but all the pale one managed to produce was a deep bronchial gurgle. The longer nothing happened, the more I was struck by the way in which each one of them exhibited a distinguishing aspect that allowed one to peer into the deepest reaches of his character. The thin one stared, looking as if he were having to contrive his own fate. The gray one rubbed an eye in such a way that it made a loud popping noise under the lid. And the young one swayed within himself as if he were a tightrope walker dreaming on the palms of his hands.

· · ·

The more time I spent with them, the slower my senses began to crawl, the more strongly the typical imposed itself on the individual, the more garrulous the expressions became. Soon the room was droning, full of the desire to proclaim, the superfluous speeches of their postures and faces, and I felt the most profound need to shake off all of these life stories that had attached themselves to me like water nymphs stuck in dried mud. I did not want to know, I did not want to hear anything about the runaway brain, the purple-veined cheeks, the bulging eyes, and not a thing about the damned lies of fragile brows! . . . To my good fortune, at the very last moment before I myself would have become a victim of this deadly time-lock, I detected a bright, narrow slit of daylight behind the back of the bearded one, a door barely ajar, that just had to lead to outside. The sun had briefly broken through the cloud cover again and intensified the infiltration of light that had barely been visible until now. With one last, determined effort, already half-crippled, I dragged myself in the direction of the inviolate glow, and my sense of relief was enormous once I actually did reach the exit, which led me out into the open air. Outside, the refracted light of the late afternoon was blinding and I shielded myself behind a raised arm. And then I saw that I was in the small, though somewhat dusty, garden I had been trying to reach, and here, a used up delight, it was enclosed by a white wall the height of a man. Dark mossy water stood in the kidney-shaped pool, which lay in the middle of the garden. Dusty, dry rhododendron bushes, yellowed palms, colorless nut trees formed the sparse remains of what was once a luxuriant retreat. The urban grayness had spread itself over the plants like a powdery dew and robbed them of all livelier hues. Here, all the more sharply, all the more brilliantly, the ruby red evening gown worn by the woman from the ferry pierced through its fallow surroundings. She stood at the end of a gravel path overgrown with weeds and was staring intently out over the edge of the wall. Though considerably sobered by the sullen group at the table, the extraordinary time-lock I had managed to escape, I rushed to my mistress full of joyous anticipation, hoping finally to engage her in conversation and to get to know her. And what wasn't I hoping to ask and to find out! But I had hardly approached within two meters of where she was standing before I bumped into what might have been an invisible wall, and fell to the ground. Confused, embarrassed at my clumsiness, I immediately got back onto my feet to try for a second time, and headed resolutely in her direction. But before I had gotten within an arm's length, I fell again, as if I were being forced aside by a magnetic field that kept me totally separated from her. And since she did not seem to have taken notice of me at all, I was now resorting to the dizziest of contortions in order to reach her; the more directly I approached her, the more obliquely was I shunted off to another corner of this desolate garden. "Mero!" I finally called out to her in desperation, but she didn't seem to hear me either, as she moved not an iota and calmly continued to look out over the edge of the wall. Then, suddenly, I heard her voice. She was very close to me, surrounding me in almost every dimension. But I didn't know where she was coming from. It was extraordinarily difficult for me to establish a connection between these gentle tones and the person who was standing there at the wall in a fiery evening gown, entirely cut off from me, and seeming to be immersed in protracted observation. Am I to believe that Mero was able to steer her voice through the airs at will, and that it found its way to my ear like a bee to a calyx, without ever losing its soft tones?

"My friend," she said to me with the same tender and stern intonation she had used before when she was giving her instructions for love, "I can see that many things here still confuse and upset you. Don't worry! From now on you will be fine. Because you are now a part of me. You *are* a blissful memory. The only thing you might still find unsettling: except for *that*, you are no longer anything. In the world, you no longer exist. For the fact that you currently exist as you do, you may give thanks to the industrious substances of my thought processes. You now belong in my corona. You have entered into *my* time, and from now on you no longer have to concern yourself with any other existence."

While Mero was revealing her fantastic and truly breathtaking gift, I found myself having to admit that I had for the most part already become the being she had described, someone obsessed, someone who had been run through with the blade of her pleasure, and crippled. To this extent, I was spared the absolute horror her statement might otherwise have engendered in me – when I heard it I was already experiencing the salutary effects of having all but lost any sense of self. Still, the process had not yet been quite wholly accomplished. A diminishing residue of the conscious "I" was still evident and remained alert – and, unfortunately, still very sensitive to pain, as well. With it, I attempted to pursue the logic of this mysterious entrancement, insofar as it was still possible for me to do so, and to explore the nature of the huntress from her inner realms.

A creature of her mind, I was now in contact with many phenomena and some of the external circumstances of the life on which she had expended some portion of memory, even though much had been discarded in ruins or was only barely visible. As a young girl, after the early death of her mother, Mero had traveled with her father, a West German trade attaché, to countries far and near, wherever his assignments took him. Some years ago, in the course of these many moves, she finally reached Ankara, where her father rose to the rank of vice consul and decided to settle down in the city. This is where the happy, even excessive, relationship she had enjoyed with her father, up until now, underwent a palpable cooling off, as he had decided to remarry, thus requiring his maturing daughter to adapt to a subordinate position in the new family unit. At this time, and unquestionably as a consequence of this affront, the first outbreak of her unhappy gift occurred. Her murderous memory committed its first crimes. Even then, all she had to do was to surround herself with her little "corona" of soulless lovers to cause her father's reputation and stature to fade away into twilight. Thereupon, he, a sober and proud man, issued Mero the most uncompromising of directives. When none of this helped, he decided to house the vagabond under another roof, and finally, issuing an even more severe ultimatum, to move her out of the diplomatic quarter altogether. Her evil talent was in no way subdued under this regimen of prohibitions and punishments, on the contrary, it became even stronger. Now, completely cut off from father and home, she took it upon herself to go even further away and moved to Istanbul, of course, not without the hope of making a richer "harvest" and, most importantly, of having the opportunity to make even finer selections. Since then she has been nesting in the ruins of this deserted coffeehouse and has considerably expanded her arachnoid rounds out over the heights of the Golden Horn. Here, for the most part, she has been attracted to heavily trafficked areas and popular tourist sights, on whose edges and in whose rest areas she patiently waits and keeps watch. For it was here where fatigue, moments of quiet joy, homesickness, or daydreaming brought about the kind of weakness in one's conscious state that would allow her and her thieving senses to easily invade. Obviously, her victims were without exception loners, adventurers, tramps, artists, pilgrims, and sometimes even businessmen traveling alone. She had an unerring nose for the scent of loneliness. Her capture technique was almost always the same. She never approached her victims head on, or made an offer of her not inconsiderable feminine charms. In every case, she affected capture through a silent caressing approach from the side, relying entirely on the infatuating effect of her consorting stride; and no one had ever resisted. In every man she had touched a deep, unfulfilled obsession to make love to *one* woman, who is his first and his abiding, his unknown and his intimate love.

Of course, there was always one essential requirement: the victim had to be in the right mood. The kind of mood that cut him off from himself and everything else of his own. The thin one, for example, was caught while viewing the collection of the sultans' robes in the Topkapi Seraglio, where blinding magnificence of fabric and precious stone had already half transported him into the realm of *The Thousand and One Nights*. Mero stung once a man was sufficiently distanced from his normal and median disposition, whether it was tending higher or lower. Thus the bearded one fell when, elated at having concluded a portentous business transaction, he was pacing back and forth in the hotel lobby, not knowing how to give expression to his joy. And me, I was an especially easy prey when after my friend's funeral I set off to cross the Bosporus totally immersed in the melancholy demeanor of one left behind. You must imagine what transpired here: how the joy of having Mero in my arms collided with my intensely active grief, how both atoms of feeling abruptly fused with one another into a life amalgam, so highly excitable and so intense, that not even the most powerful act of will would suffice to ever split it again into its original constituents.

So there I sat with my sweet grief. Like the thin one and his oriental fantasy; the bearded one and the exhilaration of success. The young one and his homesickness. The gray one and his existential doubt. Every one of us was now nothing more than embodied thought; we consisted of the exuberance of a memory, which *she* was keeping, and woe be! should it ever be erased or even blocked for any length of time – there would no longer be us. We were the creatures of an everlasting hour. The time-dimension in which Mero had stored us was also our prison, this cell in which we would tirelessly persist from now on. It was, as viewed from the outside, that dreary back room in which my comrades had been sitting under a dim lamp and quietly holding their conventicle. I now found my place among them. And weren't we sharing a magnificent hour? Weren't we basking – enhanced and nourished by Mero's happiest memories – in a much haler light than the everyman loafing around on the *outside* ever had? Elevated to a state of passion, *and* exposed, we were in need of a secret secluding, external restraint of our freedom of movement. Just as there are people who have never left the chamber of a grand love, and have even floated through the rest of the world in this one room. In our innermost being all we ever collect are captivities, and from them we build the structure of our existence, from so many cast off cells, and every cramped passage, we know, is also a placenta, it bears us over and over again.

· · ·

Of course it was the dazed and dependent portion of my conscious self explaining my situation to me, in these or similar terms. And yet, there also remained a small, lowly stump of vigilant reason. It had been fervently concentrating on change and movement.

More and more often now, in the distance, I heard the simple and plaintive song that had awakened me from my sleep as I lay in the apricot-colored room, exhausted from my "everlasting hour."

It was a strong, high-pitched girl's voice, which most often rose from behind the garden wall in the early evening, and its words reached me half sung and half shouted. The others in her dull group seemed not, or no longer, to notice. But from time to time these tones gained a stronger influence over me. Even though I did not understand the words, the voice clearly seemed to be conveying an entreaty to me, and it also seemed that she had chosen song only after thousands of words had been shouted in vain. No, her song was not useless art, it was pure entreaty.

Every time I heard it I was overcome by an extraordinary restlessness; it was like a soft rustling in the high treetops of the lucid soul. It drew me irresistibly into the garden, and I even succeeded in raising myself out of my twilight, away from the table and out of the dim circle of light, and even though one of the obsessed, in retracing the steps I had once taken with the *last* of my strength. Of course I never got any further than that point where I had bumped up against Mero's sphere, and I was not able to reach the white garden fence, let alone climb over it.

And each time I was forced to realize that I was hardly able to get out of the back room before the singing abruptly broke off, and then, with a plummeting tone, fell completely silent.

Still, one day I undertook a most arduous task, something that almost bordered on the cunning and the actions of a free will. Even before the hour when the song usually arose, I actually succeeded in dragging myself out into the little garden, which was as desolate and depressing as it always had been in the late afternoon haze. A facile and independent conscious self will hardly be able to imagine what unspeakable difficulties I, under the sway of indolence, in the chains of devotion, overcame to make what was truly my own decision, without, I might add, the stimulus of the song exciting the senses, but simply and entirely out of my own innermost motives and leaden foresight. But then, stepping behind the house, shuffling along the squalid gravel path in the direction of the wall, it happened, and all of my heaviness and lethargy suddenly burst apart in a solemn and silent explosion, the urn of my existence shattered into a thousand pieces and a boundless gazing poured forth. It was, as we lay in each other's eyes, the girl, who was there leaning over the wall, and I who had finally caught up with her. Caught up with none other than the younger Mero herself, a girl of little more than sixteen years, a young creature with a lustful gap between her front teeth, leaning up against the wall with her bare forearms, the carefree child who was not allowed over the wall by her older self, in fact, had never even been once allowed in; this precious and immature being whom the experienced woman had always chased away out of fear, concerned that she might be a robber or a thief, or even a rival.

But as I stood facing this girl, our time-dimension and direct gaze became shared, and we enveloped one another. As if I had been whisked across, I found myself on the other side of the wall right next to the overturned bicycle, the empty school bag, and the open reader to whose honey-sweet edges the wasps were clinging. From this vantage point I could now see the plump body leaning over the wall, the bottom swelling out over the jeans, the half-bared back under the hitched up sweater, the delicate birthmark above lacy blue panties. Then, almost simultaneously, I was also inside the garden and walking up to her; I was able to overcome the invisible barrier, I was able to take new first steps, and then instantly I was back outside on the curb and her two legs hung spread apart in front of me, her bare feet turned inward and resting up against the jagged stone of the garden wall, her toes scratching the coarse mortar. Still I was allowed only a fleeting glimpse before I was standing in the garden again, looking into her bright, round face. Already so near that I could touch her soft child's hair – if I had not just at that moment, fulfilling my desire to see her backside completely bared *in front* of me, been transported back over the wall, where I immediately jumped up from the edge of the street, pulled her belt out of its loops, and peeled her jeans off down to her ankles. But, without being able to enjoy the perplexed look on her face, I was incapable of taking my pleasure with this bare backside. So I walked up to her in the garden and introduced myself. That concluded, there was nothing else on my mind and I was immediately back out on the other side of the wall wholly occupied in opening her lovely thighs with a hard tongue, and a firm sucking well of mouth. Now I could see an amused realization passing over her face, and that her hips twitched with joy. She, for her part, leaped out of her previous position, freeing herself from the edge of the wall with an incomparable agility, and immediately crouched down in front of me, took my protruding root in her small hand and, with it, filled the frothy O of her lips. Barely having accomplished this, she began to sense from the depths of her open thighs how urgent her desire was to be touched – and how much I missed burying my face between her soft cheeks. So, in an instant, everything was transposed, and she was bending over in front of me, supporting herself on her elbows on top of the wall, and offering me her joyful, defenseless backside. We surrendered ourselves to a singular arrangement in which I, the one nonseeing, gave pleasure to her, the one holding lookout above, and my submerged face lit up her eye. But at the same time her empty, inquiring mouth and my rigid, single answer longed painfully for one another, and at the very moment of ecstasy she was again crouching in front of my knees enveloping my one-syllable reply with the tenderest of inquiries. We flew one to the other with the speed of the wind, the speed of spirits, and between offering and acting, between yielding and invading, our pleasures alternated from one blink of an eye to the next. These unimaginably swift turns became a dance of union the wondrous likes of which no two people have ever experienced before.

But just as I was about to be carried away by entirely unanticipated life forces, the body suddenly closed itself off beyond the wall, everything choked and stopped functioning. I heard someone calling my name. It was the older Mero calling me from the garden. Aha, the spider from her desolate arena! Could it be that I had never really escaped her? She called my name a second time and drew me across the arc of its sound, rudely dragging me through the air. Still, I was still able to catch a glimpse of my fleet love as she slumped down in front of the wall, awkwardly, motionless. I landed on my backside on the gravel path with a spitting, hissing mistress circling around me. But, having been so painfully interrupted at the height of my ecstasy, I begged her to have mercy and to work on me the delight she, as a young girl, had withheld. She did not understand what I meant, but could only see that I needed her touch more than a thirsting man needs water. Still angry and indignant, she gathered up her ruby red skirts and crouched over me in sullen magnanimity. And I hurriedly entered the same, and yet no longer the same, body, only to find that my disappointment and her indifference were putting the consummation of my reply in serious danger. In hopes of encouraging us both, especially myself, I began to tell her about the lusty prelude to this encounter, and confessed to her I had been betraying her with none other than herself, and that we had pursued our pleasures like shameless sylphs, that she was the one singing outside the wall every day, living so longingly over the wall, her own youth languishing on the outside, wanting nothing more than to reside in here with her!

However, my words, with which I had hoped to set her petulant crouch in motion, had nothing but the most painful of consequences! She merely dropped onto me deep in contemplation, and no matter how vigorously I twisted and turned I could not bring her out of it. Then suddenly she got up, still selfishly lost in thought, and left me lying there alone on the uppermost promontory, from where there was no going back and no going on. And I would have remained trapped on this craggy peak of desire forever, a petrified priapic column, if it had not been for an entirely unexpected turn of events, wonderfully consoling, releasing me from the rawest and most foolish elements of my desire, and cleansing me forever.

For at that very moment, the woman from the ferry appeared in her usual location, where she held watch over the wall almost daily, and called out her own name in the most primal and timid of voices, as if it had never crossed her lips before.

Unlike me, the young girl did not come flying over the wall angrily buffeted on an arc of sound, and did not land on her back on the hard gravel path, all fours in the air like an upended bug. Rather, the younger Mero came very slowly into view; first her hands appeared over the parapet, followed cautiously by forehead and eyes, and then she awkwardly hoisted herself onto the wall. It seemed hardly possible that with this same chubby creature I had just been sharing maddeningly swift intoxicating moments that had transformed our pleasure taking into the frenzy of nymphs. A healthy awkwardness had returned to her limbs, as befit the idle shapes of her pre-adult body. Now the older Mero hesitantly approached the figure of herself as a girl; and it was impossible to tell what kind of a reception she would give her. But finally, as she stepped up to the perimeter, she reached out to the younger one with both hands in order to help her down off the wall and into the garden that had been closed to her for so long. A short while later I finally saw the two women standing face to face, the mature one smiled affectionately at the early one, who, for her part, admired the older one blankly. It took some time for them to bring their mutual discoveries into equilibrium. But once they had, they embraced and held each other close, as if there had never been a more devoted pair.

The genuine reconciliation between these same, and yet in experience as well as expectations so completely different, souls, having truly been brought about through the agency of my unyielding desires, I was not only deeply touched at the sight of this most peaceful of scenes, and liberated from what remained of my drives, but at that very moment my mind began to breathe freely again. I sensed myself being released from Mero's memory, slowly and easily. Then suddenly, as if after a long winter's freeze, my finer senses began to stir, and even in their most remote points began to expand and open, and I found myself back in a life that was somehow richer than how I had actually lived it; in which there were admittedly many omissions, but many complete chapters too, and innumerable encounters and affirmations, of which I had not always been aware. Now they were appearing again in the abundance of consciousness, and I found myself in the reassuring company of all of those missed and long forgotten figures, all of the ones so well received, who had at one time or another crossed my path. A convalesced consciousness, that's what it was, more expansive and profound than it had ever been, thanks to the good sight of this odd pair, more closely joined than almost any other among humankind, for neither man and wife nor parents and children could be more painfully parted and more devotedly reunited than the younger and the older Mero had been.

.   .   .

Now, one after the other, the rest of the obsessed, the silent group of men who had been sitting at the table in the back room, trotted out. Still dopey, they looked all around and then up into the air, and straightened their suits, like men who had slept too long during the day. Still, these wasted comrades, having just crawled out of Mero's dungeon, having just barely escaped smashing apart in one of the recesses of her mind, they promptly came to themselves exhibiting a full complement of imperfections. Hardly half-awake, they were already buddies, like neighbors at a campground, they were noisy and draped themselves across the old, worn-out garden furniture and, as their powers of speech returned, one soon proved to be a bigger braggart than the other. The thin one, the gray one, the young one, the bearded one and the pale one, the silently ecstatic prisoners, and now they were shooting off their mouths again, and the heightened state of passion in which they had once been captured, and then imprisoned for so long, immediately disappeared once they began arguing about who had gotten the most for his money.

Now, for the first time, I became aware of being completely free and could sense that no one was heeding my presence in the least. One more time, almost affectionately, I looked over at the powerful woman from the ferry, who was strolling through the garden, her youth at her side, paying not the least bit of attention to the rest of us. They had a lot to work out. And whether or not they really would get along and stay together, that depended on the extent to which the two shrewd but opposing guardians of human life: expectation and experience, could come to an understanding.

For my part, I preferred not to associate with anyone and looked for a quick and inconspicuous way to get out of Mero's house. This was no longer an idle and difficult decision to be dragged out of oneself. Now everything went almost too smoothly. A little later, after a taxi had brought me back to my hotel and I had got ready to leave, I stood in front of the wide window of my unused room and looked out over the Bosporus in the direction of the cemetery of üsküdar. There was still a crackling hot haze lying over the city. But I felt particularly calm and collected, and in a way restored, as if I had had a profound and beneficial rest.

I, who know full well that in its raw form this substance called "reality" is nothing more than one single radical change, an impossible alchemy, I now find a healthy pleasure in distinguishing among things according to fixed shapes and consistent contrasts. So it was of no particular note that my profound grief at my friend's death had almost completely lifted, like a breath of air on a pane of cool glass. And now I was leaving the city on the Golden Horn, with the reassuring conviction that I was traveling in my friend's true and good-natured company, ready to allow myself to be infected with the joy of one who knows the *whole* truth.

. . .

"Please, wait! Keep quiet!" I shouted, defending myself against the two male listeners who couldn't hold out one single moment longer and immediately attacked my story with pointed questions and clever observations. "No, believe me! There is nothing more to say, to confirm or to interject. *This* cannot be told in any way other than it was. It is completely contained in my telling and it simply sounds the way it sounds, sometimes more sinister, at other times more gentle. I am very well aware of the fact that it doesn't completely connect with masculine cognition any more than it does with feminine instinct. It eludes one while conflicting with the other. It is simply another confirmation of the detachment and the errancy of erotic thinking, which knows no certainties, but is affected only by the fluctuation of attraction and repulsion felt toward a person, a topic or a thing. It is truly the crass antithesis of a masculine possession of knowledge. Much more like a mirror, it envelops everything but retains nothing. It allows for tumultuous inconsequence, the abrupt succession of mutually exclusive evidence and feeling; it is born by the feminine need to touch the other, in order to avoid having to be *logical*. But it also encompasses respect for the continual occurrence, the repetitions of lust, for events that are torn out of history and cannot be told, that make us sigh and then sigh to God, because each time we touch a person in our misunderstanding way, we try to go far beyond that and make ourselves part of a divine delight, but in the end what we are seeking is nothing more than syncope, the interruption of existence in a cry, in a sensual whimper, in a twisting of hips, and not another *person*. One single stirring night of love can set us adrift forever; anyone who has ever really loved one woman well will want to love every woman. He will have touched the formless and anonymous fundament of love, and the very next morning, when he goes out onto the street, he will have to make every effort to keep from immediately running off with the next woman he sees, because they will all be coming up to him with smiles and glances, as if they were literally being attracted by his joyful radiance or by the light of desire streaming out of him. And this is how we sustain ourselves – we men with the weak memory of a beautiful woman, we unhappy ones, no: we who have been stripped of our happiness, because there will have been One Time when we were profoundly touched – so we sustain ourselves throughout our entire earthly existence with the beginnings of love, with those triumphal and unbounded *beginnings*, through which all history and all social history slips away, and we become part of an immutable good-time. Inevitably, what follows from beginnings is history, sober and raw, and it dissects us into the most painful of contradictions. How many disillusioned faces I have looked into, and how painful it has been! Very often now, in the harsh early morning, I see them in the garden mists, the mute circle of dancers, my bitter lovers, all of whom had once created a beginning with me – and each of whom was once the one and only! They wander silently through the gray skies, and they truly are terrible half-breeds, malformed monsters, the misbegotten offspring of sensual pleasure and melancholy, recalled in the frenzy of a fragrance, a similar face, a rediscovered gift – oh, this silent, hungry pack! But not a single one of them accessible; unmoved and pompously aloof, they observe my desperate attempts to beg their forgiveness. Oh, my friends, wait! Just one word! . . . They are only empty shadows of my pathetic addiction to beginnings; soulless creatures of my delight. How terribly I have diminished people! I have done nothing but fabricate beginnings, selfish and incorrigible, infatuated with all things initial, and incapable of loving anyone close to me, I am much more apt to trade her in for the next, lovely stranger. Sick, wild, crazy for any woman whom I have just caught sight of, and do not have to comprehend; thirsting for blindness and illusion; creating life out of delusion, and new life out of disappointment. . . . Still: what is the use of one new passion after the other, of incomprehensible enthusiasm? Nauseating, a defect of the soul, a lack of wisdom. And I, already an aging and brittle daydreamer, who now from time to time loses desire more quickly than before, and following each lost desire becomes more fanatical, must I keep losing my way for another twenty-five years in this evocative garden of wonders, full of marvelous illusions, inexhaustible approaches and eternally unresolved endeavor? Behind every window an astonished stranger, behind every strutting step a generous acceptance, behind every bitter tone a scream of unity! And every empty hand is looking at me with one large, sensitive eye. Because eyes are everywhere, in hands, hair and hips, the eyes of knee and chest, of neck and shoe, all emitting lighthouse glares . . .

"The one dark spot of human sexuality is now, and always will be, the open face. The more profound phenomena, the faces of the face have always earned my obedient respect, they have interrupted my desire and lulled it into *pure* reluctance. The face – assuming it is open and observant – deflects blind drives, it remains one last impregnable bastion of innocence, of dark perception, of devout reverence. And this certainly contributes to all of the confusion that arises when out there, in the civilized realm of the street, we are seduced by the most natural of stimuli, the overstated posterior, only later to experience, on the inside, behind the curtains, the flip side of temptation, the warning: the face. Can we ever speak of true consummation as long as our pleasures are taken at the threshold of innocence, as long as the face is the guardian of the ass, and respect the censor of desire?

"How often have I not fallen in love with a bright and observant face, one that spoke, and awoke in me all of my sincere desire – only to quickly leave it behind, completely distorted. Because the eyes of the body looked right past it, impassive and blind. Or, the other way around, I had fallen for a beautiful body, a tall and slender figure, and found myself looking into a flesh and blood face I didn't even want to kiss, it was so impure, so morose and obscene. My desire drifts between these two opposing forces, and redemptive equilibrium will always be out of reach. And will prevent me from ever having a lasting relationship with one, individual person. No matter how devoted I am to the human face – how many of those who were once close to me haven't I already forgotten! How quickly forgotten! New ones keep coming. And many of them achieve their true luminescence only in passing. Once they appear in a crowd and then disappear, they have already conveyed their happiest message. New ones keep coming. Unlike those who truly love, I will never seek the *one* through the many. Every One only reminds of the Many."

·   ·   ·

At this point I stopped. It seemed to me that I had gone on much too long and imprudently with my pronouncements for anyone who did not share my feelings to follow. And in fact, Hans-Werner, the conciliator, was the first to raise a sober objection and gave me clearly to understand how little he himself was concerned with the cross I was having to bear.

"You present yourself to us as a man tormented by desires of the flesh, Leon. But I have a suspicion that you find much greater pleasure in entertaining an exciting theory about lust and desire than you actually do in wholly surrendering yourself to it. And it appears to me that you're genuinely obsessed with the ideal. You deify the face and damn the ass. But people have both. And as long as you allow yourself to be so hung up on ideals, you won't be seeing or getting *any*. As long as you continue to entertain what always appears to be a better idea, everything that lives and breathes, every real thing will seem all the worse and all the more impoverished for it."

"But it's not the idea," I protest earnestly, "or anything else contrived, that first inflicted the torture of the ideal on us. On the contrary, the body came first. The body is the original ideal, the ideal incarnate, which we were indeed allowed to grasp in our hands and experience through all our senses, we did not have to question its concrete existence. And just such a body seared our souls with its indelible brand. In one moment it suffused our primal, dreamlike concepts with its presence, as sure as it was whole, and since then we have not been able to find any peace. Our ideas are only a belated rearguard action that seek to thwart our senses and subdue our passion."

"No," the melancholy Almut interrupted our exchange, "the body, no matter how lovely or voluptuous it may be, is not and never has been the primary standard for our perception of the ideal, upon which – I will gladly admit – we are modeled. But everything we know about ideals we have learned through great works of art, and only through these works that have endured for centuries and withstood everything transitory. I have to ask myself what the 'ideal body' might have looked like that could have moved you so deeply and unsettled your entire existence. But I am convinced that it was, more likely than not, a rather ignoble mass; something that would rot and decompose. It is only under conditions of extreme coldheartedness – the coldhearted-ness of an inconstant man – that this most beautiful of bodies can be preserved, and it is only in such a frozen, lifeless state that you will be able to keep it from aging and decay. But you have to understand, Leon, that is not the truth of these shoulders, this ass, and these hips. Come on, free yourself from your inconsolable desires! Hans-Werner is right: otherwise you won't be able to hear or see the wonder in anything, you will be unmoved by any-thing that is truly exalted. And all you'll be left with is a twitch, in your soul as well as your sex, your own closed system of arousal and ecstasy. You'll end up like some randy amphibian mounting every round thing in your path until you finally find a sweet little female. How did you put it just now: twenty-five more years of making love? My dear Leon, it's about time that you started look-ing for something more permanent; something that doesn't have to be any less wondrous than your female on ice; something that satisfies your need for beauty and appearances but also demands of you a more generous and a more lasting passion. It's time you recovered from your first twenty-five years of perpetual arousal, from a quarter century of poundingly high pulse rates. But for now, just listen to me and let me tell you my own story. Even if I haven't got an 'ideal body' to offer you – no polite protestations required! – I do want to talk concretely about an area of the living world where you can still find this body in its original form – in painting and in sculpture. After listening to all of you tell your stories, one after the other, and getting to know the enemy of society, nature's friend, and the reluctant seducer, I will without further ado introduce you to a woman crippled by art, to myself, to yet another person with a cross to bear, though I hesitate to make use of this oppressive metaphor. If possible I'd like to get you to thinking about the voluptuous and naked woman in the painting by Rops, where she's been nailed to the cross of the Savior and is hanging lustfully suspended over Saint Anthony. . . . Well, we all know this clearly isn't the way to lead you into temptation."

· · ·

ALMUT'S STORY

"Lady Fury, Lady Doll, Lady North – they were the ones, not I, who brought you into the world, my child!" This is what my mother would sigh every time she found me sullen, obstinate, and unwilling to come to lunch. At such times, these three women of my genesis were to see to it that I bestirred myself, because she, my mother, had in any case lost whatever influence she might once have had over her child. Again and again, I was banned to the realm of this fable told throughout my childhood, the legend of my own life created by my mother to explain the origin of those aspects of my character that she found incomprehensible or disturbing. And here I should point out that my mother was not a German; she had been born into a Danish merchant family, and, while still very young, she followed my father to the south of Germany where he ran a painting business, first in Passau and then later in Regensburg. But the more difficult her life became and the more time she spent surrounded by an uncongenial landscape, the more vital the memories of the ghost stories and legends of her northern home became. In fact, these tales had come to dominate both her intellect and her emotions to such an extent that our difficult everyday life was extensively populated, and all but overrun, by trolls and sprites, a red horse, a glass smithy and a vast array of other bizarre phantoms. In my mother's mind everything banal and troublesome was transported into an entrancing magical setting, entirely without effort or conjuration. She expanded on old themes at will and invented new hobgoblins and spooks whenever the existing supply proved either insufficient or unsuitable. My father only laughed; it amused him and seemed not to cause him the slightest concern. But for me it was often too much to bear. Lady Fury, Lady Doll, and Lady North were hardly the most endearing of companions, and not the sort of characters suited to cheer up what was in any case a rather timid nature. My mother depicted them as three red-, gray-, and white-gowned apparitions, who had entered our house the day after her arrival and settled down on our sofa like three little insurance agents, who, while they were serene, would not be turned away; each sitting under one of the large, Danish plates that had been mounted on the bright blue walls and were decorated with motifs from the merchant marine. "Three real entities!" as my mother often stated emphatically, thus exhibiting the proper measure of respect for our supernatural visitors. They had nothing less portentous to propose than that they take me, a sickly preemie whom neither parents nor doctor expected to survive, under their healing wing. In return, they demanded an interest in my person to last the whole of my life. As capricious as she was, my mother continued to assert that at this critical juncture, when she was solely concerned with saving the life of her baby, she was left with no other choice but to enter into this questionable pact. And she was fully aware of the fact that Doll, Fury and North in no way embodied the characteristics one might wish to engender in a child. However, in matters of life and death, those life spirits come to the fore and are among the most highly prized, which otherwise, in cases of normal weight and full-term pregnancies, might be negligible, or even fail to appear at all. When in need, we would have to content ourselves with the best available caregiver, even one who might proffer bitter medicine. So, Lady Fury promised to energize my tired blood. Lady Doll, on the other hand, vowed that she, the one to be emulated, would take the greatest care to introduce me to the hard and serious side of life. And finally, Lady North committed herself to inject an appropriate measure of masculine toughness into my tiny frail being. Thus it was that my mother gave me into the care of three problematic geniuses, receiving in return a healthy if seldom cheerful child. Or shall we say: this is the fable in which she clothed her profound dismay at the little girl who was so incompatible, so ill-tempered and such a nuisance. I was never, at any time, held directly accountable for those aspects of my person or behavior that displeased her. Instead, without fail, she would call upon our miserable little insurance ladies to assume whatever blame was to be assigned. Her imaginary homemade spooks were to be held accountable for each and every imperfection. And even though I was often pleased at the sight of their faces and their veils, their gift to me, my life's fable, in all its harshness, alienated us from one another. And it caused me early on to doubt the utility of an all too lively fantasy and a storyteller's flair.

As a natural consequence of my discontent with my mother, I turned more and more often to my father for solace and care, and even exhibited an entirely different demeanor in his presence. To this quiet and kindly being, this diligent, art-loving craftsman, I was the ever-obedient daughter. I was fascinated with everything he did, although the profession he practiced had little to offer a young girl.

My father was by upbringing and training a painter of murals and architectural ornamentation. Of course, he accepted contracts that required him to do such things as clean facades and hang wallpaper, but his true enthusiasm was reserved for the murals on the walls of old inns and farmhouses in the environs of Regensburg, near and far. This is where he had earned his reputation, and there was no one who could restore an old fresco the way he could, or bring an old mural back to life where it had been concealed by some drab, contemporary veneer. On his own, over the years, through his study of the history of architecture and mural painting, as well as the various techniques of conservation, he had acquired a fundamental appreciation of art. In addition, he possessed a great gift for his craft, a sure sense of color and form, and above all the perception of "another time." He seemed to feel it was almost a moral obligation, not simply to restore an old ornament to its so-called original state – this being often nothing more than splendid deception – but he captured the essence in its truest form, he simply allowed it to surface, but never to gush forth, never to belie its origin. He came to be looked upon as a skilled and versatile artisan not only in our community but throughout lower Bavaria, and he was often called upon to give advice even on projects where conservationists, well-schooled and under contract to the state government, were already at work. It was not long before he himself was entrusted with the restoration of church vaults, the ceilings of city hall chambers, and castles in the countryside.

My father was especially skilled at painting figures. To be more precise, the iconography of the late eighteenth century was so familiar to him and so accessible due to his profound affection for it that he could, if called upon, easily cover a facade with a mural in that genre. And still there was always a kind of freedom and individuality that emanated from his cartoons. Legendary saints, various depictions of the madonna (our servant girl sat for him) all bore obvious traces of his personal style, even though they were wholly shaped and painted in the spirit of another time, and even though my father was nowhere near becoming an artist in his own right. Tiepolo was and always remained his mentor, and a continual object of his study. Painting a sleeve or a mantle with copious folds, he always repeated to himself: "Tiepolo's shadows."

Of less interest to him, but in much greater demand, was the light-hearted architectural ornamentation of the Bavarian Baroque. For the most part, well-to-do innkeepers were the ones who wanted faux columns and cornices on the facades of their buildings. He often took on such projects, but it was for business reasons rather than inclination.

. . .

One morning, shortly after I had turned fourteen and had recently been confirmed, my father stood me up, took my measure from head to toe and announced: "Today you're going up on the scaffolding with me." Full of joy, I clapped my hands and would have liked nothing more than to have fallen into his arms, if only he had considered this acceptable behavior. But from this moment on, I would be put to the test as his apprentice, and as the master's daughter I could expect neither special favor nor tenderness. Thus, at the first blush of womanhood, having been given the apprentice's cap, pants and smock, I disappeared into rugged, masculine attire.

As I adapted to this lofty environment with ease, suffering neither dizziness nor childish distraction, my father began immediately to instruct me in the fundamentals of his craft. Before entering into my apprenticeship, I had already learned to mix dry pigment into a lime solution. And I understood that the most important part of my job would be holding his tray of paint pots ready: white, ocher, English red, greenish umbra, the favored earth tones he had to apply in haste, while the plaster was still wet. But it was up here, directly at the walls, that I first learned to perform the most important tasks on my own: to prime a surface, to attach a cartoon with perforated outlines, and, with the help of a sack full of coal dust, to transfer the drawing to the wall and quickly paint in the outlines. Up here on the scaffolding, my father provided constant explanation and commands. I noticed a desire to instruct that had until now been unapparent in this essentially silent being. Up here, at these heights – I can still remember how we stood facing the sallow remains of a sundial on the gable of a country villa in Amberg – up here, he suddenly began to deliver himself of all of those thoughts that had occurred to him during the course of his work, and that, with complete equanimity, he had previously kept to himself down on solid ground, at home. It seemed as if he were intent on imparting to me, literally loading me up, in the shortest possible time, with everything he had learned and taught himself, and even those things of which he had nothing but an enthusiast's inkling, a demanding desire. He was not so much concerned that I master the technical aspects of his craft as he was that I appreciate the artistic, even the moral and symbolic significance of his work. At the time, I was still too young and unknowing to really understand him. Still, it was obvious to me that he was profoundly affected by what he did and that it informed him mind and soul. Bringing what had been hidden back into the light of day, and sustaining it, recalling, capturing, what had all but vanished – a craft that served such a purpose, as my father saw it, could not help but have a positive impact on our contemporaries, serving a universal emergence of the beautiful and the preceding, which every man might enjoy. Not only did he sustain a most abiding admiration for the skill and the aesthetic sense of the old builders, and the fresco and decorative painters, but he also believed firmly in the salutary effect of actually coming into contact, through one's own fingertips, with forms and colors that had been applied to surfaces in centuries past. The painstaking discovery, the creative, revealing process these old works underwent in his hands, and the new murals he created in their spirit – all this had affected his naive and tractable mind so profoundly that in an almost religious sense he truly was awaiting the "Coming of Art." Just as it appeared to him out of the old masonry, it would also emerge from under the "false plasterwork" and finally make its *advent* known to everyone. My father simply could not comprehend how any normal person could be unaffected by beauty, by the works of art created in "another time"; or how he could possibly survive his everyday life without attending to the precious gifts that earlier ages continued to hold in store for us. Most of the time, as he went about his work, he was filled with a sense of satisfaction and sometimes even an intense feeling of joy. But then, all of a sudden, the "eyes of the past" were glaring at him. They had hardly returned to life and radiance in his hands before turning their merciless gaze his way. At such times, the high standards set by the artisans of the past seemed to weigh on him and he felt himself profoundly wanting.

"What are we in the eyes of the past?! We really have very little to show for ourselves. We achieve the best we can do when we bring an old work to light and keep it from ruin. And this is the sum and substance of our mastery."

The rigorous and devout zeal with which he pursued his work also led to a number of technical advances developed along the way to better protect the restored frescoes against weathering and decay. This is how we came to be concerned, early on, with the dangers of increasing levels of air pollution, exhaust gases and toxic substances. Everything my father heard about pollution caused him a great deal of anxiety, but also encouraged his inventiveness, even if it was only out of his concern for the future of his murals. For the most part, we avoided using the more common dispersion paints, which adhere to a surface of a wall like a thin rubber membrane and are relatively long-lasting but lacking in expressive qualities. What my father wanted was to allow the paint to combine directly with the wet plaster, as had been done in the past, and this is why we used the significantly more delicate, mineral-based paints. Having made any number of test batches and reflected on their chemistry, he mixed his colored powders in with a potassium-based solution and produced a paint that could withstand the affects of carbon monoxide, the pollutant he most feared at the time.

Every work he produced or restored was to last until the end of time. And even if mankind should die out long before, the best it has to offer, the good it created, its works of art, must survive and perhaps even serve as an example or a model for a better race.

.   .   .

The next few years, in which I spent every school holiday and every vacation up in the scaffolding with my father, were – I may now say – the happiest of my life. You see, I too am one of those disabled veterans of happiness, who at one time experienced happiness in its essence, and from then on remained essentially untouched by the watered-down solutions later life was to offer. Despite the petulant tones that my mother let escape from time to time – it was clear to her that during this period I was under the influence of Lady North, of masculine toughness and cold light, the other two spooks being overshadowed for the present – there was never a serious confrontation as to whether or not a young girl like me should be dressed in men's overalls and crawling all over the facades of old buildings in whatever the weather might be. I even believe now that she had come to terms with the fact that I, perhaps after having taken advantage of a technologically advanced education, would most likely carry on in the profession for which my father had already given me such extensive preparation.

But things turned out differently. I did not follow in his footsteps. I could not bring myself to do so. I was about to graduate from high school when he died. I had no idea where to turn. He had not even reached sixty years of age by the time his sickness had consumed the organs inside, where I had assumed there was nothing but glowing life energy. I was no longer able to orient myself. It seemed as if he had led me into the outer courtyard of an enormous palace, with every conceivable beauty and secret of life being held in store for me, but then he suddenly disappeared from my side, leaving me alone before a labyrinth I dared not enter without his guidance. This splendid but incomprehensible construct with its countless chambers, halls and colonnades, its strange goings-on and unknown laws frightened me, and I beat a cowardly retreat back to the entrance. Turning my back on them once and forever, I would now have to forsake all of those treasures only he could have brought to me. Get out of this halfway induction so abruptly interrupted! And get out of my dark Regensburg where the church steeples stood in ranks, where so many murals constantly reminded me of *him*. I dropped out of school and, without really being much interested, applied to get into a translation institute in Heidelberg. Almost consumed in pain and paying no heed to my mother's tears and laments, I left my parents' house and shook off all my training, the prologue to an apprenticeship in mural painting.

I never knew how miserable a person could be until I actually left my hometown for the first time and had to make my own way in completely alien surroundings. Cheap and dreadful lodgings, the arduous initiation of my studies at the language school, which I, in complete disregard of every inclination and talent, had brought upon myself, only served to make me regret my thoughtless resolve all the more bitterly. I often holed up for days in my cubicle, especially on cruel weekends, pulling my blankets up over my head, so desperately unhappy I was not even able to squeeze out a single sob. Adding to my grief and homesickness was the difficulty of finally having to act like a proper young woman. I had not been used to dressing or behaving in a particularly feminine way. But now, seeing myself out among all the young ladies of the institute, I felt like a lost, clumsy little country girl. It was a genuinely difficult time for me. In hindsight, what may seem to have been the most natural of transitions was lived out as an utterly desperate catastrophe. Still, as is often the case when we are young, we suffer hard and deep, but not all too long. My natural curiosity overcame the empty tear-filled gaze, ambition and a desire to fit in began to rule the day. Lady Doll, Lady North, and Lady Fury managed to achieve an all too rare unanimity and effected an exuberant regeneration of my life forces.

In addition to the required English courses, I also decided to take Spanish and Portuguese, and, full of unwavering ambition, went to every class and lecture from then on.

And here I feel compelled to note that since my father's death - this may sound a little strange – I have not even been near a work of art or an architectural landmark. I didn't even want to go to Heidelberg Castle. I marched disinterestedly through the streets of the Old Town only when they could not be avoided; the oldest and most celebrated restaurant, the library, the Town Hall – not one of these buildings could slow me down or arouse the slightest bit of genuine interest. I preferred to eat in the basement of the Kaufhof department store rather than under the storied arches of a beer hall, or in an old German tavern. I could only really breathe freely in the new shopping streets and on concrete sidewalks. Actually, back then, Wolfsburg or Salzgitter would have been much better places for me. A morbid fear of coming into contact with any work of art, or of being observed and tested by the "eyes of the past," kept me in the meanest parts of town and in the new housing developments, and suppressed my natural awareness of my surroundings. Things even went so far that one day, when I got a ridiculous postcard of the Isenheim Altar, I couldn't look at it and just tore it up and threw it in the wastepaper basket.

Little by little, as time passed, my hypersensitivity abated. Maybe it was because my studies took up so much of my energy, and I was so determined to prepare for a good job, that one day I walked down an old street lined with historical buildings and found myself completely unaffected. The dulling of my artistic senses had progressed so far that it no longer mattered to me whether I was standing in front of the Marstall or the offices of the German Automobile Association. They were both simply buildings like so many others, strangely alike and contemporary in some vague way. All I wanted now was to finish my language studies as quickly as possible. I wanted to get a job where I could do well, be competent, strong, perfect. I knew I would be happy to be a foreign-language clerk in a large trading company. My studies had gone relatively well and I was expecting to finish with good grades and strong recommendations.

. . .

I got my first job with a shipping company in Duisburg. But the work there was not nearly as challenging as I had hoped. Everything was a little too lethargic and disorganized, so it wasn't very long before I gave notice. There followed a series of attempts to support myself abroad, as a conference interpreter, as an administrative assistant for German construction companies in Spain and overseas, I even accepted temporary assignments for government agencies and research institutes, and engaged in any number of other activities over a few restless and eventful years. I went places, met people, gained experience in my profession, and became fluent in three languages, but I still was not as indispensable for any one person as I had hoped to become.

In these first years of my work life, moving restlessly from one place to another, constantly looking for a new job, I lived cut off from my roots, from my father's time, I lived a life oblivious to my past. Submerged in a sphere I had never intended to be a part of, I spent my time with people, and in social circles, whose ideas and lifestyles were fundamentally different from my own. But I managed to move among them unobtrusively and with ease, almost as if I were a secret agent, the only difference being that I was unaware of having any covert mission. Throughout this time a thick insulating membrane continued to allow me to proceed unaffected by anything of artistic beauty. I had not visited one museum, not a single art gallery, no historical site in any foreign country. No painting hung on any of my apartment walls, there was nothing but suspended, creeping greenery.

My fiancé at the time – I'll call him that since we had a more or less continuous relationship for a number of years – my fiancé was not the kind of person who might have led me back into aesthetic realms. He simply wasn't interested. Of course, he was better educated and more sensitive than any of the other businessmen I had met, but he was totally blind to art. His vacations – and his vacations from me – were dedicated to athletic activity; he rowed at his club, and climbed high mountains, alone. He worked in the overseas sales division of our company, a textile factory in Rheydt; I had followed him there.

Then, one day – as usual, on our annual shopping trip to northern Italy, we made a stop in Florence – I could hardly believe my ears when he suggested that we spend a free afternoon in the Uffizi. Of course, he was simply fulfilling some perceived cultural obligation rather than expressing a suddenly ardent interest in art. In any case, I agreed to go along, innocently, happily, and without giving it a further thought.

We departed the entrance hall by means of an elevator that took us to one of the upper floors of the huge administrative palace and immediately found ourselves fighting our way, inasmuch as we had one in mind, through a teeming mass of humanity. We came entirely unprepared and, at first, when we arrived at the gallery, we simply let ourselves be carried along by the streams of visitors. The countless bands of tourists, school classes, the criss-crossing guided tours, the loud lectures in barely articulated foreign tongues, the masses of visitors gawking indifferently and then trotting on while children played hide-and-seek among them, all of this made it practically impossible to get to see a picture or to spend a quiet moment in contemplation. For me the mixing and the shoving began to grow more and more threatening. The congestion was smothering; I broke into a cold sweat, I was desperately afraid I was going to lose consciousness. It happened in those overstimulated moments shortly before an actual loss of consciousness, my secret broke free of its massive seals and indifference fell from my soul like a shadow. In these moments I felt my sad and somber psyche splitting open and liberating the younger, unformed being I once was – the young girl was there again, the helper, vulnerable and nothing but vulnerable; pure, raw, and completely uninhibited. It was in this state that I approached the Simone Martini and found myself anchored to that spot. And even when a renewed torrent of visitors threatened to carry me away, I fought my way back with all of my strength to this glorious shore of the *Annunciation*. The picture held me in its spell, it rid me of my false gestures, it peeled away my decorous shell, the bourgeois camouflage of my existence. There I stood utterly helpless and naked in its countenance. And then they appeared, shouting and glaring at me, the eyes of the past would not let me out of their sight! No way to escape, I grew dizzy, I slumped to the floor. My fiancé must have been looking for me since I had never gotten out of the Trecento Gallery. Maybe he had even noticed I was trembling, and that tears of fear and joy were running down my cheeks. So, luckily, he was there at my side to help me up and lead me out of the gallery. I let him believe that the crush of the crowds had been the sole cause of my collapse. I neither wanted nor was able to explain what had really happened. The incident was never mentioned again, and for the duration of the trip we managed to amuse ourselves sufficiently with other banal pursuits and he soon forgot the Uffizi.

But I had been deeply moved by Simone Martini and his rays of light. And they continued to affect me. I was not able to settle back into my healthy and innocuous everyday life. I came more and more to the conviction that since climbing down off my father's scaffold I had been making a singularly futile attempt at flight, boring an emotional hollow, like a tunnel, through my life. But what in the world was I to do with this overwhelming force? I was not an artist, I didn't even have the talent to be a Sunday painter, or the simple ability to pretend to paint in such a way that I might have been able to free myself from this exalted sensation. Lady Doll of my mother's circle of spooks had left me completely unprepared for times such as these.

But one thing had changed: my indifference to beauty would not continue. Without altering my external life in any significant way, I now began to concentrate on finding ways to bring artistic beauty back and integrate it into the practical everyday world where I worked and my fiancé lived, to keep it and hold on to it for the sake of my own personal happiness. But things were simply not going to be that cut and dried. Supernatural powers rarely condescend to a peaceful coexistence with us. As we have seen in other instances of radiation damage, the Uffizi event first expressed itself as a burn and the serious aftereffects appeared later. They first showed up in my relationship with my fiancé. Strange disturbances began to take place. I had always belonged to him completely, I had followed him. Maybe it was my blind physical dependence on him that had made it impossible for me to clearly understand his mind, or even his views. Of course, I knew that his feelings for me were coarser and more superficial than my feelings for him. Still, he had come to me first, he had chosen me and he was committed to us. Unfortunately, he never told me that he loved me. You make me happy, is what he said. But never: I need you. Maybe the genuine passion he showed should have been enough. He never tired of me. After all, the development of my more feminine characteristics had not been particularly encouraged. I had never dared hope that a man would ever desire and take the awkwardly self-conscious body of my father's apprentice. But he had done so. And for that alone, for the fact that he had liberated me from my sense of physical clumsiness, I was thankful and indebted to him. Perhaps, too deeply, because my physical awakening did not result in a proud and easy self-assurance, but rather in a coy and obsessive submissiveness brought on by lust and fear. My whole being was focused on him. Even my cool rationality, my practical mind took cognisance mainly of the things my strong lover told me, and only the things he knew were worth knowing. I even found it exciting to mouth his clichés and his opinions, I copied him, I literally transformed myself into his kind. Clearly, Lady Doll was pulling all the strings here and holding me firmly in her hands.

But, one evening, not long after we returned from our trip to Italy, I saw my fiancé behind a strange face as he came through the door.

"What are you doing?!" I screamed angrily. He didn't know what I meant, and he certainly had no malign intentions. But I had seen his pure contempt, the quiet undermining of me in his eyes. My fiancé had long ago succeeded in making a worthless person of me.

. . .

We often lose ourselves in another person, fall in love only, as it were, to give *shape* to our own misery, to capture it in concrete form. All the desire, all the sweet deception, serve only to allow us to confront our bitterness in flesh and blood. Instead of realizing the truth immediately and saying: leave this stranger alone! Don't touch him. You're not really interested in him at all. No, we tell ourselves: ah, what a handsome man! He has so much to offer. He is the kind of man who could protect a woman from all evil. . . . And, before we even know it, we've dragged an innocent human being into the tragic reflection of our own image.

I do not clearly recall what happened following that evening I "caught sight" of my lover. Strangely enough, all I can remember is that on the evening before this little drama took place I was in my room watching a large, dark green cicada. A cricket. A locust. It was sitting on an orange-colored pillow. I watched it for a long time. So, this was the archetype of a parasite. The way it sat there, absolutely still, it might have been a monument to a grasshopper. And it might suddenly vault into the air. Its slender femurs bent sharply up toward the ceiling. Its feelers lay stretched forward on the pillow like the a toreador's downturned dagger. What was this embodiment of being before the leap? A mantis? So many names for this insect that always looks like another insect! We fear the inhuman suddenness of its leap. The absolutely abrupt is its weapon against us.

. . .

On a rainy summer day, a Wednesday I had taken off, I drove to Düsseldorf to go shopping. Right as I drove onto the expressway, I noticed rust red placards mounted on almost every available light pole and every tree all down the median strip. They were announcing the opening of an exhibit of American painting, and white arrows pointed the way to the hall. Very matter-of-factly, without the slightest hesitation, I obediently responded to the signs, turned off the road to Düsseldorf and followed the arrows. As I drove on, I began to be able to distinguish individual names on the posters, the names of the artists, I supposed, whose works were going to be on exhibit for a number of weeks. Sam Francis,

Morris Louis, Kenneth Noland, Jackson Pollock, Mark Rothko. All names I had never heard of before in my life. At first I was certain this was going to be a show of very exotic works, maybe even Native American art. I was getting very curious, and, at any rate, I had been entirely diverted and distracted by the rowdy and confusing red rumblings on the placard. I parked the car in the space where I had been directed, and shortly thereafter I was climbing the stone stairway that led into the exhibition hall. After buying my ticket, I had to climb a second set of stairs because there was nothing to see on the ground floor except the artists' sketches and drawings. I wanted to see the paintings first. Once on the upper floor and behind a tall glass door, I looked around and saw there were no other visitors, and there was such an inviting stillness, a deep lull in the street noise and the affairs of the day, I felt somehow as if I were making my way up to exalted sacrificial grounds, to a sacred sanctuary. But having once reached my destination, I was bitterly disappointed. I did not find the pictures I was expecting to find. They weren't at all the kind of pictures in which you could find beauty, or the human form in its most inspired aspects. All I found were broad, monotone fields of color or muddled mazes or harsh bright stripes or fading, crisscrossed strokes, loud green, red and brown, wild, exploded ornament. So, this was the abstract painting of which I had seen so little until now. The Simone Martini began to glow within me sending out its intense rays. I walked past canvasses, many of them two to three meters long and almost as high, I went down every corridor, around every corner of the exhibition in search of some kind of opening, some secret entrance that would lead me to the precise canons of these totally inscrutable games. But I found no way. Upset and confused, I looked for a bench where I could sit down and rest. I thought about how I should respond to these imposing aliens. I still wasn't ready to give up. Without really having noticed, but not entirely by accident, I had stopped and sat down in front of the darkest and most powerful work in the entire collection. It was so threatening that even when I passed by it the first time I cringed, instinctively. You can well imagine how frightened I was when I raised my head and suddenly found this massive body of color looming over me, and this monster . . . I could not understand what it was supposed to be. Almost the entire canvas was dominated by a broad funnel-shaped eruption of color, moss-green, burnt umber, and, in one spot, flame red. A dark exuberance, an existence hurled into the heavens, a gushing electrical discharge with tiny flames flickering across the crest. I could not believe I was standing in front of an inanimate painting. I leaped to my feet, and was enveloped by a painful, deafening din, the beating heart of an unimaginable colossus swelled and rumbled over me, the enormous pulse expanded before my eyes and was about to beat, making me into a tiny, fleeting bacterium of time, and my life into a sudden, abrupt leap . . .

I didn't feel any hatred toward the work. But I had to defend myself. The dark, overwhelming pulse was about to crush me. All I had with me in my handbag was this small scissors. As silly as it may have seemed, it was a desperate struggle to the very end. Holding the scissors in my fist, I lunged point first at the canvas. I ran the scissors through its throat. I stabbed the beast again and again, but the more I stabbed the more enraged it became. I twisted and turned in its suffocating grip, and kept struggling, I ripped and tore at the sailcloth opening deep wounds. Then, two lame old guards came hobbling in; they screamed for help, trembling and cursing they grabbed me by the arm, pulling and tearing at it as if it alone were the perpetrator.

I was beside myself, but I was not out of my mind. I knew what I was doing. I was fighting for my life. It was reported that I had tried to destroy an outstanding creation of contemporary American art. But no one can destroy a true creation. And all I had done was damage a picture.

Today, I know that Morris Louis has forgiven me. I have spent a lot of time studying his works. I have been astounded and amazed. He had already been dead for some time when I committed my act.

Having committed an offense of this sort, it is not easy to get oneself treated like an ordinary criminal. An art assassin is different, say, from a political assassin, and is generally thought to be suffering from a psychological disorder, or at least to have been temporarily insane at the time of his crime. So, as I was sinking into the embarrassed embrace of my fiancé (he had been summoned to my rescue) my first concern was to find a way, with the help of his lawyer, to avoid imminent transfer to a mental ward. I intended to take full legal responsibility for the act I had already confessed to, and was ready to be put into pretrial detention. I wanted to atone for my crime, through all the nights of the world, but not to be put into analysis, for God's sake, not to be driven into psychiatry's endless labyrinth of exculpation and excuse. I felt the threat of a hellish plunge into the boundless inner self with its interminable tortures. The criminal court, on the other hand, would hold me accountable to a hard secular order without destroying my sense of right and wrong.

The reality of the situation turned out to be somewhat more simple and straightforward. Of course, the presiding judge released me on my own recognizance until my trial, and I was not to be sent anywhere. But to my bitter disappointment, I also learned that in the eyes of law my offense was a minor one, indeed, being nothing more egregious than "property damage." And, since this was a first offense with no criminal intent, there was absolutely no question of my having to serve a prison term. The worst I might expect was a fine of a few thousand marks. I found the prospect depressing. Even the certificate issued to my defense attorney by the court psychiatrist seemed to confirm my worst fears. The argument was being made, in the strongest possible way, that I had been *incapable* of understanding the nature of my crime. The author of the report indulged himself in the most bizarre of psychological analyses, he was downright crazy about my madness, or the behavior he considered to be my madness. My own statements, my own clearly stated motives, were totally ignored. Numerous examples of art assassination were recounted, the religious symbolism underscored, the subject was defamation of the church, a slaughter of images, the destruction of "false idols," even poor Herostratos's burning of the temple at Ephesus. But it was impossible for me to recognize my own true motives and impulses among all of those mentioned. My act had absolutely nothing to do with fanaticism or a desire for fame. Having confronted an alien timeframe I was forced to defend myself. That's all. But no one understood. Even my own attorney could not accept my explanation. He kept insisting that I formulate a *simple*, political motive. He believed that this was probably the only kind of statement that could keep me from being sent to a mental hospital. After all, it wouldn't be that difficult to understand what I had done as a *simple*, anti-American act, and not an attack from the left wing, but from the right, all in the cause of a truly German aesthetic. By now the courts must have taken note of the fact that the damaged painting was part of a *purely* Jewish-American movement in modern art. . . . I said that I'd rather be put in an insane asylum than to identify myself with such a loathsome viewpoint.

My fiancé also responded with a shameless and cowardly offer of help. He would be ready to pay for all of the court costs, if, going forward, I promised to find "my own way." Translation: I was to get out of his life. Well, he got his freedom *gratis*. I took leave of both my legal counsel and my embarrassed fiancé.

. . .

At the actual trial, there was little mention made of the more or less obscure motive for my deed. My court had, as they say, a social consciousness. It took into account how much I had already suffered, losing both a fiancé and a livelihood (I no longer worked at the textile company) and concluded there would be no need for further punishment. I was released. Of course, I was not pleased at this outcome, but I was relieved – considering the threat of psychiatric incarceration I had been facing. I had gotten off lightly; all too lightly, it seemed to me, how could this outrageous and fateful incident in the museum have faded away into oblivion while at the same time my own private failure in love had become a public penalty. My own sense of retribution had in no way been satisfied.

In the meantime, I had managed to contact the people who had been hired to repair the picture I had damaged. At first I avoided actually looking at the painting or observing the conservators at their work. Instead, I often met them in the evening and asked detailed questions about the progress of the restoration. There were five freelance conservators, among them two women, who had formed a kind of association and worked on large-scale projects as a team. Because each of them was an expert in his own field and brought his own special skills to the effort, there was always an opportunity for useful exchange, even when there was no immediate demand. The conservator, for example, could learn from the art historian and the X-ray technician from the monuments keeper; each was familiar with the latest advances in his field.

My victim, they told me, had now been completely cleaned and inspected for overall signs of aging. And once they had determined that it would be unnecessary to reenforce the entire canvas, the huge painting was hung in the workshop and the actual repair work could begin. The gashes and wounds I had inflicted were carefully combed out and smoothed around the edges. Strips of fabric were found to precisely match the strength, weave, and threadcount of the stretched sailcloth, and, once these edges were combed and scraped thin, a wax-based glue was applied and they were affixed, under vacuum pressure, to the back of the canvas, filling in the offending holes. This completed, the actual restoration of the painted surface was undertaken; filling in the gashes; the delicate retouche, or, as they preferred to call it, the inpainting, which required them not only to determine the precise color values and glazes, but even the tiniest brush stroke, each of which contained a trace of the energy and the enormous propulsion of the entire work. Without being able to apply the slightest exuberance to their task, they had to capture ecstasy in its inert atomic form and cautiously renew it. This painstaking process took more than two weeks, but finally, one evening, they could report on the happy conclusion to their project, completed to the satisfaction of all involved. No one could have been more relieved or more profoundly thankful than I was to hear this news. And not only that, I was now able to turn to these intelligent, healing people and they received me in a friendlier, more straightforward manner than anyone ever had, when by all rights they should have looked upon me as a barbarian, some kind of savage assassin. But they never did. They truly spoiled me with their gentle understanding and their genuinely forgiving ways. But the real reason I became so attached to them was to be found in their craft itself and the way it unexpectedly led me back to my own roots. In the company of these young conservators I began to recall so much of what I had learned from my father. Here, his work, his fervor, and his knowledge had found a worthy, modern continuation. The naive and courageous loner now seemed to me to be the struggling stalk from which a colorful team like this might blossom with its richly developed techniques and skills, its fruitfully intertwined talents.

These people, close friends in their private lives, complete strangers to mistrust and smug self-satisfaction, had begun to accept me; and the time we spent together was not really even affected by the fact that, day in and day out, while I did absolutely nothing to help, they were intently absorbed in ameliorating the aftereffects of my assault. Of course, they asked questions from time to time, but not as if this were an interrogation, they were simply interested and did not hesitate to contribute their own general stories and enlightened opinions. And I told them everything there was to tell about my own life, I described the happy days I spent with my father going from village church to inn, to town hall, to castle tower, learning to do much of the kind of work they were doing, if only in a very primitive way. I told them about the sad times as well, my digression, my repressed aptitudes, and my abandoned calling. The disheartened self-denial that had allowed me to lead a perfectly counterfeit life for so long. All five of them listened very attentively to everything I said, even though they could not easily empathize with my melancholy and harsh self-criticism. Through affiliation and alliance they came to share many opinions and views, theirs was a natural, unified state in which only those things that struck them as benevolent and constructive were recognized and taken to heart. When I introduced them, as best I could, to the mythology of my birth, the story of Lady Fury, Lady Doll, and Lady North, they didn't know whether they should laugh or feel sorry for me. And here I was just about to bare the innermost reaches of my being, as I was convinced that Lady Fury had had me under her complete control when I attacked Morris Louis. Oh no, the five responded, it is easy to see that anyone this superstitious must really believe they were destined to do evil. Anyone who had suffered under these precepts would somehow have to find a way to give vent to the sinister and destructive elements within. I would never, they believed, be able to find my way back to my feminine and creative powers unless I found a way to liberate myself from these malignant notions.

For their part, they, so even-tempered, demanded that I return to my thwarted beginnings and rebuild my connections with those years that, in my words, had been the happiest of my life. My sense of beauty and my skill at painting had been so well nurtured then, and now they would have to be renewed and restored through good practice. They were ready to help me in any way they could, and, if I wished, even to accept me into an apprenticeship and train me in the techniques of modern restoration. Of course, this meant that I would be required to take on some defined task and work as part of the team instead of standing around and getting in the way. But as talented and experienced as they believed I was, I could always find a way to be helpful to one of the other of them, or even undertake to do some of the preparatory work.

These sincere and welcome words truly did revive my spirits. I was going to be able to work with them! I could not have imagined anything more wonderful. I immediately blushed in embarrassment and thankfulness. I wildly promised to perform every possible trivial task. Here it is clear that the weakest aspect of my character had just be exposed: as soon as anyone showed a sincere interest in me, I immediately responded with blind submission. There was nothing else I could do, I had to treat "the man with the good voice" as my superior. Of course, as the team was very sensitive to false humility, my behavior displeased them, it disrupted their collective harmony. They responded by pointing out that there could not possibly be anything trivial, or any trivial task. In view of the precise correlation and complementary relationship between research and practice, every facet of their work would be accorded the same value and relevance. And I was requested to contain my subservient inclinations. That wretched sense of well-being, which had already caused me to suffer bitterly, since the wish to serve – here on earth and throughout my painfilled lifetime – has always been taken advantage of and woefully abused, and can no longer be fulfilled with dignity.

But the powerful attraction emanating from the group and its shared sense of good reason helped me to escape the traces of my past ways. For a time, at least, with the example of their refined sense of cooperation constantly in view, I was able to free myself from old patterns of behavior.

For the next few weeks and months I felt as though I had returned to the years of my youth. Day in and day out, a mood, a smell, a turn of speech, some sort of sign coming to me from home; maybe because I suddenly had to learn so much in such a short time, the way one only does in one's younger years; but maybe it was also because I was following the conservators from artwork to artwork, from place to place, just as I had done with my father. Participating in the silent exchange of glances the colleagues used to communicate among themselves, I also felt that I had regained the status I had when I stood at the Master's side, and even though he seldom looked at me, his arm was dependent on the sure and steady reach of my hand. The immediate understanding achieved through eye contact characterized a higher plane, the modern technological interdependence, and beyond that it seemed to me to be the living expression of a way of work free of authoritarian tendencies and without conventional hierarchical structures.

Moreover, I found myself having to master a series of tasks, none of which I could ever have imagined back at the time we were busily painting away. Of course, I had heard that it was possible to use infrared light to expose and examine a painting in the minutest of detail. But I was truly amazed at the degree to which technical devices had become commonplace in looking for early signs of damage to the varnish, or lumping in the paint layer, and deciding on corrective measures; in analyzing a pigment down to its trace elements; in preventing the warping of a wooden base, and all other manner of equally delicate refinements. The condition of a painting was no less painstakingly examined than that of a human organism. There were countless X rays, laboratory tests, and preventive measures. And a knowledge of such things as analytical chemistry and computer science was absolutely essential, and this expertise was as necessary as expertise in art history and painting. But of all the contemporary procedures, the one that impressed me most was the technique used to make two pictures out of one. This took place when it was discovered that a complete second picture had been painted over the work of an old master. And now, we really were able to perfectly separate the two layers of paint, and, in removing one layer from the other, give the world a new old work of art.

Now, for the first time, I understood how important this teamwork really was. There were so many technical advances and new discoveries that a single master, even the most experienced, would never have been able to keep up with them on his own. The work of these young men and women, each of them a recognized expert in his field, might be compared to the good, honest craft of my father as Rembrandt's painting might be compared to Tyrolian folk art.

Still, there was something that these advanced specialists did not have, something very fundamental, it seemed to me. A bonding agent that couldn't be obtained through chemistry or the most expensive equipment; a more profound adhesion to the work of art than could be accomplished in the most perfect of restorations.

In other words, what I missed in them was a genuine sense of awe. I was brought up with it and it was natural for me, since the first time I had climbed onto the scaffolding with my father and had been allowed to share his exultant joy in a beautifully ornamented facade. His means may have been primitive, and his tastes simple, but this fundamental passion, this sense of wonder and awe were given to me at an early age. It has always been the only means by which I can appreciate a work of art, by which it influences my senses and even the essence of my life.

The team members had often researched and studied a painting or a piece of sculpture from a distance before ever having laid an eye on it. But even then, once having confronted it, it seemed to me that what they saw was only the "object," they took its measure with eyes sensitized to search out the hidden and the invisible, and they never allowed themselves to be overwhelmed by its splendor, its beautiful form, or its magnificence. I really believe that they have never felt the gaze of the infamous eyes of the past. Consequently, they never had cause to worry and were able to rely confidently on their talents.

No, they had never found a master. Having grown up at a time when we are more often trained by critical programs than by experienced people, they never felt the need for anything else. And it was just this kind of undirected education that allowed them to develop their just manner, to an association of equals in which no one attempted to gain control over another.

Nevertheless, I came to see the shortcomings of this wonderful independence; where there are no masters, there is no awe, unlike those instances where something higher and exemplary is recognized. Finally, I had to conclude that they clearly had no sense of the *power* of the works they were dealing with, and they began to seem to me like a handful of busy elves, cutting away at the toes of a giant, filing and polishing in the firm conviction that they were simply working on a obscure piece of molding. But, woe unto them if the giant should ever raise his foot . . .

After I had been working for about a half a year with the young conservators, their cool, absorbed mode of operating began to seem more and more negligent to me, and my own appreciative sense of the artworks began to suffer. A about-face in my relationship to the group was inevitable and not long in coming, it took place on one of our trips.

One day, in the workshop of the Stockholm National Museum, we were working on a painting by Georges de la Tour that depicts a kneeling Hieronymus. One of the two women on the team was busy examining the fundament for so-called pentimento, possible sketches and studies that might be found under the paint layer. Overwhelmed by the powerful tableau, I asked her if the physical immediacy of the tall old saint didn't make her feel somewhat self-conscious? Close enough to smell, this sunken, naked, old-man's body, its arms and legs long and withered! And at the same time: so endlessly far away from today, the posture he had assumed, the hermit kneeling in repentance and self-flagellation! But it was just as a penitent that he appeared so noble, upright, even victorious. I asked my diligent colleague if she hadn't got the same impression from the painting as I had, that true dignity flowed from humility, that pain and privation lent an intense splendor, and wasn't this thin, emaciated arm the strongest and most supple, as long as it was being raised in self discipline?

The occupied party raised her eyes from the X-ray microscope and took a quick look at the foreground of the object in order to reassure herself that she was sitting in front of the same painting of which I had just given her even more of a promise than a description. She replied that the painter was well-known as a late mannerist; he had liked to use theatrical light effects and was following in the footsteps of Caravaggio, the painter he considered his master. I could see nothing but tenacity and the worry that she might not be able to get to the bottom of what was being asked of them. As if to protect herself from every possible manifestation of the picture, she immediately pulled two macro-photos out of her kit and explained some of the characteristics of craquelé in the primer coat, noting that it looked very much like the crackled surface on a bed of dried mud.

. . .

As everything that might possibly be a source of trouble or disagreement was to be openly discussed in the group, it was now my turn to voice my misgivings and my objections.

"To me, it seems that the more detailed the work our projects have required," I explained, "the more superficial they have become. Put more concretely, we are making the most magnificent works of art more and more threadbare every time we submit them to radical inspection. We are making less and less of an effort to recognize their vital presence and to value their beauty. Of course, our clients are happy with our work, and neither the so-called experts nor the public have anything to complain about. There are no demands being made for anything beyond what we have to offer. It is only the works themselves and their masters who are unhappy with us. And this is not the first time I have had this feeling. They have often resisted our corrective techniques, and I have seen a work of art shooting a painful grimace out from under a restored coat of varnish. Even the most modern and meticulous procedure results in something incongruous, an imperfection from which the work will never be freed. Because we are missing the spirit. Because everything we do to them is only superficial.

"No, what we are doing cannot be considered masterful in any way. Not one of us produces great work. Of course, it isn't even possible, because none of us can, or can be allowed to, advance his own abilities beyond those of the integrated unit. We think and see, we act and hope in a circumscribed equilibrium of talents. But this not only brings about a valuable distribution of expert knowledge, it also leads to an averaging of intelligence and aesthetic sense. And in this way, from the very outset, we stifle the development of any outsider or innovator, any eccentric character, any nonconformist and therefore bolder talent. We have become so tractable and are so full of respect and deference that when we confront something greater than ourselves, we can no longer acknowledge it, and perhaps cannot even recognize it. A kind of hubris of our well-adapted, contemporary intelligence that masks the true nature of our spiritual poverty. It tricks us into thinking that we really are on the same plane with the delicate work we are healing, when in reality all we are doing is handling it, fingering it, restoring it with a few good tricks. But we are and will remain nothing but unsuspecting journeymen. And just at that point, where we show ourselves to be the most successful, all we have done is proven what talented forgers we are!"

I was attempting to unnerve my mild-mannered colleagues, and to unsettle their consciences. But this circle could not be so easily perturbed. Again, I was surrounded by the gaze of large, good-natured eyes, and it almost seemed to me that they were attempting to silently transport me into a new age of innocence, an amalgam of forgetfulness and perfection.

"We have noticed," one of them finally replied, "that you have often seemed overwhelmed by whatever was done in the past, or considered exemplary, or created by a master. There's nothing good or useful in this. Perhaps you feel this way because you have never defined a secure center in your life, from which you can respond knowingly and with quiet self-assurance to the 'Greats,' as well as to the artworks and cultural values of the past. You are still looking for that center, but somehow you believe you'll find it in a world order that has long since disappeared and can never be restored. 'The Master,' as good and precious as it may sound, he is never going to return to take you by the hand and lead you through life. Not even works of art will show you your place in the world. On the contrary, you are running the danger that what is old and beautiful is only going to grow more and more overpowering, and begin to look like a dismal idol, the more ungrounded you feel yourself and the longer you continue to chase after a *calling* that no longer exists and can no longer be carried out, when there is a practical, highly-qualified *job* to be had, that will fulfill the same goal much better: keeping works of art alive. Furthermore, we believe that every era, insofar as it is capable of making a living transition, will and must develop its own legs or whatever organ of transport is required. In our association, for example, we have not only achieved a high level of individual skills, but as an entity we have also developed a *spirit*, which is no less worthy than that of any of the old masters, at least as far as craft is concerned, and we have no need to judge ourselves in terms of the creativity, which is not a part of our work. In our lives as well as our work, we have built a complex, multifaceted and organically inspired protocol – even this is a 'cultural value' – and can easily include it in a structure in which 'everything is in its place,' the same way you seem to assume it can only be found in hierarchical systems of the past. Our system is more sophisticated and complex than the old one, but it can much better meet the needs of a quickly changing world, and through this flexible fitting the individual becomes much stronger and experiences an enhancement of his capabilities. We believe that your real doubts about us are based on something quite different. You have always wanted to track down and understand the works at their creative core, actually, what you really wanted was to have them come to life again through you. That is why you have never wanted to see only the practical craft in our restorations, but instead you have always wanted to perform an artistic act of succession. This is neither the ideal nor even the repressed ambition of our work."

I had listened to them very carefully, but it soon became clear that we were no longer aiming at a common understanding. Inwardly, I had already distanced myself too far from the team. Nothing of what they were saying to me now could possibly make any sense. And I did not hesitate very long before letting them know that I intended to leave, in as conciliatory a fashion as the rules of the association allowed. When they heard this, they were neither particularly surprised, nor did they try to convince me to change my mind. Rather, they had a suggestion to offer, which itself caused me considerable embarrassment. They felt I could, of course, leave at any time I wished; but, after everything that had brought and kept us together, our separation should not be proceeding in such a trivial and offhand manner. What they wanted to do was give me a small job – a good-bye present, a master's examination – that had just recently been received, and that I was to complete entirely on my own without any outside help. It was a minor piece of work, but not without charm, and they were certain I would be able to handle it. In the New Castle in Stuttgart that had in part been decorated by the Bavarian fresco painter Zick, there was a single sopraporte, a scene over the hall doorway, to be restored. After the war it had been repainted according to an incorrect drawing, and now, finally, the original motif was to be restored.

I was being offered a job, to be carried out as I saw fit, requiring that I subordinate myself completely to a Baroque master of some standing and faithfully recreate what he had painted. At first I didn't know how I should react to this proposal. On the one hand it was a challenge, and on the other a threat to my fragile self-esteem. However, after brief reflection, the decision was made: I could not do anything but accept. I was already too intensely involved with the job to be able to think up any cogent reasons not to take it.

· · ·

Shortly after that I arrived in Stuttgart, equipped with recommendations and certificates that indicated to the curator of monuments that I was a member, tried and true, of the highly respected collective. I was immediately received with great courtesy and then led directly to my assignment. Unfortunately, the hall in which the sopraporte was to be replaced was dominated by a magnificent ceiling painting, also an original work by Zick, but one that had been replicated, after the war, in accordance with the correct design. For the most part, the restoration had been well done, even though it would fail to meet contemporary standards of color matching and light values. It was a typical restoration of the late 50s. There was no way I could use it as a model for my own work. On the contrary, it would be a burden to have such a mediocre copy constantly floating over my head. So, I decided that the first thing I would do was follow the master to a location where his works still existed in a condition much closer to their original state. I visited the cloister church in Wilbingen near Ulm, as well as others he had painted in the same area. The longer I spent studying the Zick frescoes, the more difficult my assignment began to appear. I could now clearly see that in the paintings on the ceiling of the hall the true signs of the master had been almost wiped out, and I could not and would not make use of this questionable imitation in any way. On the other hand, I had to be careful not to allow the small secco painting over the door to contrast too starkly with the ceiling. Naturally, I couldn't ignore advances in modern technique and simply reach back to the methods of the past, and, in any case, the first thing I had to do was reveal the original scene with meticulous care before making any attempt to adjust to the previous restoration. It took a full two weeks for me to complete my conscientious, and increasingly timid, preliminary studies, until finally one morning I was able to make my entrance into the castle hall with a finished cartoon, and climb onto the scaffolding, which had already been built, and where pots for my wash and my paints had been set out. Barefoot, dressed only in jeans and a smock, I took up my position and stood there, a woman soon to enter her middle years, alone for the first time at such lofty heights. There was no more father, no more intimate of any sort, who could have given me guidance or answer my questions. Only this strange little office man who had been assigned to me was hanging around down on ground level, not saying a word, leaning back on a window sill so as not to let me out of his blurry, squinty-eyed sight. First I had to remove the existing medallion, a rural scene with peasantry, encircled by a garland relief, and then I washed the exposed surface.

As long as I was working on this, I did not doubt that I had taken the correct approach to my task and that, step by step, I would be able to complete it. My own hand seemed to me to be conducting itself with more care and skill than I was managing to muster, it gave me courage and my work began to take on a sure form. But once the decorative painting had completely disappeared, the field had been entirely cleaned, and the dull, bare mortar emerged, I was suddenly seized by a horrible dizziness. And it glared at me like an extinguished mirror! It was gone. There was nothing in front of me – I was nothing. I thought: you can't do anything here, you can't put anything in his place! Suddenly, my head was swimming. Lady Doll, Lady Fury, Lady North were all screaming at me. Morris Louis was screaming. I thought: you're just here to destroy again, to obliterate and expunge. You can't give anything back!

I was trembling, my knees went weak, I had to sit down on the plank. I dipped a brush around in the pots, for show, so that the gloomy little office man wouldn't get suspicious. Now, what I had to do was give the impression of being able to do a routine job like this very meticulously, but without any unnecessary exertion. In order to hide my agitation, I picked up the cartoon and pretended I had to correct something in my sketch. It – actually, the old Zick design – showed a pair of winged cherubs on the banks of a river, a stand of bushes and a tree in the background, and then a cupid with bow and arrow. A most undemanding motif. The first step in the process was to paint in a pale white primer coat. So, I got up and was intending at least to get the bare patch of wall covered. But no sooner was I standing in front of the empty medallion than my entire body was overcome by paralysis. It was as if I had been walled in. I could not even raise my arm to paint in the primer. The naked eye gaped at me. Suddenly, I heard my father speaking, and the comforting tone of his voice terrified me. . . . "Look! There is nothing that can compare with autumn colors. And still, we humans are not satisfied to simply observe this wonder. We want to be able to mix them ourselves. Then the painters, well, they want to do even more, they want to add something unique and incomparable of their own to our multicolored world. And that's what matters, my child. Maybe we don't have to love life, but we have to try to make something of it. Whatever we create ourselves, it, in return, gives us . . ."

I couldn't stand looking into this non-mirror any longer. I climbed down off the scaffolding and told the office man that I had to chase down some special color and wouldn't be able to get back to work until the next day.

During the night, I had a remarkable dream. I lay bent forward with my head on a tabletop. A long time ago there had been a big banquet in this hall and there were all kinds of bugs crawling away over me. Then a June bug appeared. It flew into my hair. But my head was covered with multicolored streamers and confetti. And my hair was all stuck together from drinks that had been poured over my head. The bug got tangled up and stuck. I tore it off of my head along with a handful of paper and hair. I went to the window and threw the bug out. But suddenly I was in my fourth-floor apartment in Rheydt. And the bug was so glued up and incapacitated that it couldn't fly and plummeted helplessly toward the ground. Just shortly before crashing into the sidewalk, it suddenly recovered its ability to fly. And now, growing larger and larger inside the wad of hair and streamers, it slowly rose into the sky and flew up to my window. But I was standing with my back to the sill, leaning up against it just like the little man from the curator of monuments had done all day long. And behind me, a huge and powerful insect appeared in front of the window pane. Its furry body kept banging dully up against the glass. It only wants to cuddle up to you, my dream said, and like a begging dog it pushed its gray nose into the pane of glass. But when I turned around to look at it, it caught me in its thousand-faceted eye, the size of a football field, and I saw the terrible, fractured reflection of myself.

. . .

The next day, in the early hours of the morning, before the man from the monuments office arrived, I was up on the scaffolding and standing in front of the exposed patch over the door. But this time, as if I had already overcome the worst, I was suddenly able to work *with abandon*. I applied the white primer in one pass, covered the nothingness and went bravely on. Once the priming coat was dry, there was nothing to keep me from attaching the cartoon and transferring the outlines of the sketch to the wall. At this point, the office man appeared, noted with satisfaction the progress I was making, and grinned, as if he had known all along that this is how it would be. My inhibitions had been overcome! I could feel it. I could finally act, convey, produce, and fill the void. Courage and skill carried me forward and I soon had the river, the forested banks, sky, and background painted in and then did not hesitate applying the tricky incarnation of infatuated children and the cupid. But once I had done this, as I was finishing off my last stroke, my self-possession left me and I saw what I had done. The skin tones, at least, were totally wrong. Simply awful. Can you imagine a cupid with a pale ashen complexion? Maybe it wasn't exactly ashen, but it was lifeless, gray, deathly ill. I washed the figures away and made a second attempt with a corrected mix of colors. I failed again. A flesh tone that incited fear and pity. But the more I attempted to correct what I had done, the worse it became. The gap between the bright color I had in the pot in front of me and the gloomy collapse it suffered during application became ever greater. It was absolutely hopeless. And each of my failures sneered at me full of contempt. I had absolutely no idea what I could do to bring the soft childlike flesh to life. And by then my inhibition had grown so strong that I couldn't even fake anything. Finally, after one last, half-mad attempt, I gave up. I climbed down off the scaffolding, went over to the office man and told him that I would not, and could not, finish this job. I was straightforward and brief, and with these last few words I concluded, once and for all, my long and futile effort at enduring and living overwhelmed within art's field of force. I stole away.

Later, the team, the well-balanced five, effortlessly fixed what I had left behind, and in less than half a work day the sopraporte, the pretty little ornament, was harmoniously restored to its intended place.

. . .

It was a warm day, and I sat down in front of a bar, outside on the sidewalk where tables, chairs, and umbrellas had been set up.

On the other side of the street there were the remains of a recently burned-out kiosk or shed. A sooty spray, the black reflection of a fiery explosion, arched up across the bare wall of the building next door. Underneath it were three containers overflowing with garbage. This was the view I had as I sat under my Cola-umbrella, drinking iced tea as if I were at the beach. Facing me, a wave of soot, as if Morris Louis had painted his greatest exaltation. No cars, no pedestrians passed by. The side street of side streets. But the bar friendly, so it seemed, friendly and bright inside.

This is where the lovely disheartened narrator brought her own story to a close.

It would not have occurred to any one of us, not even the reckless Reppenfries, to have jumped right in with his own thinking and positing after Almut's subdued and anguished revelation. She had caused each and every one of us to stop and think. All three of us men who had already told our stories could see that this woman clearly had surpassed us with the depth of her anguish and the intelligence of her feelings. Even though she had told her story from one single, unremittingly sad perspective. Still awash in its reverberations there was nothing we could do but keep silent. And we would have remained so for quite some time, if, at the very next moment, Paula and Dagmar, the medic's two wives who had stayed away for so long, had not come fluttering in full of excitement. "Can't you hear it? Can't you hear anything?" Paula, the sister-in-law, yelled, already indignant again. "Your dreary old stories in the early morning hours! Come on, open up the windows of your gloomy souls and let a little bit of fresh vista in!"

"Aren't you going to finally lift your lazy ear to the winds?" the good-natured Dagmar said, aping her somewhat weakly. "You can't even discern the heart's simplest and most enchanting air?"

"Will you please be quiet," the medic grumbled, "or at least stop the talk about hearing something or other in the air we're supposed to be listening to, while you're shooting off your loud mouth!"

Finally, once everything had quieted down, we really could hear something. A soft and gentle song . . . It came to us wavering hesitantly through the pale morning, swelling and then subsiding, like an ancient radio, in surges and pieces it came rolling in on us. It must be coming from the outlying garden, from far beyond the bosquet and the Baroque gardens. It seemed to be a long, ambling melody, not a pithy song. A monotonous melody, as much without beginning as without end, floated nonchalantly into the air.

> Come, o friend, in search of me.
> Go wandering astray and me will you find.
>
> Now dew is washing the dusty leaves.
> The long smoldering sunrise expires.
> Day will come soon, light and clear.

Baptized in dim sun. As if created
For the man standing in wait!

I am the flower under the bush.
I am lips on stone.
I am the gaze from the ground.

I am imbecilic and smart.
I am shameless and reserved.
I am the fruit and the half.

"It's the voice of the mail clerk," Reppenfries concluded solemnly.
"But what she's singing sounds almost like the riddle of the
sphinx."

"Yossica!" I yelled, with an involuntary sigh, sadly recalling
the rough treatment she'd just gotten at the hands of the medic,
and happy now that even though she was some distance away, she
had not broken with us entirely.

"Well, it's about time!" Paula shot my way. "You've finally
noticed something. It's for you! You're the one her endless song
has been grasping for hour after hour."

"Me? But . . . ?" I asked, astounded, and turned to the modern
man, the one I had thought was more probably called.

"Who else?" he replied, shrugging his shoulders.

"You don't mean to say," Dagmar interrupted, "that all this
time the little dear was standing here, you hadn't noticed the
slightest sign of her affection for you?!"

"No!" I answered with clear conscience and heart, "I really did
not notice it in the least. Not for as long as we were here in clear
view of one another, standing next to each other, there was not
even the faintest rustling between us."

"Well, then it started rustling somewhere around the outer
limits of hearing!" the medic growled. "Shortly before the sound
barrier there was a fierce rustling between the two of you."

"Come on, get on with it!" Paula prodded me. "And be quick!
Find the girl. I think she's hopelessly lost out there, somewhere
over in the informal garden, beyond the maze and the bowling
green . . ."

However, at this very same moment, something totally unexpected came to pass and caused us all together, as one, forgetting
Yossica for the time being, to turn on our heels in *one* motion.

What we saw caused us to lose our breath. Not once during the entire morning had we paid the slightest attention to the magnificent royal palace at our backs; it had been something inanimate, lying behind us like a drab gray memory. Every thought and every gaze had been aimed across the terrace and into the park, where, in this easterly direction, there was at least the shimmering intimation of a dawning, and it was there, if anywhere, some arrival might be expected. And we could not believe our eyes or our ears as the majestic bronze-fitted portal behind us opened creakily, grinding and scraping. A rush of cool musty air poured out of the inner hall. A deathly silence stretched far out to the fore. Suddenly a drumroll commenced, then subsided into a soft rustle and broke off. Shortly after that came the thundering crash of a rock and roll drum solo, an eruption of uncontrolled mournful rage. For some time, military tribute continued to alternate with youthful fury, and we knew that there could no longer be any doubt that the royal funeral ceremony had been solemnly begun. The hour had come; his majesty, the most powerful, was being carried to his grave. At the forefront came a gentle youth in a blond pageboy, wearing a black medieval coat. Arms stretched high into the air, he carried the monarch's standard and marched in mincing measure and beat out onto the terrace. Gleaming ranks of marchers carried flags and banners, followed at some distance by the pennants, emblems, crests and insignias, representing states and provinces, associations, groups, societies, clubs and circles of friends who had submitted to the rule of the powerful one, or at least felt themselves profoundly obliged. Then out in front of the coffin came a double row of young boys and girls bearing silk pillows with imperial insignias, jewels, and precious documents, as well as various burial articles; children conforming to the heavy stride of the procession more in steadfast imitation than inner conviction. The magnificent coffin, which was being carried out of the hall and through the portal, shouldered by eight loyal subjects moving forward with the tiniest of shuffling steps, flanked by an honor guard of the highest ranking dignitaries of both church and state – this was no empty show, the coffin really did contain the cadaver of the most outrageous monster and most evil German. He lay there peacefully adapted to the narrow confines of his box, as if he had never attacked countries and peoples, as if he had only dreamed his evil deeds, quietly, brutally. The last traces of color had drained from what was once a red-spotted, apoplectic face. A crushed, unearthly pale head lay on the purple pillow.

Following at an appropriate distance came the ruler's family, led by the king's mother, the consort with her children, and the next of kin. After them, the military chiefs, the upper, middle, and lower ranks of the bureaucracy; then the gray army of advisors and experts, diplomats and envoys, representatives and members of parliament, everyone lined up according to rank, as required by public protocol. Up until this point, the procession retained both the form and the pageantry common to any national funeral ceremony for a chief of state, a leader, or head of government. Up until this point, at any rate, the gathered masses had been marching in file and formation, in order and rank. But what followed was the strangest, most bizarre, and, at the same time, most authentic funeral procession ever to have been seen in German history. For immediately behind the last of the henchmen of the old regime, the simple successors began streaming in, that leaderless society surged through the portal, the people burdened with the bitterest legacy of the malfeasant, namely *us*, the graceless, the disheartened and brazen, the prosperous and impoverished, open and devious, mad and mundane, passive and overachieving, free and thoroughly, through and through, self-conscious *society*. Heading for the palace, an endless mass of humanity came crushing in from the west side, and, stretching out far beyond the front entrance road, appeared to blanket the surrounding meadows and fields. Immediately following coats of arms and family crests came the pennants and posters, armbands and protest banners held high, and the quickly changing society replaced allegiance with dissent. And while rank and rigid etiquette seemed to have established an almost spontaneous marching order at the front of the procession, those who followed appeared to recognize no such hierarchy and everyone simply milled around together. But in reality, even among these marchers there was a set adhesion of forces, and its ranks were determined by a precisely ordered system based on mutual fixation, a semiconscious dependence had supplanted obvious ranking, proclaimed regard, or open enmity. The first from among the inventors of the new moral order, the critical clean-up crew, the modern beacons, had literally affixed themselves to the backs of the very last power brokers of the old empire. They formed the immediate extension of the solemn procession and exhibited a relatively rigid alignment and formation. But now their faces were pensive and bitter. The departed spirit had robbed so many of them not only of their morals and their critical senses, but even of their very livelihoods. They recognized their desperately dependent circumstance and sensed the absolute misery of a bewildering enslavement of the opposition to its object, which had always kept them from forming one single bold thought of their own. Having been constantly, exclusively absorbed with the evildoer, they themselves had succeeded in disseminating a spiritually debilitating intelligence and were able to do nothing but finger those who ideas were different from theirs. Fixated on these model democrats and professional anti-fascists, and following right on their heels, were two groups of mostly younger people. One group was made up of the thoroughly indifferent, who openly declared that they were in no way prepared to have their lives nailed to the cross of 1933, and, thoroughly bored, they trotted effortlessly behind critical fathers who could serve them neither as role model nor bogey man. The second group, far more cleanly fixated and committed, had tightened the anti-screw one more turn. They amused themselves by spooking their predecessors, whom they considered to be nothing but hollow half-wits, with neobarbarian provocations, thus setting them in dizzy confusion, all with a minimum of cleverness and effort. In this way, the most evil of Germans was bound to his posterity into the third and fourth generation by a long chain of tyrannies. Sharing this fate, in the most expansive time-space of a reluctant morning, numerous dynasties and numerous generations gathered, and, willingly or unaware, provided the last escort.

A few attended somberly and undisguised, others were masked and presented themselves in ordinary allegories. And everything bewilderingly flowed on like a vast and gloomy carnival. Hesitantly, the sovereign day of mourning trickled away into cheerless German holidays and celebrations.

Father's day celebrants, veteran rebels, proto-anti's in striped athletic jerseys, with their circular saws, leather bags hanging from their wrists, on fire trucks with aluminum beer kegs, lying on their backs, a magnum of cognac strapped under their chins to still the thirst of followers, the men behind; the pack of "fathers" staggered along in parade. Fixated on them, full of contempt and disgust, the young cool cats, the radical narcissists, hygiene's birds of paradise, walkman dancers, inaccessible, twitching electrically. Nearby, but still some distance apart, the talkative seekers of the self, who see an extraterrestrial light at the end of the tunnel; their ego numinos. And dancing around them, a deluge of dullards swaying back and forth in limp brotherly alliance, giggling laughter of a cola intoxication; among them, accessible to everyone, adored by everyone, Deborah the child star; nymph with crumply limbs, floating elatedly in her own being, excessively lithe and addicted to touching, laughingly licking and yet so supple that she easily slipped out of any embrace. Two aging daycare workers glumly fought their way through the throngs of the good and the good-looking, two autonomous matrons in t-shirts and gypsy skirts, while behind them in their revolutionary tumbrel full of toddlers there was always one child who had to go pee-pee, and these caretakers never tired of digging "your penis" out of a little boy's pants.

And how much more stately things became as the world's Great Convictions made their appearance; when the allegories, geniuses of doctrines that have blessed mankind, approach on their drab floats, extravagantly decked out, bathed in precious black pomp. Each powerful ideal showed up arm in arm with its dominating dark side, every lousy practice held fast to its gold-brick theory. So, capitalism appeared on the arm of merciless destructive rage, Marxism on the arm of morose slavery; but in the middle of them all, a contemptuous bag of bones, Master Progress set the pace, which both – according to the motto: one acts, and the other knows what's wrong – willingly follow. Among the others in this gentle farewell procession: zealous reform, the well-meaning fanatic with brazen forgetfulness as its partner; the prophet of conservatism with his mistress contempt; national pride with his congenitally hate-filled sister of the same name; and finally the much vaunted angel of peace, who could find no partner and just kept spinning around on its own axis.

Following these chosen abstractions, these exulted characters on rolling pedestals, and at their feet again, came the surging masses, the throngs of common people, without disguise and without style. Also featured, though not really revered, were the utterly popular people, public figures, idols at home who had not really made it into the ranks of household deities, but had only managed to become a better sort of acquaintance than the average neighbor. Still, they possessed enough magnetism and intensity to attract a multitude of poor, luckless worms into their entourage. But among them, there were those who didn't really belong. The sick, the overburdened and distressed, the intellectually foundering and those poor creative beings who suddenly find themselves filled with dazzling inspiration and then weakly collapse, but not without having brightened our dull gray morning. The readers, the drinkers, the whiners and stutterers, the ones who fail their exams, the egg-bespattered worshipers of little girls, the perpetual canasta losers – ah, you lonely hearts, unhappy city dwellers, you who can no longer be disappointed: you don't deserve to be united! Free yourselves from the sweeping nets of pollsters and prognosticators barking at your heels in an attempt to truncate your lives on the basis of rationally sanitized data.

Among the luckless worms were the overly well-informed and the intellectual buffoons, who either missed everything or confused whatever they might have grasped, the thoroughly enlightened whose heads were permanently attached to the backs of their TV chairs. Many were terrified, faces pressed to the surface. There was a lot of restlessness around here. Every one of them seemed to be missing something: a child, a dog, a debtor, God, a nude model. And so the parade usherettes were kept busy trying to be of assistance to the perplexed; they kept running up and down the ranks in their slit skirts and red stockings, constantly in search of some missing creature. Some of them had two identity cards affixed to their chests. This was to indicate that not only were they there to keep order, but that they had also been recruited to conduct polls, and many of the people whom they had just assisted instantly became statistics.

And look here: the common denominator has just appeared; average households, well-fortified preserves, shopping baskets brim full with relatives, home and hobby, with vacations and week-ends, with brokerage accounts and debts and plans, and plans. Even that gnarled old worker's saw was alive and well: "My children will have a better life" – some had, after all, reserved space in their hearts for the good old future that was once such a useful aspect of dreams and hopes, before it fell victim to merciless prognostication.

Nearby were the computer types, telecommunicating denizens of the information highway, as disembodied as computer code, as spectral as teletext, a discharge of light, the internally controlled reflection of his calculator, error messages when falling in love, overdosing on pills, or approaching godliness.

Behind them are the better off. The dealers with their "and the day after tomorrow, we'll be bullish again" faces. Representatives of pharmaceutical firms, who knew nothing of their own time and who, on their jovial ascent into the next thirty years, did nothing but tell one anally oriented joke after another. In their midst, the Magus of a Good Name, ever creditworthy, possessed of longterm fiscal soundness. The man with the polar beard, a Prospero who wants to turn things around? The natural leaders, the pitiless casino types, self-righteous and ruthless, narrow-minded and brutal, ruined for their fellow man as well as God.

The dominant were becoming ever more dominant; the subaltern were becoming ever more subaltern, like caterpillars that will never turn into butterflies, and, whenever they move, a hump transverses their entire body from head to aft.

Then came the outsiders, the pathetic freaks, themselves a thriving sector. Mutual threats of suicide and these once overcome, whimpering bitches and queers, similarly well-stationed, having long set the tone in all branches of the industry of despair and entertainment. The calculatingly feminine women, caged-in and well-wed creatures, the victims of borrowed feelings, addicted to a most masculine way of thinking; shining through each of these figures, sullenly indolent, was the "body of a woman," expressionless from experience. And now and then, a lost little lioness might be seen, weary and adorable, a nymph stranded in a kiss, with her have-me, love-me, leave-me eyes.

And all along the procession, in every rank, the innumerable caretakers, psychotherapists, hosts, social workers, school guidance counselors and other true pillars of the community. Also numberless and omnipresent were: the censorious, the media smart-asses, the epochal black holes through which time flows away, blubbering through a gully.

What did we see in this tumultuous stream of a thousand apparitions, of bizarre afterbirths? Was it one nation, or nothing more than a gigantic lottery club?

Oh, Germany! Your crocheted toilet-paper covers in the back windows of your middle-class cars!

What were we seeing: a passion play or a ragtag parade? A carnival interlude or the final blowout?

. . .

The head of the funeral procession must now have been nearing the tomb where the gruesome king would be buried. It was a cavern as high as a cathedral, and for thousands of years water had been dripping steadily from the ceiling, forming a large dark lake. In accordance with the last wishes of the monarch, his remains will be submerged in these waters. The masses had already poured down over both sides of the embankment, over the terrace and out into the open grounds of the park. They had split our rendezvous in two and dissolved our faithful circle. Dagmar and Paula had been the first to be swept up. Then, with one sudden start, having traded the enemy of society for the medic, and filled with a blind passion to help, Reppenfries plunged into the milling crowds. Almut had reluctantly let herself be chased off, while Hans-Werner the Modern had attached himself to a group of scientists, they might have been biologists and students of evolution, grinning and filled with impatience, firmly in possession of a concept of the new world, which they would soon proclaim to the assembled nation so that they might finally be revered as the new Copernicuses. I had lost sight of my friends and was most likely the only one of our group still standing in the gallery. There I stood, a protestant in the flood of epiphany, a scorner in a trance. At this point, what happened right in front of my eyes was like that fleeting moment of fullness experienced by someone drowning, suffocating, or plunging to his death. I was one who had been concocted out of too many, and still I didn't want to stop *seeing*. The grimmest of bodies had begun to rise, whirling and spinning out of the deep, dank depths of castle cellars, while a heavenly band swung down out of a light well over the roof, and these merged forming one single social mass. Ah, how they tossed and rolled in a horrifying fusion. The dead with the holy, the devil with the seraphims, the damned with the saved, and they became blind, became those who can see only through the heat-sensitive sites, and rush fatuously from one body to the next, hungering for touch.

Straight through society! or so I was taught, through sewerage and cloaca is the only way to the blessed. Through run-off and cloaca to rebirth. We will all be squeezed out through the vagina again and many of us will end up like Max and Moritz, poor fairy-tale figures lying prostrate on the ground in tortured, twisted shapes.

At this moment a masked person stepped out onto the balcony on the upper floor of the palace. She was holding a tall, closed vessel in her arms. She turned to the east and paused for a premeditated second. Then, suddenly, she grabbed the cover of the jug and tore it off. Night broke out. The tin skies shattered. The throngs below held stock-still. The funeral procession faltered. The twitch of a slain fish, the flickering of a dying candle darted through the long cortege. The first milky stream of light touched us like a blind man's groping cane. Then the heavy gray mass lying over our heads was slowly pulled away. For a moment, we looked into the endless clarity of daybreak. But it was only the brief preview of a much later harmony of the hours. Already, everything had come crashing together again, darkness and light, forward and backward, early and late in violent combat.

A gusty wind burst in from the orchard and caught us up in its swelling fury. The clouds, a billowing gentle plumage only moments before, again formed into leaden, fat bellies, and into this crashing breach a pounding rain was discharged, a slave driver, it lashed out in brute force at the broad surging waves of humanity. Blades of lightning struck among them and hail stones danced around on unprotected skulls. The choppy blast of winds grew more and more rude, the wind that sought to break, rend, and ravage now showed us how we would have been dealt with if we had only been a little lighter. The fabricated nature of the bosquet and flower borders bowed under the fury of the rain.

A terrible commotion broke out on the terrace. Some, those who had not made it out through the gate, got trapped in the hall, blocked the exits; others, trying to escape the weather, struggled back up the embankment and into the castle in search of shelter and safe haven.

To keep from being crushed, I had to give up my position in the gallery. I pushed my way through breaches in the milling crowd, laboriously battled my way forward, and finally reached the balustrade on one side of the gallery. In one leap I sprang down onto a gravel path. I looked for a way to get to the edge of the oozing legions. But they kept expanding at an ever increasing rate in all directions, and I was finally forced to take flight in order not to be engulfed again.

Luckily, the tempests and the battle of the hours did not last for very long. The heavens, which had never completely lost their glow, soon opened again, unfolding slowly and calmly. "Happy and thankful feelings after the storm," so they say, and this certainly accorded with my sentiments as I ran out into the gossamer morning potential, still unsure of my destination. Daffodils and stock, wisteria and veronica, poppies and violets, no matter which beds and perennials I passed by, it seemed that their colors had just at this very moment saturated the flowering blossoms, they shone so lively and fresh after this long, dry gray, after this eternally anemic dawning. Even though most of the plantlife had been thoroughly drubbed and drenched by the rains and the storm; still, what seems to us like the lash of a whip obviously gives immense comfort to plants. But I had no time to pause in quiet contemplation, I could already hear the first footfalls of the sprawling mass of humanity behind me. I had to run. I left the clear orderly layout of the Baroque gardens, leaving the privet maze and the bowling green to the right, I crossed the small palladio bridge and entered the realm of romantic-modern, the fanciful and illusory province of the castle grounds.

Drenched and exhausted, the first thing I wanted to do was to take refuge in an old freemason's tower, which was surrounded by a melancholy group of poplars and mulberry trees. But hardly had I stepped through the Egyptian portal and dropped down onto the lowest step of the spiral stairway when a pitiful wail broke out above me in the whispering gallery. The cries of the tortured, moaning and bawling, whimpers and sighs of tormented or mortally threatened, ravaged or incarcerated, human beings emanated from every pore and chink of the hallowed structure. This cruel concert immediately drove me out of the tower, and without giving it much thought, I chose the next best path, which led me away from this insidious refuge. Of all places, I now found myself on a path that tormented me for some time with terrifying illusions, and though they turned out to be artful and harmless, were entirely unwelcome given my current state. Every time I took a step, the ground shook under my feet, and whenever I wanted to grab hold of a shrub or a branch I was jolted with an electric shock. Several times, self-detonating guns and land mines went off right in front of me, and even though they only turned up tiny mounds of earth, the noise and the report they raised made them seem genuinely life-threatening. A gothic ruin, an ornament worthy of any landscape garden anywhere, which I was now approaching with great foreboding, unable to avoid it, suddenly it burst with an enormously deafening noise, exploding into the air just as I was about to pass it by, and the flying debris would certainly have killed me if each of the multitude of tiny pieces hadn't been attached to its own string, and, having smashed up against an almost invisible screen, sprung right back into place. I could see that I wasn't going to get bored walking along this path. After the wax likeness of a hermit had leapt out at me from a log cabin, dagger raised, and I had safely circumscribed a flame-throwing obelisk, and had crossed a self-dividing pond of snakes, I finally came upon a sunny clearing and was beginning to look forward to the cheerful grassy hills with a shimmering millstream at their base, and I believed that I had reached the end of my treacherous way. But at that very same moment, I found myself wrapped in a dark swarm of hissing arrows bolting in at me from all directions. Maybe they were carrying miniature photo cells in their points, or distance sensors, in any case, as if I had been wearing some kind of magic radiation belt, they all fell harmlessly to the ground before they could hit their mark. At this point, I had had enough of these miserable and dangerous games, and, leaving the path of terror, headed straight for the meadow with its bright, gurgling stream. I walked along its banks toward the Old Mill, where I hoped to be able to recover from the gentle chicanery, the apparent punishment, all of which, it seemed, I had set off myself, having touched secret thresholds and triggers.

Unfortunately, the Old Mill did not provide the desired sanctuary, either. As in many such playful gardens of the ruling class, and common on such manicured grounds, all I found was a sentimentally rustic facade, camouflaging a shabby little bar decorated in the style of the late twenties. Even though there was not a single person in sight, the spangled room was filled with the awful stench of sweat and sex, either artificially preserved or simulated, making it impossible for me to stay. But as I made my way back out into the light of day, my attention was immediately attracted to a strangely enchanting scene that was being played out some distance away on the banks of the little stream. Two women were standing there washing themselves with great pleasure, while a third was undressing. All of this was taking place, innocently or intentionally, under the gaze of a farmer who was turning his hay in a nearby field. However, as I got closer, I saw – and what else could I have expected here! – a group of lifeless fiberglass figures moving as if in a motorized crèche, and whose obscene grace derived from a thousand little twitches.

If I had had any idea what a labyrinth of useless and exaggerated machines and tools of torture I would run into, I would have continued my flight along the plumb lines of the hedges and borders of the classical garden. Now, where was I ever going to find my way out of this total delusion? Everything was saturated with illusion, and one artifice or subterfuge followed another. For me, now that I finally wanted to head out into the morning, this magical arena, devised and laid out in the spirit of suspended time, had become an entirely closed hour; no matter how determined I was to go on my way, or run, I could not escape through its seams.

In the meantime, I had climbed a wooded rise in the hope of achieving an overview of the entire grounds, its boundaries and its potential exits. But I was not able to see very far. Once at the top of the rise, I was immediately enveloped by the dark half shell of an outdoor movie theater. Like a fossilized herd, dozens of empty chairs stood in front of the screen where a faded and silent Louis Trenker film seemed to be showing in an infinite loop, maybe forever.

Up here I was surrounded by a dense pine forest, which blocked my view and kept me from orienting myself, so my climb onto the heights had been in vain. Behind the grotto there was a fortified path heading down off the hill in broad curves, and, as my unease had become quite extreme, I made a run for it. But I had only gotten a few steps before my way was blocked by a creeping monstrosity. It was a giant turtle crossing the path, unimaginably slow, and riding on its back, which was painted to represent half of the globe, was none other than the terrible king himself, wrapped in a commanders's field coat! The same monarch who was at this very moment was being carried to his grave! The most evil German on the back of a turtle, the creeping half of the globe . . . No! I couldn't look at it any longer! Happen what may in this garden of spirits, nothing could harm me now, and I no longer cared. Of course, I could see that the man riding along atop this sedate creature was only a jester, a feeble-minded mime, a gnome in disguise, inaccessible and lost in deep imbecility. I pushed my way past this bizarre obstacle and started running again as fast as I had before. And I had already turned into the last curve at the bottom of the hill when, suddenly, a bright jingling sound stopped me in my tracks and pulled me inexorably off to the side. It was a delicate, bell-like ring, as tempting as a siren's song, and I had no idea where it was coming from. So, I left the path, crossed the embankment and went deeper into the woods in search of the enchanting sound. It was not long before I found myself standing in front of yet another fruitless and ironical attraction. There was a high, spiraling spray of silver and gold coins tumbling over a cliff down into large, revolving marble basin. There was a plaque attached to the basin and the inscription read: "My Old Age." I didn't really understand what this meant; but it seemed to me that the same frivolous disposition was being expressed in this title and the cascading coinage, as it had been all over this park of illusion. But, maybe I really didn't understand, and the irony was simply a narrow gap through which I should have been able to perceive the more profound significance of this toy. But, I was in too much of a hurry and already too tired to spend any more time on this charming little invention.

Next, my path led me into an enormous, dusty quarry, which, owing to recent experience, I approached with some trepidation. There had been no work done here for years; and three old dumpers full of coarse sand and gravel were sitting on the tracks. At the base of the quarry wall, there was a low, round hollow in the ground, a suspicious looking feature, and I would have avoided it if the big rock piles on the right, and the cliffs on the left, had not stood in my way. But now I headed straight into the most horrifying amusement I had yet encountered on this journey. On the floor of the flat pit, there were about a dozen men's heads rolling languidly around in circles. Mighty, bald skulls rubbing quietly up against one another, all with closed eyes and mumbling mouths.

Here, the sign read "My Reservoir," and visitors were kindly requested to feed the "Thinkers in the Pit." For this purpose, there was a stack of newspapers nearby from which pages were to be torn out and handed down to the heads. But I leaned over the edge of the pit and, full of pity, I reached out to them with my open hand. The bony heads seemed to sense the warmth of my blood and, like curious ducks on a pond, pushed their way toward me, letting out a soft whimper all the while. But before the first of them could reach the tips of my fingers, I drew my hand back, revulsed at the thought of their touch, and decided to throw them a few wads of crumpled newspaper. They really did snap it up and even stole the old printed pages out of each other's mouths.

In weary disgust, disheartened and despondent, I turned away from the hideous pit. Would there never be an end to this unholy park? How futile all of my running and hurrying had been! All it did was lead me deeper into confusion. Sick of all the cynical pleasures and contemptuous sensations, and fully expecting to come upon another horror at any moment, I stumbled onto a neglected old highway, which for some reason had not been fortified. The heaps of gravel that lined the way, and even the old broken-down trucks, were overgrown with weeds. Out in the open sun, and still without any hope of progress, it became more and more difficult for me to keep walking. So, it was almost with total indifference that I took note of the shadow cast by a triumphal arch that spanned the road, and which I would pass under in just a few meters, putting it at my back like so many other vulgarities I had confronted in this luna-park. I had hardly given any thought to what tortures might lay in wait beneath this arrogant construct – when suddenly the haze over my senses was lifted and I was looking out through the arch and into the open! Into truly free reality! Life! Streets! The city! They lay open before me, all I had to do was take a few more steps and I was standing right in the middle of a wonderful, modern, big city street! How could this be? How could I have left those ancient grounds so completely behind and plunged right into the bustling lifeline of a glittering city? I saw shops, video arcades, ice cream stands, parking cars, the commotion of free human beings, and even a subway grate . . .

I ran blindly at the triumphal arch in order to make good my final escape. Like a hurdler, having given his all in the last few meters, I would collapse behind the finish line and be born away on the gentle wave of a mundane, fleeting, fraternal street, and released out onto the sea of contemporary, active life. . . . A barrier beam, stronger than steel, struck my outstretched chest. Of course, it didn't hurt, but for a moment it stopped me dead in my tracks. What had happened? I was on the outside – and couldn't move. I advanced – without moving a muscle. I was among human beings – but I was not able to embrace them. I smelled, tasted, saw and heard the street – clothing, gas, waffles, hair, waste heat from department stores. Cars drove by, loudspeakers blared, people laughed, talked, smoked. I did not doubt their presence or this bursting rush of existence for one moment. And it seemed to me that even my strange limitation, my sudden impasse might be nothing more than a fleeting shock, or even a momentary paralysis of joy. If, from time to time, there hadn't been certain peculiarities popping up in this picture of street life, an alienating admixture, which somehow had no place in solid reality. There were, for example, thick white arrows that suddenly started blinking at the back of someone's neck. Mysterious markings were fashioned on passersby, or they appeared to be brightly highlighted. Sudden fading or changes of color over entire facades! And, finally, wasn't that a swarm of winged Greek letters fluttering into the air and across the street, arranging themselves into an alphabetical unit; only one single word appeared in reddish twilight colors: Elysian. I finally had to admit it to myself: once again I had bolted into the bizarre, into another trap, and I was sitting in the depths of this delusion machinery that threatened to slash my senses to bits. It was a kind of holodrome that projected images of complete, three-dimensional corporeal presence to all of my senses, as if I were moving among an entire population of reproduced figures out for an easy, relaxing day at the local shopping center. What kind of cursed being was this lonely and misanthropic despot! The Elysian fields: for him it was nothing more than a street scene. Nothing better, nothing more exalted than big city ruins! Even Eternal Peace got nothing but cynicism! . . . I just couldn't take any more. I lost my senses. I ranted and raved inside my lightbeam cage, I screamed and lashed out at the holodrome. If it wasn't going to give way, then I would have to be the one to succumb! Better a sweet death than a synthetic eternity!

Some lingering bit of beneficent life force, or maybe it was simply an electronic keypad I had accidently touched during my desperate rampage, seemed to take pity on me. When I threw myself howling to the floor, it began to give way, and as if in one of those glassed-in elevators that carry guests down to the sea from their cliff-top hotels, I descended through a cool shaft, and for a few seconds I floated so harmlessly and free into the depths that I felt quite happy. I was deposited on the soft humus floor of a forest, and as I slowly got up, I found myself in surroundings that were dark and strange, but still somehow familiar, somehow even smelling of decency. After so many forays over deceptive ground I was now somewhat clumsy and unsteady on my feet. There was a small iron door that led out of the mountain shaft and into an uninhabited, half-lit hut. I could see that it was outfitted with a variety of technical equipment. High wire winches, switches and meters, plate-ribbed porcelain insulators covered with a heavy coat of dust, and through a narrow, barred, dirt-encrusted window, a faded light illumined it all. But without stopping to rest, I went out to the front of the structure, and when I looked back at the door I saw the sign we are all familiar with, the one with the red high-voltage symbol and the warning "Extreme Danger!" I had come out through a transformer hut, the kind you so often find up in the hills above small villages or townships, at the edge of the forest.

So, here I was, standing on a broad path and seeing the day and the hour, light, weather, flies and spiders, bugs, swallows on a summer evening, and everything alien to me, everything transitory. I could hardly comprehend it. Free! – at last, and safe. Stretching up from the inhabited valley, there was a string of vacation cabins crossing through a broad hollow and running on up to the edge of the forest. The sound of lawnmowers and sprinklers, a delicate riot of radios, Ping-Pong games and barking dogs, how enchanting this nearby, thoroughly decent vacation sounded to my ear! A great relief, an exhausted bliss overcame me, and I let myself drop down at the foot of a tree. I leaned my head against the bark and was hoping to rest before going into the village to look for a place to stay for the night. Too much deception and evil wonder had spoiled my eyes, and I was hardly in any condition to look at my first human being. First, the long spell would have to be broken and vanish. I was intending to make my way down into the settlement, a man oblivious and clear-headed, just the way things took place in the famous Klingsohr fairy-tale, I should be feeling as if: *"No longer was there any stone upon any man's chest, and all burdens had collapsed in on themselves and sunk down to become solid ground . . ."*

I picked up a broken branch and poked the tip into the loose earth. I nudged a green caterpillar with my stick and it curled itself around one end. I could see how little defense its modest endowment of reflexes provided it against this irritant. Was my fate any different from this helpless creature's? A more exulted hiker was poking me, poor earthworm, with his stick. He poked me in the side and I curled up. He knocked me on the head and I curled up. He let me crawl up onto his pole and he lifted me off the ground – I curled up dizzy and scared to death.

I put the creature down on a large milkweed leaf. And when I started digging into the ground again with my little stick, it suddenly got stuck. It was as if it had been snapped at by a set of sharp teeth. The end of the stick was being tugged by something that seemed like biting teeth. The feel of it made me shudder. I pushed a broken-off fern aside, and the discovery I made there, unimaginably horrifying and lovely at one and the same time, brought me to my knees, dumbfounded and touched. In both hands, as one would caress a delicate mushroom, I picked up the enchanting face that had been lying there on the ground. Forehead and cheeks were sprinkled with freckles, and two alert, pleasure-seeking eyes, dark brown and comprehending, looked up at me. It wasn't even a whole head I was holding in my hands, but only the face, and from the ears back it had grown into a clump of earth lying loosely on the ground without any root formation. And because I could pick it up without harming any nerve endings or blood vessels, I held it close to my eyes. I could feel its breath. The warm, pale red lips twitched a little and a firm, gentle voice spoke to me.

"It's me. Yossica."

"Yes," I answered quietly, and stunned. The mail clerk, or the precious little that was left of her – the low-growing, androgynous creature, two-thirds tuber, one-third face, a being that could not move on its own and was nothing more than countenance and voice. Once she noticed how much her looks frightened me, she was embarrassed. Then suddenly, with all of the expression she could muster, she was lustful innocence, bravely seductive from afar, but dissolving in shame once the man beckoned was standing before her. And she turned her large eyes away, this modest gesture only vaguely disguising what she had already worked out in the back of her mind. But this Yossica had no back of a mind, instead only a crumbling clump of earth. What was she, anyway? A plant developed beyond its kind, or a human being reduced to its most charming state? An ennobled fruit or a degenerate transplant?

"What happened, Yossica?"

"It's half as bad as it looks," she replied, "you only have to plant me in a small piece of earth, Leon. And then I will grow back into my old form, all on my own."

"How did it happen?" I whispered urgently.

"It happened when I – oh, if you really want to know, you're going to have to listen to a rather pathetic story. Do you really want to hear it? Well, OK. I'll tell you."

. . .

THE TWO TALENT SCOUTS

After I had been so badly treated on the terrace, and you hadn't really paid any attention to me, I ran through the castle park for some time without knowing where I really wanted to go, just trying to pull myself together. To help calm myself down, I started singing one of my songs. You must know that after all those dismal years at the post office, there is nothing I wanted more than to become a really good songwriter. Actually, that's what I've always wanted to be, and somehow I know it's going to happen. After I had sung a couple of verses, two odd-looking characters suddenly stepped out from behind the bushes. They greeted me very politely, and complimented me on my voice and on the song that I had just been singing. They claimed to be talent scouts, agents and producers, professional managers and concert organizers, and whatever else. But they were not from the same agency, and were in fierce competition with one another, a fact that led me to feel all the more certain that they were genuinely interested in me. So, one of them was the agent Schwarzsicht, and the other was the agent Zuversicht. The first, the melancholy one, was a dissolute prince dressed in a white, moth-eaten cape, torn socks, and stained waistcoat. The other was a tiny little man, who stood, or pranced, on one leg and wore a red shoe on his foot, while the other leg was secured in the belt of his fine silk knickerbockers. So, here they were, Schwarzsicht, a man of some stature, and Zuversicht, a deformed dwarf. But while the former looked miserable, down and out, the latter was not only elegantly dressed, but could dance as lightly and effortlessly as a leaf on the wind.

"If you follow me," the trembling Schwarzsicht was the first to speak, "your talent will be carefully nurtured. Then, once you are mature enough and have made your breakthrough, nothing will stand in your way on your climb to legendary heights. Your art, tested to the limits and lushly developed, will easily outlive any fad."

"Ha!" the dwarf Zuversicht shouted, "just look at him, a seedy old second-hand prince! In the first place, he can't keep the promises he's just made, and even if he could, you wouldn't be satisfied. If you follow him, you will spend a long time waiting in vain for your success, and by the time you get your big break, you'll be so bitter and depressed that you'll only put off your small but loyal following. However, if you listen to me, I will not only make you into a first class singer, but even more than that, I will make you into the leading light, the trendsetter of an entirely new cultural movement."

Prince Schwarzsicht responded with shaky disdain: "You can see for yourself: here's a cripple promoting a health club! Nothing more need be said. But, what if he could do what he says he can? Those trends and movements he's so sold on, not having anything solid to offer, they come and go faster than you can get your next contract. But once you have developed into a true artist, people will keep your songs in their hearts for generations."

"To be brief, I'm offering you a soaring career," the hunchback interrupted gruffly.

"I'm offering you mature art," the clatterer countered.

"I, a mass audience," the tiny voice chimed in.

"I, a truly knowledgeable following," the shaky one added.

"I, worldwide success," little stubby.

"I, enduring fame," old slobber puss.

"All right," I finally said, "you don't have to keep upping the ante for my benefit. Just tell me what I'll have to do to avail myself of your world-class services." I knew I wasn't going to get something for nothing in this business. "Are you expecting to retire on the commission?"

"There are no financial conditions," Prince Schwarzsicht responded, "and we have no intention of entangling you in any unfair business dealings. The one demand we do have is that, as soon as you have made your decision, you commit yourself, in every way and with the most profound conviction, either to my principles or his, and that you remain committed, never wavering, never yielding, come what may, for the rest of your life. And that's all there is to it, right?" The gnome Zuversicht nodded approvingly, and said: "Yes, on this point, and only on this point, we're entirely in agreement." Here, having listened attentively to the unlike pair, and heeding a sudden inspiration, I came up with a proposal of my own. "You have both made me huge promises. If I am going to have to sign up with one or the other of you for the rest of my life, then I'm going to have to find out beforehand if your actions are as good as your words. Let's see if you can give me an example of your extraordinary capabilities, and we'll make a contest of it."

The Zuversicht midget replied: "I'm more than ready. I'm going to show you, right now, how I can cut off my own head, and while it, my head, travels once around the moon, my trunk will tear through the center of the earth, and then both of them, my head from the heavens, and my trunk from the depths, will rejoin here, right before your very eyes, and become whole again."

"And I," the gangly Schwarzsicht rushed to interject, "I will show you, in even less time, how I can incinerate myself from top to bottom, break down into ashes, travel up through the roots of this tree, fall as an acorn to the ground, and here, right at your feet, immediately regenerate my complete self."

I agreed, and before I could bat an eyelash, they had both set to work.

The gnome drew a shiny little sword from behind his back, stretched his right arm out as far as he could, let it fly back and cut off his head. At the same time, where once a threadbare prince had stood, there was nothing but a flaming bush. These bizarre events happened so fast that I didn't know which way to look. I had just caught sight of the Zuversicht trunk, through whose headless neck his blood was flowing back into his body, then, here, the gray ashes of Schwarzsicht curling into the ground, and the head of the troll again, like a satellite roaring through blue infinity, while the trunk bored through the undergrowth down toward the center of the earth.

They had both disappeared. Now, at least I knew that they were serious about their offers and had not merely been making empty promises. And I will decide for the one who first reappears, or so I told myself; still, I will have to see what kind of shape he's in when he gets back.

But in the time that it took me to think these two simple thoughts, they were both back standing in front of me. Plunging down from the heavens, shooting out of the earth, their parts rejoined, and, as promised, the two talent scouts stood side by side, unscathed, but panting hard. Given such a display of super-human speed, it was impossible for me to tell which one of them had been first. They were both looking at me expectantly, wanting to know what my decision would be. And I turned posthaste to the Zuversicht dwarf to tell him that I had decided in his favor, and would indeed follow him. This made him so happy that with one leap into the air he landed in the uppermost branch of the oak tree and started quacking out the little ditty that I would be singing from now on, given that I was pledging my allegiance to his canon.

Schwarzsicht, on the other hand, was so grieved that he fell flat on the ground as if dead. And I was overcome with such pity that I ran to him and explained that I had only pretended to choose the other, his rival, and that I really wanted to follow him. In a flash, Schwarzsicht pulled himself together and was back on his feet, offering me his bony hand.

"If you mean what you say, and you truly are ready to commit yourself to my canon, then all you have to do is duplicate the same trivial feat that I myself performed just now before your very eyes. If you are at one with yourself and know your own mind, nothing can happen to you and you will accomplish it with ease. Then we shall be wholly united in our purpose."

I agreed. I snatched the incendiary device with which I would momentarily set myself aflame. At the same time, but not without giving a wink to the lopsided prince, I beckoned the elegant gnome and he came scampering suspiciously down out of the tree.

Now, Master Zuversicht, too, demanded that I reproduce his daring exercise in order to prove my fealty. Without letting Schwarzsicht catch sight of the transfer, I had him slip me his weapon and then I withdrew a few steps, back away from both of them.

I felt that there was nothing to keep me from swearing allegiance to both tenets at once. And who wouldn't want to be both an immortal artist and a darling of the masses? Why should I be so imprudent as to subordinate and unnaturally restrict my talent, which I knew to be considerable, by committing myself to one single principle? And since I knew myself to be equally devoted to both world views, I was convinced that my body would grow back out of the earth at the same time my head came falling out of the sky. So, before either agent could intervene, I had already put both the sword and the incendiary to their intended uses.

I immediately sensed an enormous thrust, in part propelling me through the earth, in part hurling me into the air; blasted from one principled orbit into the other. But this violent shift of pathways caused my parts to lose a portion of their attractive properties, thus making it impossible for them to rejoin. And so it came to be, that, in the end, only this bit of face grew out of the ground. You see, the two principles had clashed unmercifully and lost their magical powers. Once my journey had ended, and I, having failed to regenerate, lay clinging to the earth, a low-growing weed that would not easily find its way back into the heights, the two talent scouts appeared on the scene and immediately understood that I had shamelessly deceived them both. They could see that, on the one hand, I had truly been initiated, but was, on the other, no longer of any use to either of them. This made them furious, and they tore me out of the ground by the roots behind my ears – I suffered pain like no other pain ever suffered by a mortal being. They threw me in a high arcing trajectory out of the park. And I ended up here, lying among these dissolute ferns of the forest, where I am always having to defend myself against their unwelcome approaches. I bit through the neck of one of them not long ago, so that he'd stop molesting me with his sticky fronds.

. . .

Having heard Yossica's story, I was no less at a loss than before. Still, I was amazed at how anyone in such an unfortunate state could chatter on so cheerfully.

"And now?" I asked, guardedly.

"Well, now – now I sing better than I used to," she answered, "now my voice carries a lot further."

"It's just that you can't perform anywhere," I said, somewhat sarcastically, "not even the post office would take you back now, in your condition there's no way you can sort letters."

"Right. There's always something that isn't quite the way it ought to be." And along with these words, I was met by a wounded, dejected look.

"What's going to happen now?" I asked, soberly. She expressed a shrug of the shoulders through the corners of her mouth. A pause ensued. She lowered her eyes at the exact angle that would suggest she was still able to see below herself.

Obviously, she was thinking: why doesn't he say it himself? I, for my part, was wondering what she really wanted to hear from me. In this way, we traded a few mute presumptions.

"Take me home with you," she finally demanded.

"Home, with me? Just where do you suppose that might be?" I replied, having been frightened into attentiveness.

"Don't you have a garden?"

"Of course not. I don't even have my own apartment." A direct challenge had yet to be made, but still, with the instinctive talkativeness of a loner, I marked my territory. I dumped the entire rubbish of my unregulated existence out in front of her and shoved the passport of a free seeker in her face, the way I had done so many times before in order to escape the stifling grasp of a person or a duty. Revealing myself to get out of something or other, I'd had a lot of practice at that.

But Yossica, the warm face, saw through all of my defensive confessions with hopeful eyes, and my image, that of a new and thoroughly changed man, was valiantly reflected in them.

"All I need is a little patch of earth," she explained, unmoved, "with some good sun and not too much acid in the soil. I could grow back again in an environment like that, with very little attention."

"I own nothing," I replied curtly.

"Then find us something!"

Her left eyebrow rose a little, her lips parted, she took on a slightly ironic air, to which would certainly belong the crossed legs of a woman sitting up straight in her chair, resting lightly on her elbows while her wrist hung loosely from the arm, long slender fingers whose tips were being held and lightly squeezed by the other hand, while the attached forearm lay across the upper thigh.

Would she ever be sitting in front of me this way, so engagingly reserved, in such a properly adaptive posture as she was now communicating?

Yossica really was able to create for me every imaginable physical attraction, even though there was now nothing for me to touch or embrace. Only this foreground of a truly obstinate being!

And now, as it had become impossible to leave it lying here on the forest floor, there was nothing I could do, garden or no garden, body or no body: I grabbed the head formation and tucked it under my arm. It seems, however, that I failed to take appropriate care and Yossica let out a short, sharp cry. I had hurt her! Scared and touched, I lowered my head toward hers and begged her pardon. She granted it with a fleeting smile, even though her eyes were filled with tears.

. . .

Then her deep, melancholy, unwavering gaze met my eyes and quietly filled me. We slowly emerged each from the other's deepest memory. I kissed her on the mouth. I closed my eyes. How long had I been holding them open! Since the procession and the death of the king, in storms of abstinence, under the spell of the terrace, in the midst of the funeral procession, and finally all through my garden exodus, I had not once rested or shaded my eyes.

I closed my eyes . . . I was a man arising – collecting himself; one who after a long, long time arose from his watch, was delivered from inertia, and inexorably attracted by steps not yet taken. No purpose, only face.

THE TOWER

· ·

It turned into a gray, rainy weekend and we decided to stay in the city. In any case, I was on call all day Saturday and wouldn't have been able to leave home until late afternoon. I had to stay by the phone in case some editor came up with an odd photo request for the Monday edition. Of course, the two older ladies who worked for me in the archive were both on duty, but since they had steadfastly refused to be involved with any computer training, they couldn't use the new reference system. And it took them hours to find things by hand. At least, it seemed that way to me once I had gotten used to how much time I was saving and how much more quickly I could now access our inventory. The way they went about their work, following routines of a vanishing era, it seemed to me there was just something very contrary, even defiant, about their "old time." Sometimes they literally got on my nerves, simply because these nerves are much more attuned to electronics than to mechanical things.

· · ·

So, Yossica and I would only have had Sunday for an excursion to the cabin. I would have had a couple of hours of fishing, and she would have fiddled around with a few of her songs, feeling discontent because we still didn't have a sound studio out there. With the time it would have taken to drive there and back, the whole thing would have been a rather short-lived pleasure, and we just decided not to do both, especially since the weather forecast had not been particularly encouraging.

· · ·

I had been in a strange mood for a number of days. Even though I got along well with Yossica and our life together seemed to be showing no signs of fatigue, I occasionally thought about the times I was on my own and saw people and places through more wondering eyes. Every routine intimacy with another person threatens our inherent openness to the world, limits our capability to form a wider variety of contacts. While it may well make us stable and unafraid, it certainly makes us less receptive to new and profound experience.

I was well aware that I had arranged everything around me in order to be able to live the next thirty years in the same way I was living now. Was that the whole point of the great electronic Time-Savings?

Ah, I was simply unhappy. I was staring into emptiness. I nostalgically recalled a certain few mild days at the end of one winter where we are leaving a hotel in a strange city and the low-hanging clouds are being buffeted by the winds, for a while it's drizzling and then it stops, suddenly a blinding flood of light over the city, a silent opening fanfare hastening your stride, passing the little shops by, down old sidestreets among all the busy people, who, with their purposeful gaits, intently running their errands, give the clear impression of all being involved in one, common, agreed-upon task. They know where they are going, they have their time firmly under control. But you are passing through these streets for the first time, brushing up against the hem of their routines, drifting aimlessly along the edges of other people's workday.

. . .

It was Yossica, by the way, who read the announcement to me out of the newspaper that Saturday. It was on the back page, under the heading "Visitors in our City," and in the list of prominent persons who were staying in the first-class hotels. What she read was: "Ossia, German comic, in the Tower-Bellevue Hotel."

For a moment, I felt my heart beat fast, the way it sometimes does when you hear something about a painfully lost love out of your past.

Ossia. This man, to whom I was once so close, in the meantime a famous star, a celebrity, a public figure. My friend, my teacher!

Alfred Weigert. He was still using that name when I knew him. Before he invented the movie character and adopted the Ossia identity for himself. When I was very young, and worked for a short time in the theater, he promoted me with every ounce of his energy. He, the older and respected director, was convinced he had discovered a real talent in me, and maybe I really did have it, but it didn't carry very far, it wasn't even enough for me. But, anyway, when he shot the first Ossia film, I became his assistant, or as everyone liked to put it then: his critical colleague.

Yossica never seemed to get tired of hearing this story, and over the past few years we had gone to see all of his films, several times. With four films, he had actually succeeded in firmly establishing the popularity of his comic hero. And even though he is basically a difficult, eccentric person, he really caught on with a broad spectrum of the public. The Germans had literally devoured the fool in him. They loved the clown of their august ideals. It may seem, in the popular mind, that this is not much of an achievement, especially when it is so easy to rise above the masses, and even the abysmally vacant talking heads who do the evening newscast are celebrities. But there truly is a difference between appearing like a faded specter, an eyewash, in front of the TV camera, and actually gaining admission into people's hearts, into their human mind. And, in my opinion, this is what Ossia had succeeded in doing. Maybe he really was the last comic who was not created by the parody, the total self-reflection of the media, who didn't consist of what had already been filmed before. He had the strength of character and the good fortune to invent an original, a universal but still unmistakably distinct persona whom everyone immediately recognized because they could see themselves in him. He was someone who profoundly belonged to the Germans. In the same way Tati's Monsieur Hulot at first belonged to the French, and Woody Allen above all to New Yorkers, even though they were later to become world famous. This not only required a happy inventiveness, it also required a vulnerable courage, to create a comic figure based entirely on the German conscience, and which did not pander to the cheapest instincts of its fellow citizens, neither relying on crude slapstick, nor hiding behind the smirk of intellectual vacancy. Ossia was also a secret reincarnation straight out of German legend and poetry, a seeker of truth in the "costume of contemporary nerve-endings," a fool of noble will and ideals; one who always carried great mischief inside and often used it to comically threatening effect, while, in the end, consistently finding a way to make his peace with the happier, more life-affirming inclinations of humankind. A pedantic dreamer, a Prussian ne'er-do-well, and no matter what glowing terms the newspapers may have chosen to use; a cross between Parsifal and Paracelsus; "the man with the gentle eyes of a Rilke and the thick skull of Hidalgo," is how our rag once put it.

Of course, it wasn't easy to describe the effect he had. In spite of all the laughter, he really was able to touch people. They followed his peculiar simple-mindedness, they took it to heart when Ossia reached his skinny hand out across a particularly horrifying abyss of history in order to find reconciliation with German figures of noble character with whom we had long ago lost touch, be it a Hagen von Tronje or the faithful Eckart vom Venusberg. When he turned to the heroic Germans this way and became a part of their succession, as a comic, it was often risky baggage he was taking on and delivering with a stagger and a stumble: traditions that had long ago gone dormant in the memory of the nation, and that were being reawakened through the impact of laughter. Not only his outward appearance, but the entire character of his comic presentation often did bring to mind the adventures of the knight as melancholy soul. In *Not as a Couple*, for example, at a party in a penthouse garden, he acted just as if he were in a medieval rose arbor. Or, he would ceremoniously climb into an apple tree in order to pay court to a particular blossom he had fallen madly in love with. In another scene, he freed a lovely young giantess from an airplane hangar where frightened citizens had confined her, stole gallantly away with her without knowing where he was taking her and how he might still unlucky passion for everything about her that was physically large (in *Report for a Committee*). Ossia played the role of the last Knight of the Holy Order of the Individual. No, he not only played this role, he himself, Alfred Weigert, fervently and pigheadedly believed that the strong individual has always been, and will continue to be, able to accomplish almost anything, as long as he allows himself to be guided solely by high ideals and grandiose intention. Bubbling up out of this deep-rooted conviction, out of this powerful fallacy, was the source of his talent. And this source was holy. No one was allowed to pollute it. I learned this lesson the hard way, when I dared to cast the omnipotence of the individual in doubt, and couldn't stop picking at Ossia, the character he had created. I was, as I said, very young back then, just a little past twenty. I had focused my entire attention on the forms, symbols, rituals and institutions, the entire "social mechanism" we are made up of, and that regulates our lives even in its most intimate aspects. For me, the individual had long since fragmented into his constituent parts. I was so stupid as to have believed that it was my role to reveal true "intelligence" to an artist. Today, it would be easy for me to laugh about it. If there weren't also good reason for me to be ashamed. Alfred's influence was important right from the beginning, but my arrogant views did a lot to keep me from seeing that. I had been very skeptical about Ossia's mission as a German comic. And what could he have needed more during those hard times, in the beginning, than someone who believed in him? At the time, I was a very unhappy person, hanging around the theater, vacillating, dissatisfied with everything and much too taken with my own critical views. My first attempt at directing, while it had not been a failure, met with noticeably little response. I didn't want to stay in the theater. I told myself that it didn't fulfill my expectations and demands. In truth, I had let myself be thoroughly intimidated by the two actresses I had been working with and it had scared me off for good. Their merciless games, their bloody instinct for the jugular, the way they attacked me instead of their roles, made it obvious to me that I was not the right man for this appallingly vain and erratic business. My true interest in people and their relationships suffered irreparable damage on that stage. All the pretense and show got in my way. By the way, the two wildcats were – at first, Yossica couldn't believe that I had worked with such famous people when I was so young! – Pat Kurzrok and Margarethe Wirth, the two stars who worked in almost all of the Ossia films, the child-woman and the lady, the brash bigmouth and the beauty, the kind of female team that had more or less become a trademark feature of the gaunt hero's films and surrounded him with a strange aura of reluctant erotic power. They had even been in the first film, *Not as a Couple*, which I had worked on as well. It was a somewhat theatrical comedy in which Ossia liberated his world from a mysterious and contagious emotional illness, the so-called pair-dread, which plagued contemporary, vulnerable man and kept him from ever being alone with only *one* other person. Whenever there was the danger of such a naked vis-à-vis, he either took flight or made elaborate arrangements for security and a chaperon. Even in the development of certain intimate events, the presence of a virtuous third person became essential. Later, especially in *Montanus*, Pat and Mag created an entrancing pair, in what was perhaps his most beautiful film. I had introduced him to the material for this film early on, and he had picked it up again and really made something of it, long after our fight. He played a forklift driver in a cold storage locker who becomes the founder of a very worldly revival movement, and accompanied by his two prophetesses, Priscilla and Maximilla, his "disciples of love," he makes a pilgrimage, or something more like a road tour, through our sloshed and apathetic society. The sequence at the end of this film was truly unforgettable for anyone who saw it: an entire field full of tall sunflowers, standing in formation and at attention, march out at Ossia's command, and, like a true army of the sun, head into the dark wasteland of the city . . .

. . .

Like many others of his famous colleagues, he came relatively late to the character and role that made him famous, and then only after much preliminary study and many lengthy detours. At the time, he still thought it was impossible for a man to be seriously funny before turning forty. And that was also about the same age at which he felt that his stage career had come to an end, and he turned himself into a comedic character. As I have already mentioned, he spent a lot of time playing around with his character, there were innumerable false starts. And, at this point, he finally wanted to put everything on the line, and that is what kept driving him. Not just to be the director, the interpreter, but also author, star, filmmaker, in short, the one and only source of everything. His first production was an unexpectedly big hit at the box office, and from then on he was able to get all of the funding he needed to keep working, just as he had always wanted. He was able to produce everything he planned and had been preparing for so long, one elaborate project after the other. Over a period of ten years, he was able to produce six big films, which made the Ossia role, the outsider-German, the heroic fool, an almost legendary figure. However, he did not appear in his two last films, and neither of them was a success. They weren't very funny either, and his public was disappointed. He had suddenly felt an overwhelming urge to try something entirely new – using barely recognizable plots and moving the story forward in fragmented sequences – without seeing that this was putting him on the well-worn road toward a sterile modernism. *Remembering Till* and *Klingsohr*, especially, were filled with all kinds of difficult and ponderous nonsense, propagating a kind of mean world-weariness that could never have been part of his earlier work. The captivating fantasy and the easygoing pace were sorely missed in these last two films, as was Ossia himself, the hero, the central and defining character.

A good twelve years older than I am, he'd have to be about fifty now. For a while, there had been some talk about a jubilee production long in the works, a film that would overshadow everything the master had yet achieved. There were just a few minor financial glitches that were delaying the start of filming for a couple of weeks. This was the rumor that had been floating around in the press for about a year and a half, and I think we can assume that the production company itself had been leaking the stories in order to raise expectations and keep public interest alive.

· · ·

When Yossica read in the paper that Ossia was in town, she couldn't get it out of her mind and kept suggesting that we stop by and see him, if "only" to say hello.

But somehow the idea of meeting him after such a long time didn't quite sit right with me. Would there be anything left of my Alfred Weigert? So much success and the adoration of millions don't leave a person unchanged, they shape him, relentlessly, according to their own dictates. Could people like us even get through to him? Especially someone like me, who had wronged him so grievously. Believing firmly in himself and others, he had grabbed the brass ring. I, on the other hand, had doubted him and others, and myself above all, had always withdrawn from my talents and aspirations, finally immersing myself in essentially meaningless work in a trivial enterprise. Of course, I had a job, but it could hardly be called a career. I had not been lazy, but mine had been one long passage through a maze. Through all my searching and searching I had certainly gained experience, but before I could put it all together I had spent my best energies. And that's why I was ashamed to meet him face to face. He had been my teacher. I had done him no honor.

· · ·

But Yossica really wanted to meet him, the famous man. So, we used my nonstandby Sunday, another cloudy day when the city air was particularly sultry, to make an outing to the Tower-Bellevue.

This much discussed masterpiece of postmodern hotel architecture was in itself worth a visit, this national luxury tower that had already been home to so many prominent guests, and where meetings of profound import had taken place. In addition to normal hotel quarters, there was also a number of larger and smaller apartments available to guests in residence. Most of these were business people from abroad, wandering evangelists, airline pilots, and television personalities, as well as a few lonesome rich people who liked company, especially of a better sort. The tower was located about fifteen kilometers north of the city and more or less formed the center of a future megalopolis already on the drawing boards, and the tower was a landmark rising high above the not yet existent metropolis, belonging to an urban area slowly consolidating on both the left and the right banks of the Rhine. We were somewhat startled to find that immediately upon entering the beltway around the city, we were drawn into the wake of this new, rapidly expanding megacenter. We, inhabitants of the urban core, now found ourselves rushing like remote suburbanites toward the inner reaches of the shadow city. The design and the features of the entire complex were already so present that, as we passed through undeveloped fields, small factories, and picked-over forests, we couldn't help imagining ourselves driving along a boulevard lined with shops, banks, apartment buildings, and parks. This intense vision of a new city was generated solely by the mighty tower at the far end of the boulevard; far and wide it was the only structure to be seen, its radiance almost regal along the empty streets, which all led its way. But the streets also seemed like assembly lines, like an expansive apparatus constructed for the purpose of developing and settling a city. But the unquestioned center, defined by the strangely shimmering column, enveloped all of the consolidating areas and forced them to turn toward a new inner space, to a new center. It was a tower of pink granite sheathed in bronze-colored glass; a slender construct, rising a good one hundred and fifty meters into the air, flowing into a slightly widened, pedestal-like base, which resembled the lower trunk of a tree. This building had nothing in common with the bulky rectangles, the lifeless corn-flake boxes of an earlier high-rise era. Everyone who saw this tower was heartened. It seemed enchantingly light and mingled delicately with the sky. It played with every ray of light; picking up the faintest celestial shimmer and creating something new. There was even something sublime about it, though not at all like the solemnly pointed finger of a church. Still, it would be difficult to imagine any other contemporary, secular building with a spiritual luminescence anything like this. The tall tower seemed immovable, while consisting of nothing more than thousandfold refracted light, immovable like the faith that had constructed it; a cathedral of luxury and anonymity, it was as if our crude affluence had finally found inspired form.

. . .

Yossica and I entered the tower, each of us through one of the four revolving glass doors that stood across the front entrance. Reflexively, we each continued along our own separate way as if we didn't even belong together. It was so large and wondrous, the mesmerizing echoes of the lobby took each of us into its spell. We were met by a cool stream of cessation and leisure, it was like stepping onto the coast of another time, of a brilliant, perpetual sleepiness. It was about midday and there were very few people to be seen. They were lost in the broad expanses of the lounge and the reception area, they were swallowed up by white leather easy chairs, almost blinded by so much artificial clarity, or they relaxed in the glittering distance down in the garden of the atrium, which could be reached from the lobby along an elongated marble stairway. There was a glass-covered piazza, a complete little city with boutiques and shopping arcades, sauna, cinema, restaurants and a travel agency. The square was enclosed by bamboo, which shot out of the ground several meters high, and from its midst an exuberant waterfall dropped over a cliff, rumbling but not thunderously. Not far away was a frozen pond that was used as an ice-skating rink. This was "Tower City." Here, all of the walls reached way over anyone's head and were covered with honey-colored marble, rivers of polished brass flowed along banisters and lamps, and illuminated bands of cut glass encompassed fountains and long flower beds containing bizarre, chalk white bouquets.

Once I had slowly taken in this cool and peaceful, this posh and accursed place, it also became clear to me why Ossia had chosen it, of all places, as his retreat. Here, you were in a perpetually semi-dormant time-space, where moments expanded without bounds, similar to what we had seen in his last two films when the camera's gaze clung to a sensory detail until it began to "speak," until the gaze became a scene. He had shown us this physical mysticism in many pictures, he almost preached it. Something similar was happening in this environment, more or less of its own accord. The languid scene, the magnifying glass of time, generated its own indigenous form of perception. In the empty, lily-white Nobel restaurant, a young woman wearing a flowered, strapless dress was sitting alone at her table. She was pouring wine, sip by sip, from a bottle into her glass, and quickly drinking up. She sat with her back to the front window, bent over in a sad posture, her fore-arms folded over her thighs. But in front of her, like a raptor keeping watch over his prey, the waiter was standing perfectly straight, a handsome boy with his white apron tied around his middle and his serving cloth held in both hands at his back. With a blank and empty gaze, he looked out through the tall window into the garden of the atrium, which was itself encased in glass. The one staring out and the one leaning toward him, not a single word between them, perhaps nothing, never anything in the least. Only in *form* one fate, in attitude a distorted pair. These were looks I could easily have collected for Ossia.

At the front desk, we had to ask for the manager personally, as no other employees had the authority to so much as put through a phone call from an unannounced visitor to the artist. They kept referring to him as "the artist," because it was difficult to say "Mr. Ossia," and "Ossia," as he was known to the entire rest of the world, would have seemed too familiar and hardly indicative of the kind of respect due. No, of course, we had nothing to show him, no appointment, no invitation or references. The front desk manager, a rather pudgy South American, hastily took our mea-sure and even took his glasses off his nose. It was clear to me that there was nothing we could do. He stood there stolidly, his arms folded across his chest, and glanced regretfully at his guest list. He couldn't even put a call through for us. All of this simply served to confirm my suspicion that it had become impossible to approach Ossia like any ordinary mortal. I would have turned around and left immediately, but Yossica was adamant. She leaned over the desk, somewhat casually in the direction of the manager, and began to tell, as well as invent, our story, the histo-ry of a long friendship and work together. But all that effort resulted in nothing more than the little round man putting his glasses back on in order to look down the front of Yossica's blouse, and pushing the frames up with an ugly curl of his nose; it looked as if he were trying to hide his lecherous intent behind a grimace. But in the end, Yossica too got nothing more than a shrug of the shoulders. He had his explicit instructions from the artist . . .

At this moment we were oddly interrupted. One of the revolv-ing doors was shoveling a pack of willowy young women into the lobby. They could easily have been taken for expensive mannequins if they hadn't all been wearing the same bright pink gown with a broad hood across the back. There were twelve of them in all, two of them black. As they approached us they formed a flying wedge, in the shape of a plowshare, and blithely cut their unswerving way through the lobby. Quietly singing a monotone melody, they had the air of something a little like a religious revival. They passed right by the reception desk and headed directly for the bank of elevators. At this point, an obsequious unrest broke out among the porters. Our front desk manager left us abruptly and made a dash for the telephone exchange. Apparently, someone was to be notified of the arrival of these beauties, or possibly warned at the very last minute. To me, however, they seemed like the vestal virgins of the tower, like temple maidens. Yossica and I followed them without hesitation, simply mixing in among them as they distributed themselves among the elevators. We found ourselves standing with four of them in one of the transparent capsules that moved freely up and down the inner wall of the tower. They sang on, subdued, but without interruption. In their blissful ecstasy, they were completely and utterly inaccessible. I tried to get through to one of them, anyway, as it seemed to me that the girls knew their way around the tower and were probably on their way up to a floor for special guests. The Creole I asked about Ossia simply nodded and smiled sweetly while whispering a ribbon of her endless song into my ear. But she didn't answer. I had long ago lost all interest in continuing the search for my well-shielded, all too famous friend, but unfortunately Yossica was not about to ease off. When the elevator stopped at the thirty-seventh floor, we were received by two burly gentlemen from hotel security. Inconspicuously, but with resolute force, they pushed the singing maidens back into the cabin, after politely allowing us to disembark. The detained women defended themselves with ever louder voices, and swelling song. It came to a slight tussle between the security personnel and the unsuffered vestal virgins, or whoever they might be, but just shortly before the elevator door closed and they were about to descend again, the creole called out to us: "Four-O-One!" At first I thought she meant that I should call this number immediately in order to get them some help, or to inform somebody, but where, and about what? But then it occurred to me that at the very last moment they had given us the number of Ossia's apartment. As it turned out, 401 was on the very floor we had just reached, the one where the cheerful women were not allowed. From the outside, the doors of the residences looked no different from any other hotel door, except that the interval between them was greater, and they were equipped with doorbells. At the end of a long hallway finished with soundproof tiles, we suddenly found ourselves standing in front of 401. My mouth went dry, and my heart was in my throat. Was it like me to break through the security screen erected to protect an important personage, a popular public figure, from thoughtless intruders? Should I be ignoring all common decency just so Yossica can satisfy her curiosity? I looked at her; a bit too displeased, perhaps, she guessed what I was thinking. She shrugged her shoulders. All right, if you really don't want to . . . I rang the doorbell. An electric door opener responded immediately. It was as if the inhabitant were anxiously awaiting someone's arrival. We entered a generously proportioned vestibule, illuminated by sharp cut crystal chandeliers. A passageway led between two tall pillars, mirrored on all four sides, over flat steps and down into a sunken oval living space carpeted in moss green. Delicate ivy tendrils clung to the white walls, an abstract light tree made of stainless steel stood on a glass pedestal in which gold fish swam, and next to the salmon-pink leather couch there was a luxuriant arrangement of pampas grass and bundles of wheat. It was a mix of hothouse style and techno-design similar to what we had already seen downstairs in the atrium of the hotel. The only difference was that here there was a net of personal disarray cast all across the cold splendor. The entire window wall was covered with a pale translucent trompe l'oeil; a golf course with an oceanfront view.

. . .

"Pat?" Ossia yelled from the next room.

So, he was waiting for her. The door was slightly ajar and I pushed it open. Ossia was sitting up in bed wearing his bathrobe; he was surrounded by innumerable scraps of notepaper, sketches, photos, and newspaper clippings. He had a little writing desk in front of him, the kind that bedridden patients use. The blinds had been pulled down and the closet doors were all wide open. I believe that this was the first time in my life that I had ever looked into a face of a man scared to death. He seemed to think we were kidnappers or hostage-takers. And I, too, was profoundly shocked by the way he looked, and Yossica hid shyly behind my back. "This is why he no longer appeared in any of his films!" was the first thought to shoot through my mind. It was almost as bad as seeing a very close friend who had been horribly maimed in an accident. That man on the bed, lying awkwardly among his pillows, was barely recognizable as the same man who had once invented and played the gaunt ascetic-clown. This was an obese monster. A colossus with a waterlogged face, fatty chin, half-bald head, with long thin strands of hair sticking to the nape of his sweaty neck, with tiny eyes behind wrinkled bulges. This Ossia was so malformed that he could no longer fit into his character. That starkly comic figure known by the name of Ossia simply no longer existed. But how in all the world could a narrow, birdlike head have swelled into this balloon skull? How had a sharp-boned skeleton ever come by such a bloated belly? Was he sick or was he trying to escape his epiderm?

"It's me. Leon," I said in a husky voice.

"Well?" he asked timidly.

It was embarrassing to me in front of Yossica that he didn't recognize me.

"Leon Pracht. I was your assistant, once."

"Aha." He looked around quickly, still distrustful and suspicious, never looking directly at me. "When was that?"

"When you were shooting *Not as a Couple*."

"Hmm," Ossia roared. "Where have you been keeping yourself all this time, my boy?"

I had to laugh. The jovial inquiry, made so faintheartedly, almost wimpishly, produced a genuinely comic effect. When I laughed he immediately became friendly. Upon hearing such tones he was wide awake. You could literally see the show animal in him stir and chase off the yellow belly. He sat up in his pillows and turned a lens our way, looking to see if the time for an amusing little number had yet arrived.

"My God, Leon! I didn't recognize you at first" – and I genuinely doubted that he had done so in the meantime! – "a lot of people come up here. Mostly crazies. Or worse. They walk right in and say: 'I just wanted to let you know . . .' Know? Know what? I ask. They don't know. They gawk around the room. Know what about whom? They don't know . . ."

Now Ossia began to set his massive body in motion. He did an impression of his annoying visitors. And as he did he was obviously taking pains to display the comic advantages of his new, weighty figure. Still, it was painful for me to see how he was hiding behind his performance in order to avoid having to answer any questions about the Ossia we had come to find.

"Or they come in and say: 'Eh, I think eh I believe eh it seems to me, I just wanted to say that for me, in the final analysis your films don't really represent a genuine search for identity.' Or they come in and say: 'I am someone who would like to ask you a couple of questions. Brief questions. North/South?' – Don't know. – 'East/ West?' – Don't know. – 'Peace, microelectronics, sex and significance?' – Don't know. – 'But especially you and the burning questions of our time . . .' – Listen! Why in the hell are you asking me? Do you think I'm some damned political convention? I-do-not-know. Or they come in and I say: Get the hell out of here! But they just stand there and grin. – Didn't I make myself clear?! – They grin, they shake their index finger in the air, and say: 'Oh, I can see right through this little act. I see right through it!' What act? I'm not acting. And if you please, I would like to be left alone. – They say: 'I understand you very well. I understand exactly what you mean' – and don't move an inch. Those are the psychological ones. They rest their hands on their hips and seesaw back and forth on their heels. They know for certain that we always want the exact opposite of what we say we want . . ."

Now, Ossia was riding a wave. Yossica laughed the way she laughed when she was at the movies. She even applauded. Suddenly the doorbell rang. Ossia, who had gotten up out of bed in order to perform, now sank back into his pillows, pushed the button for the door opener and began to dig vigorously around in his notes. For a moment he reminded me of John Gielgud, playing the old writer in Resnais's *Providence*, lying sleepless on his bed, drinking chablis without pause and babbling on about his rowdy family.

Pat Kurzrok entered the room. She was wearing jeans and a plaid flannel shirt. Her hair had grown long and she was wearing it tied back at the nape of neck. She was smaller and more graceful than I remembered her. Pat, even back then, fifteen years ago, was more popular than Margarethe, who was more beautiful, but also more melancholy. In the meantime, Kurzrok had become the darling of the masses. Loved by millions, there was also something of the millions in her; she radiated a mysterious universality. She threw a pile of fresh towels in Ossia's direction and left. Without a word, without so much as deigning to look our way.

I asked if Pat was living here in the tower, and Ossia nodded.

"Sometimes she works somewhere else, on the outside. Sometimes in television, sometimes on tour with a theater company. But she always comes back. She comes back, has diarrhea for days, throws up and claims that she hears voices as long as she's here with me. She loses ten pounds, and then she disappears again. Recovers from us, and then misses us like crazy. That's the way it happens every time. I really have to do something for her. It's about time that I did another film with her."

At this moment, a kind of paralysis seemed to overcome him. He slipped down off the pillows and lay flat on his back. He stared up at the ceiling and I heard him quietly moaning. "What can this be? What does it mean? What can it possibly be?" He didn't seem to be able to move. I asked him if there was anything we could do to help. If maybe we shouldn't go?

"Leon Pracht," Ossia whispered and looked over at me out of his stiff posture. "Sounds like the name of someone in a novel by Julien Green. Are you a Catholic Jew, or something?"

"No," I said, embarrassed.

"No. A child of reconciliation, maybe?"

In the meantime, I had become convinced that he really did recognize me. He knew exactly who I was. And he wanted to avoid any discussion of the past, no matter what. But this might have had something to do with Yossica. He appeared not to have taken any notice of her at all. He edited her out and turned his complete attention toward me, toward someone he knew. That pained me for her sake, and it was very impolite of the artist. I should have prepared her for this. I knew how inhibited he was around women he wasn't working with. Apart from that, he fumbled around like a recalcitrant little boy. But the effect was very insulting.

"Everyone's in the tower," Ossia murmured, "everyone living under one roof. Now Walther's here too." Walther was his camera man. "And slowly, all of them'll come crawling out of their stuffy little living nooks, their failed marriages, friends, close acquaintances, all of the biographical leading lights. At least the ones who can afford it, the ones who made something of themselves, they'll move in here, settle in. They'll come crawling from every era and every direction, my doctors, my actors, my sports friends, the author of children's books, my ophthalmologist, my old piano teacher, my gas station attendant, the countess Meerapfel and the cook from the Schwanenhof. Everyone under one roof. Squeeze a little closer together! The ones who are still there: a little closer together. Only a few people left . . ."

He was just fantasizing, as if he had to assure himself of the remaining mobility of his brain, his mouth, and his jawbones. Finally the attack appeared to ease up a bit. He lay both hands, right and left, on top of the loose scraps of notepaper and sketches.

"Every story," Ossia explained, "is an outrageous incursion into the creative disorder of life's abundance. Everything I have to say is: a pile of stuff. The sole form of expression that approaches truth: a pile of stuff."

Then, in consternation, he quickly added: "I have to do something for Pat or she'll run away from me."

"And what about Margarethe? Does she live here too?" I wanted to know.

"No. She got married. To a leather goods magnate. She stopped working a long time ago." He pulled a thick bound album, a sketchbook, out from under the bed and untied the strings. "Here I have everything I need." The volume was stuffed full of slips of paper and photos, enhanced with countless drawings and notations.

"Woman as a comic figure. The attractive fool. Sense of form, irresolute, quick. On her own. Mortgage banker or real estate agent. The beauty and the inherent defiance of things. The slapstick devil. Elementary masculine spirit out for revenge because she's so beautiful and independent. The ideal figure and swarms of realistic mosquitoes. The female comic must touch our frightened inner child, who only wants to see adults behaving in a safe and 'noble' way. Adults must not fall, must never be drunk, must never engage in sexual intercourse. Just as in those we look to for protection, the objects of our desire must also exhibit moderation in their daily lives. If his lover stumbles, a man's inner child will be frightened. We're going to have to make our lovely mama trip up again, Leon."

Here, he read a few episodes from his collection out loud, sketches for Pat as a comic figure. If I understood him correctly, the whole thing was a kind of faun's journey through a house of horror, and the "love interest" kept being frightened and molested from all sides. An earnest, sensual heart in the midst of an utterly hopeless world full of the trickery and deceit of erotic stupefaction. Human beings who only satisfied one another frailly, and offered up their prematurely aged sexuality the way others might blow paper party favors in your face. Against this background, Pat appeared as a mythical figure from an heroic age of desire. But everything she touched in her burning desire, man or woman, was transformed into an androgynous being in her arms, into an unattainable, mounted sexual hybrid. For the time being, it was nothing but a loosely organized list of encounters floating around in Ossia's head. Before it could be turned into a really good film, there would have to be a succinct story line and the requisite, "compelling" opportunities for laughter. When he asked me if I could imagine Pat in a fantastic fabrication of this sort, I encouraged him at first and told him I liked the idea and the basic elements of the material, and singled out a number of items I found particularly worthy of praise. But then I also raised the concern that the entire thing might not turn out to be very funny at all.

"It'll be funny when I make it that way," he answered brusquely. "Once I'm completely convinced about something, and I make it, it'll be funny. But I'm not completely convinced. This isn't really anything for Pat. She won't be able to do it. She isn't the type I need for this role. Margarethe would be a lot better. But she's not really quick enough. A comic woman has to be able to be fast. The whole thing is a greedy ruin. It devours every improvement. Nothing going to come of it. I should just drop it."

I suddenly saw how miserable and desperate this comic had truly become. A kind of Howard Hughes, whose wealth is measured in plans, hidden and protected in his secret power center, ruling over a ghostly imperium of ideas and sketches, treatments, gags and storyboards; however, it was a world that was being continually threatened by enormous indecision, by the malady of free choice and vacillation. The artist had become one with the silence of his unformed subject matter: Plans, nothing but plans.

． ． ．

Again a burst from the doorbell. A certain Carmela came waltzing in, a rather brightly painted young woman with a platinum blond pageboy, mustard-colored spots on her cheekbones, and wearing pink overalls. She bowed and clapped in time to her own chant: "Os-sia! Os-sia! Get-up! Get-out!" She immediately began organizing things, opening the blinds, closing the closet doors, plumping up pillows, and, all in all, treating the artist as if he were some little truant. Amazingly enough, Ossia went along with all of it, though he did slow her down and allow as how she had already had an adequate impact on arrangements in his bedroom.

"You promised me that we'd go to the movies, and go downtown to buy a parakeet."

"Carmela, please, be reasonable," the fat man grumbled, "I never go into the city. You know that. Entire streets blocked off, houses surrounded by police, exits bricked up, burning wrecks everywhere, dump trucks overturned, torn-up pavement, looted stores, caps and masks torn to pieces, an explosive device in every fire extinguisher, the air polluted with smoke and tear gas, the helicopters circling like vultures over the carcass of the city, and government troops running all over pet shops – do you seriously believe we're going to be able to buy a parakeet in the city?"

"But you promised me," the slender woman whined and stamped her foot. All of a sudden, she was a pouting child, even though she had made her entrance as a mama intending to shoo her lazy darling out from under the covers. I was shocked at this capricious, affected behavior and it seemed to me to be almost emotionally disturbed. After a brief back and forth, in which Ossia reaffirmed his determination not to get up, and, under no circumstances, to leave the tower, the chic little creature broke out in a stream of muffled tears and her cool painted face twisted into an ugly little-girl grimace. She ran out of Ossia's room, totally dazed. I didn't understand what had happened. How could such a trivial incident drive a grown human being to such bitter and genuine despair?

"It is true," Ossia said, having noticed my discomfort, "there seems to be some kind of strange emotional fad, or whatever you want to call it, making its way around the tower. It seems to me that everyone's becoming increasingly childish. Not long ago, five of them over there were sitting around my table for hours, reciting some kind of 'eeny meeny miney mo' rhyme. They sang lullabies. Played hide-and-seek and pin-the-tail-on-the-donkey. And they kept doing it until they were all transported into a misty sense of well-being. Of course, I don't know what's happening on the outside, but I can imagine that in those areas where there is no convincing blueprint for the future, where optimism and energy are lacking, such abrupt regression into the infantile is almost inevitable. And especially here, where practically nothing is happening and endless waiting dominates. These people are all clinging to me, and they're spoiling my work atmosphere. They don't think Ossia is funny at all. The only time these infantile souls can laugh is when one of them sticks his tongue out, or looks cross-eyed at the tip of his nose." I asked him if Carmela was an actress. "Huh. Some kind of groupie. The proverbial girlfriend of the dolly operator, or something like that. But she's poison to me. Some women you sleep with and afterward there's a kind of revulsion that spreads through your veins like a sexual disease. And then you can't do it with anyone any more."

I looked at Yossica somewhat embarrassed. I felt it was very inappropriate for him to be making jokes man to man, as if she weren't even here.

"No, she's not for me," he continued, "but she might be okay for Houdebich. I'll send her to him in the asylum for a little incision!"

Finally, he even seemed silly to himself and giggled in little convulsions. Claus Houde – he referred to him sarcastically by his legal name – was a fellow comic who had managed to make a number of rather successful films over the past few years. After having worked in Ossia's shadow for a good long time, he had even succeeded in surpassing him in the public's favor – in part, of course, because there had been no film *with* Ossia for so long. But one day, a tragic event took place that initially disrupted his career. Apparently in a fit of emotional disorientation, he had attacked his life's companion with a garden shears and badly wounded her. The newspapers – especially the ones in our area – made this unfortunate story their own and had spent an inordinate amount of time snooping around for a deeper meaning. Ossia took the opportunity to ridicule his colleague's sensational fame, and he was certainly not free of petty envy when he remarked that the comic's art alone would never have been enough to arouse such great public interest. "Did you read what one of them wrote? 'The darkness falling over this man's soul will close the curtain on German comedy in the twentieth century!' Houdebich, him of all people! A cheap clown. A second-rate mask. That's all we need, to have a fathead like that setting the standards. I'll tell you something: he was not in the least bit crazy. He had been wanting to slit his wife open for a long time. That was Houdebich in one of his saner moments . . . I saw them together, I know the two of them. She built up her regime of terror over the years. And the more famous he got, the worse it became. There was nowhere he could go. There wasn't a damn thing he could do. He couldn't even curl the tips of his moustache without her swatting him across the paws. It's just like your wife trying to keep you from masturbating. But that's how things were for poor Houdebich – the German Wonderface." Ossia was really back in form again, and was just about ready to regale us with a series of Houdebich vignettes. But it was already late afternoon, and I told him that it was about time that we were on our way. But, in the end, I couldn't help drawing his attention to Yossica. I told him about her unusual evolution, her talent as a songwriter, and that she was just about to enjoy her first solid successes. I also told him that she was the one who convinced me to make this visit, and she knew all of his films and was always running off to see one. But none of this helped. He simply couldn't bring himself to look her straight in the eye. A brief nod, a tired and indulged thank-you was all he managed to spare for her.

We had already taken our leave and were climbing through the sunken living room crater when he called out to me again.

"Believe me, Leon, I want to do something. I absolutely have to and I want to. But I need someone to talk to. I've got too much stuff. Too much. I have to find the right material, the only possible material, do you understand? Why won't you try coming back to work with me again?"

He looked at me with the burdens of the world in his eyes. Suddenly, under this gaze, I was again standing there as the young man who once had to stand his own ground, but failed. But now my position was totally different. He was placing a trust in me that I had not sought. And this was not a look of confident, principled inquiry, but one of very wounded and timorous expectation. Still, I felt myself immediately transported back to the time of my apprenticeship. I gave an indefinite answer. I wanted to have a chance to think it over. I still had my work in the photo archive, and it was steady work. Ossia insisted that we make arrangements to meet again. He hadn't even shown me his best material . . .

On the way home, I kept trying to get beyond the existing Ossia and back to the skinny beanpole of a hero I knew from his films. But my memory of that character was entirely blocked by the corpulent and bloated inhabitant of the tower, the captive colossus in restless repose on his bed, attempting to organize a shapeless, possibly intractable substance, to extract form from a flight of fantasy. I took one hand from the steering wheel and reached for Yossica's arm.

"Well, what did you think of Ossia?" I assumed that this personal encounter with the man she so admired must have been disappointing and offensive.

"I think he's a degenerate and very real," she answered.

"What do you mean by 'degenerate'? Is it something superficial, his physical appearance?"

"Yes. But I also mean his entire lifestyle. This hotel, the luxury, the people around him. And most of all, I think he's a misanthrope. There wasn't any sign of that before in his films."

"Oh, I think there was. Ossia, the comic character, as eccentric as it was, entwined around a higher ideal, was always attributing false and indolent conventions to his milieu. He never made any attempt to respect the poor and piteous existence of his fellow man, but was always trying to set himself above everyone else. Of course, someone like this isn't necessarily a degenerate example of his kind."

"But there's nothing particularly good about a misanthrope!"

"No. There isn't. But somehow we seem to need them. You'll find all sorts of them hiding behind their comic masks. They're all there: hypochondriacs and depressives, some hate the state and some hate civilization, and let's not forget the ones who hate women. But worst of all are the ones who hate themselves. The best of them are born suicidals, who, thank God, usually choose to flee from themselves before taking the final step."

"And you think that a misanthrope like that can really be a darling of the masses? He must feel that all the adoration and respect he gets is just simply proof of how ignorant and crude his public really is, and in the end he'll be hating himself most of all."

"Oh, don't believe that," I said, amused at her circuitous logic, "Ossia is quite happy with just about anyone who thinks he's funny. The more who do, the better. Still, he is the idol of all the clandestine misanthropes, who, together, make up his public. This society only dreams antisocial dreams. About the fiercely eccentric, the noble, but totally outrageous loner. Then, when a whole theater full of fans laughs as one at this character, he's actually created a community, uniting all the little misanthrope wannabe's with their own kind."

"You think laughing is really all that compassionate? I think that a full, throaty laugh is always combative and aggressive. A smile is the only thing we really have to give our fellow man. It was given to us to make strangers feel conciliatory. But, it seems to me that a big laugh is nothing more than ugly arrogance, and a fundamentally different impulse from smiling. Our language should be able to express the difference more clearly."

"But just now, you yourself were laughing out loud at Ossia. He certainly wouldn't have thought it any friendlier of you if you had only smiled. And there's another point we can't forget. You just met a rather pathetic, venomous, and vain man, where you were probably expecting to encounter a kind and generous genius. But you shouldn't really allow yourself to think any less of him. Above all, he's an artist, and he's achieving a higher level of grace than the polite, socially correct kindness of the man on the street ever does. But I'm still worried about how eccentric he's gotten, both about his own character and about all of the work he's done up until now. Is it because the character has somehow gotten away from him, because of illness or the good life or just weariness, so much so that he no longer has the confidence to appear on the screen? Or maybe it's the other way around, and his awkward disfigurement was the result of sheer fright at the gigantic pharynx of the broad masses? It would be impossible for us to imagine what an immense burden that is.

"An artist with a small following may well allow himself to become narrower, and ever more esoteric, and his fans will simply become all the more adoring. But popularity is a large and inconstant treasure, and a movie comic, an almost legendary figure, is always under enormous pressure, he belongs to millions, he has to please them – or go down. But what Ossia's trying to do now, and what he has actually done in two unsuccessful films, looks to me like a desperate guerilla action against the legions of reigning expectations, against the regime of a taste he himself introduced, and then established, with the consent of the masses. Now, what's looked upon as breaking new ground is not really a creative stimulus. It's nothing more than an attempt to elude the danger of copying yourself. And this kind of escape action will never lead to a good film. What he refers to as his 'new form' – complex and open, radical and fragmentary – is actually the ruins of his old form. No one can credibly be both gardener and mole in the same garden. In that case, I prefer someone who repeats himself honorably, rather than subversively infiltrating his own works and blowing them to bits. It seems to me that once someone has enjoyed the favor of the broad public, he can never be an outsider again. There is no way back to the noble few. Connoisseurs, snobs, and cultists won't pay any attention to him in any case. The new, the spray of sparks, the glittering splinters, unchecked moments – even in great abundance they are nothing more than a brief image of the moment. In the final analysis, we experience a thousand disconnected moments as fleetingly as one, single moment. The sum of infinitely many glimpses without a story, without a plot, without a climax, is striving toward a memory span of a value approaching zero, and can barely be differentiated from a prompt and immediate forget response. As far as I am concerned, contemporary aesthetic extremes of any sort are bound to have a similarly brief life span, especially if their only purpose is to destroy conventions. They don't develop with time, their hyperactivity leads merely to decay. And later, when there's real change, and something fundamental has transformed of its own necessity, then we look back and what we see is silly, empty gesture."

. . .

"But who is creating the movement in the middle? It doesn't just occur on its own. It's always the extremists, the outsiders and the rebels who bring about these kinds of transformations! And, as far as new forms are concerned, Ossia's moments, for example, we'll have to withhold our judgment for a while. Maybe we just don't have the right kind of recall for glimpses, splinter-speak, and particle fields, but that doesn't begin to exclude the possibility that in the future people will be better at it than we are. I can easily imagine that there will be a time when humans won't be able to deal with any of the more expansive forms. They may no longer possess the kind of grid for time and attention that would allow them to appreciate an entire novel or a film story. Instead, their minds will divide a work up into entirely different kinds of perceptive fields, sorting it according to forces and stimuli we simply don't know, perceiving it in tiny, and the tiniest, of events and lucid flashes. These days, I often have a much sharper and persistent image of a film that may seem confused but still presents a deeper and unequivocal view of things, as opposed to a clean, slick story that I can't even recall after a couple of hours. But I know that you look at these things very differently, Leon, and that you have developed a deep revulsion for whatever seems muddled and disjointed. You even prefer the pleasing to the extreme (or what you consider to be extreme), you can sense a stable form in what is pleasing."

"The pleasing and the extreme," I repeated, disgruntled, and weighed her words. "In the movies I prefer those who are pleasing to those who are simply smug and arrogant. And I consider it extreme to blithely ignore the principles of film, which must also be the principles of what is pleasing. And even the claim of an exacting and serious aesthetic, which must be observed in other arts, can only be partially acknowledged in film. Right from the beginning, film has always naturally striven for a conciliatory success, embracing the craft and the art, the box office and aesthetics, and where, otherwise, everything on the brink of disintegration, and its opposite, the ennobled, are mutually exalted. Mass appeal in no way inhibits genial work, nor must a work of art be in any way inaccessible to a broad public. And the relatively short history of film is rich in examples of such successes, from Chaplin to Hitchcock, from Kubrick to Spielberg. And these are not merely instances of happy circumstance, they represent the apex of the filmmaking art. But this great cultural achievement, this preeminent rite of filmmaking, which combines the precious with the common, is already nothing more than a distant memory in the minds of today's directors, it might as well have taken place in a film Renaissance. For some time now, the most important forces in filmmaking have been pulling each other in opposing directions, and there are very few cases in which a fortuitous reunification is at all possible. And where a vigorous middle is lacking, the outer edges collapse toward the center, characters from the margin become the nucleus, eccentrics become the archetype. In the absence of precept, the arbitrarily subjective thrives. For me, film in the hands of interest groups, minorities and mini-minorities, auto-biographers and diary manufacturers, disintegrates into triviality. Without the struggle for high convention, there is no film."

. . .

I had all the rest of Sunday evening to argue with Yossica about the movies, and the popular as opposed to the engrossing, with more and more examples (and provocations) to support our various points. Of course, I could see that she was quietly projecting much of what we were discussing onto her songwriting, and it was clear to both of us that there were two kinds of careers to be made in music, either a career where you remain a lifelong hot tip, or you develop a broad public appeal. On this evening, a conflict arose between us, and it grew according to its own laws until our long debate finally turned into a petulant quarrel and degenerated into personal attack. Yossica accused me of being too flippant and claimed that this was merely the arrogance of someone who "had managed to find his way out."

Of course, what she really wanted to say was: such pompous views about movies weren't really credible in someone who hadn't been able to accomplish anything in the field.

I didn't respond. I could see how I was slowly withdrawing and becoming disheartened. Though I often wished to escape, it was precisely at such times that I sensed the reality of having merged with Yossica in so many ways. Nothing much happened in our little corner of the world, but we observed the happy exchange of the light of day with the rustlings of the night. Still, the sudden reacquaintance with my teacher had stunned me. I had immediately become pretentious, negligent of that much younger person who had chosen me to be her mentor and her advisor, who made me feel older and more mature than I was, made me act more masculine and reliable than I wanted to be.

I asked Yossica, now that she seemed to have such a low opinion of me, if she really thought it was such a good idea for me to reestablish my relationship with Ossia and start working with him on his new script. She gave me a very kind and deliberate answer, along with a good dose of stiff backbone and tedious advice: "Look, you put everything you had into badmouthing Ossia. You held him accountable for every little weakness you could come up with. But don't you see how senseless it is to be this critical of someone you're still so close to? The only real way to do him justice is to share important work with him."

I told her that any work like that would have to be taken seriously and that it would demand an enormous amount of time, making it almost impossible for us to do things together the way we had been. She replied that it was also time for her to concentrate on her own projects, her songs and her little concerts. Was I supposed to understand this as a withdrawal or an accommodation? As she spoke, she was looking at me, trusting and full of warmth, and I had no doubt that inwardly we had come to an agreement. But it wasn't completely clear what it was.

• • •

THE PRINCE AND THE COYOTE
(From Ossia's Sketchbook)

Martin Rhein, in the role of the Prince of Denmark, had already been standing seventy-five long evenings on the same stage with his persecutor, his tormentor, his creature, a victim of this man's sick surveillance, and suffering the mysterious palpations and sapping of enervating bondage, until finally he could not stand it any more and requested the theater management one morning to immediately find a replacement for the Norwegian Captain, and if they did not he would refuse to do even one more performance, even if this meant he ran the risk of having to pay a stiff fine.

Evening after evening, during the performance of one of mankind's greatest tragedies, another no less inevitable, though hardly sublime tragedy took place, the miserable "Story of the Fall," induced by the cryptic devotion with which a supporting actor held the hero of the scene in his grasp, and then strangled him. Mysteriously, over time, this madness of one man toward a better man became life-threatening for both. Like parasite and host, the great actor and his little colleague, by now a totally *fixated* creature, were inseparable. But what would it mean to have one's profoundest desires stilled by this proud manhood, this last surviving ruler, the star of this stage? And which desires are they? Fixated being, an existence. The only *Form* in which admiration and the superiority of the other can be acknowledged. A form of psychological distress, of unacceptable behavior. A system which ruthlessly demands of the sovereign that he follow through with his gesture of submission, while at the same time not allowing the meeker ones to do the same. In this case, the gesture is repressed in the vilest and most painful of ways, transformed into an illness and self-abasement, and is then expressed as aggression and threatening behavior, even toward the object of admiration and desire.

The prince is powerless against the laser emissions and the network of bondage; they can bring down his strength, his superiority, even his role, *his* Hamlet.

"What do you want?" the Prince asks his tormentor.

"Nothing," the coyote answers, quietly.

"I can't give you anything of mine."

"No!" the coyote says, astounded. As if that had any relevance at all! The hero's ability to understand the creature is obviously limited and meager. He merely feels himself harassed and cornered. This circumscribes his view, his knowledge of human nature, his brotherly interest. . . .

Unmistakable sign, when a woman wants to show you she's interested: she mimics your distinguishing characteristics with subtle and gentle humor, playfully repeating your words and expressions, a smiling mirror. And this is what the coyote did at first with the prince. How did he make himself liked? He showed himself to be quite *taken*, he was always at hand when he was needed, he only conveyed good news, he reported only the flattering remarks others had made, he was curious, he could listen exceptionally well, and he asked intelligent questions. With magical deftness he found his way into the innermost reaches of his master, and he made himself indispensable. But it all ended with telephone terror, with letters into which he smeared the last drop of his soul's pus; through deceitful surveillance and persecution, through threats of murder. Then he claimed he always meant well.

.   .   .

Famous people will have to die! They will have to disappear. They will be executed. Ossia had always known it. Coyotes are on the prowl everywhere. Unsettled by too many billboards, too many idols, too many superhuman characters, they howl into the wind by night. Too much famous. It isn't really murder. It is divine liberation from sinful images. The fall of the outrageously popular. The twilight of the idols has already begun. Image murders are on the increase. A horrible sense of reason has gripped the masses. "No!" the leading anonymities yelled, "we don't need you any more. For the longest time, you were the morons of our desires. Now it's over, we've come to our senses, and the bells are tolling your last hour!"

The prince is at the end of his rope. He is about to attack his exterminator with both fists. But the latter evades his swing with a lightning fast move, and finishes tying his shoes. I knew it! A cowardly run for it, at the very last moment! You can't even get at this creature with a punch or a boot. It withdraws, disappearing into the contours of a primeval gesture of appeasement, and there's no way to attack, you're helpless.

.   .   .

I am filming – more and more often, I enter the house of the invisible treasures. I have to find it here, the concealed ray-eye, the diadem never before seen.

We live on particles and we communicate in particles. An immense flow of particles determines if two people will be interested in each other, or if they will simply get out of each other's way. A *Star Wars* of power impulses in one single glance. Biochemistry of the fluidium or a wave theory of emanation, how long will it be before we have it? It is getting more and more difficult for me to perceive the entire shape of a person, I am always subject to his direct *influence* and I see it. The way a bee sees ultraviolet and not red, because it is more sensitive to shorter wave lengths, and that is the way I am forced to see radiated desire and currents of will, only vaguely recognizing the overall image.

I would like to try to work with thermographic photos of people. We are now able to photograph temperatures on the surface of the earth, why not erotic temperatures as well, attractive forces, among the exotic populations in the hotel lobby, for example. I would like to know what they look like: the detail of their mutual regard? None of us passes by another unaffected. Unfilmed reality, as yet unseen by the eye of any camera. The hero? The faceless being. No one who knows all that much about where he's come from and where he's going. A man of multiple and random character. A being of many persons.

.   .   .

No one understands me. No, no one understands that a filmmaker, a comic . . . is looking for phenomena, *phenomena!* and not gags. That he really wants to see through the eye on the top of his head, with a light cell, the toad stone, the shivah organ. (According to an old interpretation, a primal sense lost in the course of evolution. An external organ in early reptiles, with the development of the cerebrum became internal and suppressed, surviving as pineal gland. Very interesting. So, the forehead, the spiritual eye, is supposed to have been transformed into a hormone which regulates sexual maturation. Cell tissue which combines light and sexuality. The earthworm's "gaze into the heavens" *is* its testimony . . .)

Why shouldn't he stroll through society's meadow and see through his third eye? Looking into the face of a fellow citizen, he will be able to determine his overall condition, where this person has come from, he will perceive him in the *phenomenon* (in a nano-second) of a time-confederate.

Complex circuitry of face and history. Moments, the wafer-thin, thousandsfold chips of micro-psychology.

. . .

Carmela is undressing. Her arms crossed and raised above her head, she pulls off her sweater, pushes down her unzipped jeans, and plucks her cotton socks off the tips of her toes. There is something genuinely chaste about this grasping and twisting. They come from a time when the little girl was sitting alone in her room and taking off her daytime dress. And they haven't changed. They are the same today as they were back then. So, while you are lying here on the bed shivering in anticipation of the touch of a naked body, it has wrapped itself in primordial motions, innocence, the aura of the early days of childhood.

Almost unimaginable, that a woman can still disrobe in front of her lover in solemn innocence. And: that a man wouldn't chortle at the scene, and not find it disconcerting that the woman in front of him was disrobing "out in the open." Still, the disrobing continues, neither lascivious nor demure, but as if no one else were present. And the clothing that is being peeled off! A sweater, maybe an undershirt, a pair of socks, bright-colored panties, snug jeans. After one tube passes successfully over a calf, my lover hops on one naked leg, her jeans still stuck on the other, and then finally kicked off to the side. That's how it looks. It is not exactly the dance of the seven veils.

. . .

All subject matter is erotic metamorphosis. Desire itself is the subject matter, short-lived and volatile.

That is why a dream is such an attractive little bit of earth, because there, and only there, all desire is allotted its appropriate level of volatility. Appearing-touching-consummating-ending. High, almost time-free intensity. Dreams do away with objects. They are pure accordance, resolution.

Stories of transformation must be an ablution into *pure* sexuality.

. . .

I don't want my film lost in the fog. Put pictures into a world overflowing with pictures. I am searching for a symbol, not for the typical or revealing camera angle. But film is not capable of capturing the classical symbol. Photography is all it really possesses: anything which cannot be photographed, does not exist. Film does not know anything about the invisible. At best it may incorporate surreal montage. But there's not really anything more we can wrest from that. It has become the sole property of music video. I want film to be something entirely different from a journey. I want it to have a place to stay. You must allow everything creative the space of a house.

. . .

I will come back to this, and I am finding it more and more restricting that we have neither the terms for, nor a hold on, this region of the spirits which surrounds each of us, this damned fluidium. Only mystification. We have absolutely no data or established knowledge about something of vital significance, something we depend on to make our most fundamental decisions. And still, I feel more and more strongly that beyond the consciousness we now perceive, there is another. It will open whole new worlds. It will open the eye on our foreheads. And in the future, a physics of spiritual particles will research the elements of the fluidium.

. . .

In the Middle Ages, the blink of an eye, the ictus oculi, was thought to be the fundamental time-atom. And now: the hour in a glance. The universe of a glimpse, with its highly integrated links, its compact-history, its networked time. Romantics of the electronic revolution. Neofragmentists. Masters of emission. All external aspects reduced, everything at the nucleus proliferating.

. . .

Ossia could keep young people amused, as long as he was in good spirits and felt he was carrying on the struggle in the wasteland of distraction, as long as he was attempting to save love from total communication, and the unformed life from the well-lit Hades of TV channels. And even though for a time I may have been looked upon as another Don Quixote, let me note that my struggle was solely that to preserve the arms of the windmill. Ossia, the crooked, shaky frame of the last subject, was at the very end of a long chain of heroes born too late. But even I had to learn that the individual can never be employed again as a comic figure. We exist and *experience* more and more in "structures." They are our contemporary heroes. And hopefully, they will provide the required measure of comedy. There will always be laughter, in every time, and on every level of existence.

I remember a young boy, just a little guy barely twelve years old, who came to me – I think it was after *Montanus* – and said: "Some day I would like to do something as great as what I just saw in the movie theater." There, in tears of recognition, the oath of succession and of continuation was sworn. A role model can still be the basis of a continuing tradition. However, in order to do that, he must be willing to let himself be overwhelmed. And this is just the attribute I find lacking in all the self-promoters, the do-it-yourselfers, the handymen of art. Of course, they all go to work without an idol. And their achievements show it. Art is not something to be produced for personal use.

. . .

It seemed odd, but when I was still driving around Germany, I noticed how many young people no longer look up at a stranger coming their way, no longer feeling it necessary to exchange a friendly glance. Not that they are shy or inhibited, on the contrary, nowadays they're quite fearless as they go trotting along their way. Maybe that's just it, and an elastic self-assurance, a persistent sense of solidarity which has allowed the consideration we used to show for a stranger to become expendable. His sudden appearance provokes neither fright nor curiosity. It will simply be ignored. In other countries you can still swim in gazes. Similarly, speaking has become a matter of monologues in monotone. Things moderately abstract, reports on one's general condition predominate our conversations; we are constantly in the process of articulation and almost never in conversation. I and General Awareness somehow seem to be quite compatible. I and You, on the other hand, are very fond of interrupting each other, and seldom have much to say about anything unless it's an echo of popular opinion, or, more likely than not, a demand.

. . .

Where the eye loses its social vigilance and is no longer required to make a lightning fast judgment, distinguishing between friend and foe, beauty and ugliness, useful and insignificant, then it also loses its brilliance and its sharpness, and will not even begin to shine from within. When the eyes of a young actor are this weak and dim, there will be very little for an audience to see. Only the eye of actor can expose a film.

. . .

"The Interviewer," Segment 112.

Pat meets Otto Stundemund

Pat: Mr. Stundemund. How would you, personally, evaluate the following three statements? Which one most nearly expresses your own feelings? (A) A heating engineer, twenty-three years old, states: "I like to go to the sculpture garden in the afternoon, and when I know no one is watching, I fool around with Roman statues." (B) A traveling spice salesman, fifty-five, states: "I like to send my wife pornographic telegrams, and I get a real thrill when the girl in the telegram office reads it back to me." (C) A communications engineer, thirty-seven, states: "I limit my sexual contacts strictly to the members of my lotto club." Mr. Stundemund, can you please give us your reactions according to the following pattern: xx/leaves me feeling indifferent; xy/I find it repugnant; xyz/I can empathize.

Stundemund: Please, don't ask me any more questions. These constant sex surveys are just causing us all a lot of pain.

Pat: Would you like to take a little break now?

Stundemund: These awful definitions, the empty ideals lurking behind these questions . . . . No, I've had more than enough.

Pat: But you said you were willing to take part in our survey?

Stundemund: Under the pretext of wanting to understand this problem or that, I expressed a willingness to participate – and I have very often participated, for a time I even immersed myself in statistics, I virtually hunted down every survey being conducted and I am probably the most researched citizen of this country, because I was addicted to the question per se. But now I've had enough. I can't do it anymore.

Pat: Mr. Stundemund, we are currently approaching a problem, the so-called Partnership Breakdown, which has recently been attracting a great deal of attention in interviews everywhere, but about which we have very little factual information. If I understood you correctly, you are somewhat uncomfortable with my questions?

Stundemund: Miss, you are a pain. Do I have to say any more?

Pat: Can you tell me if the pain becomes stronger when my questions touch upon certain taboos, for example –

Stundemund: Oh, as far as I am concerned, anything even approaching the subject is taboo. We cannot talk about it. We just can't!

Pat: I understand what you're saying very well. But I think we are almost at the point of establishing new patterns of behavior, you can't withhold your opinions now.

Stundemund: My statements on the subject would grotesquely distort your statistics. They would totally blow the curve.

Pat: But we need to understand your motives! This concerns a lot of people. Everyone wants to know what's going on. They want to be able to talk about it. It is of the utmost importance for all of us, for the whole society.

Stundemund: The society, my dear friend, is not nearly as important as you may think it is.

Pat: We want to show people that no one is an outsider, that everyone is normal. No matter what he feels, no matter what he achieves, no matter how he loves. Everyone has to know that he is normal. This is the kind of reassurance people need now that we're standing on the threshold of a new age . . .

Stundemund: Another new age? Didn't we just have – ? Is this the second or the third or which industrial revolution are we living at the moment? (End Segment 112/Stundemund)

．　．　．

The new, the new!, that's what the ladies and gentlemen of the tower are demanding and yelling at me from every one of their chambers. The new! That's what the little girls want to see now, the pretty ones and the ones with faces like potato pancakes. Bring on the artist and have him perform for us how we're supposed to confront this new world never before seen.

Overwhelmed by gloom, he must nevertheless perform one more pioneering feat: the household comic, the bitter dreamer, shuffling along across the parquet, the hero of the flushing WC, the bread slicer, the goldfish bowl and the wastepaper basket, into which he has already dumped countless cards with the most beautiful views in the world.

. . .

The most honest feeling I could express in my film would be a grand restfulness, and the film itself: a powerful closing of eyelids. Full of hope that the whole apparition would turn into a *Reality!* Into a good, sensible character. That it would all end up in something good, something human!

TWO

I met Ossia a second time. We agreed to meet in the French restaurant in the piazza of the Tower-Bellevue, on the edge of the urban-tropical atrium. This is where, on my first visit, the erect waiter, and the woman bent forward over her table, had appeared to me behind their window as a tableau in a game preserve, here in this deceptive place happenstance seemed premeditated, and even the most ordinary behavior obtruded embarrassingly.

It was early afternoon when I arrived, this time on a Friday, and the restaurant, La Caravelle, was quite full. Shortly before the weekend, and a number of business people were sitting together eating their lobster or poached salmon as they sealed one or another favorable contract. The room was dominated by the stiffly relaxed air that settles in after deals are done. The mostly young men would not leave, but kept a suspicious eye on one another, all the while exchanging jokes and wisecracks.

Ossia was waiting for me in a booth near the back of the boat-shaped dining room. He had dressed for the occasion. An anthracite-colored suit with vest, and underneath, a steel blue silk shirt with an open collar. The hair on the side of his head was combed deliberately up over his bald spot, as if it were meant to be working in opposition to his pendulous sideburns. So his face remained puffy and fat, even though the skin, now cleanly shaved and powdered dry, looked somewhat tighter. The first look with which he welcomed me was so full of tender expectation that it completely tied my heart up in knots. But there was already a glimmer of protective contempt smoldering in his eyes, just in case I disappointed him. As openly and completely as he had delivered himself up to my judgment, he still had to retain the option of deeming me an ignoramus and a turncoat, and simply dismissing me. I was ashamed of my careless dress; I came in jeans and a sweater. He had sent some excerpts from his sketchbook a week ago, and I was carrying them in a plastic shopping bag from Kaufhof.

This time Ossia drank. Like Gielgud, in the Resnais film, he was having a good chablis. However, it was only a half-bottle standing in front of his massive body, and looking particularly short and comical given the large capacity of the drinker. Self-consciousness was obvious on both sides. I buried myself in the menu but without being able to concentrate on any one of the flamboyant entries. Ossia poured me a glass of wine. He asked about Yossica, and I politely conveyed her regards. Again silence. Maybe I would have been better off coming right to the point and talking about the business at hand, frankly and openly. But I don't really think I could have pulled it off. I definitely needed an innocuous lead-in. Apparently, Ossia was having similar thoughts. He was searching for something easy to talk about in order to lessen the tension between us. Unfortunately, what he came up with was Yossica. "I always thought," he said, mischievously but tense, "you always wanted to marry a woman with humor. A woman you could find amusing. Now you have an angel who can't even stumble." I looked at him with what I hope was extremely cool astonishment. "Yes, yes," he continued, "she is the embodiment of a virgin. I mean, the concept, the way she presents herself, her whole manner and behavior. Weren't you in love with Pat at one time?" He kept digging himself deeper into his conversational hole. And his face contorted into a foolish grimace. Hoisted eyebrows, pinched nostrils, oblique wrinkles across his forehead, an expression of forced irony. Only the sad eyes remained unchanged.

"Your Yossica would like to be someplace else. I could see it. She really wants to be someplace else. You'll see."

Actually, I could have kept the whole thing brief. But, first of all, I didn't have the courage, and second, I felt it my duty to discuss his work with him in detail. I was prepared to do that, and I wanted to get on with it.

What could he possibly have against Yossica? The woman who had for so long been holding me by the hand, firmly and calmly – why should she ever let go? I had tried to understand her thoughts and feelings as best I could. Her intentions, even when I didn't share them, were always kind, based on trust, fairness, and optimism, all healthy attributes which could easily stand up to Ossia's bitter wit.

I looked out of the window coldly. He had better be careful not to say one more critical thing about her. The waiter came and we agreed to order a large portion of crayfish.

Outside, not far away, we could see the make-believe pond with its oblong skating rink. A young woman and her little daughter were skating there in quiet, uniform strokes. Both wore only shorts and light sweaters. The woman had her brunette hair tied back, and the high, white boots with their blades made the slim, supple figure look even taller. The daughter followed closely on her mother's heels and adapted herself to the pendulum beat. A scratchy old skater's waltz was being played over the loudspeakers. And in the way the two of them glided along on their easy track, upper bodies motionless, legs swinging evenly, hands folded over their backs, it looked as if they were moving along immersed in exuberant thought.

I bent down to get the copies of Ossia's sketchbook out of the plastic bag. I put the materials for a late film on the table and moved both hands over the stack of papers. For me, this motion was nothing more than a way to get to my first words, but in his eyes it seemed to have a somewhat different meaning. I noticed him sit up straight, a serious mien coming over his face; actually he was expecting the best.

"Well, what's the bad news," he said, almost relieved and happy. I didn't go into it there, even though it would have made sense to pick up on the words "bad news." Being somewhat at a loss, but mustering all of the good will I possibly could, I grabbed for the pieces from his sketches and notes that had made the strongest impression on me, and began to praise them profusely, with what I believe to be credible grounds. Of all of the pieces I read, I felt that the story about the interviewer, Pat as a pollster, was the most appropriate one to work on and develop fully. The heavy, aching, famous man snapped at this little chunk of good like a street dog on the edge of starvation. It trickled through him, was warming, and he could barely hold back tears of joy. I encouraged him to pay more attention to Pat during the dialogues, and to be careful not to keep giving the lion's share of the gags and word-play to her partner; after all he was supposed to be developing the star role for Pat, not for himself.

"Of course. You're entirely right," he said, in overzealous approval. But he wasn't interested in hearing another word.

He was on again. Without any regard for our elegant surroundings, he made space for himself and put on a performance. "Look, what do you think of this . . . ?"

Before I could turn around, a veritable torrent of scenes poured over me, all brief numbers, of which he apparently had an endless supply in store, or they simply came to him as he performed.

"Pat and companion in restaurant. She keeps bending down under the table. The man: stop bending down under the table all of the time. I'm sure you haven't lost anything. You just want *me* to bend down, because that's what a gentleman is supposed to do when a lady has lost something under the table. The next time you do it, I'm going to remain sitting ramrod straight. You're not going to keep getting me down on the floor! What are you looking for, anyway? – Pat: A stamp. – Man: A stamp! – Pat: Well, it can wait until after dinner. – Man: After dinner! Crawling around on the floor is the last thing I'd be thinking of doing! . . . Or what do you think of this? Pat goes into a laundromat – "

Of course, I had to laugh. I always had to laugh at Ossia. He thought that I was with him, and had been all along. That he had convinced me and that we would make the film together, finally the film! The grand, jubilee production. What an extraordinarily earnest man he still is! I thought as he kept juggling his unfinished numbers into the air. He certainly was not lacking the courage to make himself look silly. But it is just these things, going wrong, missing the mark, attempting in vain, which now make him seem so mature and beyond compare. It transports him back into the realm of an almost tragic naivete. While I was studying his sketchbook, it always seemed to me that what he really wanted was for me to look into his heart. Look here, the pages seemed to be saying, I want to do all of this and I can't any more. Countless, mutually energizing beginnings lay scattered throughout these pages. These rough drafts and reflections – or, at least the sections he sent me – pleaded for my help while revealing his failures. Perhaps this exercise was not so much about our working together as it was about somehow preparing a gracious and merciful end to his loneliness, his agonizing and fruitless drive to create. It is possible that my judgment was too harsh and too arrogant. But I believed that with these papers I had received the encrypted missive of an imprisoned soul, the secret message of a talent seized and carried off.

"By the way, what do you think of my little drama about the actors?" he suddenly asked. I knew he meant *Prince and Coyote*, and I told him that as far as the story had been developed, I liked it quite a lot. Just that there didn't really appear to be any role for Pat in it. And of the two male leads, Coyote, the treacherous servant, would be a dream role for him. But I didn't know if he could really play it now . . .

"Of course. You're right. It can't possibly be anything for me."

For a moment, it almost seemed as if he had forgotten his real agony, the fact that he himself could no longer play, would never again ever dare to play.

"But there's a lot of material here. What do you think?" Ossia asked, somewhat unsettled now.

"In the acting drama?"

"Yes. And the other things, too. I mean in this whole pile here."

"Yes, Ossia. There's all kinds of potential here. It just has to be developed in the right way."

At first he seemed satisfied with that observation. "You're absolutely right. I'm going to get to work on the 'Interviewer.' Real disciplined. I'm only going to let things in that really fit the story. I want to do this one. So, Pat's going to go through these interviews . . . You know, Leon, the whole thing could have a more or less casual form. You know, you always have to work a little bit according to the bag-of-surprises principle – "

"Ossia!" I interrupted him. "Just cut the episodic crap! You've got to find your way to a big, coherent story again. Only a big story with real, tenable suspense can allow for diversion and assorted skirmishes."

Ossia winced slightly. But I didn't let up. I had to tell him everything, and described, reprovingly and urgently, all of the talents for cinematic storytelling in which he was really incomparable, I praised him effusively for his work in *Montanus* and *The Fish*. But the more glorious my retrospective became, the more the artist closed himself off to it. Very quietly and determined, he had erected his barricade.

"The older one gets, the less he feels bound to logical consistency. The order in which one perceives things begins to appear more and more random, their relationships almost arbitrary, and it is only through easy, playful experience that we can ever hope to track down its mysterious precepts. I have to obey my intuitions even if it has begun to seem like dilution of form. To build on my earlier work would result in nothing more than an imitation of a form which artificially denies my broadened experience, and my entirely different interests and observations. Artificial is what the process would be, and not in the least creative."

I kept my mouth shut. At this point, I could have reminded him of his last two films, those barren cornucopia, each a baffling bag of surprises.

"But maybe we can do something," he started up again, "that is light, with a lot of variety, and also very solid at the core. Exactly the way you want it, Leon. Look, there's a lot of material here, right, a lot of good, imaginative beginnings." He was virtually begging for a few encouraging words, he had pre-chewed them for me.

Ossia! My friend, my teacher! I wanted to shout, I cannot help you! Just take this awful power away from me and do not make yourself dependent upon the judgment of a person who, in your presence, will always be irrelevant! Of course I am badly mistaken and cannot adequately comprehend the worthwhile, perhaps even extraordinary, pieces in your sketchbook. Hasn't it become clear that I am simply too stupid, too limited and inflexible? My unloved profession, the aimless wandering around with an abandoned career, all my many repressed desires, how could that not help but cloud my view! And hadn't my taste already been poisoned with malice, so that from the very outset it was impossible for me to find anything good in Ossia's pages? Ah, I didn't even know what precipices and snakepits lay beneath the best of my knowledge and the best of my conscience. But I had spent a long time, a very long time, reading these sketches in sad amazement, looking and looking again for the one, unmistakable, unstoppable idea among all of these scattered pieces. But I found neither germ cells nor seeds, only matter in precipitous disintegration.

In the end, I had also come to believe that Ossia himself did not really intend to make a new film. He was far too lost in pondering. Maybe his worries about Pat drove him to plans and sketches.

The worry that he might lose her too, the way he had lost Margarethe, for whom filmmaking was now history, and whose departure from the delicately-balanced group of three, the trademark of his early work, had left the ship of Ossia's art badly listing. He had drawn his best energies from centering, from positioning himself on the balance beam.

What difference did it make if now and then he was struck by a few good ideas, the best of which struck only him – an Ossia who had long ago ceased to exist.

. . .

I had kept quiet for a while and owed him a response. In the meantime he had reached back for my first words of praise and was now beginning to repeat my critical objections too, filling the vacuum my lack of response had created. He did it with a perfectly servile obsequiousness, like a second-rate Hollywood director trying to reassure his moody producer. "Of course, we have to make sure that Pat takes the lead in the interviews. *She* certainly has to be the comic figure. I made a mistake there. We're going to have to make a hardened runner out of her, aren't we. What would you think if we picked up the segment with the erotic house of horrors again, you know, the segment I read to you a while ago."

"Ossia!" I suddenly said, in a resolute tone of voice, and he looked over at me, shocked.

"I'm not going to work with you on this film."

It was as if I had hit him over the head with a sledgehammer. He turned as white as chalk, he closed his eyes, he stuttered out some confused stuff. He crashed. I sensed his courage plunge. I was frightened by the power my words had.

"Have you really thought it over carefully?" he asked in a trembling tone.

I started to tell him why I had come to this decision and not another. I put many too many words to work explaining the simple and brutal truth that I had neither the desire nor the resolve to get myself involved in an absolutely hopeless project. In attempting to make myself as clear as possible, I only succeeded in being all the more hurtful and inconsiderate toward a man who had once shown me so much kindness. I even trotted Yossica out and claimed that at this difficult turning point in her life, I had to stand by her. Just as she had once helped me, when I, having been rudely jolted out of my artist dreams, had sought footing in an unforgivingly everyday world. But even if I had framed my argument more carefully, I would still have arrived at the same refusal, no ands, ifs, or buts. In any case, the distance between us was growing word by word.

I believe he had chosen me for this last grand attempt to test the strength of his personal and artistic appeal one more time. It ended up a shipwreck. And he really looked as if he would not recover from it any time soon. He would not make this film alone.

. . .

Actually, at this point I was expecting that Ossia would put an end to our conclave. I feared the last, indelible look in his eyes with which he would take his leave from me forever. But, to my surprise, something entirely different took place. He ordered a large bottle of white burgundy, a Batard Montrachet 1979, and he turned his attention to the next course of our dinner, since the poached turbot was no longer available. The short Algerian waiter suggested sole in a champagne-tarragon sauce, and we ordered it. "Listen, Leon," Ossia suddenly said, as if we were intending to go ahead with the whole project, "if we do this house of horrors, then we'll really have to get Pat moving. We're going to have to put her right in the middle of a very brutal Pac-Man. She's going to have to bolt across the screen just like a little LCD-man, in perpetual motion, instantly doing the right thing everywhere. Babies will be falling out of the windows of burning high-rises, and will have to be caught, or they will turn into little angels ascending into heaven. If moles are not beaten back into their holes with hammers, the entire financial district will collapse. She is going to have to dash madly around an electronic fairy tale with no way out. A woman made of flesh and blood in this totally raw and fiery synthesized world in which the horizon is always changing color and, mercilessly, you must play with everything you've got, or you will be lost . . ."

I didn't laugh. He withdrew back into himself ever so slightly. But now it looked as if he were slowly yielding up a great and powerful exertion. The most painful phase of his misery of ideas was diminishing. His face became quite clear, and a cool cheerfulness came over it.

"OK, OK. You don't like it. Let's drop it. That scene is out."

I looked over at the skating rink again and watched my two

ice-skaters, who in the meantime had allowed themselves a break and were resting on a bench. Stretched out at an angle, the child was lying up against her mother's hip, the heavy bladed feet hanging wearily toe to toe. Half in slumber, she was sucking on a straw attached to a carton of milk, or possibly fruit juice. But the tall, slender woman was resting lightly on her right elbow against the back of the bench, and, having assumed a graceful pose, allowed her exhaustion to fade. These were not my fellow citizens. Upright and lithe, the young woman was the picture of modern, bourgeois beauty, whose style and bearing were the obvious inheritance of a long, unbroken family history. Neither doll nor lady, but a mysteriously relaxed phenomenon in whom physical grace, heritage, and womanly pride were easily combined, in a way which would never be possible in our profoundly crippled country.

. . .

I had also drunk some of the "airy wine," as Ossia called it, and he suggested that I would do well to "breathe deeply in this well-ventilated hall of our mountain lodge."

Then he leaned over the table toward me, and said with a painful pride: "It must get to the point where nothing is possible anymore. Absolutely nothing. Every idea must cut itself off. That's when the real work can begin. But first we have to get things to that point! You know, once you're at a certain level, you don't make mistakes anymore. A master acts with phenomenal skill when it comes to the how and the what, the naming and referring. He does only the right thing. Instead of sinking into the depths of despair, as poets did in earlier times, today a filmmaker must be more like a formula-one driver, a master of the now, a record holder in the instant, driving through his course at breakneck speeds. What is important here, in matters of life and death, is the complete consignment of the spirit to skill. On what is both the highest and the narrowest lane of existence, you have to perform faultlessly. In an enhanced state of danger, you can't allow for any bad luck. With hallucinatory precision, at speeds as high as 180 miles per hour, Jackie Stewart could distinguish individual faces in the stands. You have to be in an elevated state of seeing, and then everything comes out perfectly even: what you see and what you have to say."

"But Ossia," I responded instinctively, "being faultless is not the answer! It is the exact opposite of the true freedom you need to really get started. An obsessive drive for perfection is the last thing we need. It's not going to get you one step closer to your film."

"Oh, but it will, Leon. Mistakes are for torn souls, unsure of themselves and the world. It all depends on whether or not you are in an exalted state of seeing. Just look at the cinema. The dreary flood of images. All they're showing is celluloid makework. Sometimes cute, sometimes critical, always a nice little attraction. Somebody speaks to your problems and it makes you feel good. Greater, earlier, more masterful films can no longer be appreciated; no one understands them.

"The older I get, the clearer it becomes to me that all great films, all great works of art, are friends among themselves, and I can see that now their contact consists of a slow leavetaking, a parting, waving good-bye for the last time. And what wouldn't we give to be a part of this evening exchange of regards! It would feel so good to be able to close even a very small gap. . . . But it's already too late, Leon. We will never again enter the happy realm to which these works are retiring, where, beyond epochs and spaces, an informed society lives on. Gods, heroes, poets, film people. Eichendorff at the side of Buñuel. Griffith arm in arm with Klio and Ingrid Bergman. They have all left. They've put everything behind them and now, having discharged their finest obligations, they're strolling around in perfect retreat. But look: *there* they are and they are still shining brightly! It makes me very sad to think that we no longer have entry into this peaceful enclosure, and that theirs is unfortunately a closed society . . ."

While he was talking, I found myself thinking about the skinny outsider in whose guise he haunted his early films. And even though this character was often quite morose, we still had to laugh at him. However, the pleasure-mound seated across the table from me could no longer "play out" his troubles at will, he had become one with them. The comic had devoured his comic figure and it had provided him a generous layer of sorrowful flab.

The airy wine kept on flowing and the supply was replenished. There was also a second main course, a warm lobster pie, but at this point I could no longer keep up, and I couldn't even look at the various deserts Ossia had delivered to our table.

Then, suddenly, as if he had broken through a thin layer of ice,

he simply sank into a drunken stupor. And he became very sentimental. He wanted to tell me about his old mother and how they
had only recently reconciled. He dissolved in homesickness and
yearning for his boyhood and kindergarten, acting as if he were
sitting in a tower, in deepest exile, even though he obviously
resides in the best middle Germany has to offer.

It had become almost impossible to speak to him anymore. His
feelings were reeling around in his heart. He was displaying the
opposite of his art, his was now unintentional comedy; the massive
man in a fog of insipid reconciliation, trying his very best to find a
way back to his little old mother.

Finally, he raised himself with some difficulty, and the little
waiter rushed to his side to take the chair away. And one more
time, he had reached an absolute and final decision: "I'll do something about my mother. With Pat. And with Margarethe. And
with you. I'll get you all together – I'll get them all together
again." With the broad and gentle arms of a man reconciled, he
pulled us all together, gathered up everything that was precious
and dear to him.

Somewhat abashed, I held the excerpts from his sketchbook in
my hands and wanted to give them back to him.

"Just hold on to them," Ossia said, "and one day you'll look at
them again. And maybe then, Leon Pracht, you will be astounded."

He walked over to me and scribbled something on the empty cover
page of the photocopies. In shaky outlines the old Ossia emerged.
He drew the sad, gaunt figure with the tails of his dress coat
flapping. He raised an invisible hat from his head and bowed to a
dolphin growing out of his toes, and offering its flat head in greet-
ing. It was the logo of *The Fish*. He wrote a short dedication
beneath it and pressed the packet into my hands. "Today, in a
world without appropriate headgear," it read, "the kind of hat we
ought to be tipping in a gesture of farewell is the least of our worries."

He went with me as far as the front lobby. Outside, a beautiful
late summer afternoon lay over the plain of the future city center.
It had been raining, and feathery plumes of steam were rising off
the asphalt. I tried to convince Ossia to drive down to the Rhine
with me and take an hour's walk in the fresh air. At first, he
looked at me, astonished; then he smiled and declined. There was
nothing I could do. He wouldn't, he couldn't bring himself to leave

the tower even temporarily. You could tell by the way he moved among the people here. He clung to the hotel traffic as if it were a ventilator flap. He was receiving artificial respiration, he was absolutely dependent on this ventilation of comings and goings, of familiar and ever changing faces.

We stood next to one another for one more awkward moment, looking into the low-lying sun which radiated a cool beauty from behind the tinted glass windows.

"I'll be back," Ossia said, quiet and somber, "and you're going to see it."

How was I supposed to respond? I embraced him. Then I turned and walked quickly walked toward the entrance, pushed myself into the revolving door and let myself be turned out.

The sun was shining, gentle and good; it was still pleasantly warm. I didn't look back. In the first few minutes after I had stepped out of the lobby, I could feel nothing but a great relief. I was simply happy to have left the illusory light and the stale chill of the tower behind me.